**Abo

Maisey Yates is the *New* ... over one hundred romance novels. An avid knitter with a dangerous yarn addiction and an aversion to housework, Maisey lives with her husband and three kids in rural Oregon. She believes her trek to her coffee maker each morning is a true example of her pioneer spirit. Find out more about Maisey's books on her website: maiseyyates.com, or find her on Facebook, Instagram or TikTok by searching her name.

Debbi Rawlins has written over fifty books for Mills & Boon since 1994, in several different lines. She lives in rural, beautiful Utah with far too many rescued cats and dogs. Although she hasn't lived there for years, she still misses her home state of Hawaii. She's currently working on a western series, one of her favourite genres.

USA Today bestselling author **Catherine Mann** has over a hundred books in print in more than twenty countries with Mills & Boon and other imprints. A six-time *RITA* finalist, she has won both a *RITA* and Romantic Times Reviewer's Choice Award. A mother of four, Catherine lives in South Carolina with her husband, where they enjoy kayaking, camping with their dogs, and volunteering at a service dog training organisation. For more information, visit: catherinemann.com

About the Authors

... a *New York Times* bestselling author of

A Cowboy for Christmas

MAISEY YATES

DEBBI RAWLINS

CATHERINE MANN

MILLS & BOON

First Published in Great Britain 2025
by Mills & Boon, an imprint of HarperCollins*Publishers* Ltd
1 London Bridge Street, London, SE1 9GF

www.harpercollins.co.uk

HarperCollins*Publishers*
Macken House, 39/40 Mayor Street Upper,
Dublin 1, D01 C9W8, Ireland

ISBN: 978-0-263-41916-0

MIX
Paper | Supporting
responsible forestry
FSC
www.fsc.org
FSC™ C007454

This book contains FSC™ certified paper and other controlled sources to ensure responsible forest management.

For more information visit: www.harpercollins.co.uk/green

Printed and Bound in the UK using 100% Renewable Electricity at CPI Group (UK) Ltd, Croydon, CR0 4YY

HOLD ME, COWBOY

MAISEY YATES

To KatieSauce, the sister I was always waiting for.
What a joy it is to have you in my life.

One

"Creative photography," Madison West muttered as she entered the security code on the box that contained the key to the cabin she would be staying in for the weekend.

She looked across the snowy landscape to see another home situated *far* too close to the place she would be inhabiting for the next couple of days. The photographs on the vacation-rental website hadn't mentioned that she would be sharing the property with anyone else.

And obviously, the example pictures had been taken from inventive angles.

It didn't matter. Nothing was going to change her plans. She just hoped the neighbors had earplugs. Because she was having sex this weekend. Nonstop sex.

Ten years celibate, and it was ending tonight. She had finally found *the one*. Not the one she was going to marry, obviously. *Please.* Love was for other people. People who hadn't been tricked, manipulated and humiliated when they were seventeen.

No, she had no interest in love and marriage. But she had abundant interest in orgasms. So much interest. And she had found the perfect man to deliver them.

All day, all night, for the next forty-eight hours.

She was armed with a suitcase full of lingerie and four bottles of wine. Neighbors be damned. She'd been hoping for a little more seclusion, but this was fine. It would be fine.

She unlocked the door and stepped inside, breathing a sigh of relief when she saw that the interior, at least, met with her expectations. But it was a little bit smaller than it had looked online, and she could only hope that wasn't some sort of dark portent for the rest of her evening.

She shook her head; she was not going to introduce that concern into the mix, thank you very much. There was enough to worry about when you were thinking about breaking ten years of celibacy without adding such concerns.

Christopher was going to arrive soon, so she figured she'd better get upstairs and start setting a scene. She made her way to the bedroom, then opened her suitcase and took out the preselected bit of lace she had chosen for their first time. It was red, which looked very good on her, if a bit obvious. But she was aiming for obvious.

Christopher wasn't her boyfriend. And he wasn't going to be. He was a very nice equine-vitamin-supplement salesman she'd met a few weeks ago when he'd come by the West estate. She had bought some products for her horses, and they'd struck up a conversation, which had transitioned into a flirtation.

Typically, when things began to transition into flirtation, Maddy put a stop to them. But she hadn't with him. Maybe because he was special. Maybe because ten years was just way too long. Either way, she had kept on flirting with him.

They'd gone out for drinks, and she'd allowed him to kiss her. Which had been a lot more than she'd allowed any other guy in recent years. It had reminded her how much she'd enjoyed that sort of thing once upon a time. And once she'd been reminded…well.

He'd asked for another date. She'd stopped him. Because wouldn't a no-strings physical encounter be way better?

He'd of course agreed. Because he was a man.

But she hadn't wanted to get involved with anyone in town. She didn't need anyone seeing her at a hotel or his house or with his car parked at her little home on her parents' property.

Thus, the cabin-weekend idea had been born.

She shimmied out of her clothes and wiggled into the skintight lace dress that barely covered her backside. Then she set to work fluffing her blond hair and applying some lipstick that matched the lingerie.

She was not answering the door in this outfit, however.

She put her long coat back on over the lingerie, then gave her reflection a critical look. It had been a long time since she had dressed to attract a man. Usually, she was more interested in keeping them at a distance.

"Not tonight," she said. "*Not* tonight."

She padded downstairs, peering out the window and seeing nothing beyond the truck parked at the small house across the way and a vast stretch of snow, falling harder and faster.

Typically, it didn't snow in Copper Ridge, Oregon. You had to drive up to the mountains—as she'd done today—to get any of the white stuff. So, for her, this was a treat, albeit a chilly one. But that was perfect, since she planned to get her blood all heated and stuff.

She hummed, keeping an eye on the scene outside, waiting for Christopher to pull in. She wondered if she should have brought a condom downstairs with her. Decided that she should have.

She went back upstairs, taking them two at a time, grateful that she was by herself, since there was nothing sexy about her ascent. Then she rifled through her bag, found some protection and curled her fingers around it before heading back down the stairs as quickly as possible.

As soon as she entered the living area, the lights flickered, then died. Suddenly, everything in the house seemed unnaturally quiet, and even though it was probably her imagination, she felt the temperature drop several degrees.

"Are you kidding me?" she asked, into the darkness.

There was no answer. Nothing but a subtle creak from the house. Maybe it was all that heavy snow on the roof. Maybe it was going to collapse. That would figure.

A punishment for her thinking she could be normal and have sex.

A shiver worked its way down her spine, and she jolted.

Suddenly, she had gone from hopeful and buoyant to feeling a bit flat and tragic. That was definitely not the best sign.

No. She wasn't doing this. She wasn't sinking into self-pity and tragedy. Been there, done that for ten years, thank you.

Madison didn't believe in signs. *So there.* She believed in fuses blowing in bad weather when overtaxed heaters had to work too hard in ancient houses. Yes, *that* she believed in. She also believed that she would have to wait for Christopher to arrive to fix the problem.

She sighed and then made her way over to the kitchen counter and grabbed hold of her purse as she deposited the two condoms on the counter. She pulled her phone out and grimaced when she saw that she had no signal.

Too late, she remembered that she had thought the lack of cell service might be an attraction to a place like this. That it would be nice if both she and Christopher could be cut off from the outside world while they indulged themselves.

That notion seemed really freaking stupid right now. Since she couldn't use the phone in the house thanks to the outage, and that left her cut off from the outside world all alone.

"Oh no," she said, "I'm the first five minutes of a crime show. I'm going to get ax-murdered. And I'm going to die a born-again virgin."

She scowled, looking back out at the resolutely blank landscape. Christopher still wasn't here. But it looked like the house across the way had power.

She pressed her lips together, not happy about the idea of interrupting her neighbor. Or of meeting her neighbor, since the whole point of going out of town was so they could remain anonymous and not see people.

She tightened the belt on her coat and made her way

slowly out the front door, bracing herself against the arctic wind.

She muttered darkly about the cold as she made her way across the space between the houses. She paused for a moment in front of the larger cabin, lit up and looking all warm and toasty. Clearly, this was the premium accommodation. While hers was likely beset by rodents that had chewed through relevant cords.

She huffed, clutching her coat tightly as she knocked on the door. She waited, bouncing in place to try to keep her blood flowing. She just needed to call Christopher and find out when he would be arriving and, if he was still a ways out, possibly beg her neighbor for help getting the power going. Or at least help getting a fire started.

The front door swung open and Madison's heart stopped. The man standing there was large, so tall that she only just came up to the middle of his chest. He was broad, his shoulders well muscled, his waist trim. He had the kind of body that came not from working out but from hard physical labor.

Then she looked up. Straight nose, square jaw, short brown hair and dark eyes that were even harder than his muscles. And far too familiar.

"What are *you* doing here?"

Sam McCormack gritted his teeth against the sharp tug of irritation that assaulted him when Madison West asked the question that had been on his own lips.

"I rented the place," he responded, not inviting her in. "Though I could ask you the same question."

She continued to do a little bounce in place, her arms folded tight against her body, her hands clasped beneath her chin. "And you'd get the same answer," she said. "I'm across the driveway."

"Then you're at the wrong door." He made a move to shut said door, and she reached out, stopping him.

"Sam. Do you always have to be this unpleasant?"

It was a question that had been asked of him more than once. And he gave his standard answer. "Yes."

"Sam," she said, sounding exasperated. "The power went out, and I'm freezing to death. Can I come in?"

He let out a long-suffering sigh and stepped to the side. He didn't like Madison West. He never had. Not from the moment he had been hired on as a farrier for the West estate eight years earlier. In all the years since he'd first met Madison, since he'd first started shoeing her horses, he'd never received one polite word from her.

But then, he'd never given one either.

She was sleek, blonde and freezing cold—and he didn't mean because she had just come in from the storm. The woman carried her own little snow cloud right above her head at all times, and he wasn't a fan of ice princesses. Still, something about her had always been like a burr beneath his skin that he couldn't get at.

"Thank you," she said crisply, stepping over the threshold.

"You're rich and pretty," he said, shutting the door tight behind her. "And I'm poor. And kind of an ass. It wouldn't do for me to let you die out there in a snow-drift. I would probably end up getting hung."

Madison sniffed, making a show of brushing snow-flakes from the shoulders of her jacket. "I highly doubt you're poor," she said drily.

She wasn't wrong. A lot had changed since he'd gone

to work for the Wests eight years ago. Hell, a lot had changed in the past year.

The strangest thing was that his art had taken off, and along with it the metalwork and blacksmithing business he ran with his brother, Chase.

But now he was busier coming up with actual fine-art pieces than he was doing daily grunt work. One sale on a piece like that could set them up for the entire quarter. Strange, and not where he'd seen his life going, but true.

He still had trouble defining himself as an artist. In his mind, he was just a blacksmith cowboy. Most at home on the family ranch, most proficient at pounding metal into another shape. It just so happened that for some reason people wanted to spend a lot of money on that metal.

"Well," he said, "perception is everything."

She looked up at him, those blue eyes hitting him hard, like a punch in the gut. That was the other obnoxious thing about Madison West. She was pretty. She was more than pretty. She was the kind of pretty that kept a man up all night, hard and aching, with fantasies about her swirling in his head.

She was also the kind of woman who would probably leave icicles on a man's member after a blow job.

No, thank you.

"Sure," she said, waving her hand. "Now, I *perceive* that I need to use your phone."

"There's no cell service up here."

"Landline," she said. "I have no power. And no cell service. The source of all my problems."

"In that case, be my guest," he responded, turning away from her and walking toward the kitchen, where the lone phone was plugged in.

He picked up the receiver and held it out to her. She

eyed it for a moment as though it were a live snake, then snatched it out of his hand. "Are you just going to stand there?"

He shrugged, crossing his arms and leaning against the doorframe. "I thought I might."

She scoffed, then dialed the number, doing the same impatient hop she'd been doing outside while she waited for the person on the other end to answer. "Christopher?"

The physical response Sam felt to her uttering another man's name was not something he ever could have anticipated. His stomach tightened, dropped, and a lick of flame that felt a hell of a lot like jealousy sparked inside him.

"What do you mean you can't get up here?" She looked away from him, determinedly so, her eyes fixed on the kitchen floor. "The road is closed. Okay. So that means I can't get back down either?" There was a pause. "Right. Well, hopefully I don't freeze to death." Another pause. "No, you don't need to call anybody. I'm not going to freeze to death. I'm using the neighbor's phone. Just forget it. I don't have cell service. I'll call you if the power comes back on in my cabin."

She hung up then, her expression so sharp it could have cut him clean through.

"I take it you had plans."

She looked at him, her eyes as frosty as the weather outside. "Did you figure that out all by yourself?"

"Only just barely. You know blacksmiths aren't known for their deductive reasoning skills. Mostly we're famous for hitting heavy things with other heavy things."

"Kind of like cavemen and rocks."

He took a step toward her. "Kind of."

She shrank back, a hint of color bleeding into her

cheeks. "Well, now that we've established that there's basically no difference between you and a Neanderthal, I better get back to my dark, empty cabin. And hope that you aren't a secret serial killer."

Her sharp tongue left cuts behind, and he had to admit he kind of enjoyed it. There weren't very many people who sparred with him like this. Possibly because he didn't talk to very many people. "Is that a legitimate concern you have?"

"I don't know. The entire situation is just crazy enough that I might be trapped in a horror movie with a tortured artist blacksmith who is also secretly murdery."

"I guarantee you I'm not murdery. If you see me outside with an ax, it will only be because I'm cutting firewood."

She cocked her head to the side, a glint in her blue eyes that didn't look like ice making his stomach—and everything south of there—tighten. "Well, that's a relief. Anyway. I'm going. Dark cabin, no one waiting for me. It promises to be a seriously good time."

"You don't have any idea why the power is out, or how to fix it?" he asked.

"No," she said, sounding exasperated, and about thirty seconds away from stamping her foot.

Well, damn his conscience, but he wasn't letting her go back to an empty, dark, cold cabin. No matter that she had always treated him like a bit of muck she'd stepped in with her handmade riding boots.

"Let me have a look at your fuse box," he said.

"You sound like you'd rather die," she said.

"I pretty much would, but I'm not going to let *you* die either." He reached for his black jacket and the matching black cowboy hat hanging on a hook. He put both on and nodded.

"Thank you," she muttered, and he could tell the little bit of social nicety directed at him cost her dearly.

They headed toward the front door and he pushed it open, waiting for her to go out first. Since he had arrived earlier today, the temperature had dropped drastically. He had come up to the mountain to do some planning for his next few art projects. It pained him to admit, even to himself, that solitude was somewhat necessary for him to get a clear handle on what he was going to work on next.

"So," he said, making conversation not so much for the sake of it but more to needle her and see if he could earn one of her patented death glares, "Christopher, huh? Your boyfriend?" That hot spike drove its way through his gut again and he did his best to ignore it.

"No," she said tersely. "Just a friend."

"I see. So you decided to meet a man up here for a friendly game of Twister?"

She turned slightly, arching one pale brow. "Yahtzee, actually. I'm very good at it."

"And I'm sure your...*friend* was hoping to get a full house."

She rolled her eyes and looked forward again, taking quick steps over the icy ground, and somehow managing to keep sure footing. Then she opened the door to her cabin. "Welcome," she said, extending her arm. "Please excuse the shuddering cold and oppressive darkness."

"Ladies first," he said.

She shook her head, walking into the house, and he followed behind, closing the door against the elements. It was already cold in the dark little room. "You were just going to come back here and sit in the dark if I hadn't offered to fiddle with the circuit breaker?"

"Maybe I know how to break my own circuits, Sam. Did you ever think of that?"

"Oh, but you said you didn't, Madison."

"I prefer Maddy," she said.

"Sorry, Madison," he said, tipping his hat, just to be a jerk.

"I should have just frozen to death. Then there could have been a legend about my tragic and beautiful demise in the mountains." He didn't say anything. He just looked at her until she sighed and continued talking. "I don't know where the box thingy is. You're going to have to hunt for it."

"I think I can handle that." He walked deeper into the kitchen, then stopped when he saw two purple packets sitting on the kitchen counter. That heat returned with a vengeance when he realized exactly what they were, and what they meant. He looked up, his eyes meeting her extremely guilty gaze. "Yahtzee, huh?"

"That's what the kids call it," she said, pressing her palm over the telling packets.

"Only because they're too immature to call it fucking."

Color washed up her neck, into her cheeks. "Or not crass enough."

In that moment, he had no idea what devil possessed him, and he didn't particularly care. He turned to face her, planting his hands on the countertop, just an inch away from hers. "I don't know about that. I'm betting that you could use a little crassness in your life, Madison West."

"Are you trying to suggest that I need *you*?" she asked, her voice choked.

Lightning streaked through his blood, and in that moment, he was lost. It didn't matter that he thought she was insufferable, a prissy little princess who didn't appreciate any damn thing she had. It didn't matter that he'd come up here to work.

All that mattered was he hadn't touched a woman in a long time, and Madison West was so close all he would have to do was shift his weight slightly and he'd be able to take her into his arms.

He looked down pointedly at her hand, acting as though he could see straight through to the protection beneath. "Well," he said, "you have a couple of the essential ingredients to have yourself a pretty fun evening. All you seem to be missing is the man. But I imagine the guy you invited up here is *nice*. I'm not very nice, Madison," he said, leaning in, "but I could damn sure show you a good time."

Two

The absolute worst thing was the fact that Sam's words sent a shiver down her spine. Sam McCormack. Why did it have to be Sam McCormack? He was the deadly serpent to her Indiana Jones.

She should throw him out. Throw him out and get back to her very disappointing evening where all orgasms would be self-administered. So, basically a regular Friday night.

She wanted to throw herself on the ground and wail. It was not supposed to be a regular Friday night. She was supposed to be breaking her sex fast. Maybe this was why people had flings in the spring. Inclement weather made winter flings difficult. Also, mostly you just wanted to keep your socks on the whole time. And that wasn't sexy.

Maybe her libido should hibernate for a while. Pop up again when the pear trees were blooming or something.

She looked over at Sam, and her libido made a dash to the foreground. That was the problem with Sam. He irritated her. He was exactly the kind of man she didn't like. He was cocky. He was rough and crude.

Whenever she'd given him very helpful pointers about handling the horses when he came to do farrier work at the estate, he was always telling her to go away and in general showing no deference.

And okay, if he'd come and told her how to do her job, she would have told him where he could stick his hoof nippers. But still. Her animals. So she was entitled to her opinions.

Last time she'd walked into the barn when he was doing shoes, he hadn't even looked up from his work. He'd just pointed back toward the door and shouted, *out!*

Yeah, he was a jerk.

However, there was something about the way he looked in a tight T-shirt, his muscles bulging as he did all that hard labor, that made a mockery of that very certain hatred she felt burning in her breast.

"Are you going to take off your coat and stay awhile?" The question, asked in a faintly mocking tone, sent a dart of tension straight down between her thighs.

She could *not* take off her coat. Because she was wearing nothing more than a little scrap of red lace underneath it. And now that was all she could think of. About how little stood between Sam and her naked body.

About what might happen if she just went ahead and dropped the coat now and revealed all of that to him.

"It's cold," she snapped. "Maybe if you went to work getting the electricity back on rather than standing there making terrible double entendres, I would be able to take off my coat."

He lifted a brow. "And then do you think you'll take me up on my offer to show you a good time?"

"If you can get my electricity back on, I will consider a good time shown to me. Honestly, that's all I want. The ability to microwave popcorn and not turn into a Maddycicle."

The maddening man raised his eyebrows, shooting her a look that clearly said *Suit yourself*, then set about looking for the fuse box.

She stood by alone for a while, her arms wrapped around her midsection. Then she started to feel like an idiot just kind of hanging out there while he searched for the source of all power. She let out an exasperated sigh and followed his path, stopping when she saw him leaning up against a wall, a little metal door fixed between the logs open as he examined the small black switches inside.

"It's not a fuse. That means there's something else going on." He slammed the door shut. Then he turned back to look at her. "You should come over to my cabin."

"No!" The denial was a little bit too enthusiastic. A little bit too telling. "I mean, I can start a fire here—it's going to be fine. I'm not going to freeze."

"You're going to curl up by the fire with a blanket? Like a sad little pet?"

She made a scoffing sound. "No, I'm going to curl up by the fire like the Little Match Girl."

"That makes it even worse. The Little Match Girl froze to death."

"What?"

"How did you not know that?"

"I saw it when I was a kid. It was a *cartoon*. She really died?" Maddy blinked. "What kind of story is that to present to children?"

"An early lesson, maybe? Life is bleak, and then you freeze to death alone?"

"Charming," she said.

"Life rarely is." He kept looking at her. His dark gaze was worrisome.

"I'm fine," she said, because somebody had to say something.

"You are not. Get your suitcase—come over to the cabin. We can flip the lights on, and then if we notice from across the driveway that your power's on again, you can always come back."

It was stupid to refuse him. She knew him, if not personally, at least well enough to know that he wasn't any kind of danger to her.

The alternative was trying to sleep on the couch in the living room while the outside temperatures hovered below freezing, waking up every few hours to keep the fire stoked.

Definitely, going over to his cabin made more sense. But the idea filled her with a strange tension that she couldn't quite shake. Well, she knew exactly what kind of tension it was. *Sexual tension.*

She and Sam had so much of it that hung between them like a fog whenever they interacted. Although, maybe she read it wrong. Maybe on his end it was just irritation and it wasn't at all tinged with sensual shame.

"Why do you have to be so damned reasonable?" she asked, turning away from him and stalking toward the stairs.

"Where are you going?"

She stopped, turning to face him. "To change. Also, to get my suitcase. I have snacks in there."

"Are snacks a euphemism for something interesting?" he asked, arching a dark brow.

She sputtered, genuinely speechless. Which was unusual to downright unheard of. "No," she said, her tone sounding petulant. "I have *actual snacks*."

"Come over to my place. Bring the snacks."

"I will," she said, turning on her heel, heading toward the stairs.

"Maybe bring the Yahtzee too."

Those words hit her hard, with all the impact of a stomach punch. She could feel her face turning crimson, and she refused to look back at him. Refused to react to that bait at all. He didn't want *that*. He did not want to play euphemistic board games with her. And she didn't want to play them with him.

If she felt a little bit…on edge, it was just because she had been anticipating sex and she had experienced profound sex disappointment. That was all.

She continued up the stairs, making her way to the bedroom, then changed back into a pair of jeans and a sweatshirt as quickly as possible before stuffing the little red lace thing back in the bag and zipping everything up.

She lugged it back downstairs, her heart slamming against her breastbone when Sam was in her line of sight again. Tall, broad shouldered and far too sexy for his own good, he promised to be the antidote to sexual disappointment.

But an emotionless hookup with a guy she liked well enough but wouldn't get emotionally involved with was one thing. Replacing him at the last moment with a guy she didn't even like? No, that was out of the question.

Absolutely and completely out of the question.

"Okay," she said, "let's go."

By the time she got settled in the extra room in the cabin, she was feeling antsy. She could hide, but she was hungry. And Maddy didn't believe in being hungry when food was at hand. Yes, she had some various sugar-based items in her bag, but she needed protein.

In the past, she had braved any number of her father's awkward soirees to gain access to bacon-wrapped appetizers.

She could brave Sam McCormack well enough to root around for sustenance. She would allow no man to stand between herself and her dinner.

Cautiously, she made her way downstairs, hoping that maybe Sam had put himself away for the night. The thought made her smile. That he didn't go to bed like a normal person but closed himself inside…not a coffin. But maybe a scratchy, rock-hewn box that would provide no warmth or comfort. It seemed like something he would be into.

In fairness, she didn't really know Sam McCormack that well, but everything she did know about him led her to believe that he was a supremely unpleasant person. Well, except for the whole him-not-letting-her-die-of-frostbite-in-her-powerless-cabin thing. She supposed she had to go ahead and put that in the Maybe He's Not Such a Jackass column.

Her foot hit the ground after the last stair silently, and she cautiously padded into the kitchen.

"Looking for something?"

She startled, turning around and seeing Sam standing there, leaning in the doorway, his muscular arms crossed over his broad chest. She did her best to look cool. Composed. Not interested in his muscles. "Well—" she tucked her hair behind her ear "—I was hoping to find some food."

"You brought snacks," he said.

"Candy," she countered.

"So, that made it okay for you to come downstairs and steal my steak?"

Her stomach growled. "You have steak?"

"It's *my* steak."

She hadn't really thought of that. "Well, my...you know, *the guy*. He was supposed to bring food. And I'm sorry. I didn't exactly think about the fact that whatever food is in this fridge is food that you personally provided. I was protein blind." She did her best to look plaintive. Unsurprisingly, Sam did not seem moved by her plaintiveness.

"I mean, it seems cruel to eat steak in front of you, Madison. Especially if I'm not willing to share." He rubbed his chin, the sounds of his whiskers abrading his palm sending a little shiver down her back. God knew why.

"You *would* do that. You would... You would tease me with your steak." Suddenly, it was all starting to sound a little bit sexual. Which she had a feeling was due in part to the fact that everything felt sexual to her right about now.

Which was because of the other man she had been about to sleep with. Not Sam. Not really.

A slow smile crossed his face. "I would never tease you with my steak, Madison. If you want a taste, all you have to do is ask. Nicely."

She felt her face getting hotter. "May I please have your steak?"

"Are you going to cook it for me?"

"Did you want it to be edible?"

"That would be the goal, yes," he responded.

She lifted her hands up, palms out. "These hands don't cook."

His expression shifted. A glint of wickedness cutting through all that hardness. She'd known Sam was mean. She'd known he was rough. She had not realized he was wicked. "What do those hands do, I wonder?"

He let that innuendo linger between them and she practically hissed in response. "Do you have salad? I will fix salad. *You* cook steak. Then we can eat."

"Works for me, but I assume you're going to be sharing your candy with me?"

Seriously, everything sounded filthy. She had to get a handle on herself. "Maybe," she said, "but it depends on if your behavior merits candy." That didn't make it better.

"I see. And what, pray tell, does Madison West consider candy-deserving behavior?"

She shrugged, making her way to the fridge and opening it, bending down and opening the crisper drawer. "I don't know. Not being completely unbearable?"

"Your standards are low."

"Luckily for you."

She looked up at him and saw that that had actually elicited what looked to be a genuine grin. The man was a mystery. And she shouldn't care about that. She should not want to unlock, unravel or otherwise solve him.

The great thing about Christopher was that he was simple. He wasn't connected to her life in any way. They could come up and have an affair and it would never bleed over to her existence in Copper Ridge. It was the antithesis of everything she had experienced with David. David, who had blown up her entire life, shattered her career ambitions and damaged her good standing in the community.

This thing with Christopher was supposed to be sex. Sex that made nary a ripple in the rest of her life.

Sam would not be rippleless.

The McCormack family was too much a part of the fabric of Copper Ridge. More so in the past year. Sam and his brother, Chase, had done an amazing job of revitalizing their family ranch, and somewhere in all of that Sam had become an in-demand artist. Though he would be the last person to say it. He still showed up right on schedule to do the farrier work at her family ranch. As though he weren't raking in way more money with his ironwork.

Sam was… Well, he was kind of everywhere. His works of art appearing in restaurants and galleries around town. His person appearing on the family ranch to work on the horses. He was the exact wrong kind of man for her to be fantasizing about.

She should be more gun-shy than this. Actually, she had spent the past decade being more gun-shy than this. It was just that apparently now that she had allowed herself to remember she had sexual feelings, it was difficult for her to turn them off. Especially when she was trapped in a snowstorm with a man for whom the term *rock-hard body* would be a mere description and not hyperbole.

She produced the salad, then set about to preparing it. Thankfully, it was washed and torn already. So her responsibility literally consisted of dumping it from bag to bowl. That was the kind of cooking she could get behind. Meanwhile, Sam busied himself with preparing two steaks on the stovetop. At some point, he took the pan from the stovetop and transferred it to the oven.

"I didn't know you had actual cooking technique," she said, not even pretending to herself that she wasn't watching the play of his muscles in his forearms as he worked.

Even at the West Ranch, where she always ended up sniping at him if they ever interacted, she tended to linger around him while he did his work with the horses because his arms put on quite a show. She was hardly going to turn away from him now that they were in an enclosed space, with said arms very, very close. And no one else around to witness her ogling.

She just didn't possess that kind of willpower.

"Well, Madison, I have a lot of eating technique. The two are compatible."

"Right," she said, "as you don't have a wife. Or a girlfriend…" She could have punched her own face for that. It sounded so leading and obvious. As if she cared if he had a woman in his life.

She didn't. Well, she kind of did. Because honestly, she didn't even like to ogle men who could be involved with another woman. Once bitten, twice shy. By which she meant once caught in a torrid extramarital affair with a man in good standing in the equestrian community, ten years emotionally scarred.

"No," he said, tilting his head, the cocky look in his eye doing strange things to her stomach, "I don't."

"I don't have a boyfriend. Not an actual boyfriend." Oh, good Lord. She was the desperate worst and she hated herself.

"So you keep saying," he returned. "You really want

to make sure I know Christopher isn't your boyfriend." She couldn't ignore the implication in his tone.

"Because he isn't. Because we're not... Because we've never. This was going to be our first time." Being forthright and making people uncomfortable with said forthrightness had been a very handy shield for the past decade, but tonight it was really obnoxious.

"Oh really?" He suddenly looked extremely interested.

"Yes," she responded, keeping her tone crisp, refusing to show him just how off-kilter she felt. "I'm just making dinner conversation."

"This is the kind of dinner conversation you normally make?"

She arched her brow. "Actually, yes. Shocking people is kind of my modus operandi."

"I don't find you that shocking, Madison. I do find it a little bit amusing that you got cock-blocked by a snowbank."

She nearly choked. "Wine. Do you have wine?" She turned and started rummaging through the nearest cabinet. "Of course you do. You probably have a baguette too. That seems like something an artist would do. Set up here and drink wine and eat a baguette."

He laughed, a kind of short, dismissive sound. "Hate to disappoint you. But my artistic genius is fueled by Jack." He reached up, opening the cabinet nearest to his head, and pulled down a bottle of whiskey. "But I'm happy to share that too."

"You have diet soda?"

"Regular."

"My, this *is* a hedonistic experience. I'll have regular, then."

"Well, when a woman was expecting sex and doesn't get it, I suppose regular cola is poor consolation, but it is better than diet."

"Truer words were never spoken." She watched him while he set about to making a couple of mixed drinks for them. He handed one to her, and she lifted it in salute before taking a small sip. By then he was taking the steak out of the oven and setting it back on the stovetop.

"Perfect," he remarked when he cut one of the pieces of meat in half and gauged the color of the interior.

She frowned. "How did I never notice that you aren't horrible?"

He looked at her, his expression one of mock surprise. "Not horrible? You be careful throwing around compliments like that, missy. A man could get the wrong idea."

She rolled her eyes. "Right. I just mean, you're funny."

"How much of that whiskey have you had?"

"One sip. So it isn't even that." She eyeballed the food that he was now putting onto plates. "It might be the steak. I'm not going to lie to you."

"I'm comfortable with that."

He carried their plates to the table, and she took the lone bottle of ranch dressing out of the fridge and set it and her drink next to her plate. And then, somehow, she ended up sitting at a very nicely appointed dinner table with Sam McCormack, who was not the man she was supposed to be with tonight.

Maybe it was because of the liquored-up soda. Maybe it was neglected hormones losing their ever-loving minds in the presence of such a fine male specimen. Maybe it was just as simple as want. Maybe there was no justification for it at all. Except that Sam was actually beautiful. And she had always thought so, no matter how much he got under her skin.

That was the honest truth. It was why she found him so off-putting, why she had always found him so off-putting from the moment he had first walked onto the West Ranch property. Because he was the kind of man a woman could make a mistake with. And she had thought she was done making mistakes.

Now she was starting to wonder if a woman was entitled to one every decade.

Her safe mistake, the one who would lift out of her life, hadn't eventuated. And here in front of her was one that had the potential to be huge. But very, very good.

She wasn't so young anymore. She wasn't naive at all. When it came right down to it, she was hot for Sam. She had been for a long time.

She'd had so much caution for so long. So much hiding. So much *not doing*. Well, she was tired of that.

"I was very disappointed about Christopher not making it up here," she said, just as Sam was putting the last bite of steak into his mouth.

"Sure," he said.

"Very disappointed."

"Nobody likes blue balls, Maddy, even if they don't have testicles."

She forced a laugh through her constricted throat. "That's hilarious," she said.

He looked up at her slowly. "No," he said, "it wasn't."

She let out a long, slow breath. "Okay," she said, "it wasn't that funny. But here's the thing. The reason I was so looking forward to tonight is that I hadn't had sex with Christopher before. In fact, I haven't had sex with anyone in ten years. So. Maybe you could help me with that?"

Three

Sam was pretty sure he must be hallucinating. Because there was no way Madison West had just propositioned him. Especially not on the heels of admitting that it had been ten years since she'd had sex.

Hell, he was starting to think that *he* was the celibacy champion. But clearly, Maddy had him beat. Or she didn't, because there was no way in hell that she had actually said any of that.

"Are you drunk, Madison?" It was the first thing that came to mind, and it seemed like an important thing to figure out.

"After one Jack Daniel's and Coke? Absolutely not. I am a West, dammit. We can hold our liquor. I am…reckless, opportunistic and horny. A lot horny. I just…I need this. Sam, do you know what it's like to go *ten years* without doing something? It becomes a whole thing. Like, a whole big thing that starts to define you, even if it shouldn't. And you don't want anyone to know. Oh, my gosh, can you even imagine if my friends knew that it has been ten years since I have seen an actual…?" She took a deep breath, then forged on. "I'm rambling and I just *really* need this."

Sam felt like he had been hit over the head with a metric ton of iron. He had no idea how he was supposed to respond to this—the strangest of all propositions—from a woman who had professed to hate him only a few moments ago.

He had always thought Madison was a snob. A pain in his ass, even if she was a pretty pain in the ass. She was always looming around, looking down her nose at him while he did his work. As though only the aristocracy of Copper Ridge could possibly know how to do the lowly labor he was seeing to. Even if they hadn't the ability to do it themselves.

The kinds of people who professed to have strengths in "management." People who didn't know how to get their hands dirty.

He hated people like that. And he had never been a fan of Madison West.

He, Sam McCormack, should not be interested in taking her up on her offer. No, not in any way. However, Sam McCormack's dick was way more interested in it than he would've liked to admit.

Immediately, he was rock hard thinking about what it would be like to have her delicate, soft hands skimming over him. He had rough hands. Workman's hands. The kind of hands that a woman like Madison West had probably never felt against her rarefied flesh.

Hell, the fact that it had been ten years since she'd gotten any made that even more likely. And damn if that didn't turn him on. It was kind of twisted, a little bit sick, but then, it was nothing short of what he expected from himself.

He was a lot of things. Good wasn't one of them.

Ready to explode after years of repressing his desires, after years of pushing said desire all down and pretending it wasn't there? He was that.

"I'm not actually sure you want this," he said, wondering what the hell he was doing. Giving her an out when he wanted to throw her down and make her his.

Maddy stood up, not about to be cowed by him. He should have known that she would take that as a challenge. Maybe he had known that. Maybe it was why he'd said it.

That sounded like him. That sounded a lot more like him than trying to do the honorable thing.

"You don't know what I want, Sam," she said, crossing the space between them, swaying her hips just a little bit more than she usually did.

He would be a damn liar if he said that he had never thought about what it might be like to grab hold of those hips and pull Maddy West up against him. To grind his hardness against her soft flesh and make her feel exactly what her snobby-rich-girl mouth did to him.

But just because he'd fantasized about it before, didn't mean he had ever anticipated doing it. It didn't mean that he should take her up on it now.

Still, the closer she got to him, the less likely it seemed that he was going to say no.

"I think that after ten years of celibacy a man could make the argument that you don't know what you want, Madison West."

Her eyes narrowed, glittering blue diamonds that

looked like they could cut a man straight down to the bone. "I've always known what I wanted. I may not have always made the best decisions, but I was completely certain that I wanted them. At the time."

His lips tipped upward. "I'm just going to be another *at the time*, Maddy. Nothing else."

"That was the entire point of this weekend. For me to have something that didn't have consequences. For me to get a little bit of something for myself. Is that so wrong? Do I have to live a passionless existence because I made a mistake once? Am I going to question myself forever? I just need to… I need to rip the Band-Aid off."

"The Band-Aid?"

"The sex Band-Aid."

He nodded, pretending that he understood. "Okay."

"I want this," she said, her tone confident.

"Are you…suggesting…that I give you…sexual healing?"

She made a scoffing sound. "Don't make it sound cheesy. This is very serious. I would never joke about my sexual needs." She let out an exasperated sigh. "I'm doing this wrong. I'm just…"

Suddenly, she launched herself at him, wrapping her arms around his neck and pressing her lips against his. The moment she did it, it was like the strike of a hammer against hot iron. As rigid as he'd been before—in that moment, he bent. And easily.

Staying seated in the chair, he curved himself around Madison, wrapping his arms around her body, sliding his hands over her back, down to the sweet indent of her waist, farther still to the flare of those pretty hips. The hips he had thought about taking hold of so many times before.

There was no hesitation now. None at all. There was only this. Only her. Only the soft, intoxicating taste of her on his tongue. Sugar, Jack Daniel's and something that was entirely Maddy.

Too rich for his blood. Far too expensive for a man like him. It didn't matter what he became. Didn't matter how much money he had in his bank account, he would always be what he was. There was no escaping it. Nobody knew. Not really. Not the various women who had graced his bed over the years, not his brother, Chase.

Nobody knew Sam McCormack.

At least, nobody alive.

Neither, he thought, would Madison West. This wasn't about knowing anybody. This was just about satisfying a need. And he was simple enough to take her up on that.

He wedged his thigh up between her legs, pressing his palm down on her lower back, encouraging her to flex her hips in time with each stroke of his tongue. Encouraging her to satisfy that ache at the apex of her thighs.

Her head fell back, her skin flushed and satisfaction grabbed him by the throat, gripping him hard and strong. It would've surprised him if he hadn't suspected he was the sort of bastard who would get off on something like this.

Watching this beautiful, classy girl coming undone in his arms.

She was right. This weekend could be out of time. It could be a moment for them to indulge in things they would never normally allow themselves to have. The kinds of things that he had closed himself off from years ago.

Softness, warmth, touch.

He had denied himself all those things for years. Why

not do this now? No one would know. No one would ever have to know. Maddy would see to that. She would never, no chance in hell, admit that she had gotten down and dirty with a man who was essentially a glorified blacksmith.

No way in hell.

That made them both safe. It made this safe. Well, as safe as fire this hot could be.

She bit his lip and he growled, pushing his hands up underneath the hem of her shirt, kissing her deeper as he let his fingertips roam to the line of her elegant spine, then tracing it upward until he found her bra, releasing it with ease, then dragging it and her top up over her head, leaving her naked from the waist up.

"I…" Her face was a bright shade of red. "I…I have lingerie. I wasn't going to…"

"I don't give a damn about your lingerie. I just want this." He lowered his head, sliding his tongue around the perimeter of one of her tightened nipples. "I want your skin." He closed his lips over that tight bud, sucking it in deep.

"I had a seduction plan," she said, her voice trembling. He wasn't entirely sure it was a protest, or even a complaint.

"You don't plan passion, baby," he said.

At least, he didn't. Because if he were thinking clearly, he would be putting her top back on and telling her to go back to her ice-cold cabin, where she would be safe.

"I do," she said, her teeth chattering in spite of the fact that it was very warm in the kitchen. "I plan everything."

"Not this. You're a dirty girl now, Madison West," he said, sliding his thumb over her damp nipple, moving it in a slow circle until she arched her back and cried out.

"You were going to sleep with another man this weekend, and you replaced him so damn easily. With me. Doesn't even matter to you who you have. As long as you get a little bit. Is that how it is?"

She whimpered, biting her lip, rolling her hips against him.

"Good girl," he said, his gut tightening, his arousal so hard he was sure he was going to burst through the front of his jeans. "I like that. I like you being dirty for me."

He moved his hands then, curving his fingers around her midsection, his thumbs resting just beneath the swell of her breasts. She was so soft, so smooth, so petite and fragile. Everything he should never be allowed to put his hands on. But for some reason, instead of feeling a bolt of shame, he felt aroused. Hotter and harder than he could ever remember being. "You like that? My hands are rough. Maybe a little bit too rough for you."

"No," she said, and this time the protest was clear. "Not too rough for me at all."

He slid his hands down her back, taking a moment to really revel in how soft she was and how much different he must feel to her. She squirmed against him, and he took that as evidence that she really did like it.

That only made him hotter. Harder. More impatient.

"You didn't bring your damn candy and forget the condoms, did you?"

"No," she said, the denial coming quickly. "I brought the condoms."

"You always knew we would end up like this, didn't you?"

She looked away from him, and the way she refused to meet his eyes turned a throwaway game of a question into something deadly serious.

"Madison," he said, his voice hard. She still didn't look at him. He grabbed hold of her chin, redirecting her face so that she was forced to make eye contact with him. "You knew this would happen all along, didn't you?"

She still refused to answer him. Refused to speak.

"I think you did," he continued. "I think that's why you can never say a kind word to me. I think that's why you acted like a scalded cat every time I walked into the room. Because you knew it would end here. Because you wanted this. Because you wanted me."

Her expression turned even more mutinous.

"Madison," he said, a warning lacing through the word. "Don't play games with me. Or I'm not going to give you what you want. So you have to tell me. Tell me that you've always wanted me. You've always wanted my dirty hands on you. That's why you hate me so damn much, isn't it? Because you want me."

"I..."

"Madison," he said, his tone even more firm, "tell me—" he rubbed his hand over her nipple "—or I stop."

"I wanted you," she said, the admission rushed but clear all the same.

"More," he said, barely recognizing his own voice. "Tell me more."

It seemed essential suddenly, to know she'd wanted him. He didn't know why. He didn't care why.

"I've always wanted you. From the moment I first saw you. I knew that it would be like this. I knew that I would climb up into your lap and I would make a fool of myself rubbing all over you like a cat. I knew that from the beginning. So I argued with you instead."

He felt a satisfied smile that curved his lips upward. "Good girl." He lowered his hands, undoing the snap on her jeans and drawing the zipper down slowly. "You just made us both very happy." He moved his fingertips down beneath the waistband of her panties, his breath catching in his throat when he felt hot wetness beneath his touch. It had been way too long since he felt a silky-smooth desirable woman. Had been way too long in his self-imposed prison.

Too long since he'd wanted at all.

But Madison wasn't Elizabeth. And this wasn't the same.

He didn't need to think about her. He wasn't going to. Not for the rest of the night.

He pushed every thought out of his mind and instead exulted in the sound that Madison made when he moved his fingers over that place where she was wet and aching for him. When he delved deeper, pushing one finger inside her, feeling just how close she was to the edge, evidenced by the way her internal muscles clenched around him. He could thrust into her here. Take her hard and fast and she would still come. He knew that she would.

But she'd had ten years of celibacy, and he was pushing on five. They deserved more. They deserved better. At the very least they deserved a damn bed.

With that in mind, he wrapped his arms more tightly around her, moving his hands to cup her behind as he lifted her, wrapping her legs tightly around him as he carried them across the kitchen and toward the stairs.

Maddy let out an inelegant squeak as he began to ascend toward the bedrooms. "This is really happening," she said, sounding slightly dazed.

"I thought you said you weren't drunk."

"I'm not."

"Then try not to look so surprised. It's making me question things. And I don't want to question things. I just want you."

She shivered in his hold. "You're not like most men I know."

"Pretty boys with popped collars and pastel polo shirts? I must be a real disappointment."

"Obviously you aren't. Obviously I don't care about men in pastel polo shirts or I would've gotten laid any number of times in the past decade."

He pushed open the bedroom door, threw her down over the simply appointed bed that was far too small for the kind of acrobatics he wanted to get up to tonight. Then he stood back, admiring her, wearing nothing but those half-open jeans riding low on her hips, her stomach dipping in with each breath, her breasts thrust into greater prominence at the same time.

"Were you waiting for me?" He kept the words light, taunting, because he knew that she liked it.

She had always liked sparring with him. That was what they'd always done. Of course she would like it now. Of course he would like it now. Or maybe it had nothing to do with her. Maybe it had everything to do with the fact that he had years' worth of dirty in him that needed to be let out.

"Screw you," she said, pushing herself back farther up the mattress so that her head was resting on the pillow. Then she put her hands behind her head, her blue gaze sharp. "Come on, cowboy. Get naked for me."

"Oh no, Maddy, you're not running the show."

"Ten years," she said, her gaze level with his. "Ten years, Sam. That's how long it's been since I've seen a naked man. And let me tell you, I have never seen a naked man like you." She held up a finger. "One man. One insipid man. He wasn't even that good."

"You haven't had sex for ten years and your last lover wasn't even good? I was sort of hoping that it had been so good you were waiting for your knees to stop shaking before you bothered to go out and get some again."

"If only. My knees never once shook. In fact, they're shaking harder now and you haven't even gotten out of those pants yet."

"You give good dirty talk."

She lifted a shoulder. "I'm good at talking. That's about the thing I'm best at."

"Oh, I hope not, baby. I hope that mouth is good for a lot of other things too."

He saw her breasts hitch. Her eyes growing round. Then he smiled, grabbing hold of the hem of his shirt and stripping it off over his head. Her reaction was more satisfying than he could've possibly anticipated. It'd been a long time since he'd seen a woman looking at him that way.

Sure, women checked him out. That happened all the time. But this was different. This was raw, open hunger. She wasn't bothering to hide it. Why would she? They were both here to do this. No holds barred, no clothes, no nothing. Why bother to be coy? Why bother to pretend this was about anything other than satisfying lust. And if that was all it was, why should either of them bother to hide that lust.

"Keep looking at me like that, sweetheart, this is gonna end fast."

"Don't do that," she said, a wicked smile on her lips. "You're no good to me in that case."

"Don't worry, babe. I can get it up more than once."

At least, he could if he remembered correctly.

"Good thing I brought about three boxes of condoms."

"For two days? You did have high hopes for the weekend."

"Ten years," she reiterated.

"Point taken."

He moved his hands down, slowly working at his belt. The way that she licked her lips as her eyes followed his every movement ratcheting up his arousal another impossible notch.

Everything felt too sharp, too clear, every rasp of fabric over his skin, every downward flick of her eyes, every small, near-imperceptible gasp on her lips.

He hadn't been in a bedroom alone with a woman in a long damn time. And it was all catching up with him now.

Shutting down, being a mean bastard who didn't let anyone close? That was easy enough. It made it easy to forget. He shut the world out, stripped everything away. Reverted back to the way he had been just after his parents had died and it had been too difficult to feel anything more than his grief.

That was what he had done in the past five years. That was what he had done with his new, impossible loss that never should have happened. Wouldn't have if he'd had a shred of self-control and decency.

And now, tonight, he was proving that he probably still didn't have any at all. Oh well, just as well. Because he was going to do this.

He was going to do her.

He pushed his jeans down his lean hips, showing her the extent of his desire for her, reveling in the way her eyes widened when he revealed his body completely to her hungry gaze.

"I have never seen one that big before," she said.

He laughed. "Are you just saying that because it's what you think men need to hear?"

"No, I'm saying that because it's the biggest I've ever seen. And I want it."

"Baby," he said, "you can have it."

Maddy turned over onto her stomach and crawled across the bed on all fours in a move that damn near gave him a heart attack. Then she moved to the edge of the mattress, straightening up, raking her nails down over his torso before she leaned in, flicking her tongue over the head of his arousal.

He jerked beneath her touch, his length twitching as her tongue traced it from base to tip, just before she engulfed him completely in the warm heat of her mouth. She hummed, the vibration moving through his body, drawing his balls up tight. He really was going to lose it. Here and now like a green teenage boy if he didn't get a grip on himself. Or a grip on her.

He settled for the second option.

He reached back, grabbing hold of her hair and jerking her lips away from him. "You keep doing that and it really will end."

The color was high in her cheeks, her eyes glittering. "I've never, ever enjoyed it like that before."

She was so good for his ego. Way better than a man like him deserved. But damned if he wasn't going to take it.

"Well, you can enjoy more of that. Later. Right now? I need to be inside you."

"Technically," she said, her tone one of protest, "you were inside me."

"And as much as I like being in that pretty mouth of yours, that isn't what I want right now." He gritted his teeth, looking around the room. "The condoms."

She scrambled off the bed and shimmied out of her jeans and panties as she made her way across the room and toward her suitcase. She flipped it open, dug through it frantically and produced the two packets he had seen earlier.

All things considered, he felt a little bit triumphant to be the one getting these condoms. He didn't know Christopher, but that sad sack was sitting at home with a hard-on, and Sam was having his woman. He was going to go ahead and enjoy the hell out of that.

Madison turned to face him, the sight of that enticing, pale triangle at the apex of her thighs sending a shot straight down to his gut. She kept her eyes on his as she moved nearer, holding one of the condoms like it was a reward he was about to receive.

She tore it open and settled back onto the bed, then leaned forward and rolled it over his length. Then she took her position back up against the pillows, her thighs parting, her heavily lidded gaze averted from his now that she was in that vulnerable position.

"Okay," she said, "I'm ready."

She wasn't. Not by a long shot.

Ten years.

And he had been ready to thrust into her with absolutely no finesse. A woman who'd been celibate for ten years deserved more than that. She deserved more than one orgasm. Hell, she deserved more than two.

He had never been the biggest fan of Madison West,

but tonight they were allies. Allies in pleasure. And he was going to hold up his end of the bargain so well that if she was celibate after this, it really would be because she was waiting for her legs to work again.

"Not quite yet, Maddy," he said, kneeling down at the end of the bed, reaching forward and grabbing hold of her hips, dragging her down toward his face. He brought her up against his mouth, her legs thrown over his shoulders, that place where she was warm and wet for him right there, ready for him to taste her.

"Sam!" Maddy squeaked.

"There is no way you're a prude, Maddy," he said. "I've had too many conversations with you to believe that."

"I've never... No one has ever..."

"Then it's time somebody did."

He lowered his head, tasting her in long, slow passes, like she was an ice-cream cone that he just had to take the time to savor. Like she was a delicacy he couldn't get enough of.

Because she was.

She was all warmth and sweet female, better than he had ever remembered a woman being. Or maybe she was just better. It was hard to say. He didn't really care which. It didn't matter. All that mattered was this.

If he could lose himself in any moment, in any time, it would be this one.

It sure as hell wouldn't be pounding iron, trying to hammer the guilt out of his body. Certainly wouldn't be in his damn sculptures, trying to figure out what to make next, trying to figure out how to satisfy the customer. This deeply personal thing that had started being given to the rest of the world, when he wasn't sure he wanted the rest of the world to see what was inside him.

Hell, *he* didn't want to see what was inside him.

He made a hell of a lot of money, carving himself out, making it into a product people could buy. And he sure as hell liked the money, but that didn't make it a pleasant experience.

No, none of that mattered. Not now. Not when there was Maddy. And that sweet sugar-whiskey taste.

He tasted her until she screamed, and then he thrust his fingers inside her, fast and rough, until he felt her pulse around him, until her orgasm swept through them both.

Then he moved up, his lips almost touching hers. "Now," he said, his voice husky, "now you're ready."

Four

Maddy was shaking from head to toe, and she honestly didn't know if she could take any more. She had never—not in her entire life—had an orgasm like that. It was still echoing through her body, creating little waves of sensation that shivered through her with each and every breath she took.

And there was still more. They weren't done. She was glad about that. She didn't want to be done. But at the same time she wasn't sure if she could handle the rest. But there he was, above her, over her, so hot and hard and male that she didn't think she could deny him. She didn't want to deny him.

She looked at him, at the broad expanse of his shoulders and chest, the way it tapered down to his narrow waist, those flat washboard abs that she could probably actually wash her clothes on.

He was everything a man should be. If the perfect fantasy man had been pulled straight out of her deepest fantasies, he would look like this. It hit her then that Christopher had not even been close to being a fantasy man. And that was maybe why he had been so safe. It was why Sam had always been so threatening.

Because Christopher had the power to make a ripple. Sam McCormack possessed the power to engulf her in a tidal wave.

She had no desire to be swept out to sea by any man. But in this instance she had a life preserver. And that was her general dislike of him. The fact that their time together was going to be contained to only this weekend. So what did it matter if she allowed herself to get a little bit storm tossed. It didn't. She was free. Free to enjoy this as much as she wanted.

And she wanted. *Wanted* with an endless hunger that seemed to growl inside her like a feral beast.

He possessed the equipment to satisfy it. She let her eyes drift lower than just his abs, taking in the heart, the unequivocal evidence, of his maleness. She had not been lying when she said it was the biggest one she'd ever seen. It made her feel a little bit intimidated. Especially since she had been celibate for so very long. But she had a few days to acclimate.

The thought made her giddy.

"Now," she said, not entirely certain that she was totally prepared for him now but also unable to wait for him.

"You sure you're ready for me?" He leaned forward, bracing his hand on the headboard, poised over her like the very embodiment of carnal temptation. Just out of reach, close enough that she did easily inhale his masculine scent. Far enough away that he wasn't giving her what she needed. Not yet.

She felt hollow. Aching. And that, she realized, was how she knew she was going to take all of him whether or not it seemed possible. Because the only other option was remaining like this. Hollowed out and empty. And she couldn't stand that either. Not for one more second.

"Please," she said, not caring that she sounded plaintive. Not caring that she was begging. Begging Sam, the man she had spent the past several years harassing every time he came around her ranch.

No, she didn't care. She would make a fool out of herself if she had to, would lower herself as far down as she needed to go, if only she could get the kind of satisfaction that his body promised to deliver.

He moved his other hand up to the headboard, gripping it tight. Then he flexed his hips forward, the blunt head of his arousal teasing the slick entrance to her body. She reached up, bracing her palms flat against his chest, a shiver running through her as he teased her with near penetration.

She cursed. The sound quivering, weak in the near silence of the room. She had no idea where hard-ass Maddy had gone. That tough, flippant girl who knew how to keep everyone at a distance with her words. Who knew how to play off every situation as if it weren't a big deal.

This was a big deal. How could she pretend that it wasn't? She was breaking apart from the inside out; how could she act as though she weren't?

"Please," she repeated.

He let go of the headboard with one hand and pressed his hand down next to her face, then repeated the motion with the other as he rocked his hips forward more fully, entering her slowly, inch by tantalizing inch. She gasped when he filled her all the way, the intense stretching sensation a pleasure more than it was a pain.

She slid her hands up to his shoulders, down his back, holding on to him tightly there before locking her legs around his lean hips and urging him even deeper.

"Yes," she breathed, a wave of satisfaction rolling over her, chased on the heels by a sense that she was still incomplete. That this wasn't enough. That it would never be enough.

Then he began to move. Ratcheting up the tension between them. Taking her need, her arousal, to greater heights than she had ever imagined possible. He was measured at first, taking care to establish a rhythm that helped her move closer to completion. But she didn't need the help. She didn't want it. She just wanted to ride the storm.

She tilted her head to the side, scraping her teeth along the tendon in his neck that stood out as a testament to his hard-won self-control.

And that did it.

He growled low in his throat. Then his movements became hard, harsh. Following no particular rhythm but his own. She loved it. Gloried in it. He grabbed hold of her hips, tugging her up against him every time he thrust down, making it rougher, making it deeper. Making it hurt. She felt full with it, full with him. This was exactly what she needed, and she hadn't even realized it. To be utterly and completely overwhelmed. To have this man consume her every sensation, her every breath.

She fused her lips to his, kissing him frantically as he continued to move inside her and she held on to him tighter, her nails digging into his skin. But she knew he didn't mind the pain. She knew it just as she didn't mind it. Knew it because he began to move harder, faster, reaching the edge of his own control as he pushed her nearer to the edge of hers.

Suddenly, it gripped her fiercely, down low inside her, a force of pleasure that she couldn't deny or control. She froze, stiffening against him, the scream that lodged itself in her throat the very opposite of who she usually was. It wasn't calculated; it wasn't pretty; it wasn't designed to do anything. It simply was. An expression of what she felt. Beyond her reach, beyond her completely.

She was racked with her desire for him, with the intensity of the orgasm that swept through her. And then, just as she was beginning to find a way to breathe again, he found his own release, his hardness pulsing deep inside her as he gave himself up to it.

His release—the intensity of it—sent another shattering wave through her. And she clung to him even more tightly, needing him to anchor her to the bed, to the earth, or she would lose herself completely.

And then in the aftermath, she was left there, clinging to a stranger, having just shown the deepest, most hidden parts of herself to him. Having just lost her control with him in a way she never would have done with someone she knew better. Perhaps this was the only way she could have ever experienced this kind of freedom. The only way she could have ever let her guard down enough. What did she have to lose with Sam? His opinion of her was already low. So if he thought that she was a sex-hungry maniac after this, what did it matter?

He moved away from her and she threw her arm over

her face, letting her head fall back, the sound of her fractured breathing echoing in the room.

After she had gulped in a few gasps of air, she removed her arm, opened her eyes and realized that Sam wasn't in the room anymore. Probably off to the bathroom to deal with necessities. Good. She needed some space. She needed a moment. At least a few breaths.

He returned a little bit quicker than she had hoped he might, all long lean muscle and satisfied male. It was the expression on his face that began to ease the tension in her chest. He didn't look angry. He didn't look like he was judging her. And he didn't look like he was in love with her or was about to start making promises that she didn't want him to make.

No, he just looked satisfied. A bone-deep satisfaction that she felt too.

"Holy hell," he said, coming to lie on the bed next to her, drawing her naked body up against his. She felt a smile curve her lips. "I think you about blew my head off."

"You're so romantic," she said, smiling even wider. Because this was perfect. Absolutely perfect.

"You don't want me to be romantic," he returned.

"No," she said, feeling happy, buoyant even. "I sure as hell don't."

"You want me to be bad, and dirty, and to be your every fantasy of slumming it with a man who is so very beneath you."

That, she took affront to a little bit. "I don't think you're beneath me, Sam," she said. Then he grabbed hold of her hips and lifted her up off the mattress before bringing her down over his body. A wicked smile crossed his face.

"I am now."

"You're insatiable. And terrible."

"For a weekend fling, honey, that's all you really need."

"Oh, dammit," she said, "what if the roads open up, and Christopher tries to come up?"

"I'm not really into threesomes." He tightened his grip on her. "And I'm not into sharing."

"No worries. I don't have any desire to broaden my experience by testing him out."

"Have I ruined you for him?"

The cocky bastard. She wanted to tell him no, but she had a feeling that denting the masculine ego when a man was underneath you wasn't the best idea if you wanted to have sex with said man again.

"Ruined me completely," she responded. "In fact, I should leave a message for him."

Sam snagged the phone on the nightstand and thrust it at her. "You can leave him a message now."

"Okay," she said, grimacing slightly.

She picked up the phone and dialed Christopher's number quickly. Praying that she got his voice mail and not his actual voice.

Of course, if she did, that meant he'd gone out. Which meant that maybe he was trying to find sex to replace the sex that he'd lost. Which she had done; she couldn't really be annoyed about that. But she had baggage.

"Come on," she muttered as the phone rang endlessly. Then she breathed a sigh of relief when she got his voice mail. "Hi, Christopher, it's Madison. Don't worry about coming up here if the roads clear up. If that happens, I'm probably just going to go back to Copper Ridge. The weekend is kind of ruined. And…and maybe you should just wait for me to call you?" She looked up at Sam, who was nearly vibrating with forcibly contained laughter. She rolled her eyes. "Anyway, sorry that this didn't work out. Bye."

"That was terrible," he said. "But I think you made it pretty clear that you don't want to hear from him."

"I said I would call him," she said in protestation.

"Are you going to?"

"*Hell* no."

Sam chuckled, rolling her back underneath him, kissing her deep, hard. "Good thing I only want a weekend."

"Why is that?"

"God help the man that wants more from you."

"Oh, please, that's not fair." She wiggled, luxuriating in the hard feel of him between her thighs. He wanted her again already. "I pity the woman that falls for you, Sam McCormack."

A shadow passed over his face. "So do I."

Then, as quickly as they had appeared, those clouds cleared and he was smiling again, that wicked, intense smile that let her know he was about ready to take her to heaven again.

"It's a good thing both of us only want a weekend."

Five

"How did the art retreat go?"

Sam gritted his teeth against his younger brother's questioning as Chase walked into their workshop. "Fine," he returned.

"Fine?" Chase leaned against the doorframe, crossing his arms, looking a little too much like Sam for his own comfort. Because he was a bastard, and he didn't want to see his bastard face looking back at him. "I thought you were going to get inspiration. To come up with the ideas that will keep the McCormack Ranch flush for the next several years."

"I'm not a machine," Sam said, keeping his tone hard. "You can't force art."

He said things like that, in that tone, because he knew that no one would believe that cliché phrase, even if it was true. He didn't like that it was true.

But there wasn't much he was willing to do about it either.

"Sure. And I feel a slight amount of guilt over pressuring you, but since I do a lot of managing of your career, I consider it a part of my job."

"Stick to pounding iron, Chase—that's where your talents lie."

"I don't have talent," Chase said. "I have business sense. Which you don't have. So you should be thankful for me."

"You say that. You say it a lot. I think mostly because you know that I actually shouldn't be all that thankful for your meddling."

He was being irritable, and he knew it. But he didn't want Chase asking how the weekend was. He didn't want to explain the way he had spent his time. And he really didn't want to get into why the only thing he was inspired to do was start painting nudes.

Of one woman in particular.

Because the only kind of grand inspirational moments he'd had were when he was inside Maddy. Yeah, he wasn't going to explain that to his younger brother. He was never going to tell anybody. And he had to get his shit together.

"Seriously, though, everything is going okay? Anna is worried about you."

"Your wife is meddlesome. I liked her better when she was just your friend and all she did was come by for pizza a couple times a week. And she didn't worry too much about what I was doing or whether or not I was happy."

"Yeah, sadly for you she has decided she loves me. And by extension she has decided she loves you, which means her getting up in your business. I don't think she knows another way to be."

"Tell her to go pull apart a tractor and stop digging around in my life."

"No, thanks, I like my balls where they are. Which means I will not be telling Anna what to do. Ever."

"I liked it better when you were miserable and alone."

Chase laughed. "Why, because you're miserable and alone?"

"No, that would imply that I'm uncomfortable with the state of things. I myself am quite dedicated to my solitude and my misery."

"They say misery loves company," Chase said.

"Only true if you aren't a hermit."

"I suppose that's true." His brother looked at him, his gaze far too perceptive for Sam's liking. "You didn't used to be this terrible."

"I have been for a while." But worse with Maddy. She pushed at him. At things and needs and desires that were best left in the past.

He gritted his teeth. She pushed at him because he turned her on and that made her mad. He... Well, it was complicated.

"Yes," Chase said. "For a while."

"Don't psychoanalyze me. Maybe it's a crazy artist thing. Dad always said that it would make me a pussy."

"You aren't a pussy. You're a jerk."

"Six of one, half dozen of the other. Either way, I have issues."

Chase shook his head. "Well, deal with them on your own time. You have to be over at the West Ranch in less than an hour." Chase shook his head. "Pretty soon we'll be released from the contract. But you know until then we could always hire somebody else to go. You don't have to do horseshoes if you don't want. We're kind of beyond that now."

Sam gritted his teeth. For the first time he was actually tempted to take his brother up on the offer. To replace his position with someone else. Mostly because the idea of seeing Madison again filled him with the kind of reckless tension that he knew he wouldn't be able to do anything about once he saw her again.

Oh, not because of her. Not because of anything to do with her moral code or protestations. He could demolish those easily enough. It was because he couldn't afford to waste any more time thinking about her. Because he couldn't afford to get in any deeper. What had happened over the past weekend had been good. Damn good. But he had to leave it there.

Normally, he relished the idea of getting in there and doing grunt work. There was something about it that fulfilled him. Chase might not understand that.

But Sam wasn't a paperwork man. He wasn't a business mind. He needed physical exertion to keep himself going.

His lips twitched as he thought about the kind of physical exertion he had indulged in with Maddy. Yeah, it kind of all made sense. Why he had thrown himself into the blacksmithing thing during his celibacy. He needed to pound something, one way or another. And since he had been so intent on denying himself female companionship, he had picked up a hammer instead.

He was tempted to back out. To make sure he kept his distance from Maddy. He wouldn't, because he was also far too tempted to go. Too tempted to test his control and see if there was a weak link. If he might end up with her underneath him again.

It would be the better thing to send Chase. Or to call in and say they would have to reschedule, then hire somebody else to take over that kind of work. They could more than afford it. But as much as he wanted to avoid Maddy, he wanted to see her again.

Just because.

His body began to harden just thinking about it.

"It's fine. I'm going to head over. You know that I like physical labor."

"I just don't understand why," Chase said, looking genuinely mystified.

But hell, Chase had a life. A wife. Things that Sam was never going to have. Chase had worked through his stuff and made them both a hell of a lot of money, and Sam was happy for him. As happy as he ever got.

"You don't need to understand me. You just have to keep me organized so that I don't end up out on the street."

"You would never end up out on the streets of Copper Ridge. Mostly because if you stood out there with a cardboard sign, some well-meaning elderly woman would wrap you in a blanket and take you back to her house for casserole. And you would rather die. We both know that."

That made Sam smile reluctantly. "True enough."

"So, I guess you better keep working, then."

Sam thought about Maddy again, about her sweet, supple curves. About how seeing her again was going to test him in the best way possible. Perhaps that was why he should go. Just so he could test himself. Push up against his control. Yeah, maybe that was what he needed.

Yeah, that justification worked well. And it meant he would see her again.

It wasn't feelings. It was just sex. And he was starting to think just sex might be what he needed.

"I plan on it."

Maddy took a deep breath of clean salt air and arena dirt. There was something comforting about it. Familiar. Whenever things had gone wrong in her life, this was what she could count on. The familiar sights and sounds of the ranch, her horses. Herself.

She never felt stronger than when she was on the back of a horse, working in time with the animal to move from a trot to a walk, a walk to a halt. She never felt more understood.

A funny thing. Because, while she knew she was an excellent trainer and she had full confidence in her ability to keep control over the animal, she knew that she would never have absolute control. Animals were unpredictable. Always.

One day, they could simply decide they didn't want to deal with you and buck you off. It was the risk that every person who worked with large beasts took. And they took it on gladly.

She liked that juxtaposition. The control, the danger. The fact that though she achieved a certain level of mastery with each horse she worked with, they could still decide they weren't going to behave on a given day.

She had never felt much of that in the rest of her life. Often she felt like she was fighting against so much. Having something like this, something that made her feel both small and powerful had been essential to her well-being. Especially during all that crap that had happened ten years ago. She had been thinking more about it lately. Honestly, it had all started because of Christopher, because she had been considering breaking her celibacy. And it had only gotten worse after she actually had. After Sam.

Mostly because she couldn't stop thinking about him. Mostly because she felt like one weekend could never be enough. And she needed it to be. She badly needed it to be. She needed to be able to have sex with a guy without having lingering feelings for him. David had really done a number on her, and she did not want another number done on her.

It was for the best if she never saw Sam again. She knew that was unlikely, but it would be better. She let out a deep breath, walking into the barn, her riding boots making a strident sound on the hardpacked dirt as she walked in. Then she saw movement toward the end of the barn, someone coming out of one of the stalls.

She froze. It wasn't uncommon for there to be other people around. Her family employed a full staff to keep the ranch running smoothly, but for some reason this felt different. And a couple of seconds later, as the person came into view, she realized why.

Black cowboy hat, broad shoulders, muscular forearms. That lean waist and hips. That built, muscular physique that she was intimately acquainted with.

Dear Lord. Sam McCormack was here.

She had known that there would be some compromise on the never-seeing-him-again thing; she had just hoped that it wouldn't be seeing him now.

"Sam," she said, because she would be damned if she

appeared like she had been caught unawares. "I didn't expect you to be here."

"Your father wanted to make sure that all of the horses were in good shape before the holidays, since it was going to delay my next visit."

Maddy gritted her teeth. Christmas was in a couple of weeks, which meant her family would be having their annual party. The festivities had started to become a bit threadbare and brittle in recent years. Now that everybody knew Nathan West had been forced to sell off all of his properties downtown. Now that everyone knew he had a bastard son, Jack Monaghan, whose existence Nathan had tried to deny for more than thirty years. Yes, now that everybody had seen the cracks in the gleaming West family foundation, it all seemed farcical to Maddy.

But then, seeing as she had been one of the first major cracks in the foundation, she supposed that she wasn't really entitled to be too judgmental about it. However, she was starting to feel a bit exhausted.

"Right," she returned, knowing that her voice sounded dull.

"Have you seen Christopher?"

His question caught her off guard, as did his tone, which sounded a bit hard and possessive. It was funny, because this taciturn man in front of her was more what she had considered Sam to be before they had spent those days in the cabin together. Those days—where they had mostly been naked—had been a lot easier. Quieter. He had smiled more. But then, she supposed that any man receiving an endless supply of orgasms was prone to smiling more. They had barely gotten out of bed.

They had both been more than a little bit insatiable, and Maddy hadn't minded that at all. But this was a harsh slap back to reality. To a time that could almost have been before their little rendezvous but clearly wasn't, because his line of questioning was tinged with jealousy.

"No. As you guessed, I lied to him and didn't call him."

"And he call you?"

Maddy lifted her fingernail and began to chew on it, grimacing when she realized she had just ruined her manicure. "He did call," she said, her face heating slightly. "And I changed his name in my phone book to Don't Answer."

"Why did you do that?"

"Obviously you can't delete somebody from your phone book when you don't want to talk to them, Sam. You have to make sure that you know who's calling. But I like the reminder that I'm not speaking to him. Because then my phone rings and the screen says Don't Answer, and then I go, 'Okay.'"

"I really do pity the man who ends up wanting to chase after you."

"Good thing you don't. Except, oh wait, you're here."

She regretted that as soon as she said it. His gaze darkened, his eyes sweeping over her figure. Why did she want to push him?

Why did she always want to push him?

"You know why I'm here."

"Yes, because my daddy pays you to be here." She didn't know why she said that. To reinforce the difference between them? To remind him she was Lady of the Manor, and that regardless of his bank balance he was socially beneath her? To make herself look like a stupid rich girl he wouldn't want to mess around with anyway.

Honestly, these days it was difficult for her to guess at her own motives.

"Is this all part of your fantasy? You want to be… taken by the stable boy or something? I mean, it's a nice one, Maddy, and I didn't really mind acting it out with you last weekend, but we both know that I'm not exactly the stable boy and you're not exactly the breathless virgin."

Heat streaked through her face, rage pooling in her stomach. "Right. Because I'm not some pure, snow-white virgin, my fantasies are somehow wrong?" It was too close to that wound. The one she wished wasn't there. The one she couldn't ignore, no matter how much she tried.

"That wasn't the point I was making. And anyway, when your whole fantasy about a man centers around him being bad for you, I'm not exactly sure where you get off trying to take the moral-outrage route."

"I will be as morally outraged as I please," she snapped, turning to walk away from him.

He reached out, grabbing hold of her arm and turning her back to face him, taking hold of her other arm and pulling her forward. "Everything was supposed to stay back up at those cabins," he said, his voice rough.

"So why aren't you letting it?" she spat. Reckless. Shaky. She was a hypocrite. Because she wasn't letting it rest either.

"Because you walked in in those tight pants and it made it a lot harder for me to think."

"My breeches," she said, keeping the words sharp and crisp as a green apple, "are not typically the sort of garment that inspire men to fits of uncontrollable lust." Except *she* was drowning in a fit of uncontrollable lust.

His gaze was hot, his hands on her arms even hotter. She wanted to arch against him, to press her breasts against his chest as she had done more times than she could count when they had been together. She wanted… She wanted the impossible. She wanted more. More of him. More of everything they had shared together, even though they had agreed that would be a bad idea.

Even though she knew it was something she shouldn't even want.

"Your pretty little ass in anything would make a man lose his mind. Don't tell me those breeches put any man off, or I'm gonna have to call you a liar."

"It isn't my breeches that put them off. That's just my personality."

"If some man can't handle you being a little bit hard, then he's no kind of man. I can take you, baby. I can take all of you. And that's good, since we both know you can take all of me."

"Are you just going to be a tease, Sam?" she asked, echoing back a phrase that had been uttered to her by many men over the years. "Or is this leading somewhere?"

"You don't want it to lead anywhere, you said so yourself." He released his hold on her, taking a step back.

"You're contrary, Sam McCormack—do you know that?"

He laughed. "That's about the only thing anyone calls me. We both know what I am. The only thing that confuses me is exactly why you seem surprised by it now."

She was kind of stumped by that question. Because really, the only answer was sex. That she had imagined that the two of them being together, that the man he had been during that time, meant something.

Which proved that she really hadn't learned anything about sexual relationships, in spite of the fact that she had been so badly wounded by one in the past. She had always known that she had a hard head, but really, this was ridiculous.

But it wasn't just her head that was hard. She had hardened up a considerable amount in the years since her relationship with David. Because she'd had to. Because within the equestrian community, she had spent the years following that affair known as the skank who had seriously jeopardized the marriage of an upright member of the community. Never mind that she had been his student. Never mind that she had been seventeen years old, a virgin who had believed every word that had come out of the esteemed older man's mouth. Who had believed that his marriage really was over and that he wanted a life and a future with her.

It was laughable to her now. Any man nearing his forties who found himself able to relate to a seventeen-year-old on an emotional level was a little bit suspect. A married one, in a position of power, was even worse. She knew all of that. She knew it down to her bones. Believing it was another thing.

So sometimes her judgment was in doubt. Sometimes she felt like an idiot. But she was much more equipped to deal with difficult situations now. She was a lot pricklier. A lot more inured.

And that was what came to her defense now.

"Sam, if you still want me, all you have to do is say it. Don't you stand there growling because you're hard and sexually frustrated and we both agreed that it would only be that one weekend. Just be a man and admit it."

"Are you sure you should be talking to me like that

here? Anyone can catch us. If I backed you up against that wall and kissed your smart mouth, then people would know. Doesn't it make you feel dirty? Doesn't it make you feel ashamed?" His words lashed at her, made her feel all of those things but also aroused her. She had no idea what was wrong with her. Except that maybe part of it was that she simply didn't know how to feel desire without feeling ashamed. Another gift from her one and only love affair.

"You're the one that's saying all of this. Not me," she said, keeping her voice steely. She lifted a shoulder. "If I didn't know better, I would say you have issues. I don't want to help you work those out." A sudden rush of heat took over, a reckless thought that she had no business having, that she really should work to get a handle on. But she didn't.

She took a deep breath. "I don't have any desire to help you with your issues, but if you're horny, I can help you with that."

"What the hell?"

"You heard me," she said, crossing her arms and giving him her toughest air. "If you want me, then have me."

Sam could hardly believe what he was hearing. Yet again, Madison West was propositioning him. And this time, he was pissed off. Because he wasn't a dog that she could bring to heel whenever she wanted to. He wasn't the kind of man who could be manipulated.

Even worse, he wanted her. He wanted to say yes. And he wasn't sure he could spite his dick to soothe his pride.

"You can't just come in here and start playing games with me," he said. "I'm not a dog that you can call whenever you want me to come."

He let the double meaning of that statement sit between them. "That isn't what I'm doing," she said, her tone waspish.

"Then what are you doing, Madison? We agreed that it would be one weekend. And then you come in here sniping at me, and suddenly you're propositioning me. I gave in to all of this when you asked the first time, because I'm a man. And I'm not going to say no in a situation like the one we were in. But I'm also not the kind of man you can manipulate."

Color rose high in her cheeks. "I'm not trying to manipulate you. Why is it that men are always accusing me of that?"

"Because no man likes to be turned on and then left waiting," he returned.

The color in her cheeks darkened, and then she turned on one boot heel and walked quickly away from him.

He moved after her, reaching out and grabbing hold of her arm, stopping her. "What? Now you're going to go?"

"I can't do this. I can't do this if you're going to wrap all of it up in accusations and shame. I've been there. I've done it, Sam, and I'm not doing it again. Trust me. I've been accused of a lot of things. I've had my fill of it. So, great, you don't want to be manipulated. I don't want to be the one that has to leave this affair feeling guilty."

Sam frowned. "That's not what I meant."

She was the one who was being unreasonable, blowing hot and cold on him. How was it that he had been the one to be made to feel guilty? He didn't like that. He didn't like feeling anything but irritation and desire for her. He certainly didn't want to feel any guilt.

He didn't want to feel any damn thing.

"Well, what did you mean? Am I a tease, Sam? Is

that what I am? And men like you just can't help themselves?"

He took a step back. "No," he said. "But you do have to make a decision. Either you want this, or you don't."

"Or?"

"Or nothing," he said, his tone hard. "If you don't want it, you don't want it. I'm not going to coerce you into anything. But I don't do the hot-and-cold thing."

Of course, he didn't really do any kind of thing anymore. But this, this back and forth, reminded him too much of his interaction with Elizabeth. Actually, all of it reminded him a little bit too much of Elizabeth. This seemingly soft, sweet woman with a bit of an edge. Someone who was high-class and a little bit luxurious. Who felt like a break from his life on the ranch. His life of rough work and solitude.

But after too much back and forth, it had ended. And he didn't speak to her for months. Until he had gotten a call that he needed to go to the hospital.

He gritted his teeth, looking at Madison. He couldn't imagine anything with Madison ending quite that way, not simply because he refused to ever lose his control the way he had done with Elizabeth, but also because he couldn't imagine Maddy slinking off in silence. She might go hot and cold, but she would never do it quietly.

"Twelve days. There are twelve days until Christmas. That's what I want. Twelve days to get myself on the naughty list. So to speak." She leveled her blue gaze with his. "If you don't want to oblige me, I'm sure Christopher will. But I would much rather it be you."

"Why?" He might want this, but he would be damned if he would make it easy for her. Mostly because he wanted to make it a little harder on himself.

"Because I planned to go up to that cabin and have sex with Christopher. I had to, like, come up with a plan. A series of tactical maneuvers that would help me make the decision to get it over with after all that time. You," she said, gesturing at him, "you, I didn't plan to have anything happen with. Ever. But I couldn't stop myself. I think at the end of the day it's much better to carry on a sex-only affair with a man that you can't control yourself with. Like right now. I was not going to proposition you today, Sam. I promise. Not today, not ever again. In fact, I'm mad at you, so it should be really easy for me to walk away. But I don't want to. I want you. I want you even if it's a terrible idea."

He looked around, then took her arm again, dragging her into one of the empty stalls, where they would be out of sight if anyone walked into the barn. Then he pressed her against the wall, gripping her chin and taking her mouth in a deep, searing kiss. She whimpered, arching against him, grabbing hold of his shoulders and widening her stance so that he could press his hardened length against where she was soft and sensitive, ready for him already.

He slid his hand down her back, not caring that the hard wall bit into his knuckles as he grabbed hold of her rear, barely covered by those riding pants, which ought to have been illegal.

She whimpered, wiggling against him, obviously trying to get some satisfaction for the ache inside her. He knew that she felt it, because he felt the same way. He wrenched his mouth away from hers. "Dammit," he said, "I have to get back to work."

"Do you really?" She looked up at him, her expression so desperate it was nearly comical. Except he felt too desperate to laugh.

"Yes," he said.

"Well, since my family owns the property, I feel like I can give you permission to—"

He held up a hand. "I'm going to stop you right there. Nobody gives me permission to do anything. If I didn't want to finish the day's work, I wouldn't. I don't need the money. That's not why I do this. It's my reputation. My pride. I'm contracted to do it, and I will do what I promised I would. But when the contract is up? I won't."

"Oh," she said. "I didn't realize that."

"Everything is going well with the art business." At least, it would if he could think of something else to do. He supposed he could always do more animals and cowboys. People never got tired of that. They had been his most popular art installations so far.

"Great. That's great. Maybe you could…not press yourself up against me? Because I'm going to do something really stupid in a minute."

He did not comply with her request; instead, he kept her there, held up against the wall. "What's that?"

She frowned. "Something I shouldn't do in a public place."

"You're not exactly enticing me to let you go." His body was so hard he was pretty sure he was going to turn to stone.

"I'll bite you."

"Still not enticed."

"Are you telling me that you want to get bitten?"

He rolled his hips forward, let her feel exactly what she was doing to him. "Biting can be all part of the fun."

"I have some things to learn," she said, her blue eyes widening.

"I'm happy to teach them to you," he said, wavering on whether or not he would finish what they'd started here. "Where should I meet you tonight?"

"Here," she said, the word rushed.

"Are you sure? I live on the same property as Chase, but in different houses. We are close, but not that close."

"No, I have my own place here too. And there's always a lot of cars. It won't look weird. I just don't want anyone to see me…" She looked away from him. "I don't want to advertise."

"That's fine." It suited him to keep everyone in the dark too. He didn't want the kind of attention that would come with being associated with Madison West. Already, the attention that he got for the various art projects he did, for the different displays around town, was a little much for him.

It was an impossible situation for him, as always. He wanted things that seemed destined to require more of himself than he wanted to give. Things that seemed to need him to reach deep, when it was better if he never did. Yet he seemed to choose them. Women like Madison. A career like art.

Someday he would examine that. Not today.

"Okay," she said, "come over after it's dark."

"This is like a covert operation."

"Is that a problem?"

It really wasn't. It was hypocritical of him to pretend otherwise. Hell, his last relationship—the one with Elizabeth—had been conducted almost entirely in secrecy because he had been going out of town to see her. That had been her choice, because she knew her association with him would be an issue for her family.

And, as he already established, he didn't really want anyone to know about this thing with Maddy either. Still, sneaking around felt contrary to his nature too. In general, he didn't really care what people thought about him. Or about his decisions.

You're a liar.

He gritted his teeth. Everything with Elizabeth was its own exception. There was no point talking to anyone about it. No point getting into that terrible thing he had been a part of. The terrible thing he had caused.

"Not a problem," he said. "I'll see you in a few hours."

"I can cook," she said as he turned to walk out of the stall.

"You don't have to. I can grab something on my way."

"No, I would rather we had dinner."

He frowned. "Maddy," he began, "this isn't going to be a relationship. It can't be."

"I know," she said, looking up and away from him, swallowing hard. "But I need for it to be something a little more than just sex too. I just… Look, obviously you know that somebody that hasn't had a sexual partner in the past ten years has some baggage. I do. Shocking, I know, because I seem like a bastion of mental health. But I just don't like the feeling. I really don't."

His chest tightened. Part of him was tempted to ask her exactly what had happened. Why she had been celibate for so long. But then, if they began to trade stories about their pasts, she might want to know something about his. And he wasn't getting into that. Not now, not ever.

"Is there anything you don't like?"

"No," he said, "I'm easy. I thought you said you didn't cook?"

She shrugged a shoulder. "Okay, if I'm being completely honest, I have a set of frozen meals in my freezer that my parents' housekeeper makes for me. But I can heat up a double portion so we can eat together."

He shook his head. "Okay."

"I have pot roast, meat loaf and roast chicken."

"I'll tell you what. The only thing I want is to have your body for dessert. I'll let you go ahead and plan dinner."

"Pot roast it is," she said, her voice a borderline squeak.

He chuckled, turning and walking away from her, something shifting in his chest. He didn't know how she managed to do that. Make him feel heavier one moment, then lighter the next. It was dangerous. That's what it was. And if he had a brain in his head, he would walk away from her and never look back.

Sadly, his ability to think with his brain had long since ceased to function.

Even if it was a stupid idea, and he was fairly certain it was, he was going to come to Madison's house tonight, and he was going to have her in about every way he could think of.

He fixed his mouth into a grim line and set about finishing his work. But while he kept his face completely stoic, inside he felt anticipation for the first time in longer than he could remember.

Six

Maddy wondered if seductresses typically wore pearls. Probably pearls and nothing else. Maybe pearls and lace. Probably not high-waisted pencil skirts and cropped sweaters. But warming pot roast for Sam had put her in the mind-set of a 1950s housewife, and she had decided to go ahead and embrace the theme.

She caught a glimpse of her reflection in the mirror in the hall of her little house and she laughed at herself. She was wearing red lipstick, her blond hair pulled back into a bun. She rolled her eyes, then stuck out her tongue. Then continued on into the kitchen, her high heels clicking on the tile.

At least underneath the sweater, she had on a piece of pretty hot lingerie, if she said so herself. She knew Sam was big on the idea that seduction couldn't be planned, but Maddy did like to have a plan. It helped her feel more in control, and when it came to Sam, she had never felt more out of control.

She sighed, reaching up into the cupboard and taking out a bottle of wine that she had picked up at Grassroots Winery that afternoon. She might not be the best cook, or any kind of cook at all, but she knew how to pick a good wine. Everyone had their strengths.

The strange thing was she kind of enjoyed feeling out of control with Sam, but it also made her feel cautious. Protective. When she had met David, she had dived into the affair headlong. She hadn't thought at all. She had led entirely with her heart, and in the end, she had gotten her heart broken. More than that, the aftermath had shattered her entire world. She had lost friends; she had lost her standing within a community that had become dear to her... Everything.

"But you aren't seventeen. And Sam isn't a married douche bag." She spoke the words fiercely into the silence of the kitchen, buoyed by the reality of them.

She could lose a little bit of control with Sam. Even within that, there would be all of her years, her wisdom— such as it was—and her experience. She was never going to be the girl she had been. That was a good thing. She would never be able to be hurt like that, not again. She simply didn't possess the emotional capacity.

She had emerged Teflon coated. Everything slid off now.

There was a knock on her front door and she straightened, closing her eyes and taking a deep breath, trying to calm the fluttering in her stomach. That reminded her a bit too much of the past. Feeling all fluttery and breathless just because she was going to see the man she was fixated on. That felt a little too much like emotion.

No. It wasn't emotion. It was just anticipation. She was old enough now to tell the difference between the two things.

She went quickly to the door, suddenly feeling a little bit ridiculous as she pulled it open. When it was too late for her to do anything about it. Her feeling of ridiculousness only increased when she saw Sam standing there, wearing his typical black cowboy hat, tight T-shirt and well-fitted jeans. Of course, he didn't need to wear anything different to be hotter to her.

A cowboy hat would do it every time.

"Hi," she said, taking a step back and gesturing with her hand. "Come in."

He obliged, walking over the threshold and looking around the space. For some reason, she found herself looking at it through his eyes. Wondering what kinds of conclusions he would draw about the neat, spare environment.

She had lived out in the little guesthouse ever since she was nineteen. Needing a little bit of distance from her family but never exactly leaving. For the first time, that seemed a little bit weird to her. It had always just been her life. She worked on the ranch, so there didn't seem to be any point in leaving it.

Now she tried to imagine explaining it to someone else—to Sam—and she wondered if it was weird.

"My mother's interior decorator did the place," she said. "Except for the yellow and red." She had added little pops of color through throw pillows, vases and art on the wall. But otherwise the surroundings were predominantly white.

"Great," he said, clearly not interested at all.

It had felt weird, thinking about him judging her

based on the space, thinking about him judging her circumstances. But it was even weirder to see that he wasn't even curious.

She supposed that was de rigueur for physical affairs. And that was what this was.

"Dinner is almost ready," she said, reminding them both of the nonphysical part of the evening. Now she felt ridiculous for suggesting that too. But the idea of meeting him in secret had reminded her way too much of David. Somehow, adding pot roast had seemed to make the whole thing aboveboard.

Pot roast was an extremely nonsalacious food.

"Great," he said, looking very much like he didn't actually care that much.

"I just have to get it out of the microwave." She treated him to an exaggerated wink.

That earned her an uneasy laugh. "Great," he said.

"Come on," she said, gesturing for him to follow her. She moved into the kitchen, grabbed the pan that contained the meat and the vegetables out of the microwave and set it on the table, where the place settings were already laid out and the salad was already waiting.

"I promise I'm not trying to Stepford-wife you," she said as they both took their seats.

"I didn't think that," he said, but his blank expression betrayed the fact that he was lying.

"You did," she said. "You thought that I was trying to become your creepy robot wife."

"No, but I did wonder exactly why dinner was so important."

She looked down. It wasn't as if David were a secret. In fact, the affair was basically open information. "Do you really want to know?"

Judging by the expression on his face, he didn't. "There isn't really a good way to answer that question."

"True. Honesty is probably not the best policy. I'll think you're uninterested in me."

"On the contrary, I'm very interested in you."

"Being interested in my boobs is not the same thing."

He laughed, taking a portion of pot roast out of the dish in the center of the table. "I'm going to eat. If you want to tell me…well, go ahead. But I don't think you're trying to ensnare me."

"You don't?"

"Honestly, Maddy, nobody would want me for that long."

Those words were spoken with a bit of humor, but they made her sad. "I'm sure that's not true," she said, even though she wasn't sure of any such thing. He was grumpy. And he wasn't the most adept emotionally. Still, it didn't seem like a very kind thing for a person to think about themselves.

"It is," he said. "Chase is only with me because he's stuck with me. He feels some kind of loyalty to our parents."

"I thought your parents…"

"They're dead," he responded, his tone flat.

"I'm sorry," she said.

"Me too."

Silence fell between them after that, and she knew the only way to break it was to go ahead and get it out. "The first guy…the one ten years ago, we were having a physical-only affair. Except I didn't know it."

"Ouch," Sam said.

"Very. I mean, trust me, there were plenty of signs. And even though he was outright lying to me about his

intentions, if I had been a little bit older or more experienced, I would have known. It's a terrible thing to find
out you're a cliché. I imagine you wouldn't know what
that's like."

"No, not exactly. Artist-cowboy-blacksmith is not really a well-worn template."

She laughed and took a sip of her wine. "No, I guess
not." Then she took another sip. She needed something
to fortify her. Anything.

"But other woman that actually believes he'll leave
his wife for you, that is." She swallowed hard, waiting
for his face to change, waiting for him to call her a name,
to get disgusted and walk out.

It occurred to her just then that that was why she was
telling him all of this. Because she needed him to know.
She needed him to know, and she needed to see what he
would think. If he would still want her. Or if he would
think that she was guilty beyond forgiving.

There were a lot of people who did.

But he didn't say anything. And his face didn't
change. So they just sat in silence for a moment.

"When we got involved, he told me that he was done
with her. That their marriage was a mess and they were
already starting divorce proceedings. He said that he just
wore his wedding ring to avoid awkward questions from
their friends. The dressage community around here is
pretty small, and he said that he and his wife were waiting until they could tell people themselves, personally, so
that there were no rumors flying around." She laughed,
almost because she was unable to help it. It was so ridiculous. She wanted to go back and shake seventeen-
year-old her. For being such an idiot. For caring so much.

"Anyway," she continued, "he said he wanted to

protect me. You know, because of how unkind people can be."

"He was married," Sam said.

She braced herself. "Yes," she returned, unflinching.

"How old were you?"

"Seventeen."

"How old was he?"

"Almost forty."

Sam cursed. "He should have been arrested."

"Maybe," she said, "except I did want him."

She had loved the attention he had given her. Had loved feeling special. It had been more than lust. It had been neediness. For all the approval she hadn't gotten in her life. Classic daddy issues, basically. But, as messed up as a man his age had to be for wanting to fool around with a teenager, the teenager had to be pretty screwed up too.

"How did you know him?"

"He was my… He was my trainer."

"Right, so some jackass in a position of power. Very surprising."

Warmth bloomed in her chest and spread outward, a strange, completely unfamiliar sensation. There were only a few people on earth who defended her when the subject came up. And mostly, they kept it from coming up. Sierra, her younger sister, knew about it only from the perspective of someone who had been younger at the time. Maddy had shared a little bit about it, about the breakup and how much it had messed with her, when Sierra was having difficulty in her own love life.

And then there were her brothers, Colton and Gage. Who would both have cheerfully killed David if they had ever been able to get their hands on him. But Sam was the first person she had ever told the whole story to. And he was the first person who wasn't one of her siblings who had jumped to her defense immediately.

There had been no interrogation about what kinds of clothes she'd worn to her lessons. About how she had behaved. Part of her wanted to revel in it. Another part of her wanted to push back at it.

"Well, I wore those breeches around him. I know they made you act a little bit crazy. Maybe it was my fault."

"Is this why you got mad about what I said earlier?"

She lifted a shoulder. "Well, that and it was mean."

"I didn't realize this had happened to you," he said, his voice not exactly tender but full of a whole lot more sympathy than she had ever imagined getting from him. "I'm sorry."

"The worst part was losing all my friends," she said, looking up at him. "Everybody really liked him. He was their favorite instructor. As far as dressage instructors go, he was young and cool, trust me."

"So you bore the brunt of it because he turned out to be human garbage and nobody wanted to face it?"

The way he phrased that, so matter-of-fact and real, made a bubble of humor well up inside her chest. "I guess so."

"That doesn't seem fair."

"It really doesn't."

"So that's why you had to feed me dinner, huh? So I didn't remind you of that guy?"

"Well, you're nothing like him. For starters, he was... much more diminutive."

Sam laughed. "You make it sound like you had an affair with a leprechaun."

"Jockeys aren't brawny, Sam."

He only laughed harder. "That's true. I suppose that causes trouble with wind resistance and things."

She rolled her eyes. "You are terrible. Obviously he had some appeal." Though, she had a feeling it wasn't entirely physical. Seeing as she had basically been seeking attention and approval and a thousand other things besides orgasms.

"Obviously. It was his breeches," Sam said.

"A good-looking man in breeches is a thing."

"I believe you."

"But a good-looking man in Wranglers is better." At least, that was her way of thinking right at the moment.

"Good to know."

"But you can see. Why I don't really want to advertise this. It has nothing to do with what you do or who you are or who I am. Well, I guess it is all to do with who I am. What people already think about me. I've been completely defined by a sex life I barely have. And that was… It was the smallest part of that betrayal. At least for me. I loved him. And he was just using me."

"I hope his life was hell after."

"No. His wife forgave him. He went on to compete in the Olympics. He won a silver medal."

"That's kind of a karmic letdown."

"You're telling me. Meanwhile, I've basically lived like a nun and continued giving riding lessons here on the family ranch. I didn't go on to do any of the competing that I wanted to, because I couldn't throw a rock without hitting a judge who was going to be angry with me for my involvement with David."

"In my opinion," Sam said, his expression turning dark, focused, "people are far too concerned with who women sleep with and not near enough as concerned as they should be about whether or not the man does it well. Was he good?"

She felt her face heat. "Not like you."

"I don't care who you had sex with, how many times or who he was. What I do care is that I am the best you've ever had. I'm going to aim to make sure that's the case."

He reached across the table, grabbing hold of her hand. "I'm ready for dessert," he said.

"Me too," she said, pushing her plate back and moving to her feet. "Upstairs?"

He nodded once, the slow burn in his dark eyes searing through her. "Upstairs."

Seven

"Well, it looks like everything is coming together for Dad's Christmas party," Sierra said brightly, looking down at the car seat next to her that contained a sleeping newborn. "Gage will be there, kind of a triumphant return, coming-out kind of thing."

Maddy's older brother shifted in his seat, his arms crossed over his broad chest. "You make me sound like a debutante having a coming-out ball."

"That would be a surprise," his girlfriend, Rebecca Bear, said, putting her hand over his.

"I didn't mean it that way," Sierra said, smiling, her slightly rounder post-childbirth cheeks making her look even younger than she usually did.

Maddy was having a difficult time concentrating. She had met her siblings early at The Grind, the most popular coffee shop in Copper Ridge, so that they could all get on the same page about the big West family soiree that would be thrown on Christmas Eve.

Maddy was ambivalent about it. Mostly she wanted to crawl back under the covers with Sam and burrow until winter passed. But they had agreed that it would go on only until Christmas. Which meant that not only was she dreading the party, it also marked the end of their blissful affair.

By the time Sam had left last night, it had been the next morning, just very early, the sun still inky black as he'd walked out of her house and to his truck.

She had wanted him to stay the entire night, and that was dangerous. She didn't need all that. Didn't need to be held by him, didn't need to wake up in his arms.

"Madison." The sound of her full name jerked her out of her fantasy. She looked up, to see that Colton had been addressing her.

"What?" she asked. "I zoned out for a minute. I haven't had all the caffeine I need yet." Mostly because she had barely slept. She had expected to go out like a light after Sam had left her, but that had not been the case. She had just sort of lay there feeling a little bit achy and lonely and wishing that she didn't.

"Just wondering how you were feeling about Jack coming. You know, now that the whole town knows that he's our half brother, it really is for the best if he comes. I've already talked to Dad about it, and he agrees."

"Great," she said, "and what about Mom?"

"I expect she'll go along with it. She always does. Anyway, Jack is a thirty-five-year-old sin. There's not much use holding it against him now."

"There never was," Maddy said, staring fixedly at her disposable coffee cup, allowing the warm liquid inside to heat her fingertips. She felt like a hypocrite saying that. Mostly because there was something about Jack that was difficult for her.

Well, she knew what it was. The fact that he was evidence of an affair her father had had. The fact that her father was the sort of man who cheated on his wife.

That her father was the sort of man more able to identify with the man who had broken Maddy's heart than he was able to identify with Maddy herself.

But Jack had nothing to do with that. Not really. She knew that logically. He was a good man, married to a great woman, with an adorable baby she really *did* want in her life. It was just that sometimes it needled at her. Got under her skin.

"True enough," Colton said. If he noticed her unease, he certainly didn't betray that he did.

The idea of trying to survive through another West family party just about made her jump up from the coffee shop, run down Main Street and scamper under a rock. She just didn't know if she could do it. Stand there in a pretty dress trying to pretend that she was something the entire town knew she wasn't. Trying to pretend that she was anything other than a disappointment. That her whole family was anything other than tarnished.

Sam didn't feel that way. Not about her. Suddenly, she thought about standing there with him. Sam in a tux, warm and solid next to her…

She blinked, cutting off that line of thinking. There was no reason to be having those fantasies. What she and Sam had was not that. Whatever it was, it wasn't that.

"Then it's settled," Maddy said, a little bit too brightly. "Jack and his family will come to the party."

That sentence made another strange, hollow sensation

echo through her. Jack would be there with his family. Sierra and Ace would be there together with their baby. Colton would be there with his wife, Lydia, and while they hadn't made it official yet, Gage and Rebecca were rarely anywhere without each other, and it was plain to anyone who had eyes that Rebecca had changed Gage in a profound way. That she was his support and he was hers.

It was just another way in which Maddy stood alone.

Wow, what a whiny, tragic thought. It wasn't like she wanted her siblings to have nothing. It wasn't like she wanted them to spend their lives alone. Of course she wanted them to have significant others. Maybe she would get around to having one too, eventually.

But it wouldn't be Sam. So she needed to stop having fantasies about him in that role. Naked fantasies. That was all she was allowed.

"Great," Sierra said, lifting up her coffee cup. "I'm going to go order a coffee for Ace and head back home. He's probably just now getting up. He worked closing at the bar last night and then got up to feed the baby. I owe him caffeine and my eternal devotion. But he will want me to lead with the caffeine." She waved and picked up the bucket seat, heading toward the counter.

"I have to go too," Colton said, leaning forward and kissing Maddy on the cheek. "See you later."

Gage nodded slowly, his dark gaze on Rebecca. She nodded, almost imperceptibly, and stood up. "I'm going to grab a refill," she said, making her way to the counter.

As soon as she was out of earshot, Gage turned his focus to her, and Maddy knew that the refill was only a decoy.

"Are you okay?"

This question, coming from the brother she knew the least, the brother who had been out of her life for seventeen years before coming back into town almost two months ago, was strange. And yet in some ways it wasn't. She had felt, from the moment he had returned, that there was something similar in the two of them.

Something broken and strong that maybe the rest of them couldn't understand.

Since then, she had learned more about the circumstances behind his leaving. The accident that he had been involved in that had left Rebecca Bear scarred as a child. Much to Maddy's surprise, they now seemed to be in love.

Which, while she was happy for him, was also a little annoying. Rebecca was the woman he had damaged—however accidentally—and she could love him, while Maddy seemed to be some kind of remote island no one wanted to connect with.

If she took the Gage approach, she could throw hot coffee on the nearest handsome guy, wait a decade and a half and see if his feelings changed for her over time. However, she imagined that was somewhat unrealistic.

"I'm fine," she said brightly. "Always fine."

"Right. Except I'm used to you sounding dry with notes of sarcasm and today you've been overly peppy and sparkly like a Christmas angel, and I think we both know that isn't real."

"Well, the alternative is me complaining about how this time of year gets me a little bit down, and given the general mood around the table, that didn't seem to be the best idea."

"Right. Why don't you like this time of year?"

"I don't know, Gage. Think back to all the years you

spent in solitude on the road. Then tell me how you felt about Christmas."

"At best, it didn't seem to matter much. At worst, it reminded me of when I was happy. When I was home with all of you. And when home felt like a happy place. That was the hardest part, Maddy. Being away and longing for a home I couldn't go back to. Because it didn't exist. Not really. After everything I found out about Dad, I knew it wouldn't ever feel the same."

Her throat tightened, emotion swamping her. She had always known that Gage was the one who would understand her. She had been right. Because no one had ever said quite so perfectly exactly what she felt inside, what she had felt ever since news of her dalliance with her dressage trainer had made its way back to Nathan West's ears.

"It's so strange that you put it that way," she said, "because that is exactly how it feels. I live at home. I never left. And I…I ache for something I can never have again. Even if it's just to see my parents in the way that I used to."

"You saw how it was with all of us sitting here," Gage said. "It's something that I never thought I would have. The fact that you've all been willing to forgive me, to let me back into your lives after I was gone for so long, changes the shape of things. We are the ones that can make it different. We can fix what happened with Jack— or move forward into fixing it. There's no reason you and I can't be fixed too, Maddy."

She nodded, her throat so tight she couldn't speak. She stood, holding her coffee cup against her chest. "I am looking forward to seeing you at the Christmas party." Then she forced a smile and walked out of The Grind.

She took a deep breath of the freezing air, hoping that it might wash some of the stale feelings of sadness and grief right out of her body. Then she looked down Main Street, at all of the Christmas lights gilding the edges of the brick buildings like glimmering precious metal.

Christmas wreaths hung from every surface that would take them, velvet bows a crimson beacon against the intense green.

Copper Ridge at Christmas was beautiful, but walking around, she still felt a bit like a stranger, separate and somehow not a part of it all. Everyone here was so good. People like her and Gage had to leave when they got too bad. Except she hadn't left. She just hovered around the edges like a ghost, making inappropriate and sarcastic comments on demand so that no one would ever look at her too closely and see just what a mess she was.

She lowered her head, the wind whipping through her hair, over her cheeks, as she made her way down the street—the opposite direction of her car. She wasn't really sure what she was doing, only that she couldn't face heading back to the ranch right now. Not when she felt nostalgic for something that didn't exist anymore. When she felt raw from the conversation with Gage.

She kept going down Main, pausing at the front door of the Mercantile when she saw a display of Christmas candy sitting in the window. It made her smile to see it there, a sugary reminder of some old memory that wasn't tainted by reality.

She closed her eyes tight, and she remembered what it was. Walking down the street with her father, who was always treated like he was a king then. She had been small, and it had been before Gage had left. Before she had ever disappointed anyone.

It was Christmastime, and carolers were milling around, and she had looked up and seen sugarplums and candy canes, little peppermint chocolates and other sweets in the window. He had taken her inside and allowed her to choose whatever she wanted.

A simple memory. A reminder of a time when things hadn't been quite so hard, or quite so real, between herself and Nathan West.

She found herself heading inside, in spite of the fact that the entire point of this walk had been to avoid memories. But then, she really wanted to avoid the memories that were at the ranch. This was different.

She opened the door, taking a deep breath of gingerbread and cloves upon entry. The narrow little store with exposed brick walls was packed with goodies. Cakes, cheeses and breads, imported and made locally.

Lane Jensen, the owner of the Mercantile, was standing toward the back of the store talking to somebody. Maddy didn't see another person right away, and then, when the broad figure came into view, her heart slammed against her breastbone.

When she realized it was Sam, she had to ask herself if she had been drawn down this way because of a sense of nostalgia or because something in her head sensed that he was around. That was silly. Of course she didn't *sense* his presence.

Though, given pheromones and all of that, maybe it wasn't too ridiculous. It certainly wasn't some kind of emotional crap. Not her heart recognizing where his was beating or some such nonsense.

For a split second she considered running the other direction. Before he saw her, before it got weird. But she hesitated, just for the space of a breath, and that was long enough for Sam to look past Lane, his eyes locking with hers.

She stood, frozen to the spot. "Hi," she said, knowing that she sounded awkward, knowing that she looked awkward.

She was unaccustomed to that. At least, these days. She had grown a tough outer shell, trained herself to never feel ashamed, to never feel embarrassed—not in a way that people would be able to see.

Because after her little scandal, she had always imagined that it was the only thing people thought about when they looked at her. Walking around, feeling like that, feeling like you had a scarlet *A* burned into your skin, it forced you to figure out a way to exist.

In her case it had meant cultivating a kind of brash persona. So, being caught like this, looking like a deer in the headlights—which was what she imagined she looked like right now, wide-eyed and trembling—it all felt a bit disorienting.

"Maddy," Sam said, "I wasn't expecting to see you here."

"That's because we didn't make any plans to meet here," she said. "I promise I didn't follow you." She looked over at Lane, who was studying them with great interest. "Not that I would. Because there's no reason for me to do that. Because you're the farrier for my horses. And that's it." She felt distinctly detached and lightheaded, as though she might drift away on a cloud of embarrassment at a moment's notice.

"Right," he said. "Thank you, Lane," he said, turning his attention back to the other woman. "I can bring the installation down tomorrow." He tipped his hat, then moved away from Lane, making his way toward her.

"Hi, Lane," she said. Sam grabbed hold of her elbow and began to propel her out of the store. "Bye, Lane."

As soon as they were back out on the street, she rounded on him. "What was that? I thought we were trying to be discreet."

"Lane Jensen isn't a gossip. Anyway, you standing there turning the color of a beet wasn't exactly subtle."

"I am not a beet," she protested, stamping.

"A tiny tomato."

"Stop comparing me to vegetables."

"A tomato isn't a vegetable."

She let out a growl and began to walk away from him, heading back up Main Street and toward her car. "Wait," he said, his voice possessing some kind of unknowable power to actually make her obey.

She stopped, rooted to the cement. "What?"

"We live in the same town. We're going to have to figure out how to interact with each other."

"Or," she said, "we continue on with this very special brand of awkwardness."

"Would it be the worst thing in the world if people knew?"

"You know my past, and you can ask me that?" She looked around the street, trying to see if anybody was watching their little play. "I'm not going to talk to you about this on the town stage."

He closed the distance between them. "Fine. We don't have to have the discussion. And it doesn't matter to me either way. But you really think you should spend the rest of your life punishing yourself for a mistake that happened when you were seventeen? He took advantage of you—it isn't your fault. And apart from any of that, you don't deserve to be labeled by a bunch of people that don't even know you."

That wasn't even it. And as she stood there, staring him down, she realized that fully. It had nothing to do with what the town thought. Nothing to do with whether or not the town thought she was a scarlet woman, or if people still thought about her indiscretion, or if people blamed her or David. None of that mattered.

She realized that in a flash of blinding brilliance that shone brighter than the Christmas lights all around her. And that realization made her knees buckle, because it made her remember the conversation that had happened in her father's office. The conversation that had occurred right after one of David's students had discovered the affair between the two of them and begun spreading rumors.

Rumors that were true, regrettably.

Rumors that had made their way all the way back to Nathan West's home office.

"I can't talk about this right now," she said, brushing past him and striding down the sidewalk.

"You don't have to talk about it with me, not ever. But what's going to happen when this is over? You're going to go another ten years between lovers? Just break down and hold your breath and do it again when you can't take the celibacy anymore?"

"Stop it," she said, walking faster.

"Like I said, it doesn't matter to me…"

She whirled around. "You keep saying it doesn't matter to you, and then you keep pushing the issue. So I would say that it does matter to you. Whatever complex you have about not being good enough, this is digging at that. But it isn't my problem. Because it isn't about you. Nobody would care if they knew that we were sleeping together. I mean, they would talk about it, but they wouldn't care. But it makes it something more. And I just…I can't have more. Not more than this."

He shifted uncomfortably. "Well, neither can I. That was hardly an invitation for something deeper."

"Good. Because I don't have anything deeper to give."

The very idea made her feel like she was going into a free fall. The idea of trusting somebody again…

The betrayals she had dealt with back when she was seventeen had made it so that trusting another human being was almost unfathomable. When she had told Sam that the sex was the least of it, she had been telling the truth.

It had very little to do with her body, and everything to do with the battering her soul had taken.

"Neither do I."

"Then why are you… Why are you pushing me like this?"

He looked stunned by the question, his face frozen. "I just…I don't want to leave you broken."

Something inside her softened, cracked a little bit. "I'm not sure that you have a choice. It kind of is what it is, you know?"

"Maybe it doesn't have to be."

"Did you think you were going to fix me, Sam?"

"No," he said, his voice rough.

But she knew he was lying. "Don't put that on yourself. Two broken people can't fix each other."

She was certain in that moment that he was broken too, even though she wasn't quite sure how.

"We only have twelve days. Any kind of fixing was a bit ambitious anyway," he said.

"Eleven days," she reminded him. "I'll see you tonight?"

"Yeah. See you then."

And then she turned and walked away from Sam McCormack for all the town to see, as if he were just a casual acquaintance and nothing more. And she tried to ignore the ache in the center of her chest that didn't seem to go away, even after she got in the car and drove home.

Eight

Seven days after beginning the affair with Maddy, she called and asked him if he could come down and check the shoes on one of the horses. It was the middle of the afternoon, so if it was her version of a booty call, he thought it was kind of an odd time. And since their entire relationship was a series of those, he didn't exactly see why she wouldn't be up front about it.

But when he showed up, she was waiting for him outside the stall.

"What are you up to?"

She lifted her shoulder. "I just wanted you to come and check on the horse."

"Something you couldn't check yourself?"

She looked slightly rueful. "Okay, maybe I could have checked it myself. But she really is walking a little bit funny, and I'm wondering if something is off."

She opened the stall door, clipped a lead rope to the

horse's harness and brought her out into the main part of the barn.

He looked at her, then pushed up the sleeves on his thermal shirt and knelt down in front of the large animal, drawing his hand slowly down her leg and lifting it gently. Then he did the same to the next before moving to her hindquarters and repeating the motion again.

He stole a glance up at Maddy, who was staring at him with rapt attention.

"What?"

"I like watching you work," she said. "I've always liked watching you work. That's why I used to come down here and give orders. Okay, honestly? I wanted to give myself permission to watch you and enjoy it." She swallowed hard. "You're right. I've been punishing myself. So, I thought I might indulge myself."

"I'm going to have to charge your dad for this visit," he said.

"He won't notice," she said. "Trust me."

"I don't believe that. Your father is a pretty well-known businessman." He straightened, petting the horse on its haunches. "Everything looks fine."

Maddy looked sheepish. "Great."

"Why don't you think your dad would notice?"

"A lot of stuff has come out over the past few months. You know he had a stroke three months ago or so, and while he's recovered pretty well since then, it changed things. I mean, it didn't change *him*. It's not like he miraculously became some soft, easy man. Though, I think he's maybe a little bit more in touch with his mortality. Not happily, mind you. I think he always saw himself as something of a god."

"Well," Sam said, "what man doesn't?" At least, until

he was set firmly back down to earth and reminded of just how badly he could mess things up. How badly things could hurt.

"Yet another difference between men and women," Maddy said drily. "But after he had his stroke, the control of the finances went to my brother Gage. That was why he came back to town initially. He discovered that there was a lot of debt. I mean, I know you've heard about how many properties we've had to sell downtown."

Sam stuffed his hands in his pockets, lifting his shoulders. "Not really. But then, I don't exactly keep up on that kind of stuff. That's Chase's arena. Businesses and the real estate market. That's not me. I just screw around with metal."

"You downplay what you do," she returned. "From the art to the physical labor. I've watched you do it. I don't know why you do it, only that you do. You're always acting like your brother is smarter than you, but he can't do what you do either."

"Art was never particularly useful as far as my father was concerned," Sam said. "I imagine he would be pretty damned upset to see that it's the art that keeps the ranch afloat so nicely. He would have wanted us to do it the way our ancestors did. Making leatherwork and pounding nails. Of course, it was always hard for him to understand that mass production was inevitably going to win out against more expensive handmade things. Unless we targeted our products and people who could afford what we did. Which is what we did. What we've been successful with far beyond what we even imagined."

"Dads," she said, her voice soft. "They do get in your head, don't they?"

"I mean, my father didn't have gambling debts and a

secret child, but he was kind of a difficult bastard. I still wish he wasn't dead." He laughed. "It would kind of be nice to have him wandering around the place shaking his head disapprovingly as I loaded up that art installation to take down to the Mercantile."

"I don't know, having your dad hanging around disapproving is kind of overrated." Suddenly, her face contorted with horror. "I'm sorry—I had no business saying something like that. It isn't fair. I shouldn't make light of your loss."

"It was a long time ago. And anyway, I do it all the time. I think it's the way the emotionally crippled deal with things." Anger. Laughter. It was all better than hurt.

"Yeah," she said, laughing uneasily. "That sounds about right."

"What exactly does your dad disapprove of, Madison?" he asked, reverting back to her full name. He kind of liked it, because nobody else called her that. And she had gone from looking like she wanted to claw his eyes out when he used it to responding. There was something that felt deep about that. Connected. He shouldn't care. If anything, it should entice him not to do it. But it didn't.

"Isn't it obvious?"

"No," he returned. "I've done a lot of work on this ranch over the years. You're always busy. You have students scheduled all day every day—except today, apparently—and it is a major part of both the reputation and the income of this facility. You've poured everything you have into reinforcing his legacy while letting your own take a backseat."

"Well, when you put it like that," she said, the smile on her lips obviously forced, "I am kind of amazing."

"What exactly does he disapprove of?"

"What do you think?"

"Does it all come back to that? Something you did when you were seventeen?" The hypocrisy of the outrage in his tone wasn't lost on him.

"I'm not sure," she said, the words biting. "I'm really not." She grabbed hold of the horse's lead rope, taking her back into the stall before clipping the rope and coming back out, shutting the door firmly.

"What do you mean by that?"

She growled, making her way out of the barn and walking down the paved path that led toward one of the covered arenas. "I don't know. Feel free to choose your own adventure with that one."

"Come on, Maddy," he said, closing the distance between them and lowering his voice. "I've tasted parts of you that most other people have never seen. A little bit of honesty isn't going to hurt you."

She whipped around, her eyes bright. "Maybe it isn't him. Maybe it's me. Maybe I'm the one that can't look at him the same way."

Maddy felt rage simmering over her skin like heat waves. She had not intended to have this conversation— not with Sam, not with anyone.

But now she had started, she didn't know if she could stop. "The night that he found out about my affair with David was the night I found out about Jack."

"So, it isn't a recent revelation to all of you?"

"No," she said. "Colton and Sierra didn't know. I'm sure of that. But I found out that Gage did. I didn't know who it was, I should clarify. I just found out that he had another child." She looked away from Sam, trying to ignore the burning sensation in her stomach. Like there was molten lava rolling around in there. She associated that feeling with being called into her father's home office.

It had always given her anxiety, even before everything had happened with David. Even before she had ever seriously disappointed him.

Nathan West was exacting, and Maddy had wanted nothing more than to please him. That desire took up much more of her life than she had ever wanted it to. But then, she knew that was true in some way or another for all of her siblings. It was why Sierra had gone to school for business. Why Colton had taken over the construction company. It was even what had driven Gage to leave.

It was the reason Maddy had poured all of her focus into dressage. Because she had anticipated becoming great. Going to the Olympics. And she knew her father had anticipated that. Then she had ruined all of it.

But not as badly as he had ruined the relationship between the two of them.

"Like I told you, one of David's other students caught us together. Down at the barn where he gave his lessons. We were just kissing, but it was definitely enough. That girl told her father, who in turn went to mine as a courtesy."

Sam laughed, a hard, bitter sound. "A courtesy to who?"

"Not to me," Maddy said. "Or maybe it was. I don't know. It was so awful. The whole situation. I wish there had been a less painful way for it to end. But it had to end, whether it ended that way or some other way, so... so I guess that worked as well as anything."

"Except you had to deal with your father. And then rumors were spread anyway."

She looked away from Sam. "Well, the rumors I kind of blame on David. Because once his wife knew, there was really no reason for the whole world not to know. And I think it suited him to paint me in an unflattering light. He took a gamble. A gamble that the man in the situation would come out of it all just fine. It was not a bad gamble, it turned out."

"I guess not."

"Full house. Douche bag takes the pot."

She was avoiding the point of this conversation. Avoiding the truth of it. She didn't even know why she should tell him. She didn't know why anything. Except that she had never confided any of this to anyone before. She was close to her sister, and Sierra had shared almost everything about her relationship with Ace with Maddy, and here Maddy was keeping more secrets from her.

She had kept David from her. She had kept Sam from her too. And she had kept this all to herself, as well.

She knew why. In a blinding flash she knew why. She couldn't stand being rejected, not again. She had been rejected by her first love; she had been rejected by an entire community. She had been rejected by her father with a few cold dismissive words in his beautifully appointed office in her childhood home.

But maybe, just maybe, that was why she should confide in Sam. Because at the end of their affair it wouldn't matter. Because then they would go back to sniping at each other or not talking to each other at all.

Because he hadn't rejected her yet.

"When he called me into his office, I knew I was in trouble," she said, rubbing her hand over her forehead. "He never did that for good things. Ever. If there was something good to discuss, we would talk about it around the dinner table. Only bad things were ever talked about in his office with the door firmly closed. He talked to Gage like that. Right before he left town. So, I always knew it had to be bad."

She cleared her throat, looking out across the arena, through the gap in the trees and at the distant view of the misty waves beyond. It was so very gray, the clouds hanging low in the sky, touching the top of the angry, steel-colored sea.

"Anyway, I *knew*. As soon as I walked in, I knew. He looked grim. Like I've never seen him before. And he asked me what was going on with myself and David Smithson. Well, I knew there was no point in denying it. So I told him. He didn't yell. I wish he had. He said... He said the worst thing you could ever do was get caught. That a man like David spent years building up his reputation, not to have it undone by the temptation of some young girl." She blinked furiously. "He said that if a woman was going to present more temptation than a man could handle, the least she could do was keep it discreet."

"How could he say that to you? To his daughter? Look, my dad was a difficult son of a bitch, but if he'd had a daughter and some man had hurt her, he'd have ridden out on his meanest stallion with a pair of pliers to dole out the world's least sterile castration."

Maddy choked out a laugh that was mixed with a sob. "That's what I thought. It really was. I thought... I thought he would be angry, but one of the things that scared me most, at least initially, was the idea that he would take it out on David. And I still loved David then. But no. He was angry at me."

"I don't understand how that's possible."

"That was when he told me," she choked out. "Told me that he had mistresses, that it was just something men did, but that the world didn't run if the mistress didn't know her place, and if I was intent on lowering myself to be that sort of woman when I could have easily been a wife, that was none of his business. He told me a woman had had his child and never betrayed him." Her throat tightened, almost painfully, a tear sliding down her cheek. "Even he saw me as the villain. If my own father couldn't stand up for me, if even he thought it was my fault somehow, how was I ever supposed to stand up for myself when other people accused me of being a whore?"

"Maddy…"

"That's why," she said, the words thin, barely making their way through her constricted throat. "That's why it hurts so much. And that's why I'm not over it. There were two men involved in that who said they loved me. There was David, the man I had given my heart to, the man I had given my body to, who had lied to me from the very beginning, who threw me under the bus the moment he got the opportunity. And then there was my own father. My own father, who should have been on my side simply because I was born his. I loved them both. And they both let me down." She blinked, a mist rolling over her insides, matching the setting all around them. "How do you ever trust anyone after that? If it had only been David, I think I would have been over it a long time ago."

Sam was looking at her, regarding her with dark, intense eyes. He looked like he was about to say something, his chest shifting as he took in a breath that seemed to contain purpose. But then he said nothing.

He simply closed the distance between them, tugging her into his arms, holding her against his chest, his large, warm hand moving between her shoulder blades in a soothing rhythm.

She hadn't rested on anyone in longer than she could remember. Hadn't been held like this in years. Her mother was too brittle to lean on. She would break beneath the weight of somebody else's sorrow. Her father had never offered a word of comfort to anyone. And she had gotten in the habit of pretending she was tough so that Colton and Sierra wouldn't worry about her. So that they wouldn't look too deeply at how damaged she was still from the events of the past.

So she put all her weight on him and total peace washed over her. She shouldn't indulge in this. She shouldn't allow herself this. It was dangerous. But she couldn't stop. And she didn't want to.

She squeezed her eyes shut, a few more tears falling down her cheeks, soaking into his shirt. If anybody knew that Madison West had wept all over a man in the broad light of day, they wouldn't believe it. But she didn't care. This wasn't about anyone else. It was just about her. About purging her soul of some of the poison that had taken up residence there ten years ago and never quite left.

About dealing with some of the heavy longing that existed inside her for a time and a place she could never return to. For a Christmas when she had walked down Main Street with her father and seen him as a hero.

But of course, when she was through crying, she felt exposed. Horribly. Hideously, and she knew this was why she didn't make a habit out of confiding in people. Because now Sam McCormack knew too much about her. Knew more about her than maybe anybody else on earth. At least, he knew about parts of her that no one else did.

The tenderness. The insecurity. The parts that were on the verge of cracking open, crumbling the foundation of her and leaving nothing more than a dusty pile of Maddy behind.

She took a deep breath, hoping that the pressure would squeeze some of those shattering pieces of herself back together with the sheer force of it. Too bad it just made her aware of more places down deep that were compromised.

Still, she wiggled out of his grasp, needing a moment to get ahold of herself. Needing very much to not get caught being held by a strange man down at the arena by any of the staff or anyone in her family.

"Thank you," she said, her voice shaking. "I just… I didn't know how much I needed that."

"I didn't do anything."

"You listened. You didn't try to give me advice or tell me I was wrong. That's actually doing a lot. A lot more than most people are willing to do."

"So, do you want me to come back here tonight?"

"Actually," she said, grabbing hold of her hands, twisting them, trying to deal with the nervous energy that was rioting through her, "I was thinking maybe I could come out a little bit early. And I could see where you work."

She didn't know why she was doing this. She didn't know where she imagined it could possibly end or how it would be helpful to her in any way. To add more pieces of him to her heart, to her mind.

That's what it felt like she was trying to do. Like collecting shells on the seashore. Picking up all the shimmering pieces of Sam she possibly could and sticking them in her little pail, hoarding them. Making a collection.

For what? Maybe for when it was over.

Maybe that wasn't so bad.

She had pieces of David, whether she wanted them or not. And she'd entertained the idea that maybe she could sleep with someone and not do that. Not carry them forward with her.

But the reality of it was that she wasn't going to walk away from this affair and never think of Sam again. He was never going to be the farrier again. He would always be Sam. Why not leave herself with beautiful memories instead of terrible ones? Maybe this was what she needed to do.

"You want to see the forge?" he asked.

"Sure. That would be interesting. But also your studio. I'm curious about your art, and I realize that I don't really know anything about it. Seeing you in the Mercantile the other day talking to Lane…" She didn't know how to phrase what she was thinking without sounding a little bit crazy. Without sounding overly attached. So she just let the sentence trail off.

But she was curious. She was curious about him. About who he was when he wasn't here. About who he was as a whole person, without the blinders around him that she had put there. She had very purposefully gone out of her way to know nothing about him. And so he had always been Sam McCormack, grumpy guy who worked at her family ranch on occasion and who she often bantered with in the sharpest of senses.

But there was more to him. So much more. This man

who had held her, this man who had listened, this man who seemed to know everyone in town and have decent relationships with them. Who created beautiful things that started in his mind and were then formed with his hands. She wanted to know him.

Yeah, she wouldn't be telling him any of that.

"Were you jealous? Because there is nothing between myself and Lane Jensen. First of all, anyone who wants anything to do with her has to go through Finn Donnelly, and I have no desire to step in the middle of *that* weird dynamic and his older-brother complex."

It struck her then that jealousy hadn't even been a component to what she had felt the other day. How strange. Considering everything she had been through with men, it seemed like maybe trust should be the issue here. But it wasn't. It never had been.

It had just been this moment of catching sight of him at a different angle. Like a different side to a prism that cast a different color on the wall and made her want to investigate further. To see how one person could contain so many different things.

A person who was so desperate to hide anything beyond that single dimension he seemed comfortable with.

Another thing she would definitely not say to him. She couldn't imagine the twenty shades of rainbow horror that would cross Sam's face if she compared him to a prism out loud.

"I was not," she said. "But it made me aware of the fact that you're kind of a big deal. And I haven't fully appreciated that."

"Of course you haven't," he said, his tone dry. "It interferes with your stable-boy fantasy."

She made a scoffing sound. "I do not have a stable-boy fantasy."

"Yes, you do. You like slumming it."

Those words called up heated memories out of the depths of her mind. Him whispering things in her ear. His rough hands skimming over her skin. She bit her lip. "I like nothing of the kind, Sam McCormack. Not with you, not with any man. Are you going to show me your pretty art or not?"

"Not if you call it pretty."

"You'll have to take your chances. I'm not putting a cap on my vocabulary for your comfort. Anyway, if you haven't noticed, unnerving people with what I may or may not say next is kind of my thing."

"I've noticed."

"You do it too," she said.

His lips tipped upward into a small smile. "Do I?"

She rolled her eyes. "Oh, don't pretend you don't know. You're way too smart for that. And you act like the word *smart* is possibly the world's most vile swear when it's applied to you. But you are. You can throw around accusations of slumming it all you want, but if we didn't connect mentally, and if I didn't respect you in some way, this wouldn't work."

"Our brains have nothing to do with this."

She lifted a finger. "A woman's largest sexual organ is her brain."

He chuckled, wrapping his arm around her waist and drawing her close. "Sure, Maddy. But we both know what the most important one is." He leaned in, whispering dirty things in her ear, and she laughed, pushing against his chest. "Okay," he said, finally. "I will let you come see my studio."

She fought against the trickle of warmth that ran through her, that rested deep in her stomach and spread out from there, making her feel a kind of languid satisfaction that she had no business feeling over something like this. "Then I guess I'll see you for the art show."

Nine

Sam had no idea what in hell had possessed him to let Maddy come out to his property tonight. Chase and Anna were not going to let this go ignored. In fact, Anna was already starting to make comments about the fact that he hadn't been around for dinner recently. Which was why he was there tonight, eating as quickly as possible so he could get back out to his place on the property before Maddy arrived. He had given her directions to go on the road that would allow her to bypass the main house, which Chase and Anna inhabited.

"Sam." His sister-in-law's voice cut into his thoughts. "I thought you were going to join us for dinner tonight?"

"I'm here," he said.

"Your body is. Your brain isn't. And Chase worked very hard on this meal," Anna said.

Anna was a tractor mechanic, and formerly Chase's

best friend in a platonic sense. All of that had come to an end a few months ago when they had realized there was a lot more between them than friendship.

Still, the marriage had not transformed Anna into a domestic goddess. Instead, it had forced Chase to figure out how to share a household with somebody. They were never going to have a traditional relationship, but it seemed to suit Chase just fine.

"It's very good, Chase," Sam said, keeping his tone dry.

"Thanks," Chase said, "I opened the jar of pasta sauce myself."

"Sadly, no one in this house is ever going to win a cooking competition," Anna said.

"You keep *me* from starving," Sam pointed out.

Though, in all honesty, he was a better cook than either of them. Still, it was an excuse to get together with his brother. And sometimes it felt like he needed excuses. So that he didn't have to think deeply about a feeling that was more driving than hunger pangs.

"Not recently," Chase remarked. "You haven't been around."

Sam let out a heavy sigh. "Yes, sometimes a man assumes that newlyweds want time alone without their crabby brother around."

"We always want you around," Anna said. Then she screwed up her face. "Okay, we don't *always* want you around. But for dinner, when we invite you, it's fine."

"Just no unexpected visits to the house," Chase said. "In the evening. Or anytime. And maybe also don't walk into Anna's shop without knocking after hours."

Sam grimaced. "I get the point. Anyway, I've just been busy. And I'm about to be busy again." He stood up, anticipation shooting through him. He had gone a long time without sex, and now sex with Maddy was about all he could think about. Five years of celibacy would do that to a man.

Made a man do stupid things, like invite the woman he was currently sleeping with to come to his place and to come see his art. Whatever the hell she thought that would entail. He was inclined to figure it out. Just so she would feel happy, so he could see her smile again.

So she would be in the mood to put out. And nothing more. Certainly no emotional reasoning behind that.

He couldn't do that. Not ever again.

"Okay," Anna said, "you're always cagey, Sam, I'll give you that. But you have to give me a hint about what's going on."

"No," Sam said, turning to go. "I really don't."

"Sculpture? A woman?"

Well, sadly, Anna was mostly on point with both. "Not your business."

"That's hilarious," Chase said, "coming from the man who meddled in our relationship."

"You jackasses needed meddling," Sam said. "You were going to let her go." Of the two of them, Chase was undoubtedly the better man. And Anna was one of the best, man or woman. When Sam had realized his brother was about to let Anna get away because of baggage from his past, Sam had had no choice but to play the older-brother card and give advice that he himself would never have taken.

But it was different for Chase. Sam wanted it to be different for Chase. He didn't want his younger brother living the same stripped-down existence he did.

"Well, maybe you need meddling too, jackass," Anna said.

Sam ignored his sister-in-law and continued on out of the house, taking the steps on the porch two at a time, the frosted ground crunching beneath his boots as he walked across the field, taking the short route between the two houses.

He shoved his hands in his pockets, looking up, watching his breath float up into the dense sky, joining the mist there. It was already getting dark, the twilight hanging low around him, a deep blue ink spill that bled down over everything.

It reminded him of grief. A darkness that descended without warning, covering everything around it, changing it. Taking things that were familiar and twisting them into foreign objects and strangers.

That thought nibbled at the back of his mind. He couldn't let it go. It just hovered there as he made his way back to his place, trying to push its way to the front of his mind and form the obvious conclusion.

He resisted it. The way that he always did. Anytime he got inspiration that seemed related to these kinds of feelings. And then he would go out to his shop and start working on another Texas longhorn sculpture. Because that didn't mean anything and people would want to buy it.

Just as he approached his house, so did Maddy's car. She parked right next to his truck, and a strange feeling of domesticity overtook him. Two cars in the driveway. His and hers.

He pushed that aside too.

He watched her open the car door, her blond hair even paler in the advancing moonlight. She was wearing a hat, the shimmering curls spilling out from underneath it. She also had on a scarf and gloves. And there was something about her, looking soft and bundled up, and very much not like prickly, brittle Maddy, that made him want to pull her back into his arms like he had done earlier that day and hold her up against his chest.

Hold her until she quit shaking. Or until she started shaking for a different reason entirely.

"You made it," he said.

"You say that like you had some doubt that I would."

"Well, at the very least I thought you might change your mind."

"No such luck for you. I'm curious. And once my curiosity is piqued, I will have it satisfied."

"You're like a particularly meddlesome cat," he said.

"You're going to have to make up your mind, Sam," Maddy said, smiling broadly.

"About what?"

"Am I vegetable or mammal? You have now compared me to both."

"A tomato is a fruit."

"Whatever," she said, waving a gloved hand.

"Do you want to come out and see the sculptures or do you want to stand here arguing about whether or not you're animal, vegetable or mineral?"

Her smile only broadened. "Sculptures, please."

"Well, follow me. And it's a good thing you bundled up."

"This is how much I had to bundle to get in the car and drive over here. My heater is *not* broken. I didn't know that I was going to be wandering around out in the dark, in the cold."

He snorted. "You run cold?"

"I do."

"I hadn't noticed."

She lifted a shoulder, taking two steps to his every one, doing her best to keep up with him as he led them both across the expanse of frozen field. "Well, I'm usually very hot when you're around. Anyway, the combination of you and blankets is very warming."

"What happens when I leave?"

"I get cold," she returned.

Something about those words felt like a knife in the center of his chest. Damned if he knew why. At least, damned if he wanted to know why.

What he wanted was to figure out how to make it go away.

They continued on the rest of the walk in silence, and he increased his pace when the shop came into view. "Over here is where Chase and I work," he said, gesturing to the first building. "Anna's is on a different section of the property, one closer to the road so that it's easier for her customers to get in there, since they usually have heavy equipment being towed by heavier equipment. And this one is mine." He pointed to another outbuilding, one that had once been a separate machine shed.

"We remodeled it this past year. Expanded and made room for the new equipment. I have a feeling my dad would piss himself if he knew what this was being used for now," he continued, not quite able to keep the thought in his mind.

Maddy came up beside him, looping her arm through his. "Maybe. But I want to see it. And I promise you I won't…do *that*."

"Appreciated," he said, allowing her to keep hold of him while they walked inside.

He realized then that nobody other than Chase and Anna had ever been in here. And he had never grandly showed it to either of them. They just popped in on occasion to let him know that lunch or dinner was ready or to ask if he was ever going to resurface.

He had never invited anyone here. Though, he supposed that Maddy had invited herself here. Either way, this was strange. It was exposing in a way he hadn't anticipated it being. Mostly because that required he admit that there was something of himself in his work. And he resisted that. Resisted it hard.

It had always been an uncomfortable fit for him. That he had this ability, this compulsion to create things, that could come only from inside him. Which was a little bit like opening up his chest and showing bits of it to the world. Which was the last thing on earth he ever wanted to do. He didn't like sharing himself with other people. Not at all.

Maddy turned a slow circle, her soft, pink mouth falling open. "Wow," she said. "Is this all of them?"

"No," he said, following her line of sight, looking at the various iron sculptures all around them. Most of them were to scale with whatever they were representing. Giant two-ton metal cows and horses, one with a cowboy upon its back, took up most of the space in the room.

Pieces that came from what he saw. From a place he loved. But not from inside him.

"What are these?"

"Works in progress, mostly. Almost all of them are close to being done. Which was why I was up at the cabin, remember? I'm trying to figure out what I'm going to do next. But I can always make more things like this. They sell. I can put them in places around town and tourists will always come in and buy them. People pay obscene amounts of money for stuff like this." He let out a long, slow breath. "I'm kind of mystified by it."

"You shouldn't be. It's amazing." She moved around the space, reaching out and brushing her fingertips over the back of one of the cows. "We have to get some for the ranch. They're perfect."

Something shifted in his chest, a question hovering on the tip of his tongue. But he held it back. He had been about to ask her if he should do something different. If he should follow that compulsion that had hit him on the walk back. Those ideas about grief. About loss.

Who the hell wanted to look at something like that? Anyway, he didn't want to show anyone that part of himself. And he sure as hell didn't deserve to profit off any of his losses.

He gritted his teeth. "Great."

"You sound like you think it's great," she said, her tone deeply insincere.

"I wasn't aware my enthusiasm was going to be graded."

She looked around, the shop light making her hair look even deeper gold than it normally did. She reached up, grabbing the knit hat on her head and flinging it onto the ground. He knew what she was doing. He wanted to stop her. Because this was his shop. His studio. It was personal in a way that nothing else was. She could sleep in his bed. She could go to his house, stay there all night, and it would never be the same as her getting naked here.

He was going to stop her.

But then she grabbed the zipper tab on her jacket and shrugged it off before taking hold of the hem of her top, yanking it over her head and sending it the same way as her outerwear.

Then Maddy was standing there, wearing nothing but a flimsy lace bra, the pale curve of her breasts rising and falling with every breath she took.

"Since it's clear how talented your hands are, particularly here…" she said, looking all wide-eyed and innocent. He loved that. The way she could look like this, then spew profanities with the best of them. The way she could make her eyes all dewy, then do something that would make even the most hardened cowboy blush. "I thought I might see if I could take advantage of the inspirational quality of the place."

Immediately, his blood ran hotter, faster, desire roaring in him like a beast. He wanted her. He wanted this. There was nowhere soft to take her, not here. Not in this place full of nails and iron, in this place that was hard and jagged just like his soul, that was more evidence of what he contained than anyone would ever know.

"The rest," he said, his voice as uncompromising as the sculpture all around them. "Take off the rest, Madison."

Her lashes fluttered as she looked down, undoing the snap on her jeans, then the zipper, maddeningly slowly. And of course, she did her best to look like she had no idea what she was doing to him.

She pushed her jeans down her hips, and all that was left covering her was those few pale scraps of lace. She was so soft. And everything around her was so hard.

It should make him want to protect her. Should make him want to get her out of here. Away from this place. Away from him. But it didn't. He was that much of a bastard.

He didn't take off any of his own clothes, because there was something about the contrast that turned him on even more. Instead, he moved toward her, slowly, not bothering to hide his open appreciation for her curves.

He closed the distance between them, wrapping his hand around the back of her head, sifting his fingers through her hair before tightening his hold on her, tugging gently. She gasped, following his lead, tilting her face upward.

He leaned in, and he could tell that she was expecting a kiss. By the way her lips softened, by the way her eyes fluttered closed. Instead, he angled his head, pressing his lips to that tender skin on her neck. She shivered, the contact clearly an unexpected surprise. But not an unwelcome one.

He kept his fingers buried firmly in her hair, holding her steady as he shifted again, brushing his mouth over the line of her collarbone, following it all the way toward the center of her chest and down to the plush curves of her breasts.

He traced that feathery line there where lace met skin with the tip of his tongue, daring to delve briefly beneath the fabric, relishing the hitch in her breathing when he came close to her sensitized nipples.

He slid his hands up her arms, grabbed hold of the delicate bra straps and tugged them down, moving slowly, ever so slowly, bringing the cups down just beneath her breasts, exposing those dusky nipples to him.

"Beautiful," he said. "Prettier than anything in here."

"I didn't think you wanted the word *pretty* uttered in here," she said, breathless.

"About my work. About you… That's an entirely different situation. You are pretty. These are pretty." He leaned in, brushing his lips lightly over one tightened bud, relishing the sweet sound of pleasure that she made.

"Now who's a tease?" she asked, her voice labored.

"I haven't even started to tease you yet."

He slid his hands around her back, pressing his palms hard between her shoulder blades, lowering his head so that he could draw the center of her breast deep into his mouth. He sucked hard until she whimpered, until she squirmed against him, clearly looking for some kind of relief for the intense arousal that he was building inside her.

He looked up, really looked at her face, a deep, primitive sense of pleasure washing through him. That he was touching such a soft, beautiful woman. That he was allowing himself such an indulgence. That he was doing this to her.

He had forgotten. He had forgotten what it was like to really relish the fact that he possessed the power to make a woman feel good. Because he had reduced his hands to something else entirely. Hands that had failed him, that had failed Elizabeth.

Hands that could form iron into impossible shapes but couldn't be allowed to handle something this fragile.

But here he was with Madison. She was soft, and he wasn't breaking her. She was beautiful, and she was his.

Not yours. Never yours.

He tightened his hold on her, battling the unwelcome thoughts that were trying to crowd in, trying to take over this experience, this moment. When Madison was gone, he would go back to the austere existence he'd been living for the past five years. But right now, he had her, and he wasn't going to let anything damage that. Not now.

Instead of thinking, which was never a good thing,

not for him, he continued his exploration of her body. Lowering himself down to his knees in front of her, kissing her just beneath her breasts, and down lower, tracing a line across her soft stomach.

She was everything a woman should be. He was confident of that. Because she was the only woman he could remember. Right now, she was everything.

He moved his hands down her thighs, then back up again, pushing his fingertips beneath the waistband of her panties as he gripped her hips and leaned in, kissing her just beneath her belly button. She shook beneath him, a sweet little trembling that betrayed just how much she wanted him.

She wouldn't, if she knew. If she knew, she wouldn't want him. But she didn't know. And she never had to. There were only five days left. They would never have to talk about it. Ever. They would only ever have this. That was important. Because if they ever tried to have more, there would be nothing. She would run so far the other direction he would never see her again.

Or maybe she wouldn't. Maybe she would stick around. But that was even worse. Because of what he would have to do.

He flexed his fingers, the blunt tips digging into that soft skin at her hips. He growled, moving them around to cup her ass beneath the thin lace fabric on her panties. He squeezed her there too and she moaned, her obvious enjoyment of his hands all over her body sending a surge of pleasure through him.

He shifted, delving between her thighs, sliding his fingers through her slick folds, moving his fingers over her clit before drawing them back, pushing one finger inside her.

She gasped, grabbing his shoulders, pitching forward. He could feel her thigh muscles shaking as he pleasured her slowly, drawing his finger in and out of her body before adding a second. Her nails dug into his skin, clinging to him harder and harder as he continued tormenting her.

He looked up at her and allowed himself to get lost in this. In the feeling of her slick arousal beneath his hands, in the completely overwhelmed, helpless expression on her beautiful face. Her eyes were shut tight, and she was biting her lip, probably to keep herself from screaming. He decided he had a new goal.

He lowered his head, pressing his lips right to the center of her body, her lace panties holding the warmth of his breath as he slowly lapped at her through the thin fabric.

She swore, a short, harsh sound that verged on being a scream. But it wasn't enough. He teased her that way, his fingers deep inside her, his mouth on her, for as long as he could stand it.

Then he took his other hand, swept the panties aside and pushed his fingers in deep while he lapped at her bare skin, dragging his tongue through her folds, over that sensitized bundle of nerves.

And then she screamed.

Her internal muscles pulsed around him, her pleasure ramping his up two impossible degrees.

"I hope like *hell* you brought a condom," he said, his voice ragged, rough.

"I think I did," she said, her tone wavering. "Yes, I did. It's in my purse. Hurry."

"You want me to dig through your purse."

"I can't breathe. I can't move. If I do anything, I'm

going to fall down. So I suggest you get the condom so that I don't permanently wound myself attempting to procure it."

"Your tongue seems fine," he said, moving away from her and going to grab the purse that she had discarded along with the rest of her clothes.

"So does yours," she muttered.

And he knew that what she was referring to had nothing to do with talking.

He found the condom easily enough, since it was obviously the last thing she had thrown into her bag. Then he stood, stripping his shirt off and his pants, adding to the pile of clothing that Maddy had already left on the studio floor.

Then he tore open the packet and took care of the protection. He looked around the room, searching for some surface that he could use. That they could use.

There was no way to lay her down, which he kind of regretted. Mostly because he always felt like she deserved a little bit more than the rough stuff that he doled out to her. Except she seemed to like it. So if it was what she wanted, she was about to get the full experience tonight.

He wrapped his arm around her waist, pulling her up against him, pressing their bodies together, her bare breasts pressing hard against his chest. He was so turned on, his arousal felt like a crowbar between them.

She didn't seem to mind.

He took hold of her chin, tilting her face up so she had to look at him. And then he leaned in, kissing her lightly, gently. It would be the last gentle thing he did all night.

He slid his hands along her body, moving them to grip her hips. Then he turned her so that she was facing away from him. She gasped but followed the momentum as he propelled her forward, toward one of the iron figures—a horse—and placed his hand between her shoulder blades.

"Hold on to the horse, cowgirl," he said, his voice so rough it sounded like a stranger's.

"What?"

He pushed more firmly against her back, bending her forward slightly, and she lifted her hands, placing them over the back of the statue. "Just like that," he said.

Her back arched slightly, and he drew his fingertips down the line of her spine, all the way down to her butt. He squeezed her there, then slipped his hand to her hip.

"Spread your legs," he instructed.

She did, widening her stance, allowing him a good view and all access. He moved his hand back there, just for a second, testing her readiness. Then he positioned his arousal at the entrance to her body. He pushed into her, hard and deep, and she let out a low, slow sound of approval.

He braced himself, putting one hand on her shoulder, his thumb pressed firmly against the back of her neck, the other holding her hip as he began to move inside her.

He lost himself. In her, in the moment. In this soft, beautiful woman, all curves and round shapes in the middle of this hard, angular garden of iron.

The horse was hard in front of her; he was hard behind her. Only Maddy was soft.

Her voice was soft—the little gasps of pleasure that escaped her lips like balm for his soul. Her body was soft, her curves giving against him every time he thrust home.

When she began to rock back against him, her desperation clearly increasing along with his, he moved his hand from her hip to between her thighs. He stroked her in time with his thrusts, bringing her along with him, higher and higher until he thought they would both shatter. Until he thought they might shatter everything in this room. All of these unbreakable, unbending things.

She lowered her head, her body going stiff as her release broke over her, her body spasming around his, that evidence of her own loss of control stealing every ounce of his own.

He gave himself up to this. Up to her. And when his climax hit him, it was with the realization that it was somehow hers. That she owned this. Owned this moment. Owned his body.

That realization only made it more intense. Only made it more arousing.

His muscles shook as he poured himself into her. As he gave himself up to it totally, completely, in a way he had given himself up to nothing and no one for more than five years. Maybe ever.

In this moment, surrounded by all of these creations that had come out of him, he was exposed, undone. As though he had ripped his chest open completely and exposed his every secret to her, as though she could see everything, not just these creations, but the ugly, secret things that he kept contained inside his soul.

It was enough to make his knees buckle, and he had to reach out, pressing his palm against the rough surface of the iron horse to keep himself from falling to the ground and dragging Maddy with him.

The only sound in the room was their broken breathing, fractured and unsteady. He gathered her up against his body, one hand against her stomach, the other still on the back of the horse, keeping them upright.

He angled his head, buried his face in her neck, kissed her.

"Well," Maddy said, her voice unsteady, "that was amazing."

He couldn't respond. Because he couldn't say anything. His tongue wasn't working; his brain wasn't working. His voice had dried up like a desert. Instead, he released his grip on the horse, turned her to face him and claimed her mouth in a deep, hard kiss.

Ten

Maybe it wasn't the best thing to make assumptions, but when they got back to Sam's house, that was exactly what Maddy did. She simply assumed that she would be invited inside because he wanted her to stay.

If her assumption was wrong, he didn't correct her.

She soaked in the details of his home, the simple, completely spare surroundings, and how it seemed to clash with his newfound wealth.

Except, in many ways it didn't, she supposed. Sam just didn't seem the type to go out and spend large. He was too…well, Sam.

The cabin was neat, well kept and small. Rustic and void of any kind of frills. Honestly, it was more rustic than the cabins they had stayed in up in the mountain.

It was just another piece that she could add to the Sam puzzle. He was such a strange man. So difficult to find the center of. To find the key to. He was one giant sheet of code and she was missing some essential bit that might help her make heads or tails of him.

He was rough; he was distant. He was caring and kinder in many ways than almost anyone else she had ever known. Certainly, he had listened to her in a way that no one else ever had before. Offering nothing and simply taking everything onto his shoulders, letting her feel whatever she did without telling her it was wrong.

That was valuable in a way that she hadn't realized it would be.

She wished that she could do the same for him. That she could figure out what the thing was that made Sam… Sam. That made him distant and difficult and a lot like a brick wall. But she knew there was more behind his aloofness. A potential for feeling, for emotion, that surpassed what he showed the world.

She didn't even bother to ask herself why she cared. She suspected she already knew.

Sam busied himself making a fire in the simple, old-fashioned fireplace in the living room. It was nothing like the massive, modern adorned piece that was in the West family living room. One with fake logs and a switch that turned it on. One with a mantel that boasted the various awards won by Nathan West's superior horses.

There was something about this that she liked. The lack of pretension. Though, she wondered if it reflected Sam any more honestly than her own home—decorated by her mother's interior designer—did her. She could see it, in a way. The fact that he was no-nonsense and a little bit spare.

And yet in other ways she couldn't.

His art pieces looked like they were ready to take a breath and come to life any moment. The fact that such beautiful things came out of him made her think there had to be beautiful things in him. An appreciation for aesthetics. And yet none of that was in evidence here. Of course, it would be an appreciation for a hard aesthetic, since there was nothing soft about what he did.

Still, he wasn't quite this cold and empty either.

Neither of them spoke while he stoked the fire, and pretty soon the small space began to warm. Her whole body was still buzzing with the aftereffects of what had happened in his studio. But still, she wanted more.

She hadn't intended to seduce him in his studio; it had just happened. But she didn't regret it. She had brought a condom, just in case, so she supposed she couldn't claim total innocence. But still.

It had been a little bit reckless. The kind of thing a person could get caught doing. It was definitely not as discreet as she should have been. The thought made her smile. Made her feel like Sam was washing away some of the wounds of her past. That he was healing her in a way she hadn't imagined she could be.

She walked over to where he was, still kneeling down in front of the fireplace, and she placed her hands on his shoulders. She felt his muscles tighten beneath her touch. All of the tension that he carried in his shoulders. Why? Because he wanted her again and that bothered him? It wasn't because he didn't want her, she was convinced of that. There was no faking what was between them.

She let her fingertips drift down lower. Then she leaned in, pressing a kiss to his neck, as he was so fond of doing to her. As she was so fond of him doing.

"What are you doing?" he asked, his voice rumbling inside him.

"Honestly, if you have to ask, I'm not doing a very good job of it."

"Aren't you exhausted?"

"The way I see it, I have five days left with you. I could go five days without sleep if I needed to."

He reached up, grabbing hold of her wrist and turning, then pulling her down onto the floor, onto his lap. "Is that a challenge? Because I'm more than up to meeting that."

"If you want to take it as one, I suppose that's up to you."

She put her hands on his face, sliding her thumbs alongside the grooves next to his mouth. He wasn't that old. In his early to midthirties, she guessed. But he wore some serious cares on that handsome face of his, etched into his skin. She wondered what they were. It was easy to assume it was the death of his parents, and perhaps that was part of it. But there was more.

She'd had the impression earlier today that she'd only ever glimpsed a small part of him. That there were deep pieces of himself that he kept concealed from the world. And she had a feeling this was one of them. That he was a man who presented himself as simple, who lived in these simple surroundings, hard and spare, while he contained multitudes of feeling and complexity.

She also had a feeling he would rather die than admit that.

"All right," he said, "if you insist."

He leaned in, kissing her. It was slower and more luxurious than any of the kisses they had shared back in the studio. A little bit less frantic. A little bit less desperate.

Less driven toward its ultimate conclusion, much more about the journey.

She found herself being disrobed again, for the second time that day, and she really couldn't complain. Especially not when Sam joined her in a state of undress.

She pressed her hand against his chest, tracing the strongly delineated muscles, her eyes following the movement.

"I'm going to miss this," she said, not quite sure what possessed her to speak the words out loud. Because they went so much deeper than just appreciation for his body. So much deeper than just missing his beautiful chest or his perfect abs.

She wished that they didn't, but they did. She wished she were a little more confused by the things she did and said with him, like she had been earlier today. But somehow, between her pouring her heart out to him at the ranch today and making love with him in the studio, a few things had become a lot clearer.

His lips twitched, like he was considering making light of the statement. Saying something to defuse the tension between them. Instead, he wrapped his fingers around her wrist, holding her tight, pressing her palms flat against him so that she could feel his heart beating. Then he kissed her. Long, powerful. A claiming, a complete and total invasion of her soul.

She didn't even care.

Or maybe, more accurately, she did care. She cared all the way down, and what she couldn't bother with anymore was all the pretending that she didn't. That she cared about nothing and no one, that she existed on the Isle of Maddy. Where she was wholly self-sufficient.

She was pretty sure, in this moment, that she might

need him. That she might need him in ways she hadn't needed another person in a very long time, if ever. When she had met David, she had been a teenager. She hadn't had any baggage; she hadn't run into any kind of resistance in the world. She was young, and she didn't know what giving her heart away might cost.

She knew now. She knew so much more. She had been hurt; she had been broken. And when she allowed herself to see that she needed someone, she could see too just how badly it could go.

When they parted, they were both breathing hard, and his dark eyes were watchful on hers. She felt like she could see further than she normally could. Past all of that strength that he wore with ease, down to the parts of him that were scarred, that had been wounded.

That were vulnerable.

Even Sam McCormack was vulnerable. What a revelation. Perhaps if he was, everyone was.

He lifted his hand, brushing up against her cheek, down to her chin, and then he pushed her hair back off her face, slowly letting his fingers sift through the strands. And he watched them slide through his fingers, just as she had watched her own hand as she'd touched his chest. She wondered what he was thinking. If he was thinking what she'd been. If he was attached to her in spite of himself.

Part of her hoped so. Part of her hoped not.

He leaned down, kissing her on the shoulder, the seemingly nonsexual contact affecting her intensely. Making her skin feel like it was on fire, making her heart feel like it might burst right out of her chest.

She found herself being propelled backward, but it

felt like slow motion, as he lowered her down onto the floor. Onto the carpet there in front of the fireplace.

She had the thought that this was definitely a perfect component for a winter affair. But then the thought made her sad. Because she wanted so much more than a winter affair with him. So much more than this desperate grab in front of the fire, knowing that they had only five days left with each other.

But then he was kissing her and she couldn't think anymore. She couldn't regret. She could only kiss him back.

His hands skimmed over her curves, her breasts, her waist, her hips, all the way down to her thighs, where he squeezed her tight, held on to her as though she were his lifeline. As though he were trying to memorize every curve, every dip and swell.

She closed her eyes, gave herself over to it, to the sensation of being known by Sam. The thought filled her, made her chest feel like it was expanding. He knew her. He really knew her. And he was still here. Still with her. He didn't judge her; he didn't find her disgusting.

He didn't treat her like she was breakable. He could still bend her over a horse statue in his studio, then be like this with her in front of the fire. Tender. Sweet.

Because she was a woman who wanted both things. And he seemed to know it.

He also seemed to be a man who might need both too.

Or maybe everybody did. But you didn't see it until you were with the person you wanted to be both of those things with.

"Hang on just a second," he said, suddenly, breaking into her sensual reverie. She had lost track of time.

Lost track of everything except the feel of his hands on her skin.

He moved away from her, the loss of his body leaving her cold. But he returned a moment later, settling himself in between her thighs. "Condom," he said by way of explanation.

At least one of them had been thinking. She certainly hadn't been.

He joined their bodies together, entering her slowly, the sensation of fullness, of being joined to him, suddenly so profound that she wanted to weep with it. It always felt good. From the first time with him it had felt good. But this was different.

It was like whatever veil had been between them, whatever stack of issues had existed, had been driving them, was suddenly dropped. And there was nothing between them. When he looked at her, poised over her, deep inside her, she felt like he could see all the way down.

When he moved, she moved with him, meeting him thrust for thrust, pushing them both to the brink. And when she came, he came along with her, his rough gasp of pleasure in her ears ramping up her own release.

In the aftermath, skin to skin, she couldn't deny anymore what all these feelings were. She couldn't pretend that she didn't know.

She'd signed herself up for a twelve-day fling with a man she didn't even like, and only one week in she had gone and fallen in love with Sam McCormack.

"Sam." Maddy's voice broke into his sensual haze. He was lying on his back in front of the fireplace, feeling drained and like he had just had some kind of out-of-body experience. Except he had been firmly in his body and feeling everything, everything and then some.

"What?" he asked, his voice rusty.

"Why do you make farm animals?"

"What the hell kind of question is that?" he asked.

"A valid one," she said, moving nearer to him, putting her hand on his chest, tracing shapes there. "I mean, not that they aren't good."

"The horse seemed good enough for you a couple hours ago."

"It's good," she said, her tone irritated, because she obviously thought he was misunderstanding her on purpose.

Which she wasn't wrong about.

"Okay, but you don't think I should be making farm animals."

"No, I think it's fine that you make farm animals. I just think it's not actually you."

He shifted underneath her, trying to decide whether or not he should say anything. Or if he should sidestep the question. If it were anyone else, he would laugh. Play it off. Pretend like there was no answer. That there was nothing deeper in him than simply re-creating what he literally saw out in the fields in front of him.

And a lot of people would have bought that. His own brother probably would have, or at the very least, he wouldn't have pushed. But this was Maddy. Maddy, who had come apart in his arms in more than one way over the past week. Maddy, who perhaps saw deeper inside him than anyone else ever had.

Why not tell her? Why not? Because he could sense her getting closer to him. Could sense it like an invisible cord winding itself around the two of them, no matter that he was going to have to cut it in the end. Maybe it would be best to do it now.

"If I don't make what I see, I'll have to make what I feel," he said. "Nobody wants that."

"Why not?"

"Because the art has to sell," he said, his voice flat. Although, that was somewhat disingenuous. It wasn't that he didn't think he could sell darker pieces. In fact, he was sure that he could. "I don't do it for myself. I do it for Chase. I was perfectly content to keep it some kind of weird hobby that I messed around with after hours. Chase was the one who thought that I needed to pursue it full-time. Chase was the one who thought it was the way to save our business. And it started out doing kind of custom artistry for big houses. Gates and the detail work on stairs and decks and things. But then I started making bigger pieces and we started selling them. I say *we* because without Chase they would just sit in the shop."

"So you're just making what sells. That's the beginning and end of the story." Her blue eyes were too sharp, too insightful and far too close to the firelight for him to try to play at any games.

"I make what I want to let people see."

"What happened, Sam? And don't tell me nothing. You're talking to somebody who clung to one event in the past for as long as humanly possible. Who let it dictate her entire life. You're talking to the queen of residual issues here. Don't try to pretend that you don't have any. I know what it looks like." She took a deep breath. "I know what it looks like when somebody uses anger, spite and a whole bunch of unfriendliness to keep the world at a safe distance. I know, because I've spent the past ten years doing it. Nobody gets too close to the girl who says unpredictable things. The one who might come out and tell you that your dress does make you look fat and then turn around and say something crude about male anatomy. It's how you give yourself power in social situations. Act like you don't care about the rules that everyone else is a slave to." She laughed. "And why not? I already broke the rules. That's me. It's been me for a long time. And it isn't because I didn't know better. It's because I absolutely knew better. You're smart, Sam. The way that you walk around, the way you present yourself, even here, it's calculated."

Sam didn't think anyone had ever accused him of being calculated before. But it was true. Truer than most things that had been leveled at him. That he was grumpy, that he was antisocial. He was those things. But for a very specific reason.

And of course Madison would know. Of course she would see.

"I've never been comfortable sharing my life," Sam said. "I suppose that comes from having a father who was less than thrilled to have a son who was interested in art. In fact, I think my father considered it a moral failing of his. To have a son who wanted to use materials to create frivolous things. Things that had no use. To have a son who was more interested in that than honest labor. I learned to keep things to myself a long time ago. Which all sounds a whole lot like a sad, cliché story. Except it's not. It worked. I would have made a relationship with my dad work. But he died. So then it didn't matter anymore. But still, I just never...I never wanted to keep people up on what was happening with my life. I was kind of trained that way."

Hell, a lot of guys were that way, anyway. A lot of

men didn't want to talk about what was happening in their day-to-day existence. Though most of them wouldn't have gone to the lengths that Sam did to keep everything separate.

"Most especially when Chase and I were neck-deep in trying to keep the business afloat, I didn't like him seeing that I was working on anything else. Anything at all." Sam took a deep breath. "That included any kind of relationships I might have. I didn't have a lot. But you know Chase never had a problem with people in town knowing that he was spreading it around. He never had a problem sleeping with the women here."

"No, he did not," Maddy said. "Never with me, to be clear."

"Considering I'm your first in a decade, I wasn't exactly that worried about it."

"Just making sure."

"I didn't like that. I didn't want my life to be part of this real-time small-town TV program. I preferred to find women out of town. When I was making deliveries, going to bigger ranches down the coast, that was when I would…"

"When you would find yourself a buckle bunny for the evening?"

"Yes," he said. "Except I met a woman I liked a lot. She was the daughter of one of the big ranchers down near Coos County. And I tried to keep things business oriented. We were actually doing business with her family. But I…I saw her out at a bar one night, and even though I knew she was too young, too nice of a girl for a guy like me…I slept with her. And a few times after. I was pretty obsessed with her, actually."

He was downplaying it. But what was the point of

doing anything else? Of admitting that for just a little while he'd thought he'd found something. Someone who wanted him. All of him. Someone who knew him.

The possibility of a future. Like the first hint of spring in the air after a long winter.

Maddy moved closer to him, looking up at him, and he decided to take a moment to enjoy that for a second. Because after this, she would probably never want to touch him again.

"Without warning, she cut me off. Completely. Didn't want to see me anymore. And since she was a few hours down the highway, that really meant not seeing her. I'd had to make an effort to work her into my life. Cutting her out of it was actually a lot easier."

"Sure," Maddy said, obviously not convinced.

"I got a phone call one night. Late. From the hospital. They told me to come down because Elizabeth was asking for me. They said it wasn't good."

"Oh, Sam," Maddy said, her tone tinged with sympathy.

He brush right past that. Continued on. "I white-knuckled it down there. Went as fast as I could. I didn't tell anyone I was going. When I got there, they wouldn't let me in. Because I wasn't family."

"But she wanted them to call you."

"It didn't matter." It was difficult for him to talk about that day. In fact, he never had. He could see it all playing out in his mind as he spoke the words. Could see the image of her father walking out of the double doors, looking harried, older than Sam had ever seen him look during any of their business dealings.

"I never got to see her," Sam said. "She died a few minutes after I got there."

"Sam, I'm so sorry…"

"No, don't misunderstand me. This isn't a story about me being angry because I lost a woman that I loved. I *didn't* love her. That's the worst part." He swallowed hard, trying to diffuse the pressure in his throat crushing down, making it hard to breathe. "I mean, maybe I could have. But that's not the same. You know who loved her? Her family. Her family loved her. I have never seen a man look so destroyed as I did that day. Looking at her father, who clearly wondered why in hell I was sitting down there in the emergency room. Why I had been called to come down. He didn't have to wonder long. Not when they told him exactly how his daughter died." Sam took a deep breath. "Elizabeth died of internal bleeding. Complications from an ectopic pregnancy."

Maddy's face paled, her lips looking waxen. "Did you…? You didn't know she was pregnant."

"No. Neither did anyone in her family. But I know it was mine. I know it was mine, and she didn't want me to know. And that was probably why she didn't tell me, why she broke things off with me. Nobody knew because she was ashamed. Because it was my baby. Because it was a man that she knew she couldn't have a future with. Nobody knew, so when she felt tired and lay down for a nap because she was bleeding and feeling discomfort, no one was there."

Silence settled around them, the house creaking beneath the weight of it.

"Did you ever find out why…why she called you then?"

"I don't know. Maybe she wanted me there to blame me. Maybe she just needed me. I'll never know. She was gone before I ever got to see her."

"That must have been…" Maddy let that sentence trail off. "That's horrible."

"It's nothing but horrible. It's everything horrible. I know why she got pregnant, Maddy. It's because…I was so careless with her. I had sex with her once without a condom. And I thought that it would be fine. Hell, I figured if something did happen, I'd be willing to marry her. All of that happened because I didn't think. Because I lost control. I don't deserve…"

"You can't blame yourself for a death that was some kind of freak medical event."

"Tell me you wouldn't blame yourself, Maddy. Tell me you wouldn't." He sat up, and Maddy sat up too. Then he gripped her shoulders, holding her steady, forcing her to meet his gaze. "You, who blame yourself for the affair with your dressage teacher even though you were an underage girl. You could tell me you don't. You could tell me that you were just hurt by the way everybody treated you, but I know it's more than that. You blame yourself. So don't you dare look at me with those wide blue eyes and tell me that I have no business blaming myself."

She blinked. "I…I don't blame myself. I don't. I mean, I'm not proud of what I did, but I'm not going to take all of the blame. Not for something I couldn't control. He lied to me. I was dumb, yes. I was naive. But dammit, Sam, my father should have had my back. My friends should have had my back. And my teacher should never have taken advantage of me."

He moved away from her then, pushing himself into a standing position and forking his fingers through his hair. She wasn't blaming him. It was supposed to push her away. She certainly wasn't supposed to look at him with sympathy. She was supposed to be appalled. Appalled that he had taken the chances he had with Elizabeth's body. Appalled at his lack of control.

It was the object lesson. The one that proved that he wasn't good enough for a woman like her. That he wasn't good enough for anyone.

"You don't blame yourself at all?"

"I don't know," she said. "It's kind of a loaded question. I could have made another decision. And because of that, I guess I share blame. But I'm not going to sit around feeling endless guilt. I'm hurt. I'm wounded. But that's not the same thing. Like I told you, the sex was the least of it. If it was all guilt, I would have found somebody a long time ago. I would have dealt with it. But it's more than that. I think it's more than that with you. Because you're not an idiot. You know full well that it isn't like you're the first man to have unprotected sex with a woman. You know full well you weren't in control of where an embryo implanted inside a woman. You couldn't have taken her to the hospital, because you didn't know she was pregnant. You didn't know she needed you. She sent you away. She made some choices here, and I don't really think it's her fault either, because how could she have known? But still. It isn't your fault."

He drew back, anger roaring through him. "I'm the one…"

"You're very dedicated to this. But that doesn't make it true."

"Her father thought it was my fault," he said. "That matters. I had to look at a man who was going to have to bury his daughter because of me."

"Maybe he felt that way," Maddy said. "I can understand that. People want to blame. I know. Because I've been put in that position. Where I was the one that people wanted to blame. Because I wasn't as well liked. Because I wasn't as important. I know that David's wife certainly wanted to blame me, because she wanted to make her marriage work, and if she blamed David, how would she do that? And without blame, your anger is aimless."

Those words hit hard, settled somewhere down deep inside him. And he knew that no matter what, no matter that he didn't want to think about them, no matter that he didn't want to believe them, they were going to stay with him. Truth had a funny way of doing that.

"I'm not looking for absolution, Maddy." He shook his head. "I was never looking for it."

"What are you looking for, then?"

He shrugged. "Nothing. I'm not looking for anything. I'm not looking for you to forgive me. I'm not looking to forgive myself."

"No," she said, "you're just looking to keep punishing yourself. To hold everything inside and keep it buried down deep. I don't think it's the rest of the world you're hiding yourself from. I think you're hiding from yourself."

"You think that you are qualified to talk about my issues? You. The woman who didn't have a lover for ten years because she's so mired in the past?"

"Do you think that's going to hurt my feelings? I know I'm messed up. I'm well aware. In fact, I would argue that it takes somebody as profoundly screwed up as I am to look at another person and see it. Maybe other people would look at you and see a man who is strong. A man who has it all laid out. A man who has iron control. But I see you for what you are. You're completely and totally bound up inside. And you're ready to crack apart. You can't go on like this."

"Watch me," he said.

"How long has it been?" she asked, her tone soft.

"Five years," he ground out.

"Well, it's only half the time I've been punishing myself, but it's pretty good. Where do you see it ending, Sam?"

"Well, you were part of it for me too."

He gritted his teeth, regretting introducing that revelation into the conversation.

"What do you mean?"

"I haven't been with a woman in five years. So I guess you could say you are part of me dealing with some of my issues."

Maddy looked like she'd been slapped. She did not, in any way, look complimented. "What does that mean? What does that mean?" She repeated the phrase twice, sounding more horrified, more frantic each time.

"It had to end at some point. The celibacy, I mean. And when you offered yourself, I wasn't in a position to say no."

"After all of your righteous indignation—the accusation that I was using you for sexual healing—it turns out you were using me for the same thing?" she asked.

"Why does that upset you so much?"

"Because…because you're still so completely wrapped up in it. Because you obviously don't have any intention to really be healed."

Unease settled in his chest. "What's me being healed to you, Maddy? What does that mean? I changed something, didn't I? Same as you."

"But…" Her tone became frantic. "I just… You aren't planning on letting it change you."

"What change are you talking about?" he pressed.

"I don't know," she said, her throat sounding constricted.

"Like hell, Madison. Don't give me that. If you've changed the rules in your head, that's hardly my fault."

She whirled around, lowering her head, burying her face in her hands. "You're so infuriating." She turned back to him, her cheeks crimson. "I don't know what either of us was thinking. That we were going to go into this and come out the other side without changing anything? We are idiots. We are idiots who didn't let another human being touch us for years. And somehow we thought we could come together and nothing would change? I mean, it was one thing when it was just me. I assumed that you went around having sex with women you didn't like all the time."

"Why would you think that?"

"Because you don't like anyone. So, that stands to reason. That you would sleep with women you don't like. I certainly didn't figure you didn't sleep with women at all. That's ridiculous. You're... *Look* at you. Of course you have sex. Who would assume that you didn't? Not me. That's who."

He gritted his teeth, wanting desperately to redirect the conversation. Because it was going into territory that would end badly for both of them. He wanted to leave the core of the energy arcing between them unspoken. He wanted to make sure that neither of them acknowledged it. He wanted to pretend he had no idea what she was thinking. No idea what she was about to say.

The problem was, he knew her. Better than he knew anyone else, maybe. And it had all happened in a week. A week of talking, of being skin to skin. Of being real.

No wonder he had spent so many years avoiding exactly this. No wonder he had spent so long hiding every-thing that he was, everything that he wanted. Because the alternative was letting it hang out there, exposed and acting as some kind of all-access pass to anyone who bothered to take a look.

"Well, you assumed wrong. But it doesn't have to change anything. We have five more days, Maddy. Why does it have to be like this?"

"Honest?"

"Why do we have to fight with each other? We shouldn't. We don't have to. We don't have to continue this discussion. We are not going to come to any kind of understanding, whatever you might think. Whatever you think you're pushing for here…just don't."

"Are you going to walk away from this and just not change? Are you going to find another woman? Is that all this was? A chance for you to get your sexual mojo back? To prove that you could use a condom every time? Did you want me to sew you a little sexual merit badge for your new Boy Scout vest?" She let out a frustrated growl. "I don't want you to be a Boy Scout, Sam. I want you to be you."

Sam growled, advancing on her. She backed away from him until her shoulder blades hit the wall. Then he pressed his palms to the flat surface on either side of her face. "You don't want me to be me. Trust me. I don't know how to give the kinds of things you want."

"You don't want to," she said, the words soft, pene-trating deeper than a shout ever could have.

"No, you don't want me to."

"Why is that so desperately important for you to make yourself believe?"

"Because it's true."

She let silence hang between them for a moment. "Why won't you let yourself feel this?"

"What?"

"*This* is why you do farm animals. That's what you said. And you said it was because nobody would want to see this. But that isn't true. Everybody feels grief, Sam. Everybody has lost. Plenty of people would want to see what you would make from this. Why is it that you can't do it?"

"You want me to go ahead and make a profit off my sins? Out of the way I hurt other people? You want me to make some kind of artistic homage to a father who never wanted me to do art in the first place? You want me to do a tribute to a woman whose death I contributed to."

"Yes. Because it's not about how anyone else feels. It's about how you feel."

He didn't know why this reached in and cut him so deeply. He didn't know why it bothered him so much. Mostly he didn't know why he was having this conversation with her at all. It didn't change anything. It didn't change him.

"No," she said, "that isn't what I think you should do. It's not about profiting off sins—real or perceived. It's about you dealing with all of these things. It's about you acknowledging that you have feelings."

He snorted. "I'm entitled to more grief than Elizabeth's parents? To any?"

"You lost somebody that you cared about. That matters. Of course it matters. You lost… I don't know. She was pregnant. It was your baby. Of course that matters. Of course you think about it."

"No," he said, the words as flat as everything inside

him. "I don't. I don't think about that. Ever. I don't talk about it. I don't do anything with it."

"Except make sure you never make a piece of art that means anything to you. Except not sleep with anyone. Except punish yourself. Which you had such a clear vision of when you felt like I was doing it to myself but you seem to be completely blind to when it comes to you."

"All right. Let's examine your mistake, then, Maddy. Since you're so determined to draw a comparison between the two of us. Who's dead? Come on. Who died as a result of your youthful mistakes? No one. Until you make a mistake like that, something that's that irreversible, don't pretend you have any idea what I've been through. Don't pretend you have any idea of what I should feel."

He despised himself for even saying that. For saying he had been through something. He didn't deserve to walk around claiming that baggage. It was why he didn't like talking about it. It was why he didn't like thinking about it. Because Elizabeth's family members were the ones who had been left with a giant hole in their lives. Not him. Because they were the ones who had to deal with her loss around the dinner table, with thinking about her on her birthday and all of the holidays they didn't have her.

He didn't even know when her birthday was.

"Well, I care about you," Maddy said, her voice small. "Doesn't that count for anything?"

"No," he said, his voice rough. "Five more days, Maddy. That's it. That's all it can ever be."

He should end it now. He knew that. Beyond anything else, he knew that he should end it now. But if Maddy West had taught him anything, it was that he wasn't nearly as controlled as he wanted to be. At least, not where she was concerned. He could stand around and shout about it, self-flagellate all he wanted, but when push came to shove, he was going to make the selfish decision.

"Either you come to bed with me and we spend the rest of the night not talking, or you go home and we can forget the rest of this."

Maddy nodded mutely. He expected her to turn and walk out the door. Maybe not even pausing to collect her clothes, in spite of the cold weather. Instead, she surprised him. Instead, she took his hand, even knowing the kind of devastation it had caused, and she turned and led him up the stairs.

Eleven

Maddy hadn't slept at all. It wasn't typical for her and Sam to share a bed the entire night. But they had last night. After all that shouting and screaming and love-making, it hadn't seemed right to leave. And he hadn't asked her to.

She knew more about him now than she had before. In fact, she had a suspicion that she knew everything about him. Even if it wasn't all put together into a complete picture. It was there. And now, with the pale morning light filtering through the window, she was staring at him as though she could make it all form a cohesive image.

As if she could will herself to somehow understand what all of those little pieces meant. As if she could make herself see the big picture.

Sam couldn't even see it, of that she was certain. So she had no idea how she could expect herself to see it.

Except that she wanted to. Except that she needed to. She didn't want to leave him alone with all of that. It was too much. It was too much for any one man. He felt responsible for the death of that woman. Or at least, he was letting himself think he did.

Protecting himself. Protecting himself with pain.

It made a strange kind of sense to her, only because she was a professional at protecting herself. At insulating herself from whatever else might come her way. Yes, it was a solitary existence. Yes, it was lonely. But there was control within that. She had a feeling that Sam operated in much the same way.

She shifted, brushing his hair out of his face. He had meant to frighten her off. He had given her an out. And she knew that somehow he had imagined she would take it. She knew that he believed he was some kind of monster. At least, part of him believed it.

Because she could also tell that he had been genuinely surprised that she hadn't turned tail and run.

But she hadn't. And she wouldn't. Mostly because she was just too stubborn. She had spent the past ten years being stubborn. Burying who she was underneath a whole bunch of bad attitude and sharp words. Not letting anyone get close, even though she had a bunch of people around her who cared. She had chosen to focus on the people who didn't. The people who didn't care enough. While simultaneously deciding that the people who did care enough, who cared more than enough, somehow weren't as important.

Well, she was done with that. There were people in her life who loved her. Who loved her no matter what. And she had a feeling that Sam had the ability to be one of those people. She didn't want to abandon him to this.

Not when he had—whether he would admit it or not—been instrumental in digging her out of her self-imposed emotional prison.

"Good morning," she whispered, pressing her lips to his cheek.

As soon as she did that, a strange sense of foreboding stole over her. As though she knew that the next few moments were going to go badly. But maybe that was just her natural pessimism. The little beast she had built up to be the strongest and best-developed piece of her. Another defense.

Sam's eyes opened, and the shock that she glimpsed there absolutely did not bode well for the next few moments. She knew that. "I stayed the night," she said, in response to the unasked question she could see lurking on his face.

"I guess I fell asleep," he said, his voice husky.

"Clearly." She took a deep breath. Oh well. If it was all going to hell, it might as well go in style. "I want you to come to the family Christmas party with me."

It took only a few moments for her to decide that she was going to say those words. And that she was going to follow them up with everything that was brimming inside her. Feelings that she didn't feel like keeping hidden. Not anymore. Maybe it was selfish. But she didn't really care. She knew his stuff. He knew hers. The only excuse she had for not telling him how she felt was self-protection.

She knew where self-protection got her. Absolutely nowhere. Treading water in a stagnant pool of her own failings, never advancing any further on in her life. In her existence. It left her lonely. It left her without any real, true friends. She didn't want that. Not anymore.

And if she had to allow herself to be wounded in the name of authenticity, in the name of trying again, then she would.

An easy decision to make before the injury occurred. But it was made nonetheless.

"Why?" Sam asked, rolling away from her, getting up out of bed.

She took that opportunity to drink in every detail of his perfect body. His powerful chest, his muscular thighs. Memorizing every little piece of him. More Sam for her collection. She had a feeling that eventually she would walk away from him with nothing but that collection. A little pail full of the shadows of what she used to have.

"Because I would like to have a date." She was stalling now.

"You want to make your dad mad? Is that what we're doing? A little bit of revenge for everything he put you through?"

"I would never use you that way, Sam. I hope you know me better than that."

"We don't know each other, Maddy. We don't. We've had a few conversations, and we've had some sex. But that doesn't mean knowing somebody. Not really."

"That just isn't true. Nobody else knows how I feel about what happened to me. Nobody. Nobody else knows about the conversation I had with my dad. And I would imagine that nobody knows about Elizabeth. Not the way that I do."

"We used each other as a confessional. That isn't the same."

"The funny thing is it did start that way. At least for me. Because what did it matter what you knew. We weren't going to have a relationship after. So I didn't have to worry about you judging me. I didn't have to worry about anything."

"And?"

"That was just what I told myself. It was what made it feel okay to do what I wanted to do. We lie to ourselves. We get really deep in it when we feel like we need protection. That was what I was doing. But the simple truth is I felt a connection with you from the beginning. It was why I was so terrible to you. Because it scared me."

"You should have kept on letting it scare you, baby girl."

Those words acted like a shot of rage that went straight to her stomach, then fired onto her head. "Why? Because it's the thing that allows you to maintain your cranky-loner mystique? That isn't you. I thought maybe you didn't feel anything. But now I think you feel everything. And it scares you. I'm the same way."

"I see where this is going, Maddy. Don't do it. Don't. I can tell you right now it isn't going to go the way you think it will."

"Oh, go ahead, Sam. Tell me what I think. Please. I'm dying to hear it."

"You think that because you've had some kind of transformation, some kind of deep realization, that I'm headed for the same. But it's bullshit. I'm sorry to be the one to tell you. Wishful thinking on a level I never wanted you to start thinking on. You knew the rules. You knew them from the beginning."

"Don't," she said, her throat tightening, her chest constricting. "Don't do this to us. Don't pretend it can stay the same thing it started out as. Because it isn't. And you know it."

"You're composing a really compelling story, Madison." The reversion back to her full name felt significant. "And we both know that's something you do. Make more out of sex than it was supposed to be."

She gritted her teeth, battling through. Because he wanted her to stop. He wanted this to intimidate, to hurt. He wanted it to stop her. But she wasn't going to let him win. Not at this. Not at his own self-destruction. "Jackass 101. Using somebody's deep pain against them. I thought you were above that, Sam."

"It turns out I'm not. You might want to pay attention to that."

"I'm paying attention. I want you to come with me to the Christmas party, Sam. Because I want it to be the beginning. I don't want it to be the end."

"Don't do this."

He bent down, beginning to collect his clothes, his focus on anything in the room but her. She took a deep breath, knowing that what happened next was going to shatter all of this.

"I need more. I need more than twelve days of Christmas. I want it every day. I want to wake up with you every morning and go to bed with you every night. I want to fight with you. I want to make love with you. I want to tell you my secrets. To show you every dark, hidden thing in me. The serious things and the silly things. Because I love you. It's that complicated and that simple. I love you and that means I'm willing to do this, no matter how it ends."

Sam tugged his pants on, did them up, then pulled his shirt over his head. "I told you not to do this, Maddy. But you're doing it anyway. And you know what that makes it? A suicide mission. You stand there, thinking you're being brave because you're telling the truth. But you know how it's going to end. You know that after you make this confession, you're not actually going to have to deal with the relationship with me, because I already told you it isn't happening. I wonder if you would have been so brave if you knew I might turn around and offer you forever."

His words hit her with the force of bullets. But for some reason, they didn't hurt. Not really. She could remember distinctly when David had broken things off with her. Saying that she had never been anything serious. That she had been only a little bit of tail on the side and he was of course going to have to stay with his wife. Because she was the center of his life. Of his career. Because she mattered, and Maddy didn't. That had hurt. It had hurt because it had been true.

Because David hadn't loved her. And it had been easy for him to break up with her because he had never intended on having more with her, and not a single part of him wanted more.

This was different. It was different because Sam was trying to hurt her out of desperation. Because Sam was lying. Or at the very least, was sidestepping. Because he didn't want to have the conversation.

Because he would have to lie to protect himself. Because he couldn't look her in the eye and tell her that he didn't love her, that she didn't matter.

But she wasn't certain he would let himself feel it. That was the gamble. She knew he felt it. She knew it. That deep down, Sam cared. She wasn't sure if he knew it. If he had allowed himself access to those feelings. Feelings that Sam seemed to think were a luxury, or a danger. Grief. Desire. Love.

"Go ahead and offer it. You won't. You won't, because you know I would actually say yes. You can try to make this about how damaged I am, but all of this is because of you."

"You have to be damaged to want somebody like me. You know what's in my past."

"Grief. Grief that you won't let yourself feel. Sadness you don't feel like you're allowed to have. That's what's in your past. Along with lost hope. Let's not pretend you blame yourself. You felt so comfortable calling me out, telling me that I was playing games. Well, guess what. That's what you're doing. You think if you don't want anything, if you don't need anything, you won't be hurt again. But you're just living in hurt and that isn't better."

"You have all this clarity about your own emotional situation, and you think that gives you a right to talk about mine?"

She threw the blankets off her and got out of bed. "Why not?" she asked, throwing her arms wide. She didn't care that she was naked. In fact, in many ways it seemed appropriate. That Sam had put clothes on, that he had felt the need to cover himself, and that she didn't even care anymore. She had no pride left. But this wasn't about pride.

"You think you have the right to talk about mine," she continued. "You think you're going to twist everything that I'm saying and eventually you'll find some little doubt inside me that will make me believe you're telling the truth. I've had enough of that. I've had enough of men telling me what I feel. Of them telling me what I should do. I'm not going to let you do it. You're better than that. At least, I thought you were."

"Maybe I'm not."

"Right now? I think you don't want to be. But I would love you through this too, Sam. You need to know that. You need to know that whatever you say right now, in this room, it's not going to change the way that I feel about you. You don't have that kind of power."

"That's pathetic. There's nothing I can say to make you not love me? Why don't you love yourself a little bit more than that, Madison," he said, his tone hard.

And regardless of what she had just said, that did hit something in her. Something vulnerable and scared. Something that was afraid she really hadn't learned how to be anything more than a pathetic creature, desperate for a man to show her affection.

"I love myself just enough to put myself out there and demand this," she said finally, her voice vibrating with conviction. "I love myself too much to slink off silently. I love myself too much not to fight for what I know we could have. If I didn't do this, if I didn't say this, it would only be for my pride. It would be so I could score points and feel like maybe I won. But in the end, if I walk away without having fought for you with everything I have in me, we will have both lost. I think you're worth that. I know you are. Why don't you think so?"

"Why do you?" he asked, his voice thin, brittle. "I don't think I've shown you any particular kindness or tenderness."

"Don't. Don't erase everything that's happened between us. Everything I told you. Everything you gave me."

"Keeping my mouth shut while I held a beautiful woman and let her talk? That's easy."

"I love you, Sam. That's all. I'm not going to stand here and have an argument. I'm not going to let you get in endless barbs while you try to make those words something less than true. I love you. I would really like it if you could tell me you loved me too."

"I don't." His words were flat in the room. And she knew they were all she would get from him. Right now, it was all he could say. And he believed it. He believed it down to his bones. That he didn't love her. That everything that had taken place between them over the past week meant nothing. Because he had to. Because behind that certainty, that flat, horrifying expression in his eyes, was fear.

Strong, beautiful Sam, who could bend iron to his will, couldn't overpower the fear that lived inside him. And she would never be able to do it for him.

"Okay," she said softly, beginning to gather her clothes. She didn't know how to do this. She didn't know what to do now. How to make a triumphant exit. So she decided she wouldn't. She decided to let the tears fall down her cheeks; she decided not to make a joke. She decided not to say anything flippant or amusing.

Because that was what the old Maddy would have done. She would have played it off. She would have tried to laugh. She wouldn't have let herself feel this, not all the way down. She wouldn't have let her heart feel bruised or tender. Wouldn't have let a wave of pain roll over her. Wouldn't have let herself feel it, not really.

And when she walked out of his house, sniffling, her shoulders shaking, and could no longer hold back the sob that was building in her chest by the time she reached her car, she didn't care. She didn't feel ashamed.

There was no shame in loving someone.

She opened the driver-side door and sat down. And then the dam burst. She had loved so many people who had never loved her in return. Not the way she loved them. She had made herself hard because of it. She had put the shame on her own shoulders.

That somehow a seventeen-year-old girl should have known that her teacher was lying to her. That somehow a daughter whose father had walked her down Main Street and bought her sweets in a little shop should have known that her father's affection had its limits.

That a woman who had met a man who had finally reached deep inside her and moved all those defenses she had erected around her heart should have known that in the end he would break it.

No. It wasn't her. It wasn't the love that was bad. It was the pride. The shame. The fear. Those were the things that needed to be gotten rid of.

She took a deep, shaking breath. She blinked hard, forcing the rest of her tears to fall, and then she started the car.

She would be okay. Because she had found herself again. Had learned how to love again. Had found a deep certainty and confidence in herself that had been missing for so long.

But as she drove away, she still felt torn in two. Because while she had been made whole, she knew that she was leaving Sam behind, still as broken as she had found him.

Twelve

Sam thought he might be dying. But then, that could easily be alcohol poisoning. He had been drinking and going from his house into his studio for the past two days. And that was it. He hadn't talked to anyone. He had nothing to say. He had sent Maddy away, and while he was firmly convinced it was the only thing he could have done, it hurt like a son of a bitch.

It shouldn't. It had been necessary. He couldn't love her the way that she wanted him to. He couldn't. There was no way in hell. Not a man like him.

Her words started to crowd in on him unbidden, the exact opposite thing that he wanted to remember right now. About how there was no point blaming himself. About how that wasn't the real issue. He growled, grabbing hold of the hammer he'd been using and flinging it across the room. It landed in a pile of scrap metal, the sound satisfying, the lack of damage unsatisfying.

He had a fire burning hot, and the room was stifling. He stripped his shirt off, feeling like he couldn't catch his breath. He felt like he was losing his mind. But then, he wasn't a stranger to it. He had felt this way after his parents had died. Again after Elizabeth. There was so much inside him, and there was nowhere for it to go.

And just like those other times, he didn't deserve this pain. Not at all. He was the one who had hurt her. He was the one who couldn't stand up to that declaration of love. He didn't deserve this pain.

But no matter how deep he tried to push it down, no matter how he tried to pound it out with a hammer, it still remained. And his brain was blank. He couldn't even figure out how the hell he might fashion some of this material into another cow.

It was like the thing inside him that told him how to create things had left along with Maddy.

He looked over at the bottle of Jack Daniel's that was sitting on his workbench. And cursed when he saw that it was empty. He was going to have to get more. But he wasn't sure he had more in the house. Which meant leaving the house. Maybe going to Chase's place and seeing if there was anything to take. Between that and sobriety it was a difficult choice.

He looked around, looked at the horse that he had bent Maddy over just three days ago. Everything seemed dead now. Cold. Dark. Usually he felt the life in the things that he made. Something he would never tell anyone, because it sounded stupid. Because it exposed him.

But it was like Maddy had come in here and changed things. Taken everything with her when she left.

He walked over to the horse, braced his hands on the

back of it and leaned forward, giving into the wave of pain that crashed over him suddenly, uncontrollably.

"I thought I might find you in here."

Sam lifted his head at the sound of his brother's voice. "I'm busy."

"Right. Which is why there is nothing new in here, but it smells flammable."

"I had a drink."

"Or twelve," Chase said, sounding surprisingly sympathetic. "If you get too close to that forge, you're going to burst into flame."

"That might not be so bad."

"What's going on? You're always a grumpy bastard, but this is different. You don't usually disappear for days at a time. Actually, I can pick up a couple of times that you've done that in the past. You usually reemerge worse and even more impossible than you were before. So if that is what's happening here, I would appreciate a heads-up."

"It's nothing. Artistic temper tantrum."

"I don't believe that." Chase crossed his arms and leaned against the back wall of the studio, making it very clear that he intended to stay until Sam told him something.

Fine. The bastard could hang out all day for all he cared. It didn't mean he had to talk.

"Believe whatever you want," Sam said. "But it's not going to make hanging out here any more interesting. I can't figure out what to make next. Are you happy? I have no idea. I have no inspiration." Suddenly, everything in him boiled over. "And I hate that. I hate that it matters. I should just be able to think of something to do. Or not care if I don't want to do it. But somehow,

I can't make it work if I don't care at least a little bit. I hate caring, Chase. I *hate* it."

He hated it for every damn thing. Every damn, fragile thing.

"I know," Chase said. "And I blame Dad for that. He didn't understand. That isn't your fault. And it's not your flaw that you care. Think about the way he was about ranching. It was ridiculous. Weather that didn't go his way would send him into some kind of emotional tailspin for weeks. And he felt the same way about iron that you do. It's just that he felt compelled to shape it into things that had a function. But he took pride in his work. And he was an artist with it—you know he was. If anything, I think he was shocked by what you could do. Maybe even a little bit jealous. And he didn't know what to do with it."

Sam resisted those words. And the truth in them. "It doesn't matter."

"It does. Because it's why you can't talk about what you do. It's why you don't take pride in it the way that you should. It's why you're sitting here downplaying the fact you're having some kind of art block when it's been pretty clear for a few months that you have been."

"It shouldn't be a thing."

Chase shrugged. "Maybe not. But the very thing that makes your work valuable is also what makes it difficult. You're not a machine."

Sam wished he was. More than anything, he wished that he was. So that he wouldn't care about a damn thing. So that he wouldn't care about Maddy.

Softness, curves, floated to the forefront of his mind. Darkness and grief. All the inspiration he could ever want. Except that he couldn't take it. It wasn't his. He didn't own it. None of it.

He was still trying to pull things out of his own soul, and all he got was dry, hard work that looked downright ugly to him.

"I should be," he said, stubborn.

"This isn't about Dad, though. I don't even think it's about the art, though I think it's related. There was a woman, wasn't there?"

Sam snorted. "When?"

"Recently. Like the past week. Mostly I think so because I recognize that all-consuming obsession. Because I recognize this. Because you came and kicked my ass when I was in a very similar position just a year ago. And you know what you told me? With great authority, you told me that iron had to get hot to get shaped into something. You told me that I was in my fire, and I had to let it shape me into the man Anna needed me to be."

"Yeah, I guess I did tell you that," Sam said.

"Obviously I'm not privy to all the details of your personal life, Sam, which is your prerogative. But you're in here actively attempting to drink yourself to death. You say that you can't find any inspiration for your art. I would say that you're in a pretty damn bad situation. And maybe you need to pull yourself out of it. If that means grabbing hold of her—whoever she is—then do it."

Sam felt like the frustration inside him was about to overflow. "I can't. There's too much… There's too much. If you knew, Chase. If you knew everything about me, you wouldn't think I deserved it."

"Who deserves it?" Chase asked. "Does anybody? Do you honestly think I deserve Anna? I don't. But I love her. And I work every day to deserve her. It's a work in progress, let me tell you. But that's love. You just kind of keep working for it."

"There are too many other things in the way," Sam said, because he didn't know how else to articulate it. Without having a confessional, here in his studio, he didn't know how else to have this conversation.

"What things? What are you afraid of, Sam? Having a feeling? Is that what all this is about? The fact you want to protect yourself? The fact that it matters more to you that you get to keep your stoic expression and your who-gives-a-damn attitude intact?"

"It isn't that. It's never been that. But how—" He started again. "How was I supposed to grieve for Dad when you lost your mentor? How was I supposed to grieve for Mom when you were so young? It wasn't fair." And how the hell was he supposed to grieve for Elizabeth, for the child he didn't even know she had been carrying, when her own family was left with nothing.

"Of course you could grieve for them. They were your parents."

"Somebody has to be strong, Chase."

"And you thought I was weak? You think somehow grieving for my parents was weak?"

"Of course not. But…I was never the man that Dad wanted me to be. Now when he was alive. I didn't do what he wanted me to do. I didn't want the things that he wanted."

"Neither did I. And we both just about killed ourselves working this place the way that he wanted us to while it slowly sank into the ground. Then we had to do things on our terms. Because actually, we did know what we were talking about. And who we are, the gifts that we have, those mattered. If it wasn't for the fact that I have a business mind, if it wasn't for the fact that you could do the artwork, the ranch wouldn't be here. McCormack Ironworks wouldn't exist. And if Dad had lived, he would be proud of us. Because in the end we saved this place."

"I just don't...I had a girlfriend who died." He didn't know why he had spoken the words. He hadn't intended to. "She wasn't my girlfriend when she died. But she bled to death. At the hospital. She had been pregnant. And it was mine."

Chase cursed and fell back against the wall, bracing himself. "Seriously?"

"Yes. And I want... I want to do something with that feeling. But her family is devastated, Chase. They lost so much more than I did. And I don't know how...I don't know what to do with all of this. I don't know what to do with all of these feelings. I don't feel like I deserve them. I don't feel like I deserve the pain. Not in the way that I deserve to walk away from it unscathed. But I feel like it isn't mine. Like I'm taking something from them, or making something about me that just shouldn't be. But it's there all the same. And it follows me around. And Maddy loves me. She said she loves me. And I don't know how to take that either."

"Bullshit," Chase said, his voice rough. "That's not it."

"Don't tell me how it is, Chase, not when you don't know."

"Of course I know, Sam. Loss is hell. And I didn't lose half of what you did."

"It was just the possibility of something. Elizabeth. It wasn't... It was just..."

"Sam. You lost your parents. And a woman you were

involved with who was carrying your baby. Of course you're screwed up. But walking around pretending you're just grumpy, pretending you don't want anything, that you don't care about anything, doesn't protect you from pain. It's just letting fear poison you from the inside."

Sam felt like he was staring down into an abyss that had no end. A yawning, bottomless cavern that was just full of need. All the need he had ever felt his entire life. The words ricocheted back at him, hit him like shrapnel, damaging, wounding. They were the truth. That it was what drove him, that it was what stopped him.

Fear.

That it was why he had spent so many years hiding.

And as blindingly clear as it was, it was also clear that Maddy was right about him. More right about him than he'd ever been about himself.

That confession made him think of Maddy too. Of the situation she was in with her father. Of those broken words she had spoken to him about how if her own father didn't think she was worth defending, who would? And he had sent her away, like he didn't think she was worth it either. Like he didn't think she was worth the pain or the risk.

Except he did. He thought she was worth defending. That she was worth loving. That she was worth everything.

Sam felt… Well, nothing on this earth had ever made him feel small before. But this did it. He felt scared. He felt weak. Mostly he felt a kind of overwhelming sadness for everything he'd lost. For all the words that were left unsaid. The years of grief that had built up.

It had never been about control. It had never been

based in reality. Or about whether or not he deserved something. Not really. He was afraid of feeling. Of loss. More loss after years and years of it.

But his father had died without knowing. Without knowing that even though things weren't always the best between them, Sam had loved him. Elizabeth had died without knowing Sam had cared.

Protecting himself meant hurting other people. And it damn well hurt him.

Maddy had been brave enough to show him. And he had rejected it. Utterly. Completely. She had been so brave, and he had remained shut down as he'd been for years.

She had removed any risk of rejection and still he had been afraid. He had been willing to lose her this time.

"Do you know why the art is hard?" he asked.

"Why?"

"Because. If I make what I really want to, then I actually have to feel it."

He hated saying it. Hated admitting it. But he knew, somehow, that this was essential to his soul. That if he was ever going to move on from this place, from this dry, drunken place that produced nothing but anguish, he had to start saying these things. He had to start committing to these things.

"I had a lot behind this idea that I wasn't good enough. That I didn't deserve to feel. Because…the alternative is feeling it. It's caring when it's easier to be mad at everything. Hoping for things when so much is already dead."

"What's the alternative?" Chase asked.

He looked around his studio. At all the lifeless things. Hard and sharp. Just like he was. The alternative was living without hope. The alternative was acting like he was dead too.

"This," he said finally. "And life without Maddy. I'd rather risk everything than live without her."

Thirteen

Madison looked around the beautifully appointed room. The grand party facility at the ranch was decorated in evergreen boughs and white Christmas lights, the trays of glittering champagne moving by somehow adding to the motif. Sparkling. Pristine.

Maddy herself was dressed in a gown that could be described in much the same manner. A pale yellow that caught the lights and glimmered like sun on new-fallen snow.

However, it was a prime example of how appearances can be deceiving. She felt horrible. Much more like snow that had been mixed up with gravel. Gritty. Gray.

Hopefully no one was any the wiser. She was good at putting on a brave face. Good at pretending everything was fine. Something she had perfected over the years. Not just at these kinds of public events but at family events too.

Self-protection was her favorite accessory. It went with everything.

She looked outside, at the terrace, which was lit by a thatch of Christmas lights, heated by a few freestanding heaters. However, no one was out there. She took a deep breath, seeing her opportunity for escape. And she took it. She just needed a few minutes. A few minutes to feel a little bit less like her face would crack beneath the weight of her fake smile.

A few minutes to take a deep breath and not worry so much that it would turn into a sob.

She grabbed hold of a glass of champagne, then moved quickly to the door, slipping out into the chilly night air. She went over near one of the heaters, wrapping her arms around herself and simply standing for a moment, looking out into the inky blackness, looking at nothing. It felt good. It was a relief to her burning eyes. A relief to her scorched soul.

All of this feelings business was rough. She wasn't entirely certain she could recommend it.

"What's going on, Maddy?"

She turned around, trying to force a smile when she saw her brother Gage standing there.

"I just needed a little bit of quiet," she said, lifting her glass of champagne.

"Sure." He stuffed his hands in his pockets. "I'm not used to this kind of thing. I spent a lot of time on the road. In crappy hotels. Not a lot of time at these sorts of get-togethers."

"Regretting the whole return-of-the-prodigal-son

thing? Because it's too late to unkill that fatted calf, young man. You're stuck."

He laughed. "No. I'm glad that I'm back. Because of you. Because of Colton, Sierra. Even Jack."

"Rebecca?"

"Of course." He took a deep breath, closing the distance between them. "So what's going on with you?"

"Nothing," she said, smiling.

"I have a feeling that everybody else usually buys that. Which is why you do it. But I don't. Is it Jack? Is it having him here?"

She thought about that. Seriously thought about it. "No," she said, truthful. "I'm glad. I'm so glad that we're starting to fix some of this. I spent a long time holding on to my anger. My anger at Dad. At the past. All of my pain. And Jack got caught up in that. Because of the circumstances. We are all very different people. And getting to this point…I feel like we took five different paths. But here we are. And it isn't for Dad. It's for us. I think that's good. I spent a lot of time doing things in response to him. In response to the pain that he caused me. I don't want to do that anymore. I don't want to act from a place of pain and fear anymore."

"That's quite a different stance. I mean, since last we talked at The Grind."

She tried to smile again, wandering over to one of the wooden pillars. "I guess some things happened." She pressed her palm against the cold surface, then her forehead. She took a deep breath. In and out, slowly, evenly.

"Are you okay?"

She shook her head. "Not really. But I will be."

"I know I missed your first big heartbreak. And I feel like I would have done that bastard some bodily harm. I have quite a bit of internalized rage built up. If you need me to hurt anyone…I will. Gladly."

She laughed. "I appreciate that. Really, I do. It's just that…it's a good thing this is happening. It's making me realize a lot of things. It's making me change a lot of things. I just wish it didn't hurt."

"You know…when Rebecca told me that she loved me, it scared the hell out of me. And I said some things that I shouldn't have said. That no one should ever say to anyone. I regretted it. But I was running scared, and I wanted to make sure she didn't come after me. I'm so glad that she forgave me when I realized what an idiot I was."

She lifted her head, turning to face him. "That sounds a lot like brotherly advice."

"It is. And maybe it's not relevant to your situation. I don't know. But what I do know is that we both have a tendency to hold on to pain. On to anger. If you get a chance to fix this, I hope you forgive the bastard. As long as he's worthy."

"How will I know he's worthy?" she asked, a bit of humor lacing her voice.

"Well, I'll have to vet him. At some point."

"Assuming he ever speaks to me again, I would be happy to arrange that."

Gage nodded. "If he's half as miserable as you are, trust me, he'll be coming after you pretty quick."

"And you think I should forgive him?"

"I think that men are a bunch of hardheaded dumb-asses. And some of us need more chances than others. And I thank God every day I got mine. With this family. With Rebecca. So it would be mean-spirited of me not to advocate for the same for another of my species."

"I'll keep that under advisement."

Gage turned to go. "Do that. But if he keeps being a dumbass, let me know. Because I'll get together a posse or something."

"Thank you," she said. "Hopefully the posse won't be necessary."

He shrugged, then walked back into the party. She felt fortified then. Because she knew she had people on her side. No matter what. She wasn't alone. And that felt good. Even when most everything felt bad.

She let out a long, slow breath and rested her forearms on the railing, leaning forward, staring out across the darkened field. If she closed her eyes, she could almost imagine that she could see straight out to the ocean in spite of the fact that it was dark.

She was starting to get cold, even with the artificial heat. But it was entirely possible the chill was coming from inside her. Side effects of heartbreak and all of that.

"Merry Christmas Eve."

She straightened, blinking, looking out into the darkness. Afraid to turn around. That voice was familiar. And it didn't belong to anyone in her family.

She turned slowly, her heart stalling when she saw Sam standing there. He was wearing a white shirt unbuttoned at the collar, a black jacket and a pair of black slacks. His hair was disheveled, and she was pretty sure she could see a bit of soot on his chest where the open shirt exposed his skin.

"What are you doing here?"

"I had to see you." He took a step closer to her. "Bad enough that I put this on."

"Where did you get it?"

"The secondhand store on Main."

"Wow." No matter what he had to say, the fact that Sam McCormack had shown up in a suit said a whole lot without him ever opening his mouth.

"It doesn't really fit. And I couldn't figure out how to tie the tie." And of course, he hadn't asked anyone for help. Sam never would. It just wasn't him.

"Well, then going without was definitely the right method."

"I have my moments of brilliance." He shook his head. "But the other day wasn't one of them."

Her heart felt as if it were in a free fall, her stomach clenching tight. "Really?"

"Yeah."

"I agree. I mean, unreservedly. But I am open to hearing about your version of why you didn't think you were brilliant. Just in case we have differing opinions on the event."

He cursed. "I'm not good at this." He took two steps toward her, then reached out, gripping her chin between his thumb and forefinger. "I hate this, in fact. I'm not good at talking about feelings. And I've spent a lot of years trying to bury them down deep. I would like to do it now. But I know there's no good ending to that. I know that I owe you more."

"Go on," she said, keeping her eyes on his, her voice trembling, betraying the depth of emotion she felt.

She had never seen Sam quite like this, on edge, like he might shatter completely at any moment. "I told you I thought I didn't deserve these feelings. And I believed it."

"I know you did," she said, the words broken. "I know that you never lied on purpose, Sam. I know."

"I don't deserve that. That certainty. I didn't do anything to earn it."

She shook her head. "Stop. We're not going to talk like that. About what we deserve. I don't know what I deserve. But I know what I want. I want you. And I don't care if I'm jumping the gun. I don't care if I didn't make you grovel enough. It's true. I do."

"Maddy..."

"This all comes because we tried to protect ourselves for too long. Because we buried everything down deep. I don't have any defenses anymore. I can't do it anymore. I couldn't even if I wanted to. Which you can see, because I'm basically throwing myself at you again."

"I've always been afraid there was something wrong with me." His dark eyes were intense, and she could tell that he was wishing he could turn to stone rather than finish what he was saying. But that he was determined. That he had put his foot on the path and he wasn't going to deviate from it. "Something wrong with what I felt. And I pushed it all down. I always have. I've been through stuff that would make a lot of people crazy. But if you keep shoving it on down, it never gets any better." He shook his head. "I've been holding on to grief. Holding on to anger. I didn't know what else to do with it. My feelings about my parents, my feelings about Elizabeth, the baby. It's complicated. It's a lot. And I think more than anything I just didn't want to deal with it. I had a lot of excuses, and they felt real. They even felt maybe a little bit noble?"

"I can see that. I can see it being preferable to grief."

"Just like you said, Maddy. You put all those defenses in front of it, and then nothing can hurt you, right?"

She nodded. "At least, that's been the way I've handled it for a long time."

"You run out. Of whatever it is you need to be a person. Whatever it is you need to contribute, to create. That's why I haven't been able to do anything new with my artwork." He rolled his eyes, shaking his head slightly. "It's hard for me to..."

"I know. You would rather die than talk about feelings. And talk about this. But I think you need to."

"I told myself it was wrong to make something for my dad. My mom. Because they didn't support my work. I told myself I didn't deserve to profit off Elizabeth's death in any way. But that was never the real issue. The real issue was not wanting to feel those things at all. I was walking across the field the other night, and I thought about grief. The way that it covers things, twists the world around you into something unrecognizable." He shook his head. "When you're in the thick of it, it's like walking in the dark. Even if you're in a place you've seen a thousand times by day, it all changes. And suddenly what seemed safe is now full of danger."

He took a sharp breath and continued. "You can't trust anymore. You can't trust everything will be okay, because you've seen that sometimes it isn't. That's what it's like to have lost people like I have. And I can think about a thousand pieces that I could create that would express that. But it would mean that I had to feel it. And it would mean I would have to show other people what I felt. I wanted... From the moment I laid my hands on you, Maddy, I wanted to turn you into something. A sculpture. A painting. But that would mean looking at how I felt about you too. And I didn't want to do that either."

Maddy lifted her hand, cupping Sam's cheek. "I understand why you work with iron, Sam. Because it's just like you. You're so strong. And you really don't want to bend. But if you would just bend…just a little bit, I think you could be something even more beautiful than you already are."

"I'll do more than bend. If I have to, to have you, I'll break first. But I've decided…I don't care about protecting myself. From loss, from pain…doesn't matter. I just care about you. And I know that I have to fix myself if I'm going to become the kind of man you deserve. I know I have to reach inside and figure all that emotional crap out. I can't just decide that I love you and never look at the rest of it. I have to do all of it. To love you the way that you deserve, I know I have to deal with all of it."

"Do you love me?"

He nodded slowly. "I do." He reached into his jacket pocket and took out a notebook. "I've been working on a new collection. Just sketches right now. Just plans." He handed her the notebook. "I want you to see it. I know you'll understand."

She took it from him, opening it with shaking hands, her heart thundering hard in her throat. She looked at the first page, at the dark twisted mass he had sketched there. Maybe it was a beast, or maybe it was just menacing angles—it was hard to tell. She imagined that was the point.

There was more. Broken figures, twisted metal. Until the very last page. Where the lines smoothed out into rounded curves, until the mood shifted dramatically and everything looked a whole lot more like hope.

"It's hard to get a sense of scale and everything in the drawings. This is just me kind of blocking it out."

"I understand," she whispered. "I understand perfectly." It started with grief, and it ended with love. Unimaginable pain that was transformed.

"I lost a lot of things, Maddy. I would hate for you to be one of them. Especially because you're the one thing I chose to lose. And I have regretted it every moment since. But this is me." He put his fingertip on the notebook. "That's me. I'm not the nicest guy. I'm not what anybody would call cheerful. Frankly, I'm a grumpy son of a bitch. It's hard for me to talk about what I'm feeling. Harder for me to show it, and I'm in the world's worst line of work for that. But if you'll let me, I'll be your grumpy son of a bitch. And I'll try. I'll try for you."

"Sam," she said, "I love you. I love you, and I don't need you to be anything more than you. I'm willing to accept the fact that getting to your feelings may always be a little bit of an excavation. But if you promise to work on it, I'll promise not to be too sensitive about it. And maybe we can meet somewhere in the middle. One person doesn't have to do all the changing. And I don't want you to anyway." She smiled, and this time it wasn't forced. "You had me at 'You're at the wrong door.'"

He chuckled. "I think you had me a lot sooner than that. I just didn't know it."

"So," she said, looking up at him, feeling like the sun was shining inside her, in spite of the chill outside, "you want to go play Yahtzee?"

"Only if you mean it euphemistically."

"Absolutely not. I expect you to take the time to woo me, Sam McCormack. And if that includes board games, that's just a burden you'll have to bear."

Sam smiled. A real smile. One that showed his heart, his soul, and held nothing back. "I would gladly spend the rest of my life bearing your burdens, Madison West."

"On second thought," she said, "board games not required."

"Oh yeah? What do you need, then?"

"Nothing much at all. Just hold me, cowboy. That's enough for me."

* * * * *

HOT WINTER NIGHTS

DEBBI RAWLINS

1

"You're supposed to be dead." Staring over the woman's shoulder, Lila Loveridge stopped in the middle of touching up Penelope's dark roots.

"Don't sound so disappointed." Penelope picked up the script, with the revisions marked in a brilliant pink, and held it against her chest. "You're not supposed to see that, anyway."

Oh, for goodness' sake, she'd left it in plain sight on her lap. It was obvious she wanted her to see. "When did Jason make those changes?"

"I shouldn't be discussing this with you," Penelope said with her usual air of superiority, which was one of the many reasons the film crew didn't like her.

An icy gust shook the small trailer, and Lila shivered. The cold December wind that had been sweeping down from the Rockies for three days straight had everyone grumbling. They should've been wrapping up and getting out of Montana by now. Not camped a mile outside the small town of Blackfoot Falls, the ragtag trailers where they worked and slept powered by generators that could barely keep up with the frigid overnight temperatures.

On top of all that, they were three weeks behind schedule.

Of course delays were to be expected in the movie business. But that hadn't stopped morale from plummeting more and more each day as they got closer to Christmas. All the changes to both script and routine brought on by their new investor sure hadn't helped.

Penelope cleared her throat.

Lila glanced at her. "Did you say something?"

"I said, since you already saw the pink pages, I might as well tell you. The director thought I interpreted the role of Dominique so masterfully he said it would be a crime for my character not to be in the sequel."

Translation—Jason was still sleeping with her.

It wasn't news. Everyone on the set knew what was going on between the director and the leading lady. But for him to suddenly change the last scene of the movie? That was going to cost their small, undercapitalized, independent film more money. What on earth had he been thinking?

This wasn't like him. Lila had known Jason for almost ten years. She and her friend Erin had met him in film school. Lila truly hoped this sudden change had nothing to do with the new investor. Or with Erin's subdued mood.

No, if Erin knew something about the last-minute revisions, she would've passed it on. They'd been friends since the third grade. They told each other everything.

"Look, if my character ends up in the sequel, that shouldn't impact your role. You're only slated to be a supporting actress, after all. It'll be quite a break for someone like you."

Lila looked at Penelope with half her dark roots still showing and tried not to laugh. Sad, really. If Penelope didn't have a script in front of her, she was hopeless. Invariably she'd say something tactless or embarrassing.

"I'm not worried," Lila said, and dipped the brush into the dye solution. Frankly, it hadn't occurred to her. She was more concerned about making it home to spend the holidays with her family. "Has Jason mentioned anything about breaking for Christmas?"

Penelope checked her watch, ignoring Lila, as usual. "Would you hurry this up? I have a dinner date."

"Going to the diner?"

Penelope met her eyes in the mirror. Miracle of all miracles—she laughed, instead of looking as if all crew members were barely tolerable. "I honestly don't understand how anyone can live in this town."

"Oh, I don't know. The place has a certain charm." Lila meant it, even though she'd grown up in Southern California. The people in Blackfoot Falls were friendly, and of course curious.

Clearly Penelope interpreted the comment as sarcasm and mistook Lila for a kindred spirit. With a little smile, Penelope went back to reading the script changes.

Fine with Lila. She didn't want to make small talk. She preferred having the time to think. If she could finagle four days off, she could get home for Christmas. It wouldn't be easy. The round-trip drive would leave her with only a day and a half with the family. Flying was out of the question since she was almost broke.

The quick turnaround wasn't ideal, but it would be worth it. She'd already missed decorating the house with her mom and sister. Even though she knew that some people thought it was silly, not being with her family, everyone singing carols while they cooked Christmas dinner together, was unimaginable. Her brother's wife, Cheryl, had joined the tradition last year. For Lila, Christmas and home were synonymous.

Just as she applied more solution to Penelope's dark regrowth, a scream pierced the low hum of the crowd milling around outside.

People started yelling.

"What was that?" Penelope pushed to get up, then must've remembered what she looked like with her hair plastered to her head and sank down again.

"I don't know." Lila rushed to the window, couldn't see anything, so she went to the door.

"What is it?"

"I can't tell." Lila tried to see past a crowd of extras blocking her view. "Hold on a second." She pulled off the plastic gloves and took the three rickety steps, her beat-up Nikes touching the hard ground just as she heard the distressed neighs of a horse.

"Stand back, everyone. No one needs to get hurt." The man's deep, steady voice drifted in the chill air as smooth as fine, warm brandy.

"Right now, people." That was Erin, from somewhere in the direction of the catering truck. "Give him room."

Lila found a narrow gap in the crowd and pushed through.

A beautiful black horse reared and let out a high, extended whinny. He wasn't penned or tethered but cornered by a cowboy with longish dark hair, wearing a tan hat with the brim pulled low. The man threw a rope around the horse's neck, and the animal tossed its head and stamped the ground.

A collective murmur rose from the crowd.

"You know who that stallion belongs to?"

Lila turned to the unfamiliar voice behind her. But the older, bearded man wasn't talking to her.

"Nope," the guy next to him replied. He smiled at her and touched the brim of his hat. "Afternoon, ma'am."

They were probably locals hired as extras. Quite a few were standing by, waiting to be called for the next scene.

Lila returned his smile, then resumed watching the scene unfolding in front of her.

Moving in slowly, the cowboy whispered something to the horse. He didn't stop, just kept speaking in a low, hushed voice. Whatever it was, the stallion began to calm down.

"Is that Clint Landers? I think it is. I see his Whispering Pines trailer over there."

Lila shuddered. Partly because the stallion had a fierce look about him, but there was something about the tall, lean cowboy that had her wrapping her arms around herself to ward off another shiver.

Stepping aside, she turned to the two men. "Do you know what happened?"

"That black broke loose. Someone didn't tether him proper. He should've been left in the corral."

"What's the Whispering Pines?" she asked just as she spotted the white horse trailer.

"It's the Landers family's ranch," the bearded man said. "That fella with the stallion is Clint Landers."

Hmm. He looked to be in his early thirties. Probably married.

"Are you an actress?" The younger guy hadn't stopped staring at her.

"Not exactly," she said. "I do hair and makeup."

"Well, that's not right. You're too gorgeous not to be a movie star."

She just smiled and turned to watch the cowboy. She could've told him she was an actress. It was the truth.

She just wasn't acting in this particular film. But she'd played a few bit parts here and there, and soon enough she would make the transition from struggling wannabe to an honest-to-goodness, card-carrying member of the Screen Actors Guild. But lately, probably because of how tired she was, how tired everyone was, she wasn't quite as thrilled as she had been about her long-held dream.

The action had died down. The cowboy and the horse seemed to have reached an understanding, and the crowd started to thin.

Clint Landers.

Huh. For some reason she thought the name suited him. He was still talking to the animal in a hushed tone, and she stepped closer, wishing she could hear his voice again.

"Ma'am?"

She stopped and turned.

The bearded man had left, but the younger one, who was about her age, stood there, hat in hand. "My name is Brady." He had a great smile. "Sorry about sounding like a starstruck hayseed."

"I'm Lila," she said, but didn't extend her hand. It was too darn cold. Instead, she hugged herself tighter. "You paid me a compliment. I should have thanked you."

"Ah, no worries. You must hear stuff like that all the time."

She did, but she wasn't about to admit it, so she just smiled. After six years of trying to make it in this brutal business, she'd made peace with comments like his. But she had done nothing to earn her looks, and lucky for her, she'd been raised to believe praise was reserved for merit.

"Are you staying in town?" Brady asked.

"No. Most of us are camped out here." She spotted Erin and waved to get her attention. "I'm sorry, Brady, I'm actually working. Would you excuse me, please?"

"Sure." His smile faded as he stumbled back a step.

Erin walked up. "Are you an extra?" she asked him, and he nodded. "The director needs you on the set."

"Yes, ma'am. Bye, Lila. I hope to see you around," he said and jogged off.

"Yet another heart you've broken," Erin muttered, watching him for a moment. "He's cute."

"Yes. But the guy with the horse? Holy cow." Lila ignored her friend and watched Clint lead the horse toward the corrals. "I wonder if he's married?"

"Clint?" Erin gave her a long look. "Why, Lila Loveridge, I'm shocked. Are you interested in that cowboy?"

Lila frowned at her. "You know him?"

"Not really. I signed for some stock he's delivering. Seems like a nice guy. I was about to go thank him for saving our asses. Want to come with?" Erin's grin died as she looked past her. "What the hell is he doing?"

Lila saw right away that she meant Baxter, the new investor's nephew, with whom the crew was supposed to play nice. He was headed toward the corrals with a scowl on his pasty face. Another annoying person with an ego issue. He and Penelope would make a good—

Penelope.

Lila glanced toward the trailer. She'd completely forgotten about her. Tough. Erin was already on the move, and Lila wasn't going to miss this.

"I'm gonna kill him," Erin muttered, walking fast and glaring ahead as Baxter approached Clint.

"Please do. For everyone's sake."

Baxter was of average height, had a pudgy build and

apparently lacked enough sense to stay out of the much taller man's face.

"Look, pal, if you can't control your animals, we'll find a supplier who can." Baxter's loud warning reached everyone within a five-yard radius, which was clearly his intention.

Clint barely spared him a glance before turning back to stroke the horse's neck, as if he'd never been interrupted. Without a word, he unlatched the corral gate.

"Baxter," Erin yelled. "Stop. Now."

Lila bit back a smile. He was no match for Erin, and he knew it. In fact, Baxter was afraid of her. And he got no sympathy whatsoever from Lila. In the week since he'd joined the crew, he'd hit on her so many times, it had gone from annoying to creepy.

Baxter shot them a nervous look, then took in the group of curious bystanders. He squared his shoulders and again faced Clint, who was basically ignoring everything around him while he got the horse safely inside the empty corral.

"I'm so tempted to let the jerk get his lights punched out," Erin said in a low voice as they approached the two men. "It was Todd's fault the horse got loose, so cool it, Baxter. The animal doesn't even belong to Mr. Landers." Erin stopped, and Lila almost rammed into her.

Up close, Clint Landers was even better looking. Beard stubble darkened his square jaw and almost hid the dimple in his chin. His bottom lip was considerably fuller than his upper one, which appealed to Lila in a big way. She worked with a lot of smoking hot guys, but she couldn't recall the last time one of them made her feel all tingly inside.

"We're damn lucky he was there," Erin was saying.

The smile she'd given Clint vanished as she switched her focus to Baxter. "We owe him our thanks, and an apology from you."

Baxter's pale face flamed.

Erin wouldn't give an inch. Her glare narrowed meaningfully. Advising everyone to play nice excluded her and Jason.

"Hey, it was an honest mistake," Clint said, making sure the gate was latched before pulling off a leather work glove and extending his hand to Baxter. "No harm done."

Baxter hesitated, clearly unwilling to give in. But it was equally clear that he had no choice. What an idiot.

He made sure everyone watching caught his condescending smirk before he stuck out his hand. Clint clasped it and gave Baxter a couple of firm pumps. Baxter looked as though he was about to choke. If his face had been red before, now it was turning scarlet.

Clint pumped his hand a couple more times. "No hard feelings…pal," he said with a big smile and released Baxter's hand.

He immediately flexed it, while subtly trying to draw in some air.

"I don't think anything's broken," Erin said with a straight face.

Lila pressed her lips together and quickly turned her head. And met Clint Landers's eyes. They were brown. Light brown with gold flecks. And he had thick dark lashes that took nothing away from his rugged good looks.

The man was positively dreamy.

She needed a little air herself. But she managed to give him a smile without hyperventilating.

"Clint Landers," he said in the same deep, velvety tone he'd used with the stallion.

"Lila Loveridge." She stared down at his extended, bone-crushing hand. "Um, I don't think so."

"Come on," he said, amusement curving his mouth in a slow smile. "Live dangerously."

With a laugh, she dragged a palm down her jeans before letting his large hand engulf hers. His grip was firm, yet gentle. He was the real deal. A genuine cowboy who did physical labor, and with rough, callused palms to prove it. And those muscled arms and shoulders? Not bulk, just lean muscle. Oh yeah, he looked darn fine.

And the other thing about him—he had no problem looking a person directly in the eyes.

"Nice to meet you," she said, pulling back her hand and lowering her gaze to his chest. "You're wearing a T-shirt."

He glanced down. "I am."

Lila sighed. "It's December." Why did the really hot guys always have to be crazy? "And it's freezing."

"Also true." He glanced at the horse. "I was changing in my truck when this guy here decided to make a break for it." He held out his hand and the horse nuzzled it. "You know if he belongs to Ben Wolf?"

"No, I don't." She turned to ask Erin, but one of Jason's flunkies had pulled her and Baxter aside and was whispering something to the two of them.

Whatever it was, Baxter stopped glaring at her and Clint and gave the young man a sharp look. Then he turned toward the set, where Jason was setting up the next shot. His uncle expected a big return on his investment, and Jason's word was gospel. The project's success trumped Baxter's self-importance. It had to.

"Who's in charge of looking after the stock?" Clint's gaze flicked to Baxter. "Not that guy, I hope," he added in a lowered voice, looking back at her.

"Oh, God, no. That would be Charlie. He's the head wrangler, and he's very responsible. I haven't seen him today, but he should be around… Older guy. White hair. Wears it in a ponytail." She thought Charlie might be in town, but she glanced around anyway, because staring into Clint's eyes made it hard to concentrate on anything but him. "I don't see him. We haven't had any other incidents with animals getting loose, though."

"I'd like to speak with him before unloading my trailer."

"Erin should know where he is." Lila gestured vaguely, noticing that someone else now had her friend's ear. Fine with Lila. It gave her more time to check out Clint. "She shouldn't be long."

"I'm in no hurry." He lifted his hat and swept back a long dark lock of hair before settling the brim low on his forehead.

"Are you also an extra?"

"An extra what?"

"I guess not." She smiled. "You said you were changing your shirt so I thought… We hire local people to be in the movie."

"You're kidding."

"Most people like it. They don't say any lines and it pays practically nothing, but they get bragging rights. Hey, if you're interested—"

"No," he said quickly. "No. No way. Not me."

"You can't be camera shy."

He laughed. "Thanks anyway."

Lila jumped when someone touched her shoulder.

She instinctively recoiled when she saw it was Baxter, but then put on a neutral smile. Some actress she was.

"I need to talk to Mr. Landers," he said with an obvious lack of enthusiasm.

She looked at Erin who now stood alone, motioning with her head for Lila to join her.

Glancing back at Clint, it was all Lila could do not to sigh. "Well, nice meeting you," she said and realized she'd already mentioned something to that effect.

They exchanged smiles, and he politely touched the brim of his hat. But it was the dark penetrating look in his eyes that had her heart pounding as she turned and hurried the short distance to Erin.

"Come on," Erin said with a little smile and started walking toward the trailers that were lined up out of camera range.

"What does Baxter want with him, and where are we going?"

"You're wearing a T-shirt? Seriously?"

Lila looked at her, and Erin burst out laughing.

"Shut up." Lila shook her head and then laughed, too.

"On a shitty note, Penelope is on the warpath."

"Oh. Right. I forgot about her." God, Lila was tempted to look back at him.

"No. Hell, no." Clint's voice had raised some.

Lila and Erin looked at each other, and then they both turned to see him walking away from Baxter, who stared daggers after him. Whatever it was the creep wanted, Lila doubted it was a face full of dust kicked up by Clint's boots as he strode toward his horse trailer.

"What was that about?" Lila asked.

"Jason wants to use Clint in his next scene and said he wouldn't take no for an answer," she said absently.

As Erin continued to stare at Baxter, Lila could almost see the wheels turning in her friend's head. She and Jason's new flunky hadn't gotten along from day one. Baxter was green and unfamiliar with the film industry, while Erin knew just about everything there was to know.

Since college she'd worked nearly every job there was behind the camera. She was supposed to be showing Baxter the ropes, which was probably why she'd been so grumpy lately.

This project was important for their future in the industry. Just like Lila, Erin's big chance was coming up with the sequel. She'd been promised the first assistant director's job.

"I know you," Lila said. "You're planning something evil."

Erin smiled. "Who was it that said 'the enemy of my enemy is my friend'?"

Lila's gaze went to Clint, his back to them as he pulled on a long-sleeve shirt. "Friend? Oh, I want him for so much more than that."

2

CLINT PARKED HIS truck close to the circular drive in front of his brother's house. He got out and lifted a hand to Woody, the foreman, and a pair of Lucky 7 hired men walking toward the bunkhouse. The air was chilly, but he didn't bother grabbing his jacket since it was a short walk to the fancy wrought-iron gate. He couldn't stay long, but he had time to kill and something he wanted to get off his chest. Nathan was always a good sounding board.

After letting himself into the small courtyard, he went straight to the front door and wiped the bottoms of his boots on the mat. He rang the bell, glancing around while he waited.

The place looked nice. Even with winter threatening to roll in with a bang, his sister-in-law had spruced up the courtyard with Christmas wreaths and garland. Strings of lights were draped along the stone archway and wrapped around the porch columns.

He liked Beth a lot and not just because she'd been so good for Nathan, bringing him back to life after his first wife's death. Clint admired Beth for leaving small remembrances of Anne, like her prized roses and topiary garden. Anne had liked everything manicured and perfect, and Beth was the total opposite.

The door opened. "Hey, I didn't know you were coming over," Beth said, stepping back to let him inside.

"Yeah, I should've called first."

"Oh, please. You know better. Nathan's in his office, and I was just putting up some Christmas decorations."

Clint smelled coffee as he walked into the large foyer. Pinecones and conifer branches littered the cherry console table. A ball of string had fallen to the hardwood floor. He scooped it up and gave it to Beth.

"I decided to make my own wreaths." She rolled her eyes. "I won't make that mistake again."

"I just came from Blackfoot Falls. I saw you have the inn all decked out. It looks nice."

"Really? You don't think I went overboard?" she asked, frowning and swiping back wisps of blond hair from her eyes.

His thoughts shot straight to Lila. Not a shocker. He hadn't been able to shake the image of her the whole ride over. Her hair was a lighter shade of blond than Beth's, and Lila's eyes were blue, a real cornflower blue you just didn't see every day. She was a stunner, the most beautiful woman he'd ever seen in person. Or more like ever. He'd never been a moviegoer or had much time for TV, but if he'd seen her starring in anything, he would've remembered.

"I did, didn't I?" Beth was staring at him. "Was it the lighted Happy Holidays sign? I worried that might be a bit much."

He frowned, then recalled they'd been talking about the old boardinghouse Beth had bought and converted to an inn. "No," he said. "It looks nice. Very festive.

Sorry, I was thinking about that coffee I smell. Any chance—"

Beth laughed. "Of course. Help yourself."

Clint continued into the kitchen, poured a mug of the strong brew and took it with him to his brother's office down the hall. The door was open. Nathan was sitting at his desk working on his laptop.

"Hey, got a minute?"

Nathan looked up. "I thought I heard your voice. Everything okay?"

"Hell, it hasn't been that long since I've visited." Clint settled in the brown leather chair across from his brother.

"Yeah, but in the middle of a weekday?"

"You got me there."

Nathan's cell rang, and Clint gestured for him to go ahead and answer. It dawned on him that he wasn't exactly sure what he wanted to say. Or even how to broach the subject without sounding as if he was complaining.

Naturally the call was short—bought him all of five seconds.

Clint took a slow sip of coffee, then cradled the warm mug in his hands. "I got the talk from Dad last night."

Nathan's eyes narrowed. "Did you tell him you already know storks have nothing to do with it?"

"Hell, no. I'm not sure he and Mom have figured it out yet."

"They have three grown sons. I think they might've put two-and-two together by now."

"Stop." Clint shook his head. "There are some things a man just can't ponder. No matter how old he is."

"Amen to that. So, last night, was Seth there, too?"

"He's still in Billings."

"Partying with his old college buddies?" Nathan's

expression hardened when Clint shrugged. "When does Dad want you to take over?"

"Soon. He'd like an answer by Christmas."

His brother's brows shot up, but he quickly masked his surprise. It didn't matter. Clint knew Nathan had expected him to run Whispering Pines eventually. Everyone did. The ranch had survived everything from droughts to poor financial management to be passed down through five generations of Landerses.

Nathan was two years older and a hard act to follow. He'd begun building the Lucky 7 from practically nothing while he was still in college. And now, at thirty-five, he owned one of the most profitable ranches in the county.

"Did Dad tell you to think about it? Or was that your suggestion?"

"It was mutual. He told me to take some time off, to really think. I don't see Seth wanting any part of it. Do you?"

Nathan shook his head. "Hell, I don't know what's going on with that kid."

"He's almost thirty."

"And acting like he's ten."

Clint rubbed his jaw. Man, he needed a shave. "Think it's time for his two big brothers to have a sit-down with him?"

"Maybe after the holidays. We don't want to stir things up and ruin Christmas for Mom."

"Good point."

"I'm more concerned about you right now."

"Me?"

Nathan was studying him a little too closely. "You're not jumping at the chance to take over—" He held up a hand. "And I'm not saying you should. After you quit college, I guess I just assumed you missed ranching."

"So did I, but…" Clint hesitated. Damn, he should've thought this thing through. Not five minutes ago he'd realized he wasn't prepared. He could've talked about the weather, the Denver Broncos making it to the play-offs, the price of alfalfa… The last thing he wanted was to make Nathan feel guilty for breaking tradition. The oldest son had always taken the reins. But that didn't mean anything.

Yep, Clint should've waited. Although the talk with his dad had completely caught him off guard, and he'd been having trouble thinking straight, or about anything else—that was until he'd met Lila.

"Did you ever think about doing anything other than ranching?"

Nathan leaned back in his chair. "No, I haven't. But clearly you have."

"No. Well, nothing specific. It's just getting pretty real is all. It's a damn serious commitment."

"Hell, you've been in charge since before Dad made you foreman," Nathan said. "The men go to you when they need something, and we both know Dad likes it that way. Making it official won't change much. Unless there's something else you're not saying?"

"That's just it. I don't feel as though I'd be losing out on anything, but I don't want to just slide in because it's what's expected of me either. On the other hand, if I don't step up and Dad were to get sick again, or if Seth doesn't come around and start pulling his weight, I'd feel like shit."

"I understand," Nathan said. "So would I, but it didn't stop me from building the ranch I wanted."

Clint just nodded, but that was the difference between

him and Nathan. His brother had always known what he wanted, and Clint wasn't sure. He still loved ranching, and it would kill him if anyone but a Landers owned the land. Wasn't that enough reason for him to step up? He'd never been commitment-phobic, so why was the thought of sealing his future making him twitchy?

"Sorry to interrupt." Beth poked her head in. "I'm going to run into town for some ribbon. Do you need anything?"

"Blackfoot Falls or Twin Creeks?" Nathan asked with an amused gleam in his eye. Twin Creeks was closer to the Lucky 7 but half the size of Blackfoot Falls.

"Oh, please… Blackfoot Falls, of course. Who knows?" She batted her lashes. "I might get discovered."

Clint shot a look at his brother. The night Anne had died in the accident, she'd sneaked off to audition for a play.

Nathan didn't seem bothered, he just laughed. "Well, you call me before you sign any contracts."

"Deal," she said, padding in to give him a quick kiss. "Text me if you think of anything you want." On her way out, she squeezed Clint's shoulder. "We're having chicken and tortilla casserole for supper if you want to stay."

"Thanks. Another time." The second she was out of earshot Clint grinned at his brother. "She's got you eating casseroles?"

Grunting, Nathan leaned back. "Wait till you get married. You're gonna find yourself doing a lot of crap you swore you wouldn't do. Hey, you still seeing Kristy?"

"Not for months. It wasn't going anywhere." He shrugged. "I think she might have itchy feet. Wouldn't surprise me if she moved away from Twin Creeks."

"Is that what's got you hesitating to take over from Dad?"

"Nah." Clint shook his head for emphasis. "Anyway, it's nothing. Just thinking things through."

"You guys having any financial problems I should know about?"

"Nope." It was a fair question. Years ago their father had made some poor decisions that had nearly bankrupted them. "We're in the black."

"Thanks to you," Nathan said, his worried pucker beginning to ease. "But I heard you leased horses to the Hollywood people, so it made me wonder."

"Didn't do it for the money. Ben Wolf asked me for a favor. They wanted a couple of showy chestnuts. We have geldings with cream-colored manes and tails that fit the bill." Clint had unloaded the horses without talking to the head wrangler. For some reason, he'd trusted Erin Murphy's word the runaway stallion was an isolated incident. But he had every intention of driving back later to make sure they weren't being careless with the animals. "You ever heard of Lila Loveridge?"

Nathan frowned. "Nope. She live around here?"

Clint wished. "She's an actress. Blonde. About five-eight. I just met her. You and Beth watch more movies than I do, so I figured you might've seen her in something."

"I can look her up," Nathan said, straightening and reaching for his laptop.

"Nah." Hell, he should've thought of that himself. "She's so far out of my league, it isn't funny."

Even before seeing Nathan's startled look, Clint regretted the stupid remark. What a dumb-ass thing to say. He'd just made idle curiosity sound like it was a big deal.

Jesus.

"Some jerk asked if I wanted to be in the movie. I wouldn't have to say anything. Just stand next to a horse and look like a jackass."

Nathan grinned. "What did you say?"

"What do you think?"

Lucky for him, his brother's phone rang.

Clint stood. Perfect time to make an exit.

Glancing at the cell, Nathan said, "Sit. It's only Woody."

"I've got to go." Clint glanced at his watch and started for the door. "We'll talk another time."

"You sure you don't wanna stay for some of Beth's casserole? I guarantee she made plenty."

Clint laughed. "I heard leftovers are even better the next day," he said on his way out of the office, grinning when he heard his brother curse.

Despite Erin's assurance, Clint figured he'd go see if the head wrangler had showed up. Although if he was being honest, he wanted to see Lila again.

THE SUN HADN'T dipped behind the Rockies yet, but the sky was overcast, which meant it would get dark early. Everyone was rushing to make use of the daylight and making more mistakes. It was just one of those days. Lots of small, annoying things had gone wrong, and everyone seemed to be on edge. The two bars in town would likely be hopping tonight.

Lila wasn't much of a drinker, but even she was considering a trip into town with everyone else. A beer shouldn't cost too much.

She watched an older man transfer his chew of tobacco from one cheek to the other, and managed not to cringe. Disgusting. In the three months she'd been working on location in cattle country, she'd grown used to many unfamiliar customs. But chewing tobacco? Yuck.

The man was an extra, not an actor, but they were using him for several close-ups during the bar-fight scene. So Lila had been called to the set to make sure his fake injuries were consistent for each shot.

Initially she'd been in charge of hair, and hadn't done much makeup. But she'd been learning a lot, and she liked having the variety, so she never minded pitching in when they asked for her.

"You need to make the scar longer," Erin said, studying the photo and then the man's jaw. "Bring it closer to his ear."

"I'm back." Glenda, an intern, showed up to take over.

"Let Lila finish the scar and then—" Erin glared at the man. "Would you stop chewing?"

He stopped.

Lila and Glenda exchanged private smiles. Erin was their hero. She was never mean or petty, but if someone wanted to be coddled, they'd better look elsewhere.

Every film needed someone as smart and efficient as Erin. Especially a low-budget, indy project like this one. So much was riding on it for a lot of people—including her and Erin. The film's success could make their careers. Or conversely, bankrupt them. The two of them were low-level investors, but it had taken every penny they'd saved, every favor owed them, and they'd even taken out small loans. Lila tried not to think about that too much. It made her queasy.

She quickly went to work on the man's scar, and just as she applied the finishing touch, Erin said, "Guess who's back?"

Lila's pulse quickened. "Shut. The. Front. Door," she said, staring at her friend. Erin's teasing smile was a big hint. Had to be the cowboy Lila had been daydreaming about all afternoon. "Are you serious?"

"As a heart attack. But don't turn—" Erin sighed when Lila whipped around for a look.

"Where?" A black truck parked near the corrals hadn't been there ten minutes ago. No sign of Clint, though. "Is he—oh, crap," she muttered when she caught sight of Baxter.

Erin's expression changed completely when she saw him hurrying toward them. "What do you want?"

"That guy…Landers." Baxter was out of breath. "He's back."

"So?"

"Jason wants to use him tomorrow." Baxter was so clueless. Whatever it was he wanted, his haughty tone wasn't going to win Erin over.

"Need anything else, Erin?" Glenda asked, already backing away.

"Nope. We're good for now."

"You have to go talk to Landers," Baxter said. "Jason insists that—"

"Jason told *you* to do it. Lila, got a minute?" Erin started walking toward the set, and Lila went along with her.

"Yeah, but—" Baxter's face flushed.

Erin stopped. "But what? Landers told you to take a hike?"

Baxter's defiant glare faded. "I don't get why Jason has to have *him*."

"Well, that's a problem. You should be *getting it*. You need to understand those small details if you want to—"

Erin cut herself short. She blinked, thought a few seconds and tried to hold back a smile. "Ask Lila to do it."

Baxter's mouth tightened. It was obvious he didn't like that idea. Finally he turned to her. "Will you talk to Landers?"

"Maybe." Lila let him stew while she willed her pulse to slow down. "Okay, I'll do it. But you'll owe me."

Baxter had the nerve to look smug again.

Lila jabbed a finger at him. "Owe me big. Got it?"

Baxter grinned. "I'll take you to dinner in Kalispell."

She could only stare at him. Clearly he was insane.

"Oh." A smile brightened Erin's face. "Spencer's here."

Lila turned and waved. She really liked Spencer, and was thrilled Erin had found love and the deep sense of contentment he'd provided in her life. Knowing that helped Lila ignore the occasional pang of jealousy. Over not having someone to share a pillow with at night. Or be there to listen to the highs and lows of her day. And she missed having Erin around all the time.

"Do you mind if I leave?" Erin asked, watching her closely. "Have you got this?"

Lila gave her a big smile. "Oh yeah."

"There he is," Baxter said, peering in the direction of the corrals. "Landers."

"Big," Lila reminded him as she walked backward. "And no dinner." She turned toward Clint and hurried her pace when she saw him and Charlie shake hands.

If he went for his truck, she'd head him off.

She didn't have to do anything but keep walking. The moment Clint saw her, he stopped.

"Hey," she said, wishing she'd changed her big sloppy sweatshirt for something nicer.

"Hello again."

"I see you found Charlie."

Clint nodded. "Nice guy. Knows horses."

"That's what I've heard. Me, I don't know anything about... I saw your chestnuts."

He blinked, and it might have been a trick of the light, but his face darkened.

"Um, geldings? Horses?"

"Right. Sure."

"Did I say that wrong?"

"No." He shook his head. "I knew exactly what you meant." His gaze drifted toward the set. "You all work late every night?"

"Only when we're shooting a night scene."

Clint chuckled. "I'm sure I'll have a few more dumb questions."

Lila smiled. She liked having to tilt her head back to look at him. "You want to ask them over a beer?"

He met her eyes. His jaw clenched.

"Unless you need to get home for dinner," she said quickly. "Your wife and kids might be waiting." She paused long enough for him to deny it, but he didn't. "I'm supposed to convince you to be in the movie. So, you know, it's not personal or anything."

He actually looked disappointed. "That's a shame," he said, his mouth quirking upward. "Since I don't have a wife or kids."

"No?" She cleared her throat. "Then how about that beer?"

3

THE FULL MOON SALOON had opened in July, but this was Clint's first time in the place. He'd heard about the mechanical bull in the back and shouldn't have been surprised by the small dance floor, since he knew a live band played Friday and Sunday nights. The only music now was something by Keith Urban coming from the jukebox.

It wasn't too crowded yet. Some guys were shooting pool in the back, and half the stools at the bar were occupied by local cowboys. Clint nodded at two men he recognized from the Circle K. They nodded back, but their eyes were on Lila. That was probably true for just about every guy in the room.

"Table or bar?" he asked her, hoping she'd choose a table so they could have some privacy.

"How about that one?" she said, gesturing toward a nice corner table.

"After you."

She led the way, and he did his damnedest not to stare at her behind. Not that he could see much anyway. It looked like she'd worn the same jeans, but she'd traded the old sweatshirt he'd assumed went with whatever role she was playing, for another that was just as bulky.

She pulled out a chair that had her facing the wall. "It's going to get busy in here," she said as she settled gracefully in her seat. "I saw two stuntmen playing pool. They won't bother us, but you can bet someone from the crew will invite himself over eventually."

Clint took the chair across the table from her. Sitting with her back to the room wouldn't matter. No man with eyes in his head would be able to pass her by without a second or third look.

"I just realized something," she said with a laugh. "This is a small town. It's kind of like a big film crew where people think nothing of pulling up a chair whether you're having a private conversation or not."

"Yep, that's about the size of it."

"Shall we make a bet on whose people will interrupt us first?"

"To be clear, the waitress doesn't count, right?" He grinned at her puzzled expression.

Lila turned just as Elaine got to their table.

"Good Lord. Clint Landers." The short brunette stuck a pencil behind her ear and put a hand on her hip. "How long has it been since I've laid eyes on you?"

"It's been a while."

"Not since Anne's…" Elaine glanced at Lila and smiled.

"I think you're right," Clint said, hoping to ease the sudden awkwardness. "It was at Anne's funeral. Hard to believe it's been four years."

Elaine nodded. "I've seen Nathan a few times. He looks good. I didn't get to talk to him, though, so tell him I said hey."

"Will do."

"Well, what can I get you folks?"

Lila surprised him once again by ordering a draft beer. He told Elaine to make it two, and was about to introduce the women when another customer called for Elaine.

As soon as she left, Lila said, "Okay, I must have a serious misconception of a small town."

"You think we all know each other?"

"Yes, that, too, but how can you go four years without seeing someone?"

"Salina is a big county, and the ranches are all spread out. I don't come to Blackfoot Falls all that much, and when I do it's usually to pick up something at the hardware store. And since I live across the county line, I went to a different school than most of the folks around here."

"But you've lived in the area your whole life?"

"Other than two years of college, yeah."

"Your family is still here?"

Clint nodded and skipped the part that he still lived in the family home, sleeping in the same room he had as a kid. Sometimes it bothered him, even though it was a common practice with families who owned big ranches. But today the idea stuck in his craw.

"Do you have brothers and sisters? Nieces and nephews?" she asked, and seemed genuinely interested. She wasn't being nosy or making small talk.

"Two brothers. Nathan is older than me. Seth is younger and a real pain in the butt."

Lila laughed. "I have one of those, too," she said with a wistful sigh. "Oh, I guess Britney isn't that bad. She started college this fall and is feeling overwhelmed by life in general. But we talk a lot."

"You miss her."

"Yes. I miss everybody—my parents and brother, his wife. They all live in California where I grew up. These last three months are the longest I've ever been away from them."

Clint could just stare at her all night. She had an expressive face and skin as fine as his mother's bone china. Right now, that face was telling him he'd missed a cue.

Shit.

He cleared his throat. "I would think you travel a lot."

"Not really. And certainly not for this long. We're behind schedule. I'm not sure what will happen at Christmas."

"You mean you won't have the day off?"

"Oh, we will. Thanks to the unions. But I don't know that any of us are going to have enough time to make it home." She shrugged, as if it wasn't a big deal, and smiled at Elaine as she set down two foamy mugs.

"I'll start a tab for you folks, yes?" Elaine said.

Clint was about to agree when Lila shook her head. She dug into her pocket. "What do I owe you?"

"Elaine, I've got this." He pulled out a twenty at the same time Lila produced a handful of crumpled bills.

"I asked you to come, so my treat," she said, busy trying to straighten her money. "In fact I'm going to make Baxter reimburse me."

Clint slipped Elaine the twenty, and she quietly left to make change.

Lila looked up and twisted in her seat. "Where'd she go?"

A group who had to be movie people had just entered the bar. The short stocky guy leading the pack spotted Lila right away.

She acknowledged the hand he lifted, sighing as she

turned back to face Clint. "I thought we'd have more time before the troops descended."

"You want to leave?"

"No. Maybe they'll play pool. But if they come over, then…"

"I won't have any trouble getting rid of them," Clint said, and she gave him a peculiar smile. "If that's what you want."

"Wait. Did Elaine take your money?"

"Look, I'll be honest with you." He leaned forward. "I had to pay the check. Because I'm going to brag like hell that I had a date with a bona fide movie star, and it wouldn't be a date if I didn't pay, now would it?"

Arching her brows, she laughed softly.

"I won't use your name if you don't want me to."

"I can't tell if you're serious."

"I am." Clint looked into her pretty blue eyes and had an almost uncontrollable urge to lean closer and kiss her. He was likely to clear the whole damn table trying, but he might be willing…

"One problem." She picked up her mug and took a tiny sip. "I'm not a movie star."

"What do you mean? You're an actress, right?"

"Yes and no." Lila shrugged. "I've done shampoo commercials, and I've had tiny parts in a few TV movies. But I do have a good shot at a decent role coming up."

Clint frowned. Something didn't add up.

"Sorry to disappoint you."

"I'm not…disappointed. Just confused."

"I'm part of the crew, working as a hairstylist. And I do some makeup, too. It's a small independent movie and we're operating on a shoestring, so our jobs tend to overlap."

"But acting isn't one of yours?"

"Not for this project. But I've wanted to be an actress since I was a kid. I even went to UCLA drama school." She smiled with that same wistfulness he'd heard in her voice earlier. "Along with fifty million other wannabes. It's a tough business to break into."

Clint opened his mouth, then realized he was about to say something totally stupid.

"What?"

He shook his head.

"Come on, you've got me curious."

"I'll just say that you look like a movie star. So you've already got that part down pat."

Lila laughed. "Well, thank you," she said with a slight nod. "I'll let my parents know you approve."

Clint ducked his head. He knew he should've kept his mouth shut.

"No, don't." Lila reached across the table and touched his hand. "I wasn't being snotty or sarcastic. I promise. It's just—"

He stared at her slim pale fingers resting on top of his big, rough ones, brown like leather from working in the hot sun. Her skin was soft, her touch so light it felt like a butterfly had landed on him. She withdrew her hand, and he looked up, wishing she hadn't.

"It's just…" she began again. "In this business it's important to keep things in perspective. My looks don't define me. I can't let them or I'll end up—" Lila blushed. "Oh, jeez. I can't believe I'm telling you all this stuff." She took a hasty sip of beer and made a face. Coughed a little. Muttered something about sticking to iced tea. And coughed again.

Clint hid a smile behind his mug, drinking his beer and giving her time to recover. She thought he was disappointed that she wasn't a movie star. Not even close. It wasn't that he thought he had a chance with her. He'd be a damn fool to think she'd go for a guy like him, some hick steeped in family tradition and the routine of ranch life. But he really admired her for not using her beauty as a crutch.

She stopped coughing, pushed the beer aside and looked at him while dabbing her watery eyes.

"I saw a sign for sarsaparillas. Only two bits," he said. "Maybe we can order you one of those."

"Very funny." With a cute little smile, she leaned forward as if she had a secret to tell him. "I'll admit I'm an umbrella drink kind of girl. And if the drink is pink or blue, that's even better."

"Elaine's on her way back. Let's see what we can do about that."

"No. I can't," Lila said, laughing. "I have to get up early tomorrow."

"Okay, then, when's your day off?" He saw her smile slip and knew he'd overstepped.

This was just part of the job for her. Have a beer with him, convince him to be the silent cowboy standing around like a jackass. Yeah, no way that was going to happen.

He watched more people come through the front door—three men, and a woman with purple hair, all in their twenties, looking a lot like they needed to let off some steam. They sure weren't locals.

"Sunday," Lila said. "I'm off on Sundays. Everyone is. You know, union rules and all."

Clint had no idea how unions operated. He knew a whole lot about ranching and raising cattle. But that was it. So why had he thought about asking her to go out with him? He'd bore her to death.

"How are you two doing?" Elaine laid his change on the table. "Can I get you anything else?"

Lila smiled and shook her head.

"No, thanks, Elaine. This is it for me."

"Well, good seeing you, Clint. You take care." Elaine gave Lila a parting nod and a lingering inspection as she went to the next table.

Lila was staring at him with a furrowed brow. "I know Sundays are usually family days, so I'm guessing it won't work for you."

Clint's heart lurched. He took another gulp of beer and discreetly wiped his mouth. Hell, he hoped he wasn't misreading her. "Sunday is fine. So is Saturday night—"

"I knew it was you hiding in the corner." A guy with tattoos on his neck came up behind Lila and tugged on her ponytail. "Can't miss this hair."

She swatted his hand away just as the rest of the group converged on them.

"Have you seen Rocco?" the woman with the purple hair asked as she strained to see into the back room.

"You know if they fixed the mechanical bull yet?" a younger guy muttered without looking up from his phone.

The fourth member of the party, a tall, clean-cut man stared at Clint.

Lila huffed with annoyance. "Everybody be quiet," she said, briefly closing her eyes before glancing up at them. "Did any of you stop for one second to wonder if you might be interrupting something here?"

The three people—who weren't sizing up Clint— looked at Lila and then looked at one another. "Nah," they said at once and grinned.

"Well, you are. I'm on a date. So butt out."

They all stared at her. Even Mr. Clean-cut dragged his gaze away from Clint to gape at Lila.

Clint just kept his mouth shut.

"No, you aren't," the tattooed guy said. "You never hook up. With anybody."

"Ever." The kid had lowered his phone.

"You don't hook up, and you don't cuss. Everyone knows that."

"Goodbye, Randy," Lila said to him with a shooing motion. "And Tony. Rhonda. Davis. Goodbye. See you all tomorrow."

Rhonda gave Clint a considering look, smiled and strolled off toward the bar.

"I mean it, you guys." Lila glared at the other three when they didn't budge. "Leave."

Clint reached across the table for her hand. The softness of her skin stunned him all over again. "How about *we* leave instead?"

"Yes. Even better."

He didn't want to let go of her hand, and she wasn't trying to pull away. Her smile lit him up inside. All the way down to the deepest, darkest pit where he stuffed feelings he didn't know what to do with.

Her fingers curled lightly around his. "Ready?"

Clearing his throat, he nodded and released her hand. He scraped back in his chair and noticed the guy who'd been staring at him hadn't gone far. Lila had called him Davis. His glare had been replaced with an obnoxious smirk. Probably thinking, *you poor dumb bastard*.

Clint got that, and he could live with it. At least for tonight, and if he was really lucky, Saturday night too.

4

"SORRY ABOUT THAT," Lila said once they were sitting in his truck. "Film crews should never be released into the general population. They have no manners. No sense of—"

Clint started the engine and glanced over at her, an amused expression on his face.

"Yes, I know I'm one of them," she continued. "But I do have manners."

"They didn't bother me," he said with a laugh. "But I can't say I was sorry to get out of there, either."

"And what I said about us being on a date… I hope that didn't upset you."

"Lila." He let the truck idle and turned to look at her. "Do you honestly think I would care if anyone assumed we were on a date?"

"I don't know. If you had a girlfriend, you would." She paused, waiting for him to respond. "You don't, right?"

"No, I don't have a girlfriend. If you're free Saturday night, would you like to have dinner with me?"

"Yes."

"Good." He started to put the truck in gear but cut

the engine instead. "One more thing," he said, and leaned over the console.

His hand slipped behind her neck as he pressed his mouth against hers. Startled, her lips parted on a silent gasp. But he didn't mistake her reaction for an invitation and rush in. He took his time, his mouth warm and firm as it moved over hers, his large hand cupping her nape. His fingers exerted a slight pressure, just enough to make her ache for more of his touch.

She parted her lips a little more. His tongue slipped inside, teasing, tasting, probing, then retreated too soon. Clint just stopped kissing her and leaned back. She didn't understand what had just happened, then relaxed as a lazy smile curved his mouth.

"I could kiss you all night," he whispered, brushing the back of his hand down her cheek.

"I didn't stop you," she said, hoping the semidarkness hid her blush.

"No, I have to keep myself in check before I—get carried away." He toyed with her hair, letting a tendril curl around his finger. "I have manners, too."

She loved the smell of him. His scent was warm and musky and very masculine in a way she couldn't describe. There was a hint of soap, maybe leather, and a big helping of easygoing confidence.

"Why don't you date?"

"I don't meet many men outside the industry. And hooking up with coworkers rarely turns out well. I won't do it. People gossip about nothing as it is. I refuse to feed them anything they can distort. I'm not thick-skinned enough." She saw that he was really listening and maybe having trouble making sense of what she was telling him. "And yes, to be in this business I need to be tougher. I know that, and hopefully I'll get there."

Clint frowned, withdrawing his hand. "That would be a shame. From what I've seen, you're already firm and assertive. You don't let anyone bulldoze you. I think you're plenty tough."

"Oh, you don't know this business," she said, laughing.

"You're right. I don't know the first thing about it. What I do know is that I like you just the way you are."

Lila searched his eyes. It could've been just a line, but it didn't feel like that. "I mean, how often do you hear the word *date* anymore? Nowadays, if you even hear the word, it's usually a euphemism for sex."

"I seem to recall us both using it. That's not what I meant."

She couldn't help grinning at his offended expression. "I didn't think you did, not for a second. If I had, we wouldn't be having this conversation."

"See?" The skin at the outside corner of his eyes crinkled with humor. "You can be tough."

Lila had forgotten what a joy it was to be talking with a man she liked, who had no association with Hollywood. No hidden agendas. She had a feeling that with Clint, what you saw was exactly what you got. "By the way, I do cuss. A lot." She moved her hand to rest on his. "But only in my head." Clint laughed just as she was about to lean forward and show him how assertive she could be. "Hey," she murmured, "that counts."

"You're right." His voice had lowered, and his gaze dropped to her mouth. "We should go someplace."

"Where?"

"Anywhere but here." His flat tone prompted her to follow his gaze.

Two men were crossing Main Street, but she didn't know them.

"Have you eaten?" Clint asked. "We can grab something quick at the diner, or if you have time, there's a new steak house—"

"Sorry, I can't." She sat back. "I was teasing earlier. We do film at night, indoor scenes, especially when we're this far behind schedule. They might need me later, but I won't know until the last minute."

"Ah, but you haven't convinced me to be an extra. So your job here isn't done yet."

"That's true." She fastened her seat belt when he started the engine.

"Hey, who's that Baxter character, anyway?"

Lila sighed. "A pain in everyone's behind, but he has a rich uncle who's written us a big fat check, and now everyone has to put up with him."

"You mean the guy's in charge?"

"Oh, God, no. Baxter's just the director's glorified errand boy. He's supposed to be learning the business."

"So he gets chewed out if I don't want to be an extra? Not you. Is that right?"

"Oh, I have nothing to do with it. If you had agreed, then Baxter would owe me. That's all."

"I noticed a bunch of local cowboys standing around. I assume they've been hired. Why not use one of them?"

"If Jason, the director, sees something he wants in a particular shot, he won't let it go. Whether it's a person or a storefront or a mountain, he gets obsessed. He and Erin went to war over using Moonlight Mountain. Do you know it?"

"Sure. Who won?"

"Erin." Lila grinned like a proud mama, which made Clint laugh.

She was guessing that the way he'd handled the runaway horse, shutting out everything around him, his focus laser sharp until it was just him and the stallion, was what had drawn Jason's attention.

As they drove down Main Street, she studied Clint's profile, seeing him just as the camera would see him.

With his strong stubbled jaw and intense gaze, he was the quintessential cowboy hero. On the other hand, she could just as easily picture him as an outlaw, his face on an old West wanted poster. Either way the camera would love him.

"You know what, it might be fun," she said. "Something different."

"What?"

"Being in the film. It's not like learning a role. But I should point out that while you'd be considered an extra, you won't be just a face in the crowd like the others. The director will want some close-ups and shots of you standing alone, apart from the action. A shadowy red herring."

Clint looked at her as if she'd forgotten to brush her teeth.

Lila grinned. "There's no speaking involved, and if you're worried about looking stiff, I could coach you."

He didn't respond but turned off the highway onto a gravel road. She'd forgotten what a short ride it was between town and their camp. Out here among the bare trees, pines and thick underbrush, it seemed they were miles away from civilization. They'd been lucky to find a clearing large enough to accommodate the trailers and temporary corrals.

"Where to?" Clint asked, slowing the truck to a crawl to avoid crew members walking around in their own little worlds.

"Past the catering truck and generators." Lila pointed

to the row of trailers. "The second one. Home sweet home. God, I'm sick of that tin box."

"Is that where you work or...?"

"It's where I sleep and keep my clothes and stuff. And what's even better? I share it with two other women, one of whom happens to be a total slob."

"Why would you stay there—is the motel full?"

Lila laughed. "No. The Boarding House Inn and the motel are reserved for the director and cast, the screenwriter, what we commonly refer to as above-the-line personnel. We peons get to live like we're still in college."

"And you've been on the road for how long?"

"Three months." That it seemed more like a year probably had more to do with her recent lack of enthusiasm. "Oh, and Baxter gets to stay at the motel, but his uncle pays for that. It doesn't come out of our budget."

"Should I park?" Clint asked, sounding uncertain. "Or am I just letting you off?"

Lila glanced at the dark trailer. "My roomies aren't here. No telling what it looks like inside, but if you don't mind risking exposure to nuclear waste, you're welcome to come in."

He stopped the truck. "Okay if I park here?"

Lila chuckled. "Sure."

The slight jitter in her tummy was ridiculous. Nothing was going to happen in the stupid trailer, she thought as she climbed out of the truck. She could be called to the set at any time. Or Shannon or Diane could show up.

Lila jumped out and hurried to the door. If the place was beyond disgusting, she'd discourage Clint from coming in. "So, have I completely ruined your perception of Hollywood and all its glamour?" she asked over her shoulder.

"To be honest, I hadn't given it much thought one way or another."

Of course he hadn't. The world didn't revolve around Hollywood. Something most people in the business often forgot, including herself.

She pushed the creaky door open. It wasn't horrible inside; she'd seen it in worse condition.

"I guess I am surprised that making a movie doesn't take more people." He stopped on the first step and shook the rickety railing. "This is dangerous. It needs to be tightened," he said. "I have tools in my truck."

Lila stood just inside the door, staring at him. She couldn't quite find her voice, or breathe for that matter. It was such a kind, unexpected offer. A small gesture, and yet not really small at all considering he didn't know her.

He looked up, met her eyes and smiled.

"That's nice—but it's only three steps. No one uses the railing."

"Wouldn't take me long." He pushed up the brim of his hat, the warmth in his eyes turning them a golden brown. "And I'd feel better."

She held in a sigh. "As much as I appreciate it, my roommates could show up at any moment..."

Clint nodded. "Okay."

Lila turned and grabbed a pillow off the floor, then kicked Shannon's boots out of the way. Great. Diane had left her vibrator out. Lila dropped the pillow on it and spun to face Clint.

"So..." She shrugged. "Don't say I didn't warn you."

He eyed the two unmade beds heaped with a mix of dirty and clean clothes. Tubes of mascara, pencil liners and palettes of eye shadow and nail polish in every possible color were scattered among dirty dishes.

Oh, dear God.

Lila spotted a second vibrator too late. Really, Diane? Two of them? The hot pink one was a doozy, too. Very fancy and clearly meant to leave no nook or cranny untouched.

Huh. Weirdly interesting. Lila would have to get a better look at it later.

Of course Clint spotted it right off. He frowned, angling his head to the side, as if he was trying to figure out how it worked.

"It's not mine," Lila blurted and felt her cheeks burn.

"Okay." Clint gave a slow nod. "That's what I thought it was," he muttered, ending with a short laugh.

The place really was a disaster, and yet a minute ago Lila had decided it wasn't so awful. When had she grown accustomed to living in a pig sty? When had her standards fallen so low?

"That's my bed back there," she said, jerking a thumb over her shoulder. "I make it every morning."

He gave her a sympathetic smile, and she buried her face in her hands.

"I'm sorry. I shouldn't have let you come in here," she moaned, her voice muffled.

"Hey, it's okay. I'm not all that neat myself." He put his hands on her shoulders and squeezed lightly. "And I have two brothers, remember? Everything was always a mess at the house. You can talk to my mom. She'll confirm it."

Lila smiled a little, even though he'd just lied. His truck was spotless. She uncovered her face, but she kept her chin lowered and her gaze on his chest. "This movie is important. We've got a real chance to get a deal with a distributor and after having begged, borrowed and bartered, we're still operating on fumes. That's why we have limited crew. Those of us who've invested in the project are working twice as hard, doubling up and overlapping jobs. Doing anything and everything to make sure the film succeeds. I've put in every last penny I'd saved and then some. Erin did, too. This has been our dream since we were in the third grade."

He kept massaging her shoulders and whispering that everything would be okay in that low velvety tone that was beginning to hypnotize her into believing him.

"I'm not complaining."

"I didn't think you were."

"Oh, Lord. Why am I even telling you all this? You're a stranger."

"Sometimes it's easier," Clint said, and rubbed a knot in back of her left shoulder.

"Well, fine, feel free to unload. Whatever you want to get off your chest, go for it."

"If I think of something, I will."

"Oh, so your life is perfect? That makes me feel so much better."

He laughed, the sound a low quiet rumble that wrapped her in his warmth. "It's not perfect," he said. "More like...predictable."

Lila couldn't tell if he thought that was good or bad. She lifted her chin and was rewarded with a smile that reached his eyes. "Want to hear something really sad?"

"What's that?"

"As horrifying as this pit is, I don't care half as much as I do about not having a tub. We have a shower. A tiny stupid shower. I would kill for a tub. Any plain generic one would do."

"I'm surprised you're not sharing a trailer with Erin."

"Ah." Lila nodded. "Normally we would have. But she met someone. He lives here, actually. Spencer Hunt.

He owns Moonlight Mountain. So she's been staying with him at his ranch."

Clint's hands stilled and his brows rose. He looked shocked, confused, curious. All appropriate reactions, but only for someone who knew Erin. Lila had no idea what was going through Clint's head.

"Do you know Spencer?" she asked.

"No. I've heard of him, though. He's been volunteering at a local animal sanctuary."

"They've invited me to stay with them," she said. "But Shadow Creek is too far."

"What is it, about thirty minutes?"

"I don't have my own car, and I never know when I'm needed on the set." She skipped the part about feeling like a third wheel. And the odd feeling she'd been having just recently that something was bothering Erin. Lila hoped it had nothing to do with Spencer. But, she was sure Erin would fill her in soon. "Anyway, predictable doesn't describe my life, that's for sure."

"You have anything pressing to do right now?" His eyes were beginning to darken, a clear hint that he had something in mind for her, something she was going to like.

"Nothing at all."

He put his hands on her waist and pulled her toward him. "How badly do you think Baxter needs me to agree?"

Unprepared for the switch in gears, she laughed. "I'd say he's pretty desperate if he asked me to help. I know he's zero for three with Jason."

Clint wrapped his arms around her. "Tell Baxter to put you up in the motel in town, and I'll do whatever he wants."

Lila stared at him. "Huh?"

"With his own money." Clint paused. "Or his uncle's, I don't care which."

"But—I—" She laughed. "I can't do that."

"Why not?" He brushed a kiss across her mouth. "Would you rather I call him?"

"No." She couldn't think. Not when her body was flush against his and she could feel him getting hard. "I don't know."

"Whatever you want, Lila," he whispered, his lips searing a path to her throat.

She swayed in his arms. His strong, muscled arms. How weird was it that she didn't feel nervous with Clint? She'd never kissed a man five minutes after meeting him. Okay, it had been longer but not all that much. She was always careful about not playing into the Hollywood stereotype. She didn't play fast or loose. Actually, it just wasn't her style.

She felt the tip of his tongue trace her collarbone. Her nipples tightened. She squeezed her thighs together. Her breathing was off, and she couldn't seem to drag in enough air.

"Tell me what you want, Lila." His voice was low and rough, his breath hot on her skin.

Her sweatshirt was too thick. She couldn't feel him pressed against her the way she wanted to...

He stopped kissing her and lifted his head. The second he stepped back, she heard the laughter just outside the trailer. She recognized Shannon's loud snort.

Lila stepped back, as well.

"So, you can tell him," Clint said when they heard the doorknob turn, "or you can give Baxter my number. That's up to you." He turned and nodded causally at Shannon and Diane as they entered, both of them speechless, eyes full of curiosity.

"I have to think about it," Lila said, her voice hardly shaking at all. But she almost lost it when he took off his hat and held it in front of himself. "I'll need your number."

Her cell signaled a text. They needed her on the set.

Clint surprised her with a business card. "I should probably get your number, too."

5

THE NEXT MORNING Clint delegated the few chores he normally handled to Heath, the new man they'd hired last month. Then Clint left a note for his dad, letting him know he was taking some time off, and another note for the other three men who worked for them. He hadn't mentioned where he was headed, just that he'd be gone all day.

They'd all razz him if they knew he'd be standing around like some jackass while someone shot film of him. It wasn't as if he could keep it a secret. Eventually word would spread. He just didn't want anyone showing up to watch—or asking him why he was charging out of the house in his good clothes.

He filled a to-go mug in the kitchen and made it to his truck without anyone seeing him. But he managed to spill coffee on the new jeans he'd just put a crease in and cussed up a storm, trying to figure out what he should do about it. He decided the spot would be fine once it dried. And anyway, he didn't have time to change.

He reversed out of the garage and drove all of ten feet when he saw his dad coming from the stable. Clint considered pretending he hadn't seen him…then his dad motioned for him to stop.

Damn.

Clint let down his window. "Hey, Dad. What were you doing in the stable this early?"

"Just checking on Hazel. I thought she might be favoring her hind leg," he said, frowning as he got closer. "That a new shirt?"

"I left you a note. In the kitchen. So, how's Hazel?"

His dad chuckled, looking younger than he had in a long while. Now that he'd filled out some, his clothes were starting to fit him again, and his coloring was better. Years of stressing over finances had aged his father.

"I think she's okay. I'm not gonna call Doc Yardley yet." He paused, obviously waiting for Clint to say something. Then he smiled. "It's okay, son. You're a grown man. No need to tell me where you're going. It's none of my business."

Clint laughed. "I might've believed you if you weren't staring me down like I was sixteen again."

"I won't deny you got me curious."

"Dad, if a man puts on a new shirt and it's not Sunday—"

"It's a woman."

"That's right." Clint gave him a nod. "And that's all I'm saying about it."

"Your mom's going to be real happy."

"Only if someone opens his big mouth," Clint said and powered the window up, cutting off the howl of laughter that had him chuckling along with his dad.

He drove slowly down the gravel driveway, glancing in the rearview mirror and watching his dad dab at his eyes. How long had it been since he'd laughed like that? Too damn long. It was a great thing to hear. Despite the guilt tightening like a fist in Clint's chest.

For four decades Doug Landers had struggled with the responsibility of running Whispering Pines, choking from fear of failure and nearly destroying the legacy entrusted to him. What he knew about raising cattle, which was a hell of a lot, was equaled by how little he knew about business. But now that he saw an end in sight, he could finally breathe.

And Clint was that end.

It didn't seem to matter that he'd taken over the books years ago. And that he'd been the one going to auctions, deciding when to send the cattle to market and handling the daily operation of the ranch. Something about his dad knowing he'd soon officially hand over the reins had given him a new lease on life.

Dammit, how could Clint make any other decision but to take over?

He'd made it halfway to town before his brain finally settled. Thinking about Lila and knowing he'd be seeing her soon calmed him down some.

That she'd called soon after he'd left her last night had given him hope. Hope for what exactly, he wasn't sure. Sex would be a good start.

Damn, but he liked her. For so many more reasons than he could've guessed, considering she was beautiful and lived in a sophisticated world that was foreign to him.

After he parked in the same spot as yesterday, he checked the visor mirror to make sure he didn't have shaving cream on his face. He dragged a hand across his jaw. Smooth as a baby's behind. Hadn't missed a single spot.

Most of the people milling about were movie folks.

He didn't see Lila, though he was early. Catching sight of Baxter, Clint wondered what exactly she'd told him. By the time he'd gotten her voice mail and returned her call she was busy working, and they had all of twenty seconds to talk.

Clint decided to stay put for now. Wait until he got the chance to talk to Lila. He was dead serious about the motel being the thing that sealed the deal. Other than getting to see her, he wasn't looking forward to this bullshit. He would have rather paid for her to stay somewhere nicer, but he knew she wouldn't have accepted the offer.

He still hadn't made sense of her involvement with the film and why she'd invested her own money. She'd really confused him.

Thinking he saw her walking with Erin near the corrals, he straightened. Yep, it was her. His heart kicked into high gear. He paused long enough for a final inspection of his good boots, then he got out of the truck.

Lila spotted him right away. She waved, said something to Erin and the two of them veered toward him. He started walking to meet up with them, enjoying the snug fit of Lila's jeans and the curve-hugging sweater that showed off a lot more than yesterday's sweatshirt.

A good four yards away, Lila stopped and gaped at him.

"Something wrong?" he asked, and did a quick fly-check.

"What happened?"

Erin was shaking her head, not bothering to hide her amusement.

Clint loosened his collar. Damn shirt was a little stiff. "What do you mean?"

Lila advanced slowly. "You're not supposed to look

like this," she said, eyeing his jeans, his boots before glancing up and sighing. "You shaved. Why would you do that?"

Yes, Erin was *her* friend, but Clint looked to her for help, anyway.

Erin smiled. "Yesterday you wore faded jeans, scuffed boots. I don't remember the shirt—"

"Yeah, I was working." He swung a gaze at Lila. She was still frowning.

"Anyway," Erin continued. "That rugged, unshaven, hard-riding cowboy look you had going on? That's what Jason wanted."

Clint didn't know what to say. He rubbed his smooth jaw. "Baxter didn't say anything."

"I'm sorry," Lila said. "It's my fault."

"So…" Clint noticed people were staring. Yeah, just what he wanted—to be the center of attention. All because he'd cleaned up? There was something wrong with these people.

"Don't worry. Lila can fix you right up." Erin glanced at her friend. "Jason doesn't need him for another hour."

"He'll be ready," Lila said, checking her watch.

"Either Baxter or I will come get you," Erin told him. She turned to leave but glanced back with a grin. "Oh, and nice move getting Lila set up at the motel."

Clint wished she'd kept her voice down. A couple of complete strangers strolling by grinned and gave him a thumbs-up.

"Come on," Lila said, "and don't worry about the crew knowing. Everyone would've heard even if Erin and I hadn't spread it around." She tugged on his arm, trying to get him to move.

"Why would you let it get out?"

"Once the crew found out, which was inevitable, I

couldn't let them think Wild Coyote—our production company—was footing the bill."

"Explain something to me," he said as he walked alongside her. "You mentioned you'd invested money but you're working as a hairstylist instead of acting. Why?"

"I think I also said we don't have a big studio behind us. Erin and I met Jason and two of his friends, David and Brian, in film school. We hung out together, worked on projects together and really clicked. None of us had any connections in the business, so after school we looked out for each other—" Lila shaded her eyes from the sun and squinted at something. "Excuse me for just a sec."

She flagged down a young woman with short blue hair carrying a clipboard and then walked briskly to meet up with her. Lila's worn jeans really showed off her long slim legs, and her hair, tousled by the breeze, glinted gold in the sunlight.

Granted, he knew less than nothing about the entertainment business, but it was mind-boggling that a woman like her wasn't doing something more than grunt work behind the scenes. She wasn't just gorgeous, she seemed smart, level-headed, dedicated. The fact that he'd showed up at all, had agreed to act like a fool— and come to think of it, he didn't remember her even asking him to do it. He'd volunteered. Yes, the woman had a gift.

After she confirmed the hair-and-makeup trailer was available, they resumed walking.

"You were telling me about how you and your school buddies got to this point," he reminded her.

"Oh, right. About a year ago we realized none of us were getting anywhere and knew we had to make something happen. So we formed Wild Coyote Productions. Westerns have been in need of a revival, so that's where we're focusing our efforts. Lucky for Jason—for all of us actually—he inherited a nice chunk of money he was willing to sink into the project. That's why he's directing and not Erin. But this is still her best shot. She'll be first AD—that is, assistant director—for the sequel. David's a writer, so he and a friend collaborated on the script. Brian, Erin and I made the smallest financial contribution, but we've been working our tails off and paying ourselves just enough money to cover our expenses."

When they arrived at the trailer, Lila opened the door and peeked inside. "We have the place for thirty minutes, but it won't take that long." She turned and regarded him with a critical eye. "I don't suppose you have an old shirt in your truck."

"A T-shirt. Maybe. And an old denim jacket that I should've tossed in the rag bin."

"Oh, good." She gave him a smile that could turn winter into spring. "We'll get it later."

He followed her inside the trailer, mulling over what she'd just told him. It still wasn't clear what she'd end up getting in return for her investment.

"Go ahead and have a seat," she said, gesturing at a row of stools, and then crouched to rifle through a set of plastic drawers.

The stools were adjusted to different heights and faced a wall made up of mirrors. It resembled the beauty shop where his mom got her hair done once a month. He took a sniff. Kind of smelled like it, too.

He glanced around. More mirrors. Lots of them, on the opposite wall, some floor length, and there was even a mobile unit stashed in the corner. A few round hand-held mirrors and blow-dryers hung from nearby hooks.

"Finding anything interesting?" Lila asked, an amused lilt to her voice.

"Hollywood people sure like looking at themselves." He turned, and, momentarily blinded by a glaring white light, ducked his head. "And they want a lot of light while they do."

Lila grinned. "You're wrong. They'd prefer next to no light and that high-def be banned forever."

Yep, there were a lot of light fixtures. They just weren't turned on. The sheer number of tubes, jars and various other *stuff* lying around astounded him. Yet somehow everything seemed orderly.

"Ah." Clint didn't know what triggered it, but he finally figured out what Lila had to gain from her investment. Oddly, if he was right, he couldn't say the notion pleased him. "Will you be starring in the sequel?"

Lila looked at him and laughed. "Starring? Try supporting actress."

"Why?"

"Because no one knows who I am. We need actors the public likes or at least has heard of. Obviously they aren't big names because we couldn't afford them." She rose to her feet, gracefully, just like she did everything else. "Penelope Lane, for instance. You've heard of her, right?"

"Nope."

Lila frowned at him. "Really?"

"Really."

She turned away and flipped through a folder. "Here," she said, showing him a picture of a twenty-something blonde. "Now do you recognize her?"

"Sorry."

"Do you go to the movies at all?"

"Not much." He hated that she was staring at him like he was a dumb hayseed. No, that was unfair. She just looked surprised.

"Should I ask which movie you saw last?"

"Probably not."

Grinning, she squeezed his arm. "It's nice to know someone whose life doesn't revolve around Hollywood." She didn't move her hand, the heat from her palm seeping through the cotton shirt. "By the way, thank you."

"Just make sure Baxter holds up his end."

"I meant for fixing the railing after I left."

"Oh. Yeah." For some reason, her mentioning it embarrassed him. "It was nothing."

"And for doing this. What a kind and generous thing." She started rubbing his forearm with her thumb, then glanced at her hand and pulled away. "I should be ashamed of myself for letting you make that deal with Baxter."

"No, you shouldn't. Not when I did it for my own selfish reason."

Lila blinked at him, looking puzzled at first. And then her eyes filled with dread, as if she expected him to say something she didn't want to hear.

"Do you have any idea how much pleasure it gives me to do this? And not just because Baxter's an ass." Clint winced. "Um, it slipped."

A smile brightened her face. "Couldn't have said it better myself."

He liked the rosy flush that colored her cheeks and how her eyes sparkled. That same image of her from last night had replayed in his head and kept him up for hours.

"Darn it, Lila, I want to kiss you so bad."

"What's stopping you?"

"I didn't want you to think that I expected—" He faltered when she started to laugh. "Expected anything."

"Sorry," she murmured and pressed her lips together. "Me too. I wanted to kiss you, but I didn't want to give you the impression I felt obligated."

"Well, aren't we a pair," he said, and caught her by the waist, drawing her closer.

"Do I have to lock the door?" she asked, with an impish smile as she came up against his chest.

"You might."

"I'm supposed to be working."

"We'll get to that."

"Yes, but—"

Her lips were soft and warm. He felt the fast, steady thumping of her heart against his chest, echoing the rhythm of his own. She slid her arms around his neck as he skimmed a hand down her back. Lila was slender, but she still had enough curves to keep a man's hands itching for more.

She pushed her fingers into his hair, and when he cupped her bottom, she moaned into his mouth. He angled his head and kissed her deeply. Her tongue stroked his, fueling the need that had been burning inside him since last night. Lila moved her hips against him, and he knew there wasn't a chance she could've missed his erection.

It wasn't easy juggling good sense and desire. Maybe they *should* lock the door.

Clint thought he heard someone just outside. When Lila stiffened, he knew it hadn't been his imagination.

"To be continued," she whispered, and stepped back.

"Yes, ma'am."

His grin vanished when Baxter opened the door.

6

"WHAT'S THE HOLD UP?" Baxter looked directly at Lila and completely ignored Clint.

She figured that was probably fine with him. He was busy moving the only mobile stool around, either to give himself leg room or buying time for his erection to settle down.

The thought had her biting back a smile.

Lila cleared her throat. "What do you mean?" she asked Baxter. Echoing his deliberate rudeness, she focused on setting out her supplies without as much as a glance in his direction. "You can't be referring to Clint. Jason isn't ready for him."

Baxter responded with sulky silence.

Lila hoped it lasted for a while.

Clint finally abandoned the stool. "How's it going?" He slapped Baxter on the back and sent him stumbling forward. "I trust everything's been taken care of with the motel."

Baxter righted himself and adjusted his Ralph Lauren shirt collar. "Yes," he said. "And I prefer that our deal stays between us."

Clint glanced at her. "It makes no difference to me, but I don't see this thing staying quiet."

"Sit, please," she told Clint and shook out a plastic cape, forcing Baxter to move back. "Almost everyone knows."

"Already? Jason, too?"

"No. Not Jason," she said. "But eventually he'll find out."

"Who opened their big mouth?" With malice in his beady eyes, he glared at Clint.

"Erin and I put the word out."

Baxter turned and stared at her as if she'd betrayed him in some deep, profound way.

"What do you think the crew would say if they thought my room was coming out of the budget after asking everyone to sacrifice so much?" she asked. "You'd have a mutiny on your hands."

"I'm more concerned about what Jason will think," Baxter muttered.

"You got the job done. He doesn't care how you did it." She was about to fasten the cape around Clint's neck but changed her mind. "Would you mind horribly taking off your shirt?"

"Why?" Baxter's voice shot up two octaves.

"I was talking to Clint." She gave Baxter a wry look. "You can keep your shirt on. Please."

Chuckling, Clint started unbuttoning. She honestly hoped Baxter didn't faint. Lila wanted to get rid of him, not necessarily embarrass him. He did fine in that department all by himself.

Seeing the two men side by side, she couldn't help but feel some sympathy for Baxter. Clint was a good six inches taller, infinitely broader across the shoulders, and had nicely muscled arms and narrow hips.

To be fair, Clint wasn't an average-looking guy. But honestly, the two men didn't look as if they belonged to the same species.

He shrugged out of the shirt and she held her breath, hoping she wouldn't blurt out something stupid like, *can I lick your chest*? It was perfect. Just the right amount of muscle, just the right amount of hair scattered between his flat dark nipples. And not an ounce of spare flesh on his stomach. The hint of a six-pack was there but not *too* obvious, exactly how she liked it.

She cleared her throat and pretended she was auditioning for the role of Mother Teresa. "Let me hang your shirt so it won't get messed up," she said, modulating her voice. The sainted woman would not ogle or stammer over Clint's chest.

Clint passed her his shirt, and while she took it to the back of the trailer, she used the time to breathe deep and even. Deep and even. Deep and even. The brief calming exercise did the trick.

"You can go," she told Baxter. "Erin is coming to get Clint when it's time." She settled the cape over Clint and then fastened it at his nape. If Baxter hadn't been standing there, she might've been tempted to take a little nip. He smelled yummy.

"You're using the cape," Baxter said, sounding irritable. "Why did he have to take his shirt off?"

"Oh." She shrugged. "I just wanted to see his chest."

Clint choked out a laugh.

Baxter's pasty face turned red.

Lila was having a heck of a time controlling her own blush. Pulling off that line was harder than she'd guessed. At least she wasn't facing Clint. She leaned close to his ear and said loud enough for Baxter to hear, "Very nice, by the way."

Without a word Baxter headed for the door, but then paused with his hand on the knob. "Let me know when you're ready to check in, and I'll take you to the motel."

"I have a ride. Thanks, anyway."

Anger pinched Baxter's features. From the beginning he'd behaved like a petulant child used to having his way. And when he didn't get it, he pouted. But this was different. His hateful expression gave Lila a chill.

"Let me know if you change your mind." Casting a scornful glance at Clint, Baxter opened the door. "By the way," he said, his mocking smile aimed at Lila. "I had them put you in the room next to mine."

She held her breath until he was gone. "That's not going to happen," she muttered. "I'd rather stay in the trailer."

Her hand shook slightly. Grateful Clint couldn't see her, she pretended to fuss with the cape's Velcro fastener using the few seconds to calm down.

As she came around to face him, she saw he'd been watching her in the mirror. "I know what you're thinking," she said, busying herself with selecting the right brush. "I shouldn't have goaded him."

"Not what I was thinking."

"I'm not saying this is an excuse, but I wouldn't be giving him such a hard time if he hadn't come in throwing his weight around. He knows nothing about the business and is supposed to be learning. Instead, he makes everyone's job harder."

"I got the impression it's more personal with you."

She hesitated, not wanting Clint involved in any way. "He's asked me out a few times. Obviously I said no. But he won't leave it alone." She tried for a joke. "I figure annoying him is better than strangling him. Less red tape."

"Have you reported him?"

"Of course not. I can handle it." Right, Lila thought wryly. Because she'd done so well to that end. "I'm sorry I asked you to take off your shirt. It was unnecessary."

"I don't care about that." Clint looked serious. "How much do you know about Baxter?"

"Oh, he's harmless. I didn't mean to make a big deal of him asking me out. Lots of guys do. I ignore them." She realized how easy that was to misinterpret. "I'm impressing you left and right, aren't I?"

He cracked a small smile. "You're just stating the facts."

Lila sighed and nudged his chin higher so she could decide how dark she wanted to make the stubble. She touched the side of his face. His jaw was as smooth as could be. "I assume you shaved this morning and not last night."

"Afraid so."

"How much of a shadow will you have by late afternoon?"

"If I were going someplace that mattered, I'd have to shave again."

"Okay. That's good." She touched the other side of his face, his skin warm under her fingers. Her body welcomed the heat radiating from him, and she felt her breathing change. Uneven. Shallow. She didn't dare look into his eyes.

Except she did. And now she couldn't pull her gaze away from the dark seductive want mesmerizing her.

"How likely is it someone will be coming through that door?" His voice was low and rough.

"When?"

"In the next two minutes."

All she did was smile. Without waiting for an answer, he caught her wrist and kissed her palm. In the next second he'd pulled her onto his lap.

Surprised, Lila gasped but didn't resist. "I'll never have you ready in time."

"One kiss," he said. "That's all."

"Just one, huh?"

"Or two," he said, with a slow smile. "Your call."

She touched her lips to his but realized she was at an awkward angle. Shifting, she broke contact trying to find a better position.

He frowned at her. "Not like *that*."

"Hold on," she said, laughing. "I'm just getting more comfortable."

"No." He bit the side of her neck. "Forget comfortable. I want you on edge," he murmured against her skin. "Ready to explode."

Lila shivered. "Okay," she said weakly, closing her eyes as he trailed soft biting kisses to her ear.

Tilting her head to give him access, she put a hand on his chest. The plastic barrier frustrated her. She wanted to feel warm skin and soft hair beneath her palm. Maneuvering her hand under the cape would be impossible since she was sitting on the stupid thing.

He cupped her jaw, bringing her chin around until their eyes met. "I'll take that kiss now," he said.

Their lips touched. His arm tightened around her. The light pressure of his mouth increased, and she could feel him getting hard beneath her bottom. His tongue swept past her parted lips. She tasted coffee and the faint mint of toothpaste. His tongue stroked hers, and she eagerly met each caress with a stroke of her own. She felt weak, weightless, held together only by Clint's kiss and strong arms.

She wasn't at all prepared for his sudden retreat. Blinking at him, she tried to gather her wits. "What's wrong?"

"You didn't hear that?" He glanced at the door. "It's probably nothing," he said, releasing her, frustration in his eyes. "But we better not push it."

"No." She slid off his lap and had to clutch his shoulder to steady herself.

"You okay?" he asked, his hand going to her waist.

"Not sure," she murmured, surprised she was literally weak in the knees. No man had ever done that to her before.

She turned to pick up her stippling brush and dark eye shadow, and caught a glimpse of her flushed face in the mirror. Her eyes were bright, and her hair looked as if she'd just gotten out of bed. She quickly ran a hand through it.

The movement drew her attention to the other mirrors. She'd worked in this very trailer hundreds of times and had been totally clueless. You couldn't even blink without seeing yourself from three angles.

"Wow!" She swept a gaze all the way around, her pulse quickening. "This would be a pretty wild place to have sex."

Clint grinned. "Sweetheart, you read my mind."

THREE HOURS LATER, reminding himself he was doing this for Lila, Clint leaned against a cottonwood tree and stared off toward the foothills, trying his best to look *casually sinister*. Because if he had to do this take one more time, he was likely to use the gun stuck in the waistband of his jeans. It was just a prop, but he figured he could use the butt to beat Jason Littleton senseless. Clint wished someone had warned him the director was an asshole.

Casually sinister.

What the hell did that even mean?

"You're doing great," Erin said as she approached him. "We shouldn't be too much longer."

"Can I move? They aren't filming with you standing here, right?"

She nodded. "But don't get comfortable. You have only a couple minutes' reprieve."

"Your buddy, Jason—"

"I know. He's being a prick." Erin glanced over her shoulder. "Jason wasn't always like this. He's stressed over being so far behind schedule plus a bunch of other things. It doesn't excuse him…"

The director was early thirties. Tall, wiry, his blond hair pulled into a short ponytail. Clint knew Lila and Erin had gone to UCLA with him, and he could see the subject bothered Erin, so he let it drop.

"Lila wants you to know that when we break for lunch she'll meet you by the catering truck," Erin said, while studying the dark stuff on his jaw. "If that's okay with you."

"Yeah, sure." He felt chilly standing in the shade wearing a T-shirt and his thin, worn denim jacket. "Do you know how much longer they'll need me?"

"Most of the afternoon, I'm afraid. You're doing too good a job acting for them to let you go."

Clint shot Jason a look. He was still chewing out some poor kid holding a camera. "You mean, looking *casually sinister*?"

Erin followed his gaze and her smile looked more sardonic than amused. "Believe me, I get that you want to kill Jason. That's perfect. Keep thinking that, and we won't have to do many takes."

"I'll admit it," he said. "I was hoping the gun was loaded."

"If it was I would've beaten you to it." She clapped him on the shoulder. "Hang in there. This afternoon we'll be filming in town, so it'll be warmer."

His jaw nearly hit the ground. "Are you serious?"

"What's the problem? You didn't expect this to take so long, or you don't want your neighbors to see you?"

"Both."

She gave him a sympathetic nod. "Just remember it's for a good cause." A young woman yelled, "Places, everybody," and as Erin backed away she said, "Any chance you can take Lila to the motel this evening?"

"I'm planning on it," he said, despite not having asked Lila if that's what she wanted.

"Thanks." Erin turned and hurried toward a group of extras standing off to the side.

Clint recognized a couple of them. They were all young, looking eager and excited, and probably jealous that he'd been used in two scenes with close-up shots. Hell, he'd trade places with any of them in a hot second.

When he'd offered his services in exchange for Lila's motel room, he hadn't understood exactly what was expected of him. He would've minded a whole lot less if he was just a face in the crowd. Though he supposed it didn't matter. He'd liked seeing the way her eyes lit up at the idea of having a bathtub. He liked her, period. So yeah, he would've made the same decision either way.

Unfortunately, that didn't make the prospect of being on display for people he knew any easier. A few locals had been hired to build sets. Yesterday he'd seen them working at the edge of town. Even if they'd finished the job, wherever the crew filmed, they'd draw a crowd. He was just going to have to tough it out.

An hour later when they broke for lunch he had to remind himself of the greater good. Baxter shooting him looks that could kill didn't bother Clint. And he ignored Jason's occasional tantrums. Ironically it was Erin who made Clint want to rethink this whole movie gig as they left the set and went in search of Lila and food.

"Um, I hate to ask you this," Erin said. "But how would you feel about saying a few lines in tomorrow's scene?"

Clint snorted a laugh. "Hell, I think you already know."

She grinned. "Can I convince you to do it anyway? It pays more money."

"I don't care about that."

"Yeah, I figured."

The thing was, he liked Erin, but not enough to make an ass of himself.

After walking in silence for several minutes, Erin spotted Lila and flagged her down.

She changed course and headed toward them with a smile across her face, her hair loose and fluttering in the breeze.

"You know, Lila could take you somewhere private and help you learn your lines," Erin said.

He slanted her a look and caught her sly grin. "You wanna play dirty, huh?"

"Is it working?"

Clint turned back to Lila and sighed.

7

SHORTLY AFTER FOUR Lila had started straightening her work station. She was officially done for the day. But she knew it didn't mean Baxter or one of Jason's other flunkies wouldn't call and ask her to do something. For now, though, she wasn't arguing with Erin's directive. Not counting Jason, Erin was pretty much the boss around the set. Mostly because she was smart and very good at what she did, and that made her right 98 percent of the time.

Lately though, even Jason had been giving her a wide berth. Avoiding her when she was in a bad mood or deferring to her when it came to the crew. What troubled Lila was that Erin wasn't the moody type. Earlier Lila had flat out asked her if something was going on between her and Spencer, but according to Erin, all was fine with them. Still, something was off. Erin could be serious and focused, getting right to the point, but the detached attitude was new. And pretending everything was all right just made it worse.

She heard a brief knock before the door squeaked open.

Clint poked his head inside. "Erin told me to meet you here."

"Come in," she said, excited to see him, despite having eaten lunch with him only three hours ago. "Actually I'm finished, so we can leave."

"I'm totally down with that."

Lila grinned. "I see you still haven't caught the acting bug."

"Never gonna happen."

"I believe you." Grabbing her purse from a lower cabinet, she paused for a second. "Did Erin railroad you into helping me move?"

His mouth curved into a slow smile. "No."

"Are you sure?"

"Yes."

"You've been here all day. You must have a lot of work waiting for you at home."

"Even if that were true, do you think I'd leave you to Baxter's mercy?"

"I'm not helpless. I know how to tell him to get lost. Having said that…" She faked a shudder. "Thank you a thousand times over."

"My pleasure, ma'am," he said with a tug on the brim of his hat, looking sexy and adorable at the same time.

"I promise to pay you back, in full, with all the acting lessons you want."

His amusement vanished.

She paused. "Wow. You really don't want to…" Of course he didn't want to do that scene tomorrow. "Erin badgered you into it, didn't she?"

"Your friend should be a politician," he said, stepping back from the door and offering her a hand down the three steps.

Lila felt foolish accepting his assistance. After all, she'd run up and down them a million times all by herself. But when her fingers touched his callused palm, a tiny frisson of awareness blazed a path all the way down to her toes, and she just didn't give a flip how it looked.

"I assume we're going to your trailer to pick up your things," he said, to which she nodded. "You want to ride over with me, or would you prefer I meet you there?"

"Oh, I'm already packed. We can go together."

With a hand at the small of her back, Clint steered her in the right direction, and Lila set a quick pace, hoping to get out of there before someone called her to the set.

"You getting any grief over moving to the motel?" he asked once they were both in his truck.

"The crew thinks Baxter lost a bet. They're all very happy that I'm sticking it to him."

Clint smiled. "Where did they get that idea?"

"You know, Erin and I have been wondering the same thing."

"God help anyone who messes with the two of you."

"Darn straight." She saw his lips twitch. "You'd think after being in this business for six years I'd know how to swear. I mean, I can say the words, but not without turning ten unattractive shades of red."

"Cussing is overrated."

"It's supposed to be therapeutic. They have studies proving it's a stress reliever. Although, Erin can cuss with the best of them and I wouldn't describe her as very Zen."

"No," he agreed with a laugh. "She's more like a drill sergeant."

"Oh, she'd approve of that description." Lila smiled as he pulled the truck to a stop beside the trailer and shut off the engine. "Has Erin seemed snappy to you?"

"I'm not sure how to answer that. I'd say she's mostly all business."

"I'm sorry. That was a silly question. You don't even know her." She opened her door. "I'll only be a minute."

"I'll help with your bags."

She touched his arm when he turned to get out. "Diane might be napping. She works late tonight. I can handle my bags."

Clint nodded and stayed put. But when she emerged from the trailer a minute later, she wasn't at all surprised to see him standing just outside the door. Without a word he took both bags and deposited them on the small back seat.

"Anything else?"

"Nope. That's it."

"You travel light for a—" He cleared his throat and opened the passenger door. "How long is Baxter springing for the room?"

Lila grinned. "Travel light for a woman? Is that what you were going to say?"

"Me? Um…" He smiled. "Nope."

"Why, Clint Landers," she said, sliding onto the seat. "I bet you get away with all kinds of things with that sexy smile of yours."

His eyebrows shot up, and he looked somewhat embarrassed. "Sexy, huh? I'll take it," he said, his arm resting on the door as he bent forward. "Just don't mention it in public."

She leaned in for a kiss and realized she'd misread the move when she saw the surprise in his eyes. He responded by brushing his mouth across hers in a sweet, gentle kiss that demanded nothing more than a brief connection. Probably didn't want to embarrass her.

Clint straightened. "We'd better get going."

She noted the sudden flurry of activity around them. Anyone would've thought there had just been a shift change at a nearby factory. She couldn't explain it. If something unexpected had happened, it could mean she'd be getting a call soon and there went her evening.

After what had just happened, maybe it wouldn't be such a bad thing. Her mind kept returning to the perfunctory kiss. Had it been that long since she'd liked a guy? Had she completely forgotten how to behave around someone who mattered?

She waited until he'd started the engine before she murmured, "Sorry about before."

He reversed, and looked at her as he waited for people to clear the way. "For what?"

"I thought you were going to kiss me and I—I just misunderstood. I wasn't being pushy."

His silence made her wince inside. She turned away and watched Red and another stuntman wolf down hot dogs outside their trailer while they eyed Clint's truck.

"Lila," he said finally, "I always want to kiss you. I'm just not comfortable doing it in front of people you work with."

"Yeah," she said, unable to stop a smile. "That wouldn't be good. But it wouldn't be the end of the world, either."

A car came up behind them, and someone beeped the horn. Clint hit the accelerator but drove at a snail's pace until they were clear of all the slowpokes coming and going from their trailers.

"How many of you are part of the crew?" Clint asked once they were on the highway.

"About forty-five, I think. Indies usually have smaller crews." Lila rubbed her hands together and suppressed a squeal. "Oh, my God. I can hardly believe it."

"What?" Clint asked, glancing at her.

"I get to sleep in a real bed tonight. Soak in a tub

of warm sudsy water. Do you think each room has its own coffeepot?"

"I have no idea. The motel just opened a month ago."

"That's okay. The bed and tub are key…anything else would be a bonus."

They turned onto Main Street and passed the service station and the pawn shop.

"That inn there on the left," Clint said, indicating an older white building with a wide porch. "My sister-in-law owns it. Unfortunately the rooms only have showers."

"Too bad. It's a cute place."

The town had gone all out decorating for Christmas. The words *Season's Greetings*, lit in bright red cursive, arched over the street. Thousands of white lights were woven into green garland. Lila twisted around as they passed a sign for The Cut and Curl.

"Was that a hair salon?" she asked.

"I think it's probably more beauty parlor than salon."

"Ah. How many are there in town?"

"Just the one as far as I know."

"Huh." She noticed quite a few vehicles parked in front of the Watering Hole. Next to the bar was a bank with a beautiful Christmas wreath hanging on the door. "I bet some hairstylists work out of their homes."

"Is that what you used to do before you wanted to be an actress?"

"No, but in film school, pretty much everyone worked every job. Especially on student productions. I discovered I had some talent in that direction and I actually liked doing hair, so I picked up tips while doing different jobs on movies and commercials. Lots of wannabes work as restaurant servers or parking valets to pay the bills. At least doing hair has kept me involved in some aspect of the business while I—" She sighed. "Wait for my big break." God, that sounded so cliché.

Funny, it had never bothered her before. But for some reason, it felt like she should have found that break before she'd turned twenty-eight. Still, she hung on, clinging to her old dream with everything she had. Anyway, she'd worked too hard to get this far and give up.

At the other end of Main Street, the brand-new motel with its red roof and oversized welcome sign came into view. The big cheesy blowup Santa and snowman sitting on either side of the parking lot entrance was just what she needed.

Clint laughed along with her as they turned into the lot and pulled up to the three-story building.

"Well, it's not the Hilton." He stopped the truck. "Do you see a sign for the office?"

"No, but look at that." She pointed to the glass doors under an overhang. "They have a lobby."

"Hey, pretty snazzy."

"I'll say." She got her phone out and snapped a picture to send to her mom and sister. "Oh my, this is so exciting."

Clint stared as if he didn't know what to make of her. "How long have you been living in that trailer?"

"Too long, evidently." She felt her face heat, then she laughed and gestured to a vacant parking spot in front of a marked exit door.

He insisted on carrying both of her bags, so Lila took another picture before they entered the lobby. It wasn't much, just a small sitting area with a pair of burgundy club chairs, a brown loveseat and a few magazines on a small table. Lila's gaze went straight to the Christmas tree in the corner.

Standing over ten feet tall, it was decorated with blue

and gold ornaments and hundreds of blinking lights. The tree was real, not artificial, and she breathed in the sweet pine scent, releasing it when she felt a pang of homesickness.

She glanced at Clint. "I bet they found this tree locally."

"I'd put money on it. That's one thing we've got plenty of."

"May I help you folks?"

They turned to a dark-haired woman who was standing behind the reception desk.

"Well, for goodness' sake, Clint Landers, I didn't know that was you." She was medium height, maybe forty, with laugh lines fanning out from her blue eyes. "You need a haircut, mister."

Lila gasped. "Oh, no. Don't say that."

Clint grinned. "Hey, Patty, how you doing?"

The woman didn't answer. She was staring at Lila.

Probably thought Lila was the rudest person on earth for butting in like she had. "I only said that about his hair because—"

"Lila." Clint put down a bag and touched her lower back. "Let's get you checked in before Baxter shows up."

The warm steady feel of his hand pressed against her spine felt so much better than it should have. Exhaustion was really getting to her, that and the nostalgia of the holidays. Why else would she react so strongly to the touch of a man she barely knew?

"Lila Loveridge," Clint said, looking at her. "I assume that's how the reservation would've been made."

Lila snapped out of it and nodded.

"Is that your real name?" Patty asked.

"Yes." She smiled, not in the least surprised. It was a common question.

Patty blinked. "Heavens," she said, waving away her blush. "I'm acting like a starstruck teenager. Please pardon my manners. Just last week I scolded the day clerk for behaving like that when Penelope Lane and Dash Rockwell arrived."

"It's okay. I'm not a cast member. I'm part of the crew, the hairstylist, actually."

Patty frowned, then glanced at Clint.

He nodded, shrugged.

"Well, ain't that a shame," Patty muttered and went to work on her keyboard. "Yes, here you are. Your reservation was made by Mr. Mortimer, and you're staying for two weeks?"

Lila's unladylike shriek made Patty look up. Clint just laughed.

"Yes," she said demurely.

The second Patty returned her attention to the computer screen, Lila looked at Clint, held up two fingers and mouthed *two weeks*.

He was smiling, but faint worry lines had formed between his brows. "Mortimer? Is that Baxter Mortimer?"

"Oh, right." Lila turned to Patty. "Could you please make sure my room isn't anywhere near his?"

The woman hesitated. "Actually, he made a special request that you be put right next to him."

"That won't work." Lila bit her lip. She could see the poor woman wasn't sure how to handle the situation. But her name tag did indicate she was the night supervisor. "I know he's paying, but I'm the named guest. Shouldn't my request count more?"

She let out the most pitiful sigh.

"Look, Patty," Clint said, "if this puts you in a bind—"

"You know me, Clint. I'd be more than happy to oblige if I could. The manager handled the reservation personally. And truth be told, with my two older ones away at college, I need this job."

"I understand," Clint said, nodding. "Do I know the manager?"

Patty shook her head. "Kevin's a young fella out of Kalispell. He oversees a motel there along with this one. In fact, you just missed him."

"Maybe I could call him?" Lila knew it was a bad idea the second Patty's expression fell. "That's okay," she said. "If Baxter annoys me, I'll just go back to base camp. No problem."

"He won't bother you," Clint said in a quiet voice. "I'll take care of it."

Lila studied the strong set of his jaw, saw the confidence in his dark eyes and her heart beat double time.

"Granted, I don't know this Baxter fella," Patty said. "But I know Clint, and for what it's worth, my money's on him."

Lila bumped him with her shoulder. "Something about you I should know about?"

"Oh, honey, the stories I could—" Patty stopped abruptly after one look from Clint.

"We done here?" he said, and picked up the bag he'd set down.

"If I could just get you to sign this…" Patty slid the electronic signature machine toward Lila. "We serve coffee in the lobby all day. I was about to make a fresh pot if you're interested. And from seven to nine in the morning, we set out an assortment of muffins, doughnuts and cinnamon rolls, all made fresh right here in town."

Lila thanked her, accepted the room key and led

Clint to the elevator. Once they were inside the car, she pressed the button for the third floor. "Not too bright of Baxter," she muttered, annoyed with the man's gall. "I could do some serious damage shoving him off the balcony."

Amusement gleamed in Clint's eyes. "Something I should know about *you*?"

"Yes," she said, smiling up at him. "I like kissing. A lot." She slid her arms around his neck. "With **you**."

8

LILA FUMBLED TRYING to unlock the door. But as soon as she succeeded, her arms went right back around Clint's neck.

Managing not to lose her bags, Clint pushed the door open with his elbow and backed into the room with her clutching his shoulders. Her lips clung to his lips, and her breasts, her nice, round breasts found a home against his chest.

Damn, who knew 317 was his lucky number?

A few steps in and they cleared the door. He let it close and dropped both bags just as she pushed her fingers through his hair. She had one hell of a touch. He'd never had a spine-tingling reaction to a woman rubbing his scalp before.

He put his arms around her and held her tight, keeping his boots planted until he was sure they weren't about to take a tumble. Everything had happened so fast he didn't even know how close they were to the bed. Not that he was presuming anything. But a man could hope. And that *hope* was getting harder by the second.

No other woman had ever felt this good in his arms. Or tasted this sweet. She let out a breathy sigh as his tongue stroked hers, the intoxicating sound going straight to his cock. The sway of her hips, as if she were dancing to a song in her head, sorely tested his self-control.

He rubbed a hand down her back, stopping at the tempting curve of her bottom. He didn't want to stop. And he didn't think she'd tell him to, but for some crazy reason, he decided Lila was a woman he wanted to go slow with. He wanted to learn the contours of her mouth, see all her different smiles, make her eyes shine like they did when she was excited about something. Even something as simple as a motel Christmas tree.

It made no sense. His wanting to woo her slowly. She wouldn't be here long. Any time they spent together would be over in the blink of an eye. Lila was on the road to a bright future. She didn't have room in her life for a cowboy stuck running the family ranch.

The thought rattled him.

He'd never felt trapped by his family or the Whispering Pines, and he sure couldn't afford that line of thinking now. Not with the big decision he had to make.

Clint changed the slant of his mouth and kissed her more deeply. Her fingertips dug into his scalp with just the right amount of pressure. Her breasts pressed against the lower part of his chest, and he could feel her hardening nipples through the layers of their clothing. What he wouldn't give to see all of her, to feel the warm softness of her skin…

Her sweet, sexy moan almost undid him.

He broke the kiss. Slowly. As slowly as he could without dropping to his knees.

Lila gave a slight jerk when he moved his head back. He gently pried her arms from around his neck, and she blinked at him. "Sorry," she murmured. "I don't know what got into me."

Wishing it had been him, he held back a groan. Ordered his cock to be patient. Hoped like hell his brain still had control over his mouth.

He put it to the test with a smile first. Reasonably encouraged, he stepped back and said, "I was afraid you'd trip over your bags."

She frowned at the lame excuse.

"Look, Lila—"

She had a dark smudge on her left cheek. Or was it a shadow? He caught her chin, angling it so he could study the rest of her face.

"What are you doing?"

"You have something on your face." He rubbed his thumb over a second smear.

"Oh." She touched her cheek and grinned. "I know what that is. Come with me."

Following her, he noticed it wasn't a bad room. Done up in green-and-cream, it had a king-size bed, a table with two upholstered chairs, and a small dresser. The open drapes showed off a partial view of the Rockies in the distance.

Light flooded out of the bathroom.

He saw Lila standing in front of the sink. His gaze drifted back to the bed before he joined her.

Damn his one-track brain.

Washcloth in hand, she stared at herself in the mirror, dabbing at her nose. Even in the terrible artificial light, her skin was smooth and perfect. Before he knew what he was doing, he touched her cheek.

She turned her head and smiled at him. "Did I miss a spot?"

"I don't know." He laughed and lowered his hand. "Let's see." Of course he fixated on her lips, pink and damp from all the kissing.

"Okay, let's take care of you."

"Huh?" He met her eyes. Something crackled in the air around them. Did she mean…?

They just stared at each other for a long drawn out moment. Blood pumped hot and fast to his groin. She turned to rinse out the washcloth and then tugged him closer.

"I thought I'd gotten all of it," she said as she dabbed at his chin. "Your stubble is already coming in so it fooled me."

Clint finally understood what had happened. He took a quick look in the mirror but didn't see any of the goop she'd used earlier.

"There." She dropped the washcloth into the sink and cupped his chin. Mimicking his earlier move, she angled his face to the left, then to the right for her final inspection. "You're good to go."

"As in you want me to leave?"

"No." She shook her head, smiling. "Unless you want to." She let go of his chin and dried her hands on a towel. "I mean you did your good deed, and I'll be fine."

"Actually I was wondering if you were hungry."

She gave him a tentative look he couldn't read.

"I'd like to take you to dinner," he continued. "There's a new steak house down the street. I haven't been there yet. It opened only a couple months ago." He paused, leaving her time to say something, but she didn't. "I heard it's pretty good."

"I was pushy," she said, staring at her hands. "You know…before. I swear I'm not usually like that. I'm really not."

"Lila?"

"I'm just saying you can leave, and it won't hurt my feelings."

"Hey…"

She glanced up.

"I didn't think you were pushy. After our talk last night, I thought I had to wait until Saturday to take you out, so believe me when I say I'm as happy as a flea in a doghouse—" He stopped. Had he just sounded like his granddad? "I have no idea where that came from, so if we could just forget that bit of down-home whatever…"

Lila's laughter put the sparkle back in her eyes.

He found himself smiling back at her. And oddly, it seemed as natural as breathing for him to put his hands on her waist. "I'm going to make it real plain," he said. "You know what's going to happen between us if we stay here, don't you?"

Her smile wavered a bit. "I really like you, Clint," she said, and he knew what was coming next. "I don't think I'd mind if something did happen…"

Not what he'd expected. "You don't look all that sure," he said, "so how about we wait until you are?"

Her lips lifted in a soft smile that he brushed with a brief kiss.

He'd done the honorable thing, and it felt good. And at the same time so goddamn disappointing.

Go figure.

And now he had to take a giant step back before he screwed up everything by stealing the kind of kiss he really wanted.

LILA WOULDN'T HAVE minded walking the few blocks to the steak house if the air hadn't been so chilly. Clint found a parking spot in front of a bakery that Lila had missed earlier.

"The Cake Whisperer," she said, reading the sign as she slid out of the truck. "How cute. Looks new."

Clint nodded as he closed the passenger door. "The Full Moon Saloon opened sometime back in July. Then the bakery and steak house opened right after. Nice to see the town thriving, especially around this time of year. Speaking of which, don't you have a jacket with you?"

"Not so much for this temperature," she said, wrapping her arms around herself and trying not to shiver. Her black sweater was made of a decent weight cashmere blend, but she was foolish to have paired it with a short denim skirt in this weather.

She was sick of wearing jeans all the time, even though Clint assured her the steak house wasn't anything fancy and they would do fine. But mostly she'd wanted to look nice for him. Yeah, her chattering teeth were probably so attractive.

Looking out of place, the restaurant's flashing pink neon sign lorded over a row of early-bird specials handwritten with black marker and taped to the window. She didn't stop to have a look but hurried into the welcoming warmth of the dimly lit steak house. The heavenly smell of sizzling meat woke up her taste buds.

A middle-aged woman wearing a Frosty the Snowman sweatshirt came bustling from the back. "Evening, folks," she said, grabbing menus from a basket next to an old cash register. "Anywhere in particular you wanna sit?"

Clint glanced around. Only two tables were occupied; it was still early. "How about the corner booth? Should be fairly quiet back there."

The woman laughed. "Well, I hope it's not too quiet," she said over her shoulder as she led them to the booth. "We could use the business."

"Has it been slow?" Clint sounded surprised.

"Nah, not too bad considering it's so close to Christmas. Having them movie people in town helps a lot. A few of 'em eat here almost every night."

Lila bet she could name which ones and prayed they were held up on the set until she and Clint were gone.

"That's good," he said. "Good for the whole town I imagine."

Lila slid into the booth. The woman passed her a menu, narrowing her eyes as if she'd just seen Lila for the first time.

"You must be one of them," the woman said.

"Yes, I'm with the crew. And by the way, cute sweatshirt."

The woman glanced down. "Oh, my grandkids surprised me with it last year. I like it. Get a lot of compliments, too." The door opened, and she glanced in that direction. "You folks take your time looking over the menu. I'll be back in a jiff."

"See?" Clint said. "I don't know everyone in town."

"Just every woman under forty."

He snorted a laugh. "Now why would you say that?"

"Because you're hot," she said and laughed at his exaggerated eye roll. "If you slide a little closer, I promise not to maul you under the table."

"Sweetheart," he said in a low, gravelly voice as he leaned forward, "that's not what I'm worried about. So, I believe I'll stay right where I am."

"Really?" Lila pretended to pout. "I promise to slap your hands if you try anything."

Clint shook his head. "Just look at your menu."

She held in a laugh. "I already know what I want. A baked potato with butter, sour cream and anything else they can pile on it. And maybe a small rib eye.

Hey, wait." She frowned at the menu. "They must have dessert."

"On the back." The woman who seated them had just stopped at the table. "Shoulda told you right off my name's Irene. I can get your drinks while you're still having a look."

Lila asked for water with lemon, and Clint ordered a beer.

When more people entered the restaurant, another woman, younger, with reddish hair gathered in a ponytail, came from the kitchen to seat them.

Tempted to turn around, Lila kept her face averted. "If Jason or anyone you recognize from the set comes in, would you let me know?"

"Sure. So far it's been locals." He glanced around. "Is it a problem for you to be here with me?"

"No. Nothing like that. I'm really lucky to have this extra night off and I guess I just don't want to see anyone. Except Erin, of course." She smiled, despite the sharp pang brought on by thinking about her friend. God, she missed her so much. It wasn't just about sharing her with Spencer, although that was taking some getting used to.

"You asked me about her mood earlier," Clint said, studying her closely.

"Did I?"

"We don't have to talk about it."

Well, so much for her stellar performance. "It's just that Erin hasn't been herself lately. She's been too subdued."

"Subdued?" Clint laughed. "She must've been hell on wheels before."

"Yep. That's Erin." Lila waited until after the redhead had set down their drinks. "When it comes to the job, she gives 200 percent. She has more enthusiasm and energy than anyone I know. We've been friends forever, so we've been through a lot together. There's never been a taboo subject with us."

Irene returned with a pad and pencil. "Did I give you folks enough time to decide?"

"I'm ready," Clint said. "Lila?"

Her appetite had dwindled, but she ordered the potato and a small salad. So did Clint, along with a large cut of rib eye.

He studied her a moment. "Hey, how about we both slide in a little bit?"

Lila smiled. "Okay, but remember there's no table-cloth."

"Well, damn." He pretended to be surprised, leaning back and checking under the table. "I'll let you see my hands at all times," he said, shifting toward the center of the black vinyl seat and getting a grin out of Lila.

She'd already been sitting farther in, so sliding a few inches put her within reaching distance of his arm and leg. "Now what?"

"Well…" He paused briefly. "Now you're close enough to snitch bites of my steak."

"Ah. I hadn't thought of that," she said and burst out laughing.

People were probably staring, and she didn't care.

She noted the humor gleaming in his eyes, then looked at his large tanned hand resting on the table. She already knew his palm was rough, but his touch was gentle. And that his clever mouth could send her soaring all the way to the moon and back.

And Lord, he was patient, and considerate. She'd sensed his disappointment back at the motel, but he hadn't pushed even a tiny bit. It had been Clint who'd applied the brakes, almost as if he knew she'd been feeling fragile lately. Unsure about her career, unsure about what was troubling Erin. And worried that sinking everything into this film would turn into a colossal mistake.

She hadn't been intimate with a lot of guys, but the few she had hooked up with had never expressed concern about whether she'd been ready to take the next step. She wasn't stupid. Her looks had played a big part in their attraction to her. Except for Jason. He'd shown an interest back in college. At least he hadn't been a jerk when she'd told him it was friends or nothing.

Clint moved his hand to cover hers and gave her a reassuring squeeze. She looked into his pensive eyes and smiled. How had he known that was exactly what she needed?

"Here you go, folks." Irene placed a salad in front of Lila. "Italian on the side for you," she said, then set down Clint's, covered with blue cheese dressing. In the middle of the table she placed a linen-covered basket. "Your dinners should be up soon."

They thanked her, and as she walked to the next table over, Lila peeked under the yellow linen napkin. Smelling the golden yeast rolls brought back her appetite.

"You think they're homemade?" She sniffed and made a moaning sound that probably embarrassed Clint. "I bet they are." She knew she shouldn't... The potato she'd ordered was a huge splurge. What with her big role coming up...

"Go for it," he said, grinning.

She hesitated...until she saw the glass ramekin of pale whipped butter. Her willpower evaporated like the steam from the warm rolls.

Lila grabbed the largest one. "You're a bad influence," she said as she slathered it with butter. "All these carbs are going to kill me."

"You barely ate anything for lunch." He tipped the beer to his lips.

"Don't forget, we still have to work on your speaking part for tomorrow. You can't afford to have me conk out on you."

That wiped the humor from his face.

Lila swallowed a small piece of roll. "Although, since it's a love scene, it shouldn't be a problem. I'm guessing you'll do very well."

Clint stared back, looking shocked. "You're joking."

"I thought Erin told you."

He pointed his fork at her. "You're messing with me."

"Why would I do that?" Lila asked, eyes wide, the picture of innocence. She could be a very good actress when she wanted to be.

9

LILA WAS SHIVERING by the time they arrived at the motel. She'd recognized Baxter's car even before they turned into the parking lot. The red Beemer convertible occupied the same spot they'd vacated a couple hours ago. Just the idea of it annoyed her, which said a lot about her anxiety level lately.

"Don't tell me," Clint said, glancing at the car. "It's Baxter's."

"How did you know? The California plates?"

"It's December in Montana. How many idiots would leave the top down?"

Lila grinned. Feeling a slight pinch near her ear, she realized it had come from her jaw joint. It actually ached from smiling so much. After dinner when she'd asked if they could drive around and look at Christmas lights, he'd agreed without even a blink. Of course they hadn't been gone long. Other than a pair of residential side streets, the ranches were spread out. Christmas was obviously a big deal around Blackfoot Falls, which made Lila like the place even more.

Clint pulled into a parking spot near the door, and her pulse jumped. He could've simply dropped her off, so maybe he wanted to come to her room. Although he hadn't cut the engine, so it was hard to know for sure. Lila appreciated that he'd been chivalrous before, but now she knew exactly what she wanted.

"Do you want—"

"How will you get—"

They spoke at the same time.

Clint motioned for her to go first. And then his phone chirped.

"Go ahead," she said when he didn't bother looking at it.

"Later. It's my mom."

"Oh, did you miss your curfew?" Her teasing apparently missed the mark.

Staring at the phone, he sighed. "How many times have I showed her how to text?"

"I can get out if you want."

"No. I'll only be a minute," he muttered, then shut off the engine and answered. "What's up, Mom?" He listened for a moment, frowning. "No way. I brought up every single box you had marked." He paused, chuckling under his breath. "No, ma'am, I stacked them in the same corner I do every year. The basement's not that crowded."

Lila typed a text to Erin. Nothing important. She just didn't want to make Clint uncomfortable or have him think he had to rush.

Clint stretched his neck to the side. "Fine. I'll check when I get home," he said, then turned his head and lowered his voice. "Yes, I did. In town. I have to go." He dropped his phone on the console and scrubbed a hand over his face. "Sorry."

"Don't be." She sent her text and pocketed her phone. "I should've just gotten out."

"That would've made things worse. Believe me, there's no crisis. She thinks some Christmas ornaments are missing."

"Are you insane?"

"Maybe," he said. "Could you be more specific?"

"Definitely a crisis. How long has she been collecting the ornaments? I bet they were passed down from your grandparents. Probably even from your great-grandparents." Lila sighed. "Why are you looking at me like that?"

"You're serious."

"Well, of course I am! Those kinds of things are irreplaceable."

"Okay. I see your point. But I know damn good and well it's all there. The minute I get home—" He couldn't have looked more disgusted if he tried. "How are you getting to the set tomorrow? Can I give you a ride?"

"I think Erin is going to pick me up. Did I say something to upset you?"

"No, it's not you. It's…nothing."

"Okay." It sounded as if he might live with his parents and maybe he didn't want her to know. "What time do they want you on the set?"

"By eleven."

"Lucky you. I start at seven."

Clint snorted. "Hell, I'll have fed and watered the horses by then."

"Wow. That's right. You have a bunch of ranch things to do."

He found her hand and gave it a light squeeze. "Don't feel too sorry for me. We have some hired men to help with the *ranch things*."

"Okay, I should've said chores. Would that be more

accurate?" How crazy was it that just the feel of his callused palm could make her skin tingle?

"I like *ranch things*. I'm going to start using it."

Lila laughed. "You've never told me exactly what
you do."

"I'm the foreman, so I handle the daily operation,
ordering supplies, payroll, buying and selling cattle at
auctions. When it's roundup time, I work right alongside the guys."

"Does your father do anything?" She groaned. "I
didn't mean that the way it sounded. Honestly, that was
so rude."

Clint chuckled. "Let's just say he's semiretired..."
He looked as though he was about to say something
else but changed his mind. Whatever it was, his mood
seemed to take a dip.

Lila shifted restlessly. "Thank you for dinner," she
said. "And for getting me an amazing room."

"Amazing, huh?" He smiled. "Hey, I didn't look.
Does it have a tub?"

"Oh, yeah."

"Has to be pretty generic."

"I'm not complaining." She drew in a breath. "Maybe
you'd like to try it out with me some time..."

The moon lit most of his face. Desire flared hot in
his eyes. "No maybe about it."

Lila's mouth went dry. She knew she should say
something. Clearly it would be up to her if and when
they were to take the next step. But she couldn't seem
to think straight or even make her mouth work, which
at the moment was probably a blessing.

She hated the timing. She knew she was overly
touchy about sex being used as a favor; hard to live and
work in Hollywood and not be aware of it. Clint was dif-

ferent. Knowing with absolute certainty his generosity came without strings attached helped, but not enough. Not in this particular instance.

What had tripped her up was thanking him for dinner and the room. It was appropriate, even though she'd already thanked him, but saying it again and then jumping into bed with him? Too weird. She liked him too much to give him the wrong impression.

He'd been watching her, and when she met his eyes again, he gave her a patient smile.

"I love the name Whispering Pines," she said, feeling like the biggest wuss in the whole world.

He didn't release her hand, so he hadn't written her off as a lost cause. "It's okay. Not very manly, though," he said with a shrug and a self-deprecating laugh. "The ranch has been in the family for generations. I think it might've been my great-great grandmother who came up with the name."

"Is it very far?"

"Thirty minutes."

She waited, hoping he'd suggest taking her there some time. The invitation didn't come.

"Am I going to see you tomorrow?" he asked.

"I'll make a point of it." She curled her fingers around his hand and leaned slightly toward him.

Clint took it from there. Sliding a hand around the back of her neck, he drew her closer as he leaned over the console until their lips met. The pressure of his palm against her nape had an odd and intoxicating effect on her. She parted her lips, anxious to feel the warm stroke of his tongue, and he didn't disappoint.

She tasted his hunger as he explored her mouth, her need for him growing with breathless speed. Shifting her body so that she faced him, her hand landed high on his thigh. His muscles tensed underneath her touch, and his low, husky moan filled her mouth.

Her heart seemed to stop.

Oh, how she regretted not inviting him to her room. It was silly to be sitting out here. She'd fretted for nothing. She would make the suggestion…

He'd deepened the kiss and she could barely stay still, much less think. He sucked on her tongue, nibbled her bottom lip and teased the corners of her mouth. He tilted her chin up and changed the angle of his head, then traced his fingers along her jawline before plunging them into her hair.

The loud bang of a car door changed the tempo.

Clint didn't pull away, but he tamed the kiss and relaxed his hand. He took his time ending things, but it didn't blunt the sense of loss she felt the moment he broke away.

His mouth curved in a smile as he brushed the hair away from her eyes. And then his gaze drifted past her to something outside. Something that caused his expression to tighten, and she couldn't resist a backward glance.

Over two dozen cars crowded the small lot. But of course it had to be Baxter. Standing beside his Beemer and looking in their general direction. Between the moon and the motel's floodlights, the visibility was good if he knew where to look.

Exasperated, Lila groaned. "You think he can see us through these tinted windows?"

"I wouldn't have thought so. But he slammed the door for a reason."

She hadn't considered that, but of course. He hadn't just arrived, and he obviously wasn't in a hurry to leave. "Should we give him a show?"

Clint looked at her. "You really want to do that?"

Her inner child was all pumped to say *you betcha.* "I guess not," she muttered, sitting back against the seat. "Stupid jerk. He's probably pleased with himself for killing the mood."

Clint looked as though he was about to say something, but changed his mind. "I'll stay here in the truck until you get to your room and he leaves. I'll make sure he sees me. Hopefully he'll take off and not bother you tonight."

Lila tried to think fast. It was a good excuse to invite Clint upstairs. "Or you could come up with me."

"I could," he said with a slow nod as he searched her face. "If that's what you want."

Oh, God, she hated being put on the spot like this. Despite the fact that she'd started it. Usually she had no trouble dealing with men. No was an answer she knew well. But it was different with Clint. Darn him.

Tempted to run a hand down his fly and ask him what *he* wanted, she huffed a breath instead. "What's today? Wednesday?"

"Yep."

"Okay." She put her hand on the door handle. "I'll see you on the set, but I'm going to be busy all day tomorrow and then we're shooting a twilight scene." She lifted the handle. "Don't even think about weaseling out of Saturday night."

Clint let out a laugh. "Nope."

"Now, go find your mom's ornaments." She opened the door and slid out. "Thanks again for…everything."

By the time she closed the door, he'd climbed out and was coming around the hood.

"What's wrong?"

He pulled her into his arms and kissed her until there

was no air left. Not in her lungs, and maybe not even in the whole state of Montana. She dragged her mouth from his with a gasp.

"Good night, Lila," he whispered and let her go.

"Uh-huh," she murmured, making sure her legs weren't too wobbly before she turned and walked straight to the motel entrance, and right past Baxter without a single word.

AFTER BEING RECRUITED to do makeup on the principals some time around eleven the next morning, Lila had been bombarded with work the rest of the day. She'd skipped lunch, which wasn't unusual, but she hated that she'd gotten only a glimpse of Clint. She'd completely forgotten his scene was being shot in town.

Erin had been just as swamped. They'd met up once, briefly, but too many people had been around so they couldn't really talk. In the old days, Lila would've called her the minute she'd left Clint last night and talked for an hour, with Lila spilling everything down to the last detail.

Things were different now that Spencer was in the picture. Erin wouldn't have minded if Lila had called. If anything, Erin would be royally pissed if she knew the reason for Lila's hesitation.

Instead of their traditional postdate chat, Lila had looked at pictures of the family Christmas tree that Britney had sent to her phone. God, she hated not being there to shop and make Christmas cookies, do all the things she loved about the season.

Why did life have to throw so many curveballs at once? Being a grown-up and working in *glamorous* Hollywood had sounded like a lot more fun at thirteen.

At 4:30 p.m., Lila finally had a chance to breathe.

She'd splurged on a scrawny wreath she'd found at the small grocery store in town and had just hung it on the trailer door when Erin jogged toward her, an apple in each hand.

"You got a few?" she asked.

"Not really."

"Come anyway." Erin stopped and frowned at the wreath. "That's pretty sad."

"I know. Better than nothing."

Erin turned to study Lila. "You probably didn't have lunch," she said, handing her an apple and pulling a flattened protein bar out of her jeans pocket.

Lila wasn't interested in the bar, but she knew better than to refuse it. "Where are we going?"

"Nowhere. I just wanted a chance to talk. Walk fast—"

"And look busy. Got it."

Munching their apples, they headed in the opposite direction of the craft services table where most of the extras had gathered. Lila knew there was a good chance Clint had left. Or else he was still shooting in town, but she swept a glance around anyway.

"Do you like Clint?" Lila asked. "I do. I like him."

Erin gave her a long look and laughed. "Yeah, I know."

"What? He's really a nice guy."

"Why are you being defensive? I agree. I wanted to hear about what happened at the motel. Why do you think we're power walking in the friggin' cold?" Erin shivered and put her hood up. "Did you have sex with him?"

Lila laughed. This was the old Erin. Thank God. "He took me to that steak house in town for dinner.

Then we drove around, rehearsed his lines and looked at Christmas lights."

Erin chewed and swallowed a bite of apple. "But did you have sex?"

"No. We didn't."

"Why not?"

"I met the man two days ago. Have you ever known me to hook up with anyone that fast?" Lila slowed down and studied her friend. "What is going on with you?"

"No, you're right." Erin slowed as well. They'd passed the last trailer, and no one was within earshot. Lately, a chance for a quick chat didn't get better than this. "Clint's different—" She shrugged. "You know how you get a gut feeing about someone. I think he's a good guy," Erin said, "and it's been a while since you've hooked up with anyone, so I was hoping the two of you had clicked…"

"Are you feeling guilty because you're staying with Spencer? Because if you are, knock it off. I'm happy for you. Spencer seems great, and if you weren't making time for him, I'd have to kick your butt."

Erin grinned. "You could try."

"Wipe that smirk off your face. I've been pretty darn good about sticking up for myself and being assertive."

"Huh," Erin muttered with a thoughtful frown. "You really have. Well, at least Baxter's good for something."

"Practice?"

"Yep."

They both laughed.

"Okay, one more thing," Lila said as they started walking again. "In the interest of full disclosure, I'm very envious of you and Spencer. Not to be mistaken for jealousy. Just please don't think you have to push Clint and I together. I like him. I really do." Staring at the Rockies, she sighed. "Things were going well last night, and I know it's stupid, but part of me kept waiting for something to go wrong. Once sex entered the picture... Well, I didn't want what we had to end in disappointment because I misinterpreted the situation."

Erin nodded with understanding. She'd been there with Lila, through the tears and regret, when she'd discovered a guy she really liked had been more invested in sex with her than in her as a person.

"Of course there's always that risk," Erin said. "But I think Clint's the real deal. Hell, I don't know, maybe there's something about cowboys. They're a different breed. Spencer certainly is."

Lila smiled, wondering if Erin knew how her face lit up every time she mentioned his name. "Clint and I have a date Saturday night. I'm pretty sure it'll have a happy ending."

"Bring it home, sister," Erin said, holding up a hand.

Lila slapped a high five.

They lost their grins at the sound of Erin's name riding on the brisk wind, and turned toward the voice.

Baxter was standing near the clothes trailer.

"Jesus, he's got a cell phone and a walkie-talkie," Erin said, acknowledging him with a wave. "The dumb ass probably doesn't know how to use them."

Lila groaned inwardly when Erin started toward him. "Hey, have you got anything for me?" she asked casually as she fell into step with her. "You know, in the interest of full disclosure?"

Dread flickered in Erin's face before she looked away. She shrugged. "I don't think so," she said. "If he turns up missing, everyone would know it's me. Catch you later."

Lila's chest tightened with the grim certainty she

hadn't been wrong. Something was going on with Erin. Yet, after a twenty-year friendship and countless secrets that bonded them, she'd chosen not to share it with Lila.

Her spirits lifted when she spotted Clint. He was talking to a wrangler near the corrals. Lila didn't hesitate. She changed course and headed toward him, and the comfort she knew he'd give her.

10

CLINT LEFT THE house through the kitchen door and cursed under his breath when he saw Joe and Paxton. It was Saturday evening, for Christ's sake. By now they should've been halfway to Kalispell looking to raise hell. Yet there they were, hanging out with Murray, all three of them standing too close to Clint's truck for it to be a coincidence.

As far as he knew, Paxton and Murray were still feuding over last week's poker game. Evidently it hadn't stopped them from planning an ambush.

The old-timer was the first to spot him. Murray turned and spit on the ground beside him before giving Clint a toothless grin. "Well, now, don't you look purdy."

Joe swung his gaze around. "Hey, boss, are those new boots?"

Clint ignored them.

Paxton let out a whistle. "New shirt and new jeans, too," he said, sizing him up. "Hell, son, looks like you're getting all Hollywood on us."

"Might be he's courting someone special." Murray's

pale eyes took on a mischievous gleam. "Anything we should know about, Clinton?"

"You sound like a bunch of bored old ladies." He pushed past them and opened the driver's door, their laughter grating on his nerves.

Hell, he'd known all along word would spread that he was an *extra*. No one knew the circumstance that had prompted him to sign on. Though he supposed that didn't matter. He wondered if they'd heard about the speaking part he'd managed to bungle. What a damn disaster.

Squinting through the smoke from his cigarette, Joe said, "You gonna tell us where you're going, boss?"

If it weren't for Murray, who'd been working at the Whispering Pines since before Clint was born, he would've let his middle finger do his talking. "Look, I've told you before not to smoke near my truck. It stinks up the cab."

"See, I knew it." Murray nodded smugly. "He's aiming to impress a lady."

Clint gave the old guy a slick smile. "Next time I see Mrs. Chesterfield, I'll be sure to let her know how much you love her corn pudding."

Mention of the doting widow wiped the amusement off Murray's face. "That ain't funny, Clint. That crazy old woman won't never stop pestering me."

"That's right," Clint said and slid into the truck. Paxton started to say something, but Clint cut him off. "The two of you are fired."

Paxton and Joe laughed.

Jesus. First his mom had grilled him with the persistence of the county prosecutor. And then while he'd calculated next month's feed order and closed payroll, his dad kept giving him curious looks. What did a guy have to do to get some peace and privacy around here?

The only thing Clint had told his folks was that Lila was part of the movie crew working as the hair and makeup person. Nobody had to know she was an actress. He couldn't imagine what kind of uproar that would cause.

After all the bitter feelings and heartache following Anne's death, he wasn't so sure old wounds couldn't be reopened. His late sister-in-law had kept her obsession to be in the spotlight a secret from Nathan. And whatever the rest of the family had known or suspected, including Clint, no one spoke of Anne's audition trips out of town every time Nathan was away.

Until the car accident. A lot of angry words had been exchanged, accusations flung, rocking the Landers family's foundation to the core.

No, he wasn't about to kick up dust now. And for what, anyway? He liked Lila one hell of a lot. But nothing would come from whatever was happening between them. By the time they started shooting the sequel, finally giving her the role she wanted, he'd be only a passing memory for her.

Clint hoped he got off that easy. He'd never met a woman like her. And beauty didn't have a damn thing to do with it.

On second thought, that wasn't true. The fact that she was gorgeous did have something to do with what he liked about her. The real pretty girls he'd known had almost always centered their life on their looks. Lila wasn't vain, and she wasn't looking for a golden ticket to fame. She must've had doors flinging open left and right...for a price. Instead, she worked hard for her shot.

Fifteen minutes later, he pulled into the motel parking lot. Baxter's red convertible was conspicuously absent. Good. After yesterday's fiasco, it had gotten so Clint couldn't stand to look at the guy.

Clint knew from his earlier conversation with Lila some of the crew were still wrapping up at the set. Tomorrow everyone had the day off, including her. Clint had subtly warned his dad he might not make it home tonight and to not count on him for tomorrow.

After he'd parked the truck, he hit speed dial.

Lila answered on the first ring.

"I'm here," he said. "Are you ready or do you want me to come up?"

"Oh, definitely come up."

The excitement in her voice made his heart lurch. "I'll be right there."

He paused to check his teeth in the rearview mirror. Then took the elevator instead of the stairs and made sure his shirt was evenly tucked into his jeans.

Before he could knock she opened the door, wearing tight black jeans, a snug sweater and the best smile.

Then he noticed her hair. "What happened?"

"What do you mean?"

"Your hair…" Most of it was pinned up in back and on the left side. The rest fell to the right of her face. It looked as though the tips had been dipped in black paint.

"Oh." Lila laughed and motioned him inside. "I forgot." She closed the door. "I've been experimenting."

"With paint?"

"No." She stared at him as if *he* was crazy. "Extensions."

"Okay. I think."

Smiling, Lila took his arm and led him to the table and chairs in the corner. He sat without her asking.

She stepped back and freed the silky cloud of blond hair. Then she reached underneath and pulled out what looked like a miniature, black-tipped donkey's tail.

"See? It isn't really my hair. It's called an extension."

"Why?"

She shrugged. "It's as good a name as any, I suppose."

"Not what I meant. Why would anyone want to put that thing in their hair?"

"You'd be surprised," she said, laughing, and continued to pull out the weird-looking tails.

"You do that often?" he asked, realizing he might've sounded critical. "You know…wear that kind of stuff?"

"Not me. But I do use them in my job."

"I'm glad," he said. "Your hair is way too pretty to mess with."

"Thank you." She moved closer. Close enough that he could smell the warm sweetness of her skin. She stepped between his spread legs and put her hands on his shoulders.

Every muscle in Clint's body tensed.

"It occurred to me that we hadn't discussed what we're doing tonight."

"No." Clint cleared his throat. He'd had someplace in mind, but for the life of him he couldn't remember. "No, we haven't."

"So, I took matters into my own hands," she said, and with a single smile reduced him to a tongue-tied teenager. "Oh, wait. I'll probably forget, so I should tell you before we get started."

Get started?

His brain seemed to stop working. Lila was talking,

but he hadn't caught any of it. Somehow he equated
the words to sex, and he couldn't make himself see it
any other way.

"Okay," she said, looking disappointed. "I'll probably go. Obviously you don't have to."

He took a deep breath. "Go where?"

"Shadow Creek." She paused, frowning. "Spencer's
ranch."

Clint waited expectantly.

"You didn't hear any of it, did you?"

"Guilty."

Lila grinned. "Erin and Spencer are having a barbecue tomorrow, and the whole crew is invited."

"A barbecue in December?"

"That's what I said." She shrugged. "Erin's a bigger wuss about the cold than I am, so I figure it can't
be too bad."

Clint put his hands on her waist and watched the tip
of her tongue sneak out and wet her lips. "Does that
include Baxter?"

"He's away until Monday."

"If you're going, count me in," he said, feeling the
slight sway of her body.

Her hair was tousled from shaking it out, and he sure
hoped she'd let him mess it up some more.

"To be honest, it'll probably turn into a bitchfest
about him. But we wouldn't have to stay long."

"Let's talk about tonight."

"Talk?" The corners of her moist lips tilted up. She
leaned closer. "I had something else in mind."

"Show me."

Lila smiled, and the way she shifted made him think
she was going to sit in his lap, but she reached across
the table for a paper sack he hadn't even noticed. The
movement caused his hands to slide over her round bot-

tom. She didn't seem to care. He wondered how she'd feel about a light squeeze.

She leaned back before he could find out.

"I picked up dinner," she said. "I thought we could eat in and just... I don't know—" She lifted a shoulder. "Kick back."

"Ah, that's Marge's cooking. I can't believe I didn't smell it before now."

"You were too worried about my hair."

"Yeah, I had a couple other things on my mind." He didn't like that she'd moved back to open the bag, and he caught her hand.

"Such as?"

"Trying to figure out just how determined you are to wreak havoc with my willpower."

"I'm not doing it on purpose."

He tugged her closer, and she voluntarily planted her nice, firm bottom on his lap. Too late he realized he should've made a minor fly adjustment.

She squirmed a bit, trying to get settled. "Oh, you really are happy to see me," she said, her eyes widening.

Damned if he could tell whether she was teasing or not. For some reason he thought she might be genuinely surprised. The woman was a mass of contradictions. Maybe he was the problem. He'd never realized it before, but he had a lot of ideas about Hollywood and actors. None of them very good.

"Want to know what I would really, really like?" she whispered, her voice a soft purr.

Clint knew one thing for sure. Those big blue eyes of hers could get a man in all kinds of serious trouble. "What's that?"

LILA PRESSED HERSELF against his broad chest, seeking his warmth and strength, craving the comfort she found in his arms. Obviously she knew it was impossible to actually melt into him, but she could pretend.

Nothing about how she felt around Clint made sense. Maybe this was part of the overall grieving process over her old life. She missed the relationship she used to have with Erin, and she missed her family. And working on location for three months? It wasn't anything like she'd imagined. She didn't mind the hard work, it wasn't that at all…

Clint wrapped his arms around her, and she lifted her chin and smiled at him.

He brushed a kiss across her mouth. "I'm waiting."

"For?"

"You were going to tell me what you wanted." His gold-flecked eyes had darkened, mesmerizing her, pulling her deeper into the sensual mist.

He was turned on, no denying the bulge she felt under her backside. But his voice and actions were calm, controlled. If she said no, he would back up three feet. And then step back another two just to be sure she didn't feel threatened.

Clint was a gentleman, and she didn't use the word often or lightly. What made him interesting…he was also hot. Superhot. Or as Erin would say, hot as hell.

"Tell me the truth, Clint Landers. Women must fall for you all the time," she said, watching his brows rise. "How long does it usually take? Five minutes? Ten?"

"Never that long." His lopsided smile set off a flutter in her tummy.

Maybe Erin was right. There was just something about a cowboy.

He lowered his head until his breath danced along the line of her jaw. "You have something to tell me," he murmured, his voice deep and raspy, tickling the skin at the side of her neck.

A minute ago all she'd wanted was a kiss. "You," she whispered. "And me. Naked." She took a small nip of his ear. "In that bed over there."

She felt something stir under her butt, and a giggle slipped from her lips.

Clint looked at her with a half smile.

"Is that okay?" Lila asked, remembering the food was still warm but it wouldn't be later. "Are you hungry? Would you rather eat first?"

His gaze fell to her mouth, lingered, before he claimed it with a searing kiss. Lifting her in his arms, he stood as she clung to him, tightening her hold around his neck without the slightest misgiving over what they were about to do.

He laid her down gently, keeping the kiss intact until the last possible second. Lila was already breathing hard as if she'd been the one doing all the lifting. After unzipping her, he tried to peel her jeans down her hips.

Lila smiled at his frustration. She should've warned him they wouldn't be easy.

He narrowed his gaze. "What did you do? Spray paint this thing on?"

"They aren't called skinny jeans for nothing." She kicked off her leather ballet flats, intent on helping him. But he managed to get the job done just fine by himself.

Getting up on her elbows, she started to take off her sweater. At the rapt look on his face, she froze.

Clint's gaze traveled the length of her bare legs, then he leaned down and fingered the red silk triangle of her thong. "If I were to turn you over, I believe I'd have a real nice surprise."

"I believe you're right."

His sexy smile gave her goose bumps their own baby goose bumps. He sat on the edge of the bed and slipped a finger under the silk. Thank heavens she'd given herself a wax job last week. His exploration was getting a bit thorough…he grazed her clit and she let out a gasp.

His dark eyes glittered with satisfaction, and more. So much more. Lila didn't think any man had ever wanted her as intensely as Clint did in this very moment. Desire blazed hot in his gaze. A muscle worked in his jaw.

He slid a hand under her sweater. His palm grazed the skin between her ribs until he found a nipple and thumbed it through the silk of her bra. "This is like Christmas morning. I don't know which package to unwrap first."

"Then let me decide." She yanked his shirt from his jeans and heard a snap pop. It didn't stop her from reaching for his belt. The buckle was too tricky for her to do one-handed.

Clint stood and pulled up her sweater. She lifted her arms so he could tug it off all the way. He tossed it on the other side of the bed, his gaze sweeping over her and coming to rest on her face.

She could feel her cheeks heat. Not from embarrassment or anything like that. She was excited, happy, and so turned on her panties had already skipped the damp phase. All day she'd been distracted knowing tonight she'd be able to see more than his bare chest. And hoping she'd be allowed to touch him all she wanted.

He unsnapped his cuff and then started on the other sleeve. "You mind taking that off for me," he said, nodding at her bra.

"Since you asked so nicely." She reached behind

and found the hook quickly, then let the cups slide off slowly.

Watching her with hooded eyes, his lips parted. His nostrils flared. He'd unsnapped the front of his shirt but he just stood there, staring, barely moving.

Finally he leaned toward her, but she scooted over to the other side of the bed. "Take your shirt off."

He could easily reach her if he wanted. But his slow smile told her he'd concede this round, and he shrugged out of the soft wool shirt. When he sat on the edge of the bed to pull off his boots, Lila ditched the bra entirely and came up on her knees behind him. She dragged her hard nipples across his back as she placed a kiss on his shoulder.

Clint shuddered.

His skin was hot, feverishly hot, making her breasts prickle as she pressed against him. He yanked off the second boot and twisted around. His mouth claimed hers, the fierceness of his kiss pushing her backward.

He covered her left breast with his hand and fingered the tight nipple. His tongue continued to stroke and tease, keeping her off balance. She couldn't reach his buckle, but she wanted his jeans gone. Now.

The lofty thought blurred when he bowed his head and sucked a nipple into his mouth. The slightly rough texture of his tongue did amazing things to her sensitive skin. Firming his lips, he tugged hard at the rigid peak, and she arched upward. His swift reflex was the only thing that kept her from toppling over. His arm curled around her waist and held her tight.

It was too late. She was already falling, tumbling out of control into a bottomless pit of heat and longing with nothing to latch on to but Clint.

11

His touch was magic, his mouth as hot as the noon sun. Clint knew just where to apply more pressure and when to use his teeth and tongue. Lila promised herself she wouldn't be distracted. She'd get him naked. But then he moved his mouth to her other breast, and she lost track of her thoughts.

The moment he eased back she gathered her wits.

His lips were damp, his expression confused as he watched her scramble off the bed. She knelt in front of him and got to work hastily undoing his belt. His impressive erection made the zipper trickier.

Clint touched her hair. "Why don't you let me do that," he said, lifting her chin and brushing a kiss across her lips.

Of course she didn't want to hurt him, but she couldn't help rubbing her palm against his fly as he pulled her up.

He drew in a sharp breath and let out a shaky laugh.

Once he was on his feet, in a matter of seconds he was completely naked.

Tall and lean, he had no tattoos or visible scars. His skin had a healthy glow to it And she zeroed in on his tapered waist and narrow hips. His thick aroused cock. He was a tempting package of strong, virile male.

Anticipation shuddered through her.

For God's sake, she had to stop staring. Although he wasn't shy about checking her out while he dug into his jeans pocket.

She yanked back the covers.

He dropped some packets on the nightstand. Two or three of them, she couldn't tell, but she applauded his optimism.

When he tugged her closer, she eagerly wound her arms around his neck. His hands gripped her waist as he looked into her eyes.

"You're off tonight, right?"

"I am."

"No last-minute phone call asking you to run to the set."

"Nope." She shook her head. "I'm all yours."

"Yeah?" Something thrilling and sexy burned in his dark eyes.

"For the whole night."

"I like the sound of that." Reaching around, he cupped her butt. He squeezed and pulled her flush against him.

The searing heat of his arousal pressed hard into her skin. She felt the moisture that slicked the crown as he backed her up. Her legs met the side of the bed. The next thing she knew, she was lying on her back and he'd stripped off her thong.

Her startled gasp was part giggle. "Sneaky."

"We were taking too long."

"We have all night, remember?"

"Don't worry." His gaze swept over her legs and hips,

practically daring her to squeeze her thighs together. "I'll make good use of the time."

A tremor spiraled through her body.

He pressed his right knee into the mattress. Leaning over her, he parted her thighs and kissed her.

Right there.

Slowly, he exerted a gentle pressure before thrusting his tongue past the seam and grazing her clit.

Gasping, she bucked against his mouth.

She loved foreplay, but she wouldn't last like this for long.

Clint kept her thighs parted, his tongue breaking contact only once while he climbed completely on the mattress and settled between her legs. He looked up, his gaze drawn to her left breast. Reaching a hand to touch it, he kissed her lower belly, his dark eyes focused on her nipple. He rubbed his thumb over the jutting flesh, and she held her breath.

He moved his hand to the other breast and gave the tight bud a light pinch.

Lila moaned.

"Are you always this sensitive?"

She bit her lip and shook her head.

His brows furrowed. "Am I hurting you?"

"No." She lifted her shoulders off the mattress and caught his face between her hands. They looked at each other for a long moment before she slid her fingers into his hair and tugged at him, guiding his mouth to her breast.

He rolled his tongue over the distended nipple before it disappeared into his mouth. He sucked, blew some air on the damp flesh, then sucked again. She could tell he was holding back. Probably still worried she was too sensitive.

Clutching at his muscled arm, keeping his hand where she wanted it, she whispered, "Is that the best you can do, cowboy?"

His short, rumbling laugh vibrated against her skin and all the way to her core.

Clint did exactly as requested. And at the same time, inserted a finger inside her.

Lila jerked at the sly move. A moan mingled with laughter spilled from her lips. "Wait," she said.

He lifted his head, but kept his finger right where it was. "What?"

"I can't reach you."

Ignoring her, he bowed his head. Switching to her other nipple, he sucked it deeply. As he worked in a second finger, his thumb found her clit. She couldn't stay still, not with his thumb circling and circling, his fingers plunging in farther. But with every move, he stayed with her, increasing the pressure until want turned to a throbbing need.

She closed her eyes, squeezing them tight, willing her body to slow down. Not react so swiftly. But she'd already lost control. The ache for release was too great…

Her whimper of protest was cut short.

The orgasm hit her full force. It gripped her with the power of a tornado, tossing her around like a rag doll as the fire inside her flared. She opened her eyes to slits, but couldn't see through the red-hot haze.

Beneath her palm she felt a cord of muscle. Her fingernails were digging into Clint's arm. Unfazed by it, he stayed with her the whole time, easing back when it became too much, as if he had the ability to read her every move, her every moan.

Finally the inferno became soothing warmth that washed over her body in slow languid waves.

Her hands fell like lead weights to the mattress. She wanted to touch him, his shoulders and the muscles rippling with each tiny movement. She wanted to run her palms along the hard planes of his toned body. And she wanted to feel the long thick length of him, wrap her fingers around the smooth taut skin. But she couldn't seem to make her hands or arms work.

Clint shifted and claimed her mouth with a bone-melting kiss. "Hi," he said, his smile strained at the edges, his eyes dark with banked desire.

"Hi," she murmured, barely having enough breath to get out the tiny word.

He cupped the side of her face, and she turned her head to nuzzle his hand. A tremor passed through his body. Her shuddering response shot all the way to the soles of her feet.

His hair was mussed and his lips damp. He slid down to place a soft kiss on her inner thigh.

She widened her eyes, fully alert. He couldn't possibly—

He lapped at the moist, protective folds of her sex.

Squirming, she tried to clamp her thighs together. "Clint." Her mouth had gone dry. "Clint, stop."

His head came up instantly. "Too sensitive?"

"No, it's not that." Shifting to lie on her side, she caught his arm. "Come here," she said, patting the mattress.

Surprise flickered in his eyes, but he did as she asked and settled next to her. Stretched out on his side, elbow bent, he propped his head and faced her. Their eyes met and she smiled at him. But then she got distracted by his bulging biceps.

"Are you going to tell me what's wrong?"

"Hmm?" she murmured, staring at the bunched muscle until she couldn't stand it. She had to touch. "Nothing's wrong." She laid a hand on his arm. Beneath her palm, the rock-hard muscle tensed.

His arousal stirred against her tummy.

That's what she really wanted.

Reaching between them, she wrapped a hand around his hot hard length. One long stroke, and his groan nearly shook the bed.

She got in two more pumps before he grabbed her wrist, keeping her immobile, while he blindly reached behind and almost knocked over the lamp. Cursing under his breath, he finally had to release her so he could search the top of the nightstand.

He found a condom, managing to dodge her hand at the same time.

"Wait," she said when he tore the packet. "Not yet."

"Why?"

"Just give me a minute. Three minutes. That's all I'm asking for."

Clint looked thoroughly and adorably confused.

She slid down for a taste. Salty. Spicy. All male. She licked the head dry.

With another groan, his hands tangled in her hair. He started to pull her away, and then his hold slackened. He gulped for air. Whispered something too raw and broken for her to understand.

Closing her mouth around him, she sucked lightly at first, then harder. She moved her way down, stroking him with her tongue, but she only made it partway.

"No," he said, his voice hoarse. "Not like this."

Lila felt another tug at her scalp. This time he wasn't fooling around. Too bad. She flicked her tongue and slid down to the base.

"C'mon, Lila..." He cut off a groan and fisted a handful of her hair. "You're killing me here."

Reluctantly she released him. "I didn't make *you* stop."

He was already rolling on the condom. "Really?" he said with a cocked brow. "You're going to pout?"

"Maybe." Tilting her head to the side, she licked her lips. He surprised her by rising, making her gasp as he laid her back against the pillows and pushed her legs apart.

Slipping between them, he ran a finger along her slick wet lips. "Have anything more to say?"

Watching his nostrils flare, seeing how ready he was, her heart pounded out of control. "Please?" she whispered, struggling for air when he slid his finger in partway.

Clint leaned down for a kiss. The moment their lips touched, she felt him enter her. Just a little. He pulled back when her body tried to grip him.

She narrowed her eyes in warning.

He just smiled and rubbed her with the tip of his cock, teasing her, stroking her where she was most sensitive, small calculated movements, sliding up and down, in and out, and making her crazy.

And pushing her too close to another orgasm.

But he was torturing himself, too. She could see the strain in his face, the muscle flexing in his jaw. He wasn't going to last...

But then Lila wouldn't, either. He slipped a little ways inside her, and she rocked up to meet him.

Clint froze, his body tensing. His gaze seemed to scorch her to the core.

He thrust into her. Hard and deep. His muscled arms

shook with the effort of keeping his weight off her. He withdrew just a little, then surged into her again.

Their moans tangled and filled the room as Clint filled her, stretching her beyond the border of anything she'd experienced before.

"Ah, Christ," he murmured, and pulled her legs tightly around his hips.

She gripped him for all she was worth as he plunged inside her. He did it again and again, his hoarse groan echoing in her ears as she felt the first hint of her climax.

Clint's low primal cry was enough to trigger her release. Arching beneath him, she was beyond thinking, beyond speaking, beyond anything other than feeling him explode inside her. Or maybe it was her body that had burst into a million glittering pieces shooting into the darkness.

A tremor racked her all the way to her soul. Her lungs burned with the need for air. And yet she felt as if she were floating…

"Lila." Clint's ragged whisper penetrated the fog. He dislodged her legs from his hips.

She felt his arm slide beneath her shoulders, and he hauled her up against him, chest to chest. He put his other arm around her and before she knew it, he'd rolled onto his back, taking her with him, his cock still sheathed inside her.

Of course he wasn't hard anymore, but it amazed her that she could still feel his heft. All she seemed capable of was lifting her chin. He pushed back the tangle of hair that covered half her face, then slowly traced her bottom lip with his forefinger.

She sighed with contentment, not even trying to move. "I see you've done this before."

Clint smiled. "Yeah, a couple times."

"Good Lord. I think you've worn me out."

Her breathing was too shallow for her to be talking. She had to rest and regroup. She wouldn't turn down some water, either. A gallon would probably do it.

"Where are you going?" With a hand cupping her butt, he stopped her from rolling off.

"Water. The bathroom. And more water."

He nodded, looking so serious. "We're not done."

Lila laughed and shivered at the same time. "No, we aren't," she agreed and gave him a quick kiss before she rolled off him.

After being awake a few minutes, Clint finally opened his eyes. Moonlight poured in through the window past the partially open drapes. Careful not to disturb Lila, he barely moved. He sure was glad tomorrow was Sunday and neither of them had to work. Even if he did have to share her for part of the day.

She was laying on her side, curled toward him, one leg thrown over his, her pale hair spilling across his chest.

In a matter of weeks she'd be gone, and he didn't know if he'd ever see her again. She had a bright and busy future. Too bright to be sneaking off with a cowboy for a weekend here and there. Hell, that wouldn't be enough for him, anyway.

The notion was worrisome. That sort of thinking would only lead to trouble. So far they'd had sex twice since he'd arrived for their date. He glanced at the clock. It was 2:20 a.m. Technically, already Sunday. They'd stopped fooling around to eat cold fried chicken and cornbread. He smiled thinking about the staggering amount of honey she'd used to drown her cornbread.

The woman sure loved her sugar. Maybe that's what made her hair and skin smell so sweet. And man, the way she tasted…

Shit.

What was wrong with him, anyway? Having those sappy thoughts? He'd never been that kind of guy.

She snuggled deeper against his chest, and the flood of warmth that flowed through his body was unlike any other feeling he'd ever had.

"Are you awake?" she whispered.

"Sort of. You?"

Her laugh was husky with sleep. "What time is it?"

"Two-thirty-ish." Tightening his arm around her, he kissed her hair. Damned if he wasn't getting hard again.

Lila sighed. "It's Sunday. No setting the alarm. Yay."

"What time is the barbecue?"

"Around three. But I told Erin I'd go early to help."

Maybe he'd drop her off and run home, shower, change. "I should've brought extra clothes."

She lifted her head and looked at him with sleepy blue eyes. "Why didn't you?"

"I didn't want to jinx it."

"Jinx what?"

Clint touched the tip of her nose. "Don't give me that innocent look. Anyway, I should run home at some point. Won't take me long. I wonder what we should do in the meantime…" he said, cupping her breast.

She shivered and swelled to his touch. "Hmm, I wonder," she whispered, slowly stretching out on top of him.

12

THE WEATHER WASN'T half bad for a barbecue. Well, considering it was *December*, Lila thought. Red jumped to his feet and opened the patio door for her. Juggling two large platters, she smiled her thanks and braced herself before she stepped out onto the patio.

A light gust of cold air greeted her, but that wasn't the reason she paused by the door. She smiled as she watched Clint flip steaks and burgers on the massive stainless-steel barbecue. He looked right at home, sipping from a bottle of beer and keeping close tabs on the progress of the meat.

About half the crew had shown up. The wranglers were wandering around the barns and stable. Some of the guys were watching a televised football game in Spencer's den. With the exception of Rhonda, Davis and the new camera assistant sitting around a fire pit at the other end of the patio, the rest of the crew had gathered in the rec room to gripe about one thing or another.

Lila was having fun helping Erin in the kitchen. Mostly it was the other way around. Lila loved to cook and bake, and Erin was always much happier to have no part of it whatsoever.

Clint had dropped her off at Shadow Creek, zipped home and still arrived ahead of everyone else. Erin had put him to work assisting Spencer. The two men had hit it off right away, which made Lila stupidly happy. What did it matter? Sure it made for a more pleasant afternoon. But to expect anything beyond today? She knew better.

"Wow, you're in some serious like." Erin had come up behind her, a beer in each hand.

"No." Lila rolled her eyes and slid another peek at Clint. "Maybe." She sighed. "Okay, I'm pretty screwed."

Erin grinned. "Why? He's a good guy."

Clint must've heard them because he turned and smiled.

Lila smiled back. He returned his attention to the grill, and she sighed. "What difference does it make?" She'd lowered her voice. "I mean, I do like him and we're having fun. But you know how it is in this crazy business…" She looked her friend directly in the eyes. "What about you and Spencer?"

Erin blinked and took a sudden interest in the bottles she was holding. "Oh, here," she said, trying to pass a beer to Lila.

"You can't tell me you haven't been wondering what's going to happen once we wrap up here."

"Of course I have. But am I going to discuss it now? Here?" She glanced around, mostly for effect. "No."

"You always were a bad actress." Lila grabbed a bottle and twisted off the top.

"Never claimed to be one at all," Erin replied.

Clint glanced back at them. "The meat's done. You want to hand me that platter?"

"Coming right up," Lila said, and then to Erin, "To be continued."

"I can hardly wait."

Ignoring her, Lila moved close to Clint and kissed his jaw.

He lifted a brow in surprise.

No one had asked why he was here. Besides Spencer and Dusty, who worked at Shadow Creek, Clint was the only other outsider.

She took a whiff of the sizzling steaks. "Oh, my God, I think I'm going to faint." At his look of alarm, she grinned and set the beer aside. "These smell crazy good. How about I hold the platter while you transfer the steaks over?"

"What about the burgers?"

"I don't care what you do with those."

Clint laughed. Leaning closer as he reached for the tongs, he murmured in that low, raspy tone she loved, "I want to kiss you all the way into next Sunday." He straightened and returned to his normal voice. "Pick out a steak, and I'll set it aside for you. Medium is on the right."

She'd thought for sure he'd been about to bite her ear-lobe. "Thanks, now I'm one big goose bump, you rat."

His mouth curved in a self-satisfied, purely male grin. He glanced behind them before going to work filling the first platter. "Why do all these folks think I'm here?"

"Because Erin invited you."

"That's all?"

"I'm sure there's been talk…"

"You do realize you kissed me."

"On the jaw." She grinned and pressed her leg against his. "Only because I couldn't reach your mouth."

"Warn me next time. I'd be happy to cooperate."

"Hey, I didn't mean to desert you." Spencer's voice came from behind. "I got cornered by—"

Lila hastily moved away from Clint, as if she'd just been caught raiding the Christmas candy. She couldn't explain her reaction. Reflex?

"And now I'm interrupting." Spencer hesitated, even when Lila turned to smile at him.

"Of course you aren't. As a matter of fact, you're just in time." She held up the platter piled high with steaks. "Mind taking this to the kitchen?"

"No, ma'am. It's the least I can do after leaving Landers here to do the grilling."

Clint chuckled, and as soon as she'd lifted the second platter, he started loading that one, too. "This is a damn nice barbecue. Makes me wonder why I'm still using charcoal and an old barrel."

"Because you aren't lazy," Spencer said, laughing. "Want me to wait for that other platter?"

"Thanks, but I can manage," Lila said, but almost dropped it when Clint pushed the steaks to the side to make room for the burgers. It weighed a ton. "Didn't know you were feeding a whole regiment, did you?"

"Good thing I'm in the cattle business," Spencer said with a grin and started toward the door. "Clint, you want another beer?"

"Maybe later."

"Oh." Lila nodded to the bottle she'd taken from Erin. "That's for you. I took a couple sips."

"Thanks," he muttered, focused on scraping the grill with a spatula. "You know if there's anything else to go on here?"

"Erin didn't say." Lila could tell something was wrong, and she hated that she might've made things awkward between them. "I'll go ask."

He caught her arm as she turned. "I understand why you'd want to be cautious around the crew. I've got no problem with that," he said, and then with a self-deprecating smile added, "Not that you should care what I think."

"I'm not trying to downplay anything, but I knew you'd think that and I'm sorry. I can't tell you why I…" Lila sighed. "Half the guys have already hooked up with locals. It's practically a tradition when a movie's on location, but I never do, so…"

"It doesn't matter." He squeezed her arm, and while he tried to hide it, she caught his little satisfied smile. "Why don't you take that inside and find out if there's anything else for me to grill before I turn this off."

"Okay," she said, nodding. "Wait. What do you mean turn it off?"

"It's gas. No charcoal mess, just on, off, done. Plus it's hooked up to the line going into the house. I'm gonna steal the idea for the home I'm building."

Lila thought she'd heard wrong. "You're building a house?"

He glanced up, looking very much like a man who wanted to kick himself. It made her all the more curious. "I have plans to build. Just not at the moment."

"How exciting," she said, and meant it, if only for a second. A man usually built a house when he was ready to settle down. Start a family. Did he have a woman in mind? Clint had denied having a girlfriend, and she'd believed him. She still did. That didn't mean he wasn't narrowing down prospects. "Where will you build? Around here?"

He nodded. "You should get the meat inside before it gets cold."

"Oh. Right."

She hurried to the kitchen where Erin started firing questions at her. For a smart woman, Erin was terrible at coordinating cooking times. Lila was glad she was too busy to worry about anything but getting the food to the table without turning every dish into jerky.

Clint had done as instructed and undercooked the burgers and steaks so they could be finished in the oven. Spencer had thought of that little trick though, not Erin. Lila would've keeled over if her friend had put that much thought into anything related to cooking. But what really interested Lila was why Clint had urged her inside with the steaks. Obviously he'd regretted mentioning the house and wanted the subject dropped. And now she wondered why.

Dinner was a boisterous affair, everyone talking over everyone else as if they didn't live in one another's pockets. But finally the dishwasher was loaded, and most of the gang had settled on couches and chairs, or on the floor in the rec room. It took all of thirty seconds before the conversation turned to Baxter.

"Is the prick going to be around for the sequel, too?" Red asked just as Lila entered the room.

Clint immediately got up from the recliner he'd nabbed.

Lila motioned for him to sit back down. "We'll share," she said, and then sat on his lap.

Practically everyone in the room stared at her.

"Really, guys?" She swept her glare around. "I wish you'd paid this much attention when we needed help washing pots."

Clint's chuckle tickled her ear. She snuggled back against him, and he wrapped an arm around her as she got comfy.

Charlie cleared his throat. "I hope not," the grizzled wrangler said in his tobacco-roughened voice, referring to Baxter. "That kid's got as much sense as a hen's got teeth."

"Hell, that's giving him too much credit." Red looked at Erin as she and Spencer joined them. "Erin, you must know. Tell me that kid ain't hanging around for the sequel."

After a brief hesitation, she said, "Probably, he will."

"Probably?" Frowning, Red gave up his seat on the couch for Erin. "You don't know for sure?"

Spencer walked straight to the fireplace and took his time adding logs to the fire. He knew something. Lila had seen his jaw tighten before he'd turned his back to them. Obviously Erin had confided in him.

It was silly for Lila to feel hurt, but she did.

"Okay. Look…" Erin huffed an exasperated sigh. "He's a pain in the ass. I know that, and I'm not asking you to go out of your way to be nice to him—"

"Shiiit," the camera crew drawled in unison.

"Yeah, if I'm going outta my way," Red said, "it'll be to wrap his goddamn Beemer around his goddamn fat head."

Laughter took over. They sounded like a bunch of preschoolers. Normally Erin would've told them to shut up. Shrinking back against the couch, she looked as though she'd rather disappear.

She met Lila's eyes and quickly looked away.

"Baxter's scared of you," Tony said to Erin. "He wets himself every time you look at him. You're going to be first AD. Can't you give him the boot?"

Lila stared at her friend. Unlike everyone else, Lila wasn't waiting for her reply.

Holy crap.

Erin wouldn't look at her.

It didn't matter. Lila had already seen the telltale twitch. So tiny, it was easy to miss. For anyone who didn't know Erin inside and out.

The recent lack of enthusiasm, the avoidance, the short temper... Erin's behavior hadn't made sense. Exhaustion had nothing to do with it. What if it had something to do with the first AD's position Jason promised her? She'd sacrificed a year of her life for a shot at it.

No, that was too extreme. Jason wouldn't screw her over. He depended on her too much.

Now, Baxter, he'd been a problem from day one. Erin was angry about being saddled with him. Jason had forced the idiot on her in exchange for his uncle's money. Lila had assumed that after they wrapped, that would be the end of Baxter. Now, she wasn't sure what to think.

The timing had thrown Lila. Erin had met Spencer two months ago. And talk about falling hard. This thing with him wasn't a passing fling, so it had been easy to miss the real reason Erin's head wasn't in the game.

Baxter must be an even bigger problem than Lila had guessed. Had to be. But what was worse by far, Erin hadn't told her. Hadn't turned to Lila for comfort or help. And that cut went deep.

Clint's arm tightened around her. "Hey," he whispered, "you okay?"

"Fine." Her whole body had tensed, and her pulse ramped up. "Just tired."

"You want to go?"

"I think I do," she murmured, aware Erin hadn't looked at her even once.

THEY DROVE BACK to town mostly in silence. Clint felt helpless, something he'd just discovered he wasn't good at. He'd never been the controlling type, or maybe he'd just never been tested. Clint had pretty much run the Whispering Pines since the day after he'd quit college. Lucky for him, the operation ran exactly how he wanted it to run. On the not so lucky front, the ranch had become the sum total of his life.

Right now, he'd do just about anything to get Lila to smile.

Except he didn't think there was one damn thing he could say or do that would cheer her up.

She stared out the window at the semidarkness, fidgeting with her hands, and surely setting some kind of record for sighs per minute. He doubted she realized she was making a sound.

"I'll go beat up Baxter if you want me to," he teased, and she turned, eyes widening. "Say the word."

Her unexpected grin lit up the darkest corner of his soul. "I don't care about Baxter."

"Something sure has gotten you down."

With another sigh, she turned to look out the window again. Not many stars had made a showing yet.

"You know what we could do," he said. "Drive over to Kalispell and look at the Christmas lights. Not just downtown, either. I heard some of the neighborhoods go all out."

"Oh, that would be fun," she said, "but not tonight. I hope that doesn't disappoint you."

"Nope. I just want to see you happy."

"Oh, I'm sorry. You were great about going to the barbecue, and now I'm being a spoilsport."

"I had a good time, and I'm glad I met Spencer. Interesting guy."

Lila nodded. "I don't think I could've picked anyone

more perfect for Erin. At least that's going well, so—"
She stopped short. "So that's great."

Clint wished she would've finished what she'd
started to say. Hell, he wished for a lot of things when
it came to Lila.

She surprised him by reaching over and brushing a
lock of hair off his forehead.

"I didn't mean to startle you," she said, snatching
her hand back.

"But in a good way."

"Yeah?"

He heard the smile in her voice, and he pulled the
truck off to the side of the highway.

"What are you doing?" She straightened in her seat.
"Is something wrong—?"

His aim was bad in the darkening cab. Their lips
met clumsily. They both smiled, and then everything
lined up perfectly: lips, tongues, lightly nibbling teeth…

He touched her hair, savoring the feel of the soft,
silky strands. Her lips were soft, too, and so was her
skin. He'd given up trying to understand how it could
feel like velvet and satin at the same time. Her whispered sighs floated into the night.

Two hours ago he'd cut himself off, drank his
last beer. But it was Lila and her seductive scent he
should've been worried about. The sweet smell of her
skin intoxicated him like no alcohol ever had. It made
him think foolish thoughts. Made him long for things
he had no business wasting energy on.

Knowing he could never have a woman like her for
keeps didn't dull the want.

They were five minutes from town. He wasn't crazy
about them sitting there, making out on the side of the
highway, but there was no way of telling if she planned

on inviting him to her room. Just coming out and asking didn't feel right.

They broke apart for some air.

"Let's run away for a week," he said, the words tumbling out of his mouth before he knew it.

"Let's." She laughed. "Wait. Only a week?"

"A month?"

"Keep going."

"Don't tease me, Lila. That's not funny."

With a wistful sigh, she leaned in for another kiss. Her soft lips sent a jolt straight to his groin. "Who's teasing?"

His heart lurched. Why was he being so stupid? Just because he'd seen another side to her. Yeah, he'd been surprised when she'd taken over the kitchen the minute she arrived. The way she'd issued orders and went right to work sorting through pots and casserole dishes reminded him of his mom on holidays. The kitchen turned into a well-oiled machine, and everyone knew who was boss.

He doubted Lila was the only actor who knew how to cook, but he'd expected her to be more like Erin, who'd clearly been out of her comfort zone. She was a mini-tyrant on the set, but in the kitchen she waited like a puppy for Lila's instructions.

He caught a set of headlights in the rearview mirror. "Guess we'd better go."

Lila glanced back. "Where?"

"Anywhere you want."

She smiled. "How about Canada?"

Clint chuckled. "A minute ago I couldn't get you to go to Kalispell."

"Canada is less than two hundred miles away, right?"

The small SUV sped past them, and he eased the

truck back onto the highway. "Yep, to the border," he said, not sure what to make of her almost desperate tone. "With nothing but nowhere land on both sides."

"Sounds perfect," she said softly and kind of wistfully again. "Except we're going back to town, aren't we?"

He looked at her. "You're serious?"

She smiled. "Jeez. Would you listen to me?" she said, shaking her head. "Being so selfish. You probably have a million chores to catch up on."

No, he was the selfish prick. Something was really bothering her, and his mind kept rebounding to sex. He saw the turnoff for Cherry Point and made a split-second decision.

13

THE TRUCK BOUNCED over a pothole. Lila threw a hand out and clutched the dashboard. "Where in the world are we going?"

"Cherry Point. The best high school make-out spot in three counties. At least it used to be." Damn, he was old.

"Cherry Point. Really?" She squinted past the windshield into the gathering darkness.

"Hey, I didn't make up the name."

"I would've forgiven you if we're going to make out."

"I'm sure we'll get around to that, but first—"

Her phone buzzed.

"You might want to get that," he said, slowing down. "I can't say we'll have a signal for long."

She peered into the forest of tall, dense pines all around them. "You really are going to take advantage of me, aren't you? Or maybe I'll take advantage of you. Either works for me—or both."

Clint smiled. "Is that a yes or no on taking the call?"

"What? Oh." She shook her head, her pale hair catching the moonlight and shimmering like it had been sprinkled with fairy dust. "I know who it is. It can wait."

"I don't mind getting out and giving you privacy."

She smiled and brushed the stubborn lock off his forehead again.

He'd brought her here to talk. His brain understood, but his body responded to even her briefest touch. Talk first, he reminded himself, then...

Well, that depended on a lot of things that he'd be a fool to forget.

He stopped the truck and brought her fingers to his lips. He kissed the tip of each one before pressing his mouth to her soft palm.

"Here?" A shudder shook her shoulders as she glanced around at the eerie shadows. "This is the famous Cherry Point?"

"No. Farther into the woods."

"It's kind of spooky."

"I would never take you anywhere dangerous," he said, and she looked at him. "But if this is making you nervous, we'll turn back."

"I know you wouldn't." She curled her fingers around his hand.

"I'd always keep you safe." He touched her cheek, stroking his thumb down the velvety softness. Feeling self-conscious all of a sudden, he stopped. "Does it bother you that my hands are rough?"

"No." She gripped his wrist, preventing him from lowering his hand.

"But you're so soft..."

"I like it."

"But—"

"Clint." She moved closer. "I like it when you touch me. And when you kiss me," she said, leaning close enough he felt her breath on his chin.

His cock jerked against the denim fly.

Her lips grazed his.

"Shit," he muttered, not meaning to say it out loud. "Sorry."

"It's okay."

"I didn't bring you here for this." He ordered himself to stand down, to use his brain and not his dick.

"I don't understand."

"I wanted us to talk."

She sank back. "Talk about what?"

"Look, I know something's bothering you. And I figured out here where it's dark, you might be more comfortable and—" He shrugged, relaxed his clenched jaw. "If you need someone to listen, or if there's some way I can help..." Gritting his teeth, he scrubbed at his face. "I don't know what I'm saying. I'm way out of my depth here."

Lila's soft laugh loosened the knot coiling in his gut. "Well, sure, you used the word talk. With a woman. Ever done that before?"

"Never."

"That's what I thought." Her grin was contagious.

"Don't poke fun," he said. "It's a humbling experience."

"Yes, but now you've made it over the biggest hurdle. The first time is always the hardest."

Clint laughed. She got that wrong. The hardest part was fixing to bust through his fly at this very moment. Trying to ignore it was no picnic, either.

Her phone rang again.

Lila pulled it out of her pocket as if she dreaded the call. "It's my sister," she said, her tone flat. "She wants to know when I'm coming home for Christmas. I'll just be a minute." She sighed before answering. "Hey, Brit, what's up?"

Her voice had changed in an instant, even her expression had transformed. As if she'd slipped into a different role.

"Just flurries, mostly. I heard we might get slammed next week." She paused. "I think you should go shopping without me."

Clint did her the courtesy of turning his face away. Naturally she didn't care that he could hear her side of the conversation. Lila was acting now. Controlling the inflection of her voice. Her sister couldn't tell a damn thing about her mood. Of course, neither could he. Whatever Lila was feeling was locked tight inside.

Nathan's first wife popped into his head. It occurred to him that Anne had used her acting skills to keep his brother in the dark about a big part of her life. He had no idea why she'd been so secretive, but finding out the truth after her death had nearly done Nathan in.

Lila sure didn't owe Clint anything. They barely knew each other. He couldn't help wondering, though, if things were different, would he worry she was hiding her true feelings from him?

"I didn't say that, Britney. I can't promise, but that doesn't mean I'm not trying." A small crack in her voice had her shifting in her seat. "You know what… I should've mentioned now isn't a good time. How about I call you tomorrow?"

Clint stared out his window at a curious young buck standing several feet away in the brush.

"I am not." Lila let out a sound of frustration. Apparently she'd quit holding back. "I'm on a date, okay? Oh, God. Fine. Clint?" She held the phone near his face. "Would you please say something to my sister?"

"Um, sure. Hi, Lila's sister… Britney. Right?"

A high-pitched squeal nearly pierced his eardrum.

Lila quickly took back the phone. "Happy?" She bit off a giggle. "Shut up. Goodbye."

Britney's excited voice was still audible as Lila disconnected. She stuffed the phone in her pocket, then pulled it back out.

"I need to turn it off or she'll drive me nuts." She took care of that and said, "Where were we? You said something about making out?"

Clint shook his head. "I'm starting to worry. Everyone is shocked to see you with a man. I hope you're not one of those black widow serial killers."

Grinning, she reached over and cupped the back of his neck. "You found me out," she said, pulling him toward her. "Now I'm going to kiss you to death."

"You sound awfully chipper when you talk about murder," he said, well aware that he'd stopped trying to get her to open up to him. He felt her smile against his lips. And he did something he'd been *dying* to do all afternoon.

Clint slipped his hand under her sweater and cupped her breast. Her nipple was hard beneath the silky barrier of her bra. With a quiet whimper, she shifted so that it was easy for him to dip a finger into the cup. Soft, soft skin surrounded the stiff nipple. A pale pink normally, by now it would have turned three shades darker.

He remembered every detail from last night. How her lips and nipples flushed as her arousal heightened. And how she bit her bottom lip a lot, trying to stifle her loud moans of pleasure. When that hadn't worked, she had put a hand over her mouth. Clint had enjoyed peeling her fingers away and thrusting his tongue between her lips, kissing her long and hard until they'd both gasped for air.

After he'd worked her bra strap down her shoulder

a bit, he managed to lower the cup and free her breast. The creamy flesh almost filled his hand. She was the perfect size, not too big, and all her, nothing fake or un-natural about the feel as he kneaded gently.

He wanted to put his mouth on her. Flick his tongue quick and light the way he knew she liked it. He had offered to listen if she needed to talk. Nothing more he could do on that front. It was up to her.

Avoiding the gearshift, she pressed against him, parting her lips and welcoming his tongue with a light suction and then meeting him stroke for stroke. The sweet taste of her mouth lured him closer, deeper. The warm scent of her skin, the firm, silky feel of her round breast…

Clint stiffened against the speed and intensity of his body's response. The woman was going to send him straight into cardiac arrest.

She arched into his palm and moaned, the sound coming from somewhere at the back of her throat. Her nails dug into his forearm. Heat surged through his body. Distorted his senses. Almost made him forget they were sitting in his truck in the cold night air. As far as he was concerned, they could stay right where they were and wait for summer.

He broke the kiss and dragged in a lungful of air, hoping that would clear his head. What he got was a strong whiff of her arousal.

Jesus.

Lila cupped his fly.

He froze, braced himself. His cock throbbed. He wanted to believe he had more self-control now than he'd had as a teenager. But damn. Maybe she really was trying to kill him. It wouldn't be a bad way to go.

She applied more pressure and started rubbing him,

which caused way too much of a ruckus inside his body. He clamped a hand around her wrist, and she stopped.

"We should've gone straight to the motel," she murmured and licked his chin up to his lips.

He leaned back, but she just kept licking any part of him she could get to. Finally he put enough distance between them.

"Spoilsport," she said, sinking back. "You can let go of my wrist."

"I don't trust you."

Her lips lifted in a devilish smile. "Why?"

"You can't touch me like that."

"Like what?"

"C'mon, Lila, you can't expect me not to—"

Her free hand came at him like a bullet.

"Like this?" she asked, pressing her palm against his cock, rubbing up and down, the thick denim offering no protection.

He groaned through gritted teeth. "Goddamn it, Lila." The curse had slipped out, but she'd get no apology this time. He was about to explode with frustration. She was going to make him come, and he didn't want that. Not now. "Can we wait until we get to town?"

"Um…" She paused. "No."

Clint blocked her next move. Good to know he still had his high school football reflexes.

Calmly she reached around him and cut the engine. "Thanks," she said, looking him in the eyes, "for offering to listen. I need this more."

Absorbing the meaning behind her words, he nodded slowly.

Dumb cowboy.

Took him long enough to get it. He was her distraction. Not that he felt *used*. Or regretted any part he played in her life this last week. But he wasn't special. He'd seen how the men in the crew had eyed him. That and knowing she rarely dated had turned his head some.

For whatever reason, she felt safe with him, felt confident that he understood this was just a fling. That it would all come to an end the day the movie wrapped and she left. Or it could end tomorrow.

He gazed into her expectant eyes. "Is that so?"

Smiling, she nodded and reached for his fly.

"Hold on." He took her hand and entwined their fingers. "I didn't say you could have your way with me."

Laughter burst from her lips.

He cupped her chin and brought her face closer. "Kiss me."

She was still trying to lose the grin as she leaned forward. He covered her mouth with his, then slowly turned up the heat while he moved his hand to find her zipper. Her tongue circled his, then swept around his mouth demanding he join the dance. The kiss was supposed to sidetrack her, not him.

He had her unbuttoned and unzipped fairly quickly, and then felt her tremble. "You cold?"

"Mostly just excited."

Clint smiled at her honesty and paused to restart the engine and adjusted the vents to get the heat circulating. "Think you'd be warm enough without your sweater?"

Lila stared at him, her eyes widening as she nodded. The determined temptress was gone, leaving behind a young woman who looked unsure of herself. This wasn't the first unguarded moment he'd glimpsed of Lila. But he had a feeling these brief displays of vulnerability were rare.

He waited a few moments, but she didn't whip off her

sweater. Guess it was up to him. The space was tight, so it was awkward, but he managed to lift the sweater over her head.

Next Clint sprung the front clasp of the bra, and she did her part by letting the straps slide off her shoulders. Her smooth ivory skin glowed in the moonlit cab. The tips of her breasts were a dark rose, just as he'd expected. He touched the right one.

"Wait." Shivering, she barely got the word out. "What about you?"

He pushed her hair aside and kissed her neck. "What about me?" he murmured, and trailed his lips to her throat. Her little whimper spurred him on. Using the tip of his tongue, he traced the ridge of her delicate collarbone.

Her head fell back, and she made a soft contented sound.

Sucking her nipple into his mouth, he slipped a hand inside her jeans.

Lila inhaled with a quick shallow gasp. "Clint."

His name fell from her lips in a breathy whisper. An earthy muskiness laced her sweet scent, and a surge of lust shot through his veins. She bucked against his hand. He felt the tension slowly ease from her muscles.

He parted her with his fingers and slid them into her wet heat. Her clit had swelled. He thumbed it as he pumped his fingers in and out.

The sound of their ragged breathing filled the cab.

"Clint, what are you— Oh… God—" She'd brought her head partway up, then let it fall back against the headrest with a thump.

He smiled.

She'd said she needed this, and he was happy to give

it to her. Hell, he'd give her anything she wanted, anything that he was capable of providing, anyway.

For now, he hoped it would be the best damn climax she'd ever had—well, one of the best. What happened last night while he'd been inside her… He didn't think it was just his ego.

And after the fireworks, he was going to drop her off at the motel and then go straight home to talk to his dad. Put his mind at ease. Clint would let him know he was ready to take over the ranch. Why wait until after Christmas? What else did he have in his future besides the Whispering Pines?

Not Lila. No matter how much he fantasized or tried to read things into her sweet smiles and soft looks. This fling was just that to her. He was merely a stop on her bullet train to a big and glamorous life. And he sure as hell couldn't complain because she'd never led him to believe otherwise.

Giving his dad his word meant a lot to Clint…enough to clear the muck in his head. There'd be no more room for wishful thinking.

After that was done, he planned on spending every free minute he could with Lila. Until they'd screwed each other's brains out and he'd no longer have the capacity to understand she'd soon be gone forever. Almost like she'd never been there in the first place.

14

LILA WAS WORRIED. Definitely about Erin, that had never gone away. But now she was fretting over Clint, too. He parked the truck near the entrance of the motel. Baxter hadn't returned, or at least his car wasn't in the lot.

"Are you sure you don't want to come up?" She met his gaze. "I can return calls later. Or even tomorrow."

He smiled. "You sure do get a lot of calls and texts."

Her sister first, then her mom had called, and then Erin had texted. All of them multiple times. "Did that ruin the mood for you?" Lila asked.

"No." Clint laughed. "No," he repeated, shaking his head, then he leaned closer and kissed her lips.

He didn't linger, probably afraid of giving her the wrong idea. It was clear he wanted their date to end. She'd really hoped he would spend the night with her.

"Most of it is your fault," she said. "Everyone was calling because of you."

"What did I do?"

"Besides give me an orgasm that nearly blew my head off?" She sighed. "You think I'm selfish. But I tried getting you to—"

"I don't think you're selfish." Clint took her hand.

The light squeeze he gave it felt oddly platonic, but she liked the lopsided smile. "If I recall, I was the one who drove that particular cattle drive."

That made her laugh. "Interesting euphemism. Did you just think that up?"

"Come on," he said with another unsatisfactory squeeze. "I'll walk you to your door."

He got out of the truck, so she had little choice, other than to sit there by herself.

Clint opened her door and held it while she slid out. She couldn't help but see that he was hard, just as aroused as he'd been fifteen minutes ago. Would he still be that turned on if she'd done something wrong?

They headed for the entrance, his hand brushing against hers. It seemed he was about to take it. She saw his hesitation as clear as day.

She stopped. They both turned and faced each other. "Clint—"

"Look—" he said at the same time, then gestured for her to speak first.

Her cell phone chirped. She jerked it out of her pocket.

"Oh, shut up." She should never have turned the darn thing back on. Easy enough to fix. Her palms were damp, she realized, as she returned the phone to her pocket and looked up to find Clint studying her face.

"I think we have the same thing on our minds," he said and put his hands on her shoulders. "The timing sucks. Much as I would rather be going to your room with you, I have something very important to do. It concerns the ranch, which I've gladly neglected for nearly a week…" He smiled and lifted her chin when she slumped with guilt. "Something I plan on doing a lot more of, if you let me. But I have this one obligation I can't ignore. I realize now that I should've told you as soon as I remembered."

Relief washed over her. "Then go. I can get to my room just fine."

"I can at least walk you to your—"

"We'll probably start making out in the elevator."

"Good point." His frown was just too adorable. "Any chance I can see you tomorrow night? I don't care how late."

"Absolutely." She stretched up on her toes and kissed him. "Now, go."

His body no longer seemed tense as he pulled her into his arms. Then they started kissing, more passionately than they should in a public place. She pushed him away.

"What?" he murmured hoarsely.

"You have to go."

"Right." He reached for her again, but she'd stepped back. "God, you tempt me…"

"That's why I'm saying goodbye." She gave him a small wave as she backed toward the door. Mostly because he tempted her too. Clint made everything else so easy to forget.

Lila didn't have the responsibility of a ranch to run, but she had a duty to the film, to her career, and she owed Erin. They'd made a pact. They were in this rotten business together, for better or for worse. But even that didn't concern Lila at the moment.

When he didn't move, she turned and hurried into the motel. Once she was in her room, without even washing off her makeup or changing into her nightshirt, she called her friend.

"You didn't have to call back tonight," Erin said as a greeting. "Are you with him?"

"No," Lila said, sitting on the edge of the bed and slipping off her flats. "And we're not going to talk about Clint."

"Did something happen between you guys?"

"We're fine. It's us, Erin. Something's happened that you're not telling me," Lila said on an exhale. "And I won't pretend it's not killing me. Not anymore."

Erin allowed silence to stretch, and then she sighed. "We'll talk. But not on the phone. Tomorrow, okay?"

"That isn't fair."

"I'm not putting you off. I promise you. And please trust me that everything will be okay. But tomorrow would be better."

Lila agreed, disconnected and fell back against the pillows.

Her friend could assure her they'd talk, but she couldn't know that everything would turn out okay. Lila had a strong feeling that wouldn't be the case. And God, how she wished Clint were here to help her forget. But he was right. They tempted each other, in so many ways, and Lila sure didn't need to lose sight of her career, her future, not when she was so close.

Foolish her, she'd begun to think Clint just might be the one man she didn't want to let slip away. And yet she'd only known him a week.

One short week.

On top of that, it was the holiday season, and she was emotional about not being able to go home. That explained so much. It was for the best he wasn't spending the night, she thought, rolling over to bury her face in the pillow. Because with so much going on already, she was starting to seriously doubt her judgment.

CLINT WAS SURPRISED to see the office light on as he parked the truck. It was 9:20 p.m. He figured his dad would still be up, but not working on ranch business. It was the only time he used the office, and that was a rare occasion.

Guilt slammed Clint. Shit. He really had been neglecting his duties if his dad felt the need to step in, though he was the one who'd urged Clint to take some time off.

Not in the mood to run into his mom or grandmother, he skipped going through the house and walked to the outside entrance to the office. They never kept the door locked. He paused for a brief knock so he wouldn't startle his dad.

He was sitting behind the old oak desk with the middle drawer open and frowning. "Hi, son," he said, glancing up. "You're home early." He shoved aside a stapler and box of paper clips. "Do we have any tape in here?"

"What kind of tape?" Clint sat in the leather chair across from the desk. He wasn't used to the view from this side. Damn, they had a lot of books crammed together on the built-in shelves.

"You know…the kind your mom uses to wrap presents."

"Ah. I don't think so. Isn't there some in Mom's junk drawer?"

"I looked." Clearly agitated, he continued rifling through the desk. "She must've put it somewhere else. Probably with her wrapping paper."

"What do you need it for?"

"To wrap her Christmas present."

"You bought her something?"

His dad narrowed his eyes. "Yes, I did. Just like I've

done in the past. So, I'll thank you not to make it sound like I don't give your mom presents."

Clint laughed. "I meant it's not a vacuum cleaner or new washer. Not if you're going to wrap it."

"Wise guy. I bought tickets for a Caribbean cruise," he said, and Clint's jaw dropped. "You bought your gal anything yet?"

"You know Kristy and I broke it off months ago."

"I'm talking about the other gal," his dad said with a small smile.

"Don't have a gal, and I don't know what you're talking about."

"The young lady you spent last night with, Clint. I didn't expect I'd have to spell it out for you."

Clint sighed, wishing like hell he'd waited until tomorrow. "This is a different time, Pop. I like Lila," he said, not keen on discussing the topic with his old man. "I like her a lot. But she's not…mine."

"Why? Because she has something to do with that movie they're shooting near Blackfoot Falls?"

Clint nodded. "She's part of the crew, and when they're finished, she'll be gone."

He'd given up the search and was putting all his energy into frowning at Clint. "You know that for sure?"

"It's her job, Pop. I'm sure." Clint straightened. "Look, I wanted to talk to you. About me taking over. No point in waiting till after Christmas. We both know the answer. I'm honored you have faith in me."

"Faith in you?" He shoved a hand through his salt-and-pepper hair. "We still have the Whispering Pines because of you. I'm real clear about that," he said, when Clint shook his head. "I've always been a lousy businessman. I know my cattle, though. Just wish I'd had enough sense to let someone else handle the business end early on. Your mom's smart about that sort of thing. I was young, newly married and had too much ego to get her involved."

Clint rubbed his jaw. Sounded familiar.

"What's that grin for? Your old man was young once."

"Weren't we all?"

Doug Landers snorted a laugh. "Hell, you're still a pup. Smart as a whip, though, I'll give you that. You knew everything about auctions and keeping the books well before you went off to college. And even the cattle... Don't you tell your brother I said this, but you've always been a better cattleman than Nathan. He's good with horses."

Clint chuckled. "Come on, Pop. Give me an early Christmas present. Let me tell him you said that. You can be there to see his face."

"Yeah, go ahead, start a war. Your mom would love that." His smile faded as he looked solemnly at Clint. "What I'm getting to is this... I'm not accepting your answer. Not yet." He held a hand up when Clint started to protest. "Obviously I'm not questioning your ability. But you were right to ask for time to think it over. And I believe you still have some thinking to do."

"I don't understand what brought this on," Clint said, his insides clenching. "But I'm telling you that I'm—" He leaned back, not sure if he felt ashamed or offended. "You think I've been neglecting my job—"

"Hell, no. I told you to take time off, didn't I? Anyway, we have good men living in that bunkhouse," he said, jabbing a finger in that direction. "No reason you should be here 24/7. Not to mention you can handle the job with one arm tied behind your back. Your mom and I just want you to be sure. That's all."

Swiftly losing his sense of humor, Clint sighed. "I'm telling you I'm sure. I want to run the Whispering Pines. A Landers has held the reins for over a hundred years." Why had he said that? It had no bearing on anything. He was tired. Maybe his dad had mistaken weariness for uncertainty. "My decision has nothing to do with Seth acting out or Nathan having his own ranch to worry about. I'm telling you I'm ready."

"Good." His dad stood, and Clint exhaled. "I expect you'll still be ready in three weeks."

"Dad…"

He walked around the desk and stopped at the door. "Do me a favor, son. Pick me up some of that tape next time you're in town."

"I don't know when that'll be," Clint lied, feeling like a defiant teenager. Idiot.

"No rush." His dad tried hiding a smile. "It can wait until you go shopping for that present."

SOMETHING HAD HAPPENED on the set. Lila didn't know the specifics, only that the problem was big enough that Erin could weasel out of their talk and force half the crew to take an early lunch. Which sucked so bad because the day was already crawling.

Lila turned to go back inside the trailer when she thought she saw Clint's truck. She didn't think they needed him today, but he could be delivering horses. Straining to see around the corner, she nearly fell off the step.

"Looking for someone?"

The sound of his deep voice sent an army of goose bumps marching down her arms. She spun to face him, almost losing her balance, but he caught her by the waist.

"Someone tall, dark and handsome, as a matter of fact." She paused as he gave her the exaggerated eye roll that never failed to make her grin. "But you'll do," she added.

"You're in a good mood," he said, releasing her. "Filming must be going well today."

"Oh, no, it's a complete mess. They're at a standstill." She smiled at his puzzled expression. "I'm happy to see you," she said, considering sneaking in a kiss. "God, you're wearing your hat. Have I told you how much I love that Stetson? On you. Not the hat by itself."

Clint laughed.

"Did you get your business taken care of last night?"

"Yeah." He lifted the Stetson and resettled it on his head, looking beyond her toward the set. "Everything's fine."

"Did they call you to come today?"

He shook his head. "I had something to pick up in town and figured I'd stop by. You eating lunch with Erin?"

"We had plans to meet, but I doubt I'll see her for a while," she said, glancing toward the set. Baxter was headed their way. "Oh, great." She quickly turned back to Clint, who looked equally thrilled to see the moron.

Clint's jaw was set, his gaze fixed. Neither of them spoke. She braced for impact.

"What are you doing away from the set?" Baxter asked Clint. "They need you over there by the—" He waved a hand, clueless as usual. "Whatever they call it."

Clint's straight face dissolved, and he let out a laugh.

"They're not using him today, Baxter," Lila said, so sick of his obvious attempts to separate them. "Didn't you read the call sheet?"

His evil glower startled her, but she held firm and glared back.

"Jason and I want something for lunch." He challenged her with a dark look she'd never seen before.

"Okay," she said, shrugging. "You know where the craft service is set up."

"We're sick of that shit. Make yourself useful, go pick something up at the diner."

She opened her mouth to remind him *he* was Jason's gofer, not her. But she saw the anger in Clint's face and reconsidered.

Better not throw gas on the fire, she decided.

Baxter frowned at her outstretched palm. "What?"

"Money and the keys to your car."

Baxter scowled. "Don't you have money?"

"Nope." She waited, wiggling her fingers. "Hurry up, I don't have all day."

He pulled some bills out of his pocket and passed them to her, while he dug for his keys.

"You don't need his car," Clint said, pressing a hand to the small of her back. "I'll drive you."

"Thanks."

Baxter didn't like that at all. She tried not to let her glee show.

"Wow, a hall pass I hadn't expected," she said as they started walking. "Nice."

Clint still looked as if he wanted to rearrange Baxter's face. "What the hell is his problem?"

She shrugged. "He's jealous." It was a short walk to his truck. She glanced back a couple times, hoping to see Erin. Lila had been ready to have that talk. Since that wasn't possible at the moment, this wasn't a bad way to spend the time.

Although, she'd warned herself about relying too much on Clint.

He turned onto Main Street, and she looked at the crumpled bills. "Awesome. There's enough here for us to have lunch, too."

Clint chuckled. "How about I buy you lunch?"

"Actually I'm not hungry. Where are we going?"

"You tell me."

"Okay, the Food Mart."

Clint looked at her. "Have you had their ready-made sandwiches?"

"They're terrible. Jason will hate it." She smiled at his confusion. "Jason would never tell Baxter to send me to get lunch. That's part of Baxter's job description."

He kept driving, a smile slowly curving his mouth. "You can look so angelic. But you really are a little devil, aren't you?"

"When it comes to Baxter? Oh, yeah."

The parking lot wasn't crowded. Clint found a spot close to the front. As Lila slipped out, she caught a brief glimpse of herself in the side mirror and laughed.

"What?" he asked, coming around to hold the door. He was unfailingly polite. And not just with her. He always held a door for any woman.

"I forgot about this purple extension." She lifted it away from her own hair. "You didn't say anything."

"I've rearranged my expectations when it comes to you."

Lila waited for him to close the door. "I'm not sure if that's good or bad."

He surprised her by taking her hand. "Is this okay?" he asked, glancing at their entwined fingers as they walked toward the entrance.

"It is with me." She smiled so big her cheeks hurt.

Her parents would adore Clint. She squeezed his hand tighter.

He squeezed back. "Mom?"

"What did you say?" Laughing, Lila glanced up at him.

Clint wasn't looking at her. He'd stopped and was staring at a short, middle-aged woman with sparkling hazel eyes and the same olive skin coloring as Clint. "What are you doing here?"

The woman glanced from Clint to Lila and then at their joined hands. She smiled. "Shopping."

"Right." Clint released Lila's hand. "What's wrong with Bill's Food Town? Other than being thirty miles closer to home."

"Aren't you going to introduce me to your friend?" Mrs. Landers was studying Lila, but in a friendly way.

"Lila Loveridge meet Meryl Landers, my nosy mother."

"Oh, hush," Mrs. Landers said, sending him a reproving look.

Grinning, Lila extended her hand. "I'm so happy to meet you."

"I confess to being a bit starstruck," Mrs. Landers said as she accepted Lila's handshake. "I usually do shop at the Food Town in Twin Creeks, but I was hoping to see someone famous."

"Oh, we don't have any really big names. But I bet you've heard of Dash Rockwell and Penelope Lane."

"And you," Mrs. Landers said. "My goodness, I can't believe Clint has been keeping you a secret. You can't be the hairstylist…"

"Oh, brother," Clint muttered. "Sorry, Mom, but Lila's on a tight schedule. We need to hurry."

"Of course, I understand," Mrs. Landers said, and kept staring like so many awestruck fans.

But Lila didn't mind. For once she was sorry to be a disappointment.

"I know." His mom beamed at them. "How about coming over for dinner? That way we can visit without rushing."

"Nope," Clint said. "She works tonight."

Lila nodded. It was true. But Clint didn't know that.

"It doesn't have to be tonight. What about this weekend?"

"I'd love to," Lila said at the same time Clint said, "No can do."

His mom ignored him and patted Lila's hand. "I'm so looking forward to having you."

15

"You nervous?" Clint squeezed her hand as they lurched over the icy road on their way to his family's ranch.

"No," Lila said. "Yes. But no. Really no. Your mother was as sweet as could be. This is an amazing treat for me." She smiled at him. "What about you? Are you nervous?"

"Damn straight, I am."

She laughed. "Why?"

"You don't know my mom. She's liable to make this into a big to-do. You'd think it's Christmas come early."

"Wow, that'll make the evening even better. Erin thinks I'm nuts around the holidays. I usually start decorating the day after Thanksgiving, and I don't stop singing carols until after New Year's."

"Are you sure that's the only reason she thinks you're nuts?"

"Hey!" Lila let go of his hand so she could punch his arm. "You're really asking for trouble, you know that?"

"Yeah, well…" Clint took her hand in his again. "I knew I was in trouble the moment I met you."

"Huh." She leaned back to look at him. "Should I ask?"

He cleared his throat and muttered, "Probably not."

She sighed, grateful for the ease between them, memorizing the feel of his hand swallowing hers, the slight smile she could see half of, the warmth of the truck against the cold of the wind and the intermittent snow flurries.

When it felt like too much, Lila looked in the small backseat at her bag of treats. Yesterday she'd received her mom's care package filled with all the fixings for their traditional spiced Christmas tea along with some other goodies.

Lila had been delighted at first, but then the truth behind the gesture had sunk in. Her mom had given up hope that Lila could make it home for Christmas. She had to stop thinking about that or she'd be a complete mess.

To make herself feel better, she'd stayed up ungodly late making a big batch of her famous Rocky Road bark, using the microwave in the production trailer.

"I probably should have brought wine," she said.

"Would you stop? When Mom heard you were bringing stuff for your family's traditional tea, she was very excited. Have I mentioned she's more nuts than you about the holidays?"

"She couldn't be."

"Oh, no? Take a look at the gate."

Lila had been so busy staring at Clint she hadn't realized they'd reached the ranch. The gate was large enough for two semitrucks to pass when opened, and it looked like it was made from the pine trees that lined the roads and filled the forests. Hanging at the center was a breathtaking wreath, dotted with holly berries, dusted pinecones and a huge red velvet bow.

"Oh, I think I'm going to fit right in," she said with relief. "And you're sure it's just casual?"

"Lila. You're wearing a skirt, which by itself defies the word casual at our house. Not that I don't appreciate it," he said, eyeing her legs. "A lot."

Grinning, she bumped his shoulder. She hadn't dressed up too much. To go with the pencil skirt she'd chosen a simple cream-colored blouse with a cardigan that was festive but wouldn't be too hot in the kitchen. She'd pulled her hair back in a ponytail, just like she would have if she'd been at home.

"Look, we don't have to stay late. We can be back at the motel by ten if we don't linger over the meal."

"Good grief, we just got here. And lingering is the whole point. That and hearing embarrassing stories about you when you were a kid."

"Fat chance. I've warned everyone to keep their stories to themselves." He put the truck in Park and jumped out to open the big gate. She thought about getting behind the wheel to save him a step, but she wanted to be able to look around.

The long driveway led to a large house at the top of the rise. It was really attractive, a mix of ranch-style and Alpine, with a peaked roof atop the biggest section. And the best part—the whole exterior was decorated to the gills.

Lila took in the lights, the wreath on the door, the garlands around the porch railing and the two big rocking chairs. One thing she didn't have at home was the light dusting of real snow instead of movie-magic Snowcel, which made the whole place look like a gingerbread house. It was magical.

Clint parked the truck next to three others. As she slipped on her jacket, she noticed a barn, a couple of corrals, another big building that was probably a bunkhouse, given the smoke coming out of the chimney. The lowing of cattle chased the wind from the valley floor.

Clint carried her bag of goodies as they took the stone walkway to the front door. He touched her lower back, and she glanced at him. "Who were you waving at?" She turned to see, but caught only a glimpse of two cowboys standing outside the barn before Clint blocked her view.

"I wasn't waving," he said in a wry voice. "It's just some of the guys from the bunkhouse. Keep going."

Now, she really wanted to see who he'd flipped off, but the front door swung open before they even reached it.

There was Mr. Landers, it had to be, because he looked like the mold his son was cast from. His salt-and-pepper hair gave her a hint as to what Clint would look like as he got older. Of course he'd be just as striking.

"Welcome, Ms. Loveridge, to our humble home."

"It's Lila, and I'm so happy to be here."

"I'm Doug, Clint's dad, but I reckon you knew that."

Lila grinned. "Well, he does have your good looks."

The older man flushed and laughed.

"There you are," Mrs. Landers said, wiping her hands on a white towel attached to a Santa apron. "Nathan and Beth are already here, and Seth should arrive soon. So come on in, and let's get you two defrosted."

Her jacket was whisked away. The scent of roast beef and fresh rolls made her mouth water. The interior of the house—much more expansive than she'd expected with its high roof and fireplace in the living room—was filled with older, overstuffed chairs, pictures of horses and boys at all stages, trophies and ribbons, studio shots on the walls, and a leather couch that looked as if it had seen a couple of generations grow up.

Another Landers man joined them. He had to be Nathan and the beautiful tall blonde who followed, his wife, Beth. Introductions took less than a minute, they chatted for a few more, then Doug, Nathan and Beth excused themselves because Mrs. Landers had assigned them all *duties*.

Clint seemed pleased that he'd gotten off scot-free so he could show her around. Lila would bet anything he'd be stuck with cleanup. She decided not to burst his bubble as he ushered her into a family room with another fireplace, and a ridiculously perfect Christmas tree standing near a large window. The view was so quintessential it looked like a painted backdrop.

"It's wonderful," she said, taking Clint's hand. Some of the cute Christmas ornaments looked handmade. "Better than I even imagined."

"The house was originally built by my great-grandfather," he said, "then extended by my grandad and Dad. It's a real ranch home with enough room to house half a dozen hands, and enough supplies to last a Montana winter."

"Well, I can see it's a real hardship for you to live here."

He leaned in and surprised her with a kiss on the lips. Without even looking to see if anyone was watching. He kept it brief and G-rated, which was more than fine with her. Even so she sneaked a peek behind them.

He smiled and nodded at the window. "It's getting dark, but you can still see we have a great view of the Rockies."

"The house you want to build, would it be near

here?" she asked and saw him stiffen. "I'm sorry. Maybe I shouldn't—I won't bring it up again."

"No," he said, shrugging. "It's fine." He turned back to the window. "It's not a secret. I'm just having trouble deciding between two spots, but yeah, it'll be about a mile or so north."

"Darn, I wish we had more daylight."

"I can always bring you back out…" He met her gaze. "If you have time."

Something was making her tongue stick. Looking into his eyes often made her heart flutter. But this was different…

"Come on," he said with a small resigned smile that she hoped was her imagination. "I'll show you my mother's pride and joy."

A few more surprises met her in the kitchen. Double ovens and a six-burner stove, an island big enough for four people to work at. Laughter floated in from another room. This house, the holiday songs coming from the family room, the scents, the décor, it was all a bit overwhelming.

She had to blink back tears as she thought of her family's much smaller home in LA where her mom and dad and Brit had the tree up. Her brother was married and had his own home, but he and Cheryl lived close and would spend Christmas at the house.

"Hey," Clint said, his big hand landing softly on her shoulder. "You okay?"

"Just missing my family."

"I wish there was something I could have done about that."

"You have. Believe me. I'm fine."

"Then get in there and make that spiced tea you told

me about. I want to try it. I'm sure my mom will be back in a second."

"Yes, sir," she said, taking the bag with her to the island. First thing she brought out was the Rocky Road bark, made with semisweet chocolate, mini-marshmallows, slivered almonds and little pieces of peppermint stick and toffee. The *tray* was just a cookie sheet covered with tinfoil, but she hadn't had much to work with.

As soon as she uncovered it, Mrs. Landers, who insisted Lila call her Meryl, joined her at the island. "Oh, my. Doesn't that look sinfully delicious?"

Coming up behind Clint's mom, Beth let out a moan that made Lila blush. "What's this called? Better than Sex?"

"Oh, Beth." Laughing, Meryl swatted at her daughter-in-law as she reached for a piece.

Beth took a bite. "Oh, yeah," she murmured, eyes closed.

They all laughed, and it helped Lila relax. The three men flowed through the kitchen, snatching pieces of her bark as they got water and wine glasses to put on the dining-room table.

Clint's grandmother, fresh from a nap, appeared and was introduced. Tall and lean like her son and grandsons, she looked to be in her eighties, with wrinkles that showed the rancher's life she'd lived, her silver hair tied up in a high swirl.

"Here, honey," Meryl said, handing Lila an apron with a snowman on the front. "We don't want that pretty sweater ruined."

Most of the meal was either ready or baking in the oven. A couple dishes needed tending, and there were always last-minute details. All in all, Meryl was so organized she didn't even use a cheat sheet.

While she brought out serving bowls from the cabinets, Clint's grandmother, Shirley, sampled the Rocky Road. "I think I'm going to have to hide this bark you brought, or the men will all be stuffed before supper."

"Where are you going to hide it, Grandma?" Beth asked sweetly as she plucked a holiday apron from the drawer. "Your room?" She met the older woman's squinty gaze and burst out laughing.

"You hush up, Beth Landers," Grandma Landers said, holding up a wooden spoon.

Lila couldn't help but laugh. They were all wonderful. She could tell Clint's family all genuinely liked one another. She could hear the three men talking and laughing in the family room. And Nathan and Beth, they'd been married only a year, yet Beth already belonged.

A few minutes later, as Lila finished sautéing some fresh green beans, she caught Clint at the edge of the kitchen door. He didn't say anything; he was just checking on her, she was sure. She tried not to let him know she'd seen him, but it was impossible not to smile. He was the very best part of her life these days.

After all the crap that was going on with Baxter and Jason and her own feelings of disillusionment about show business, it was crazy how much she needed him at the end of the day. At first it had just been fun and exciting. He was so hot, yet funny and kind, a rare combination in a man. And her feelings had changed; she'd known that since the barbecue. But there simply wasn't anything to do about it. He belonged here with his family, on Landers land.

As for her, well, Lila didn't know where she belonged anymore. If it weren't for Erin, sometimes Lila swore she would just quit, walk away, pretend the twenty-year-old dream had never existed. The thought was scary, but also liberating. And that only made it twice as scary.

No matter what, though, she would remember Clint, his family and this dinner. It couldn't have come at a more perfect time for her.

The three women laughed about something, snapping her out of her gloomy thoughts.

Evidently Beth, who was working on a carrot-and-raisin salad, had told a story about Nathan and her niece Liberty. Lila was sorry she missed it. She promised herself she'd stay present, as she put together the special Spiced Christmas Tea made with star anise, cinnamon and passion fruit nectar.

"One Christmas," Meryl said, as she checked on the dinner rolls, "Clint found a dog out by the gate. A rangy looking, big old mutt who was shivering in the cold and absolutely covered in mud. Well, that boy could never turn away an animal in need, so he snuck that dog in, trying to keep him quiet in the mudroom so we'd be none the wiser. Of course he had to show his brothers. You can guess what happened.

"The dog got out, went straight for the big turkey that had been resting on the counter, took it down and went to town. When the boys tried to get the turkey back, the dog made a run for it, pretty much destroying half the dinner table and most of the presents under the tree."

"What did you do?"

"Ate cold cuts and whatever we could salvage, tied the dog up in the barn, and the boys spent most of their evening cleaning up the mess."

When she finished laughing, Lila said, "My mother could tell you a few juicy stories about my brother."

"It's just the two of you?"

"I have a sister, too. But Brit and I were angels." Lila barely got the lie out without laughing.

The other three joined in and she couldn't have felt more at home.

BY THE TIME they were all seated around the table, one empty chair for Seth, should he decide to show up, Clint was slightly buzzed from a glass of his father's best whiskey. He'd felt a little guilty about leaving Lila on her own in the kitchen, but he'd sneaked by a few times to check on her, and she'd been laughing and cooking and making herself at home.

She looked really happy. As happy as he'd seen her. It was like there were two Lilas—the actress who looked so delicate and beautiful she seemed like a different kind of human, but who would show up in purple hair or with crazy eye makeup, all business in the trailer, and putting up with the rowdy crew; and then there was this Lila, who looked as if she belonged in a home filled with family, a life of simple pleasures and down-to-earth dreams.

Funny enough, he liked both of them. All of her quirks and her mischief, especially when that wicked streak showed up in bed.

She sat between him and Beth, and those two hit it off like gangbusters. What did surprise him was that tiny Lila could eat like one of the ranch hands. Usually she stuck to salads. Tonight she had double helpings.

"Meryl tells me you're an actress," Grandma Landers said from across the table. "Nathan's first wife, Anne, she was an actress, too. Pity about the accident. She was a sweet girl. Had a real nice touch growing roses."

Clint's gaze went straight to Nathan, who was letting go of a deep breath, then to Lila. She'd obviously picked up the sudden tension around the table. Even his parents had. His grandmother hadn't meant anything by her comment, but with Beth there, the topic was tricky.

Though, Beth looked perfectly fine.

"I'm not acting in this film, Mrs. Landers. I'm part of the crew. I do hair and makeup."

"I've never been much for the movies," she said. "I like a few TV shows though. That Ellen DeGeneres. She's funny. And she doesn't curse like so many young people do."

"You're right," Lila said, "she is funny."

"Have you ever met her? I think she lives in Hollywood."

Lila smiled. "No. I haven't. But I know people who have, and they say she's very nice."

Clint relaxed. As he finished his second helping of mashed potatoes and gravy, he realized something. He'd been a little worried about tonight, but it had nothing to do with Lila not fitting in as he'd thought. Now he understood that wasn't the issue at all. Of course she fit in. He'd already seen how she acted in town, at the motel, with other members of the crew.

The real issue was that he'd already started picturing her in the house he was going to build. And that was a mistake he couldn't afford to make.

A rush of cold air hit the back of his neck, and everyone turned to the sound of feet stomping on the front door mat. Seth had made it after all. Clint hadn't thought he would. Of course he was late.

"Hello everybody," he said, sweeping off his snowy Stetson, spraying water over the floor. "It smells good in here. And I'm starving."

Their mom was up like a shot, pulling him into her

arms as if she hadn't seen him in years. Which was fine. Better to keep welcoming him home. Maybe it would stick at some point. Make him forget about whatever the hell he'd been running down to Billings for and reacquaint himself with the family. Nathan and Clint exchanged looks, but tonight wasn't the time to get into any heavy discussions.

"He looks just like you and Nathan," Lila whispered as she leaned close to Clint.

He breathed in her seductive scent and almost didn't see Seth's jaw drop when he noticed Lila. Clint hid a smile. Sure would've been a pity to miss that. They weren't competitive, not when it came to women. Sports, definitely.

"Hey, Seth." Clint rested his arm on the back of her chair. "This is Lila." To her, he said, "Seth's our baby brother."

Shaking his head, Seth snorted a laugh. He came around the table and shook her hand. "Lila, nice to meet you. What are you doing slumming it with this guy?"

"All right, boys." Meryl pulled out Seth's chair. "That's enough."

"Boys?" Clint frowned. He and Nathan looked at each other. "We didn't say anything."

"Baby brother?" Seth kissed their mom's cheek before he sat. "Nah. You weren't trying to bait me."

"What? Is that not a true statement?" Clint felt Lila's gentle touch on his thigh. "Okay. Truce."

"Fine. Truce," Seth muttered, and then laughed.

So did Nathan and Clint.

"Okay," their mom said, "Seth, I'll warm a plate for you. As for everybody else, you all better have saved room for dessert. I made my blue ribbon deep-dish apple pie and pumpkin chiffon."

"Which took second place two years running," Seth added as he got to his feet.

"Where are you going? You just got here."

Seeing the worry on his mom's face made Clint's chest tighten. He was a second away from telling Seth to shove the truce.

"I can warm my own plate, Mom," Seth said in a low voice. "I should've been on time. You go take care of dessert."

Clint glanced at his father who hadn't said one word since Seth had arrived.

Lila moaned. "I've eaten your weight in food already. And you know I can't resist pie."

Clint slid his arm from the back of her chair and draped it around her shoulders. He knew she was trying to be a buffer. "Of course you can't."

"It's only polite to have a piece of both."

He nodded.

"Does she serve them with ice cream?"

"How are you so small?" he said, laughing at the seriousness of her tone.

"Please, you know I live on salads most of the time. Which gets very old. I sure won't miss that."

The odd comment caught him off guard. "What do you mean?"

Lila blinked. "Nothing. I just— Nothing." She smiled and turned to Beth.

Nothing?

Like hell.

16

"I HAD A wonderful time." Feeling pleasantly tired, Lila settled in the truck's comfy seat.

"I'm glad you enjoyed yourself," he said. "Everyone thought you were great."

She wished there wasn't the console between them, when all she wanted was to snuggle up against him. But she made do with his hand in hers.

"Your mom's pies are amazing. I can't believe she gave me a slice of each. I really hope I don't eat them both tonight."

Clint lifted a brow at her. "You're serious."

She just laughed, then remembered her earlier remark about salads getting old. How utterly thoughtless. She'd have to be more careful and not give anyone the wrong idea.

It wasn't that she didn't trust Clint. She hadn't told anyone, not even Erin, God, especially not Erin. They'd made a pact to conquer Hollywood or die trying. They were in this stupid business for the long haul.

Lila couldn't really explain to anyone that she'd lost her enthusiasm because she didn't understand it herself yet. Of course being stuck on location for eternity had something to do with it. Plus it was the holidays, and she missed her family. If she could just make it past Christmas, maybe all the doubt would go away and she'd be back to her normal self.

"Tell me about Seth," she said. "How much younger is he than you?"

"Two years. But he acts like he's twelve."

Lila bit her lip. Clint hadn't exactly been the paragon of maturity when it came to baiting Seth.

"He got into a little trouble in college, nothing big, he moved past it. Then a year after he graduated he joined the air force. Not a single word to any of us. Told us the day before he shipped out. It about killed my mom."

"Well, obviously he isn't career military."

"No, he came home after four years."

"So he works the ranch with you?"

"Sort of…when he feels like it. He'd lived in Billings for a while and keeps running back there. He's kept himself away from the family for the most part. We're not sure what's going on with him. We've all tried talking to him, but he's not saying."

"Can't be easy for him," Lila said, laying her head back.

"Easy?" Clint gave her a sharp look. "What do you mean?"

"He's got some big shoes to fill, given how amazing you and Nathan are. I'm sure that's got to put on some pressure."

"No, Seth is smart. He was one of those kids who didn't have to study and still got better grades than Nathan and me."

"Yeah, but you guys are ranchers. I mean, how important was it to—You know what? I have no idea what

I'm talking about. I know nothing about ranchers or their mind-set or anything else."

"Maybe not," he said. "But humor me. Finish what you were going to say."

"Look, I just met your family. I feel like a dope making any kind of observation."

"An objective one is usually the best."

Lila sighed. "You and Nathan seem to be more like your dad. The ranch, the land, you take pride in the work and preserving your home for future generations." She brought her head up. "And before you get the wrong idea, I'm not saying Seth doesn't feel that way, too. Obviously I don't even know him. But coming up behind two older brothers who are making your dad and the Landers name proud...

"Well, it's got to be tough. I'm guessing grades didn't matter all that much to any of you. And of course I could be...full of beans." Lila laughed softly, hoping she hadn't offended Clint. He looked so solemn. "I hadn't even heard that phrase before coming to Montana, can you believe that?"

Clint didn't answer.

Feeling she'd overstepped and desperate to fill the silence, she couldn't think of anything to say but, "I'm sorry."

"Don't be. I'm just thinking about what you said. Seth and I had always been close, and you might have a point. I just wish I knew how to get him to open up about it."

"I have a feeling, just watching him tonight, that he misses you all. That's a start."

"I hope so. For my mom's sake." Clint smiled. "For all our sakes. What about you?" he said. "Whose expectations are you trying to meet?"

"Erin's," she said without even thinking. He probably thought she was joking. And that she had a lot of nerve dodging his question after psychoanalyzing his family. Lila sighed. "Erin's parents worked long hours, and she practically lived at our house when we were kids. She's as much a sister to me as Brit. Maybe even more, and yes, I feel horribly guilty saying that. But it's the truth. We used to be inseparable. Since she met Spencer, things have changed, so you're not getting a good picture of how close we used to be."

"I bet you're still close."

"Yes, of course, we are. Definitely. It's just that… it might sound stupid, but I really don't want to disappoint her. We've shared the same dream for twenty years." Lila felt disloyal and sad just speaking the words. "Hypothetically, because I'm not saying I want to quit, okay? I'm not. I'm just trying to answer your question. So, hypothetically, if I decided I wanted out, I would feel as if I was betraying Erin."

Clint didn't speak for about a minute. Then all he said was, "Damn."

"Yeah," Lila said, sighing. "And my parents. They've always been supportive, never once discouraged me from studying drama. They paid for my entire tuition for UCLA because they believe in me." She felt her throat tighten. She'd said too much. What was wrong with her? They'd had such a nice evening, and she was ruining everything. She forced a laugh. "I have no idea how we ended up here. I'm sorry I made this about me. Because those aren't even real issues." She paused, grasping for something else to talk about. "Why don't you tell me more about Anne? You never mentioned knowing someone in the business."

Another long silence had her feeling prickly. Did

it have to do with what she'd just told him? Or was it about Anne?

"Don't be sorry," he said finally. "I know you were trying to make me feel better about the whole Seth situation."

Whether he really believed that, she had no way of knowing, but she was grateful just to be able to breathe again.

"Anne died a few years after they were married," Clint said, and Lila winced. "Every time Nathan was out of town on business, she'd go to Kalispell or wherever the regional theater was holding auditions. She was my age, we were in school together and she loved drama class. But she'd never said anything about wanting to be an actress. According to her friend Bella, Anne had obsessed over whether she could've made it big. Nathan felt as if he hadn't known her at all. For a while, he was a wreck. Three years later he met Beth, and she turned his world right again."

"Oh, that's so sad about Anne. No wonder it got so quiet."

Clint nodded. "I have a feeling he knows everything there is to know about Beth."

"I'm sure," she said, wondering how many people at that dinner table were thinking about her being an actress. Someone who would always be chasing her dream no matter what the cost. A woman who wasn't right for Clint. Just another reason they were location lovers and nothing more.

She looked out the passenger window, her mood plummeting. She'd always tried to be honest with herself. She'd loved being with Clint tonight. With his family. It was all too easy to picture herself in his world.

Lila wanted kids. Even Erin didn't know that because Lila couldn't tell her. An actress looking for her big break didn't commit career suicide by starting a family. So, yes, they were close, and yet they weren't. Not if Lila wanted to keep a dream alive that she was no longer sure she wanted.

And then here was Clint. Gorgeous, kind, dependable, perfect.

Temporary.

Lila could just cry.

BY THE TIME they reached the motel, Lila had promised herself she wouldn't be a buzzkill. She was going to make the most of their time left together. Tonight. Every night. Every minute they could be together.

She had her jacket off before the door closed. She tossed it, wound her arms around Clint's neck and kissed him hard. She knew she'd surprised him, but he responded quickly.

He pulled her close and teased the seam of her lips until she opened them for him. His tongue swept inside her mouth. She tasted the faint sweetness of his mother's apple pie. Lila met each slow stroke of his tongue with a caress of her own and pressed closer.

Breaking the kiss, he leaned back to look at her. His dark eyes searched her face as his mouth curved in a warm smile. Was he for real?

It would be so much simpler if he weren't. She'd been asking herself that question since the barbecue. They'd met just over two weeks ago, and it was hard to separate reality from what she wanted to believe. She knew the answer. Even before tonight.

"It's okay. I know you can't stay." She'd lied. It wasn't okay at all.

"Why is that?"

"Your parents and grandmother…" She didn't understand his bewildered expression. "They'll know where you were…"

Clint smiled and slowly moved his hands up and down her back. The repetitive motion felt incredibly soothing.

"I guess we can set the alarm," she murmured, wanting to close her eyes and just feel his hands while she daydreamed.

He raised his eyebrows in question.

"In case we fall asleep."

His hands stopped at the top of her backside. "Do you have to work tonight?" he asked, frowning. "Or does this have to do with my *curfew*?"

Lila sighed. "I didn't say that."

"Listen, I hate that I'm still living with my folks, and I'd never rub anything in their faces. But I'm sure as hell not going to let them interfere with my private life."

"I understand." Lila lowered her arms from around his neck. When he didn't release her, she rested her hands on his biceps. "The thing is, I really don't want them to think poorly of me."

Comprehension dawned in his face. Briefly. And then the frown was back.

"I know it doesn't matter. They don't consider me…" She drew in a breath. What? A good prospect? Appropriate for Clint? True or not, she couldn't say that out loud.

"Consider you what?"

She hesitated. "Please don't make me say it."

"Is this about Anne?"

"No." She understood that might also be a problem. "Yes. Partly. My lifestyle is…unpredictable. Although, I do have that role in the sequel." So it wasn't as if she was chasing an illusive dream. Her hard work was about to pay off. But she knew far too many people like Anne. Always certain their big chance was around the corner. Clearing her throat, she shrugged. "I mean, they know I'm leaving soon, right?"

Clint tensed. His face. His whole body. Then he relaxed and nodded. "They do."

Lila sighed. "Well, I sure know how to ruin a party." She tried to step back, but he held her tighter.

"It's just beginning," he said with a thoroughly wicked smile as he backed her toward the bed.

Relieved, she lifted her arms to put them around his neck. He stopped her and gently pushed her sweater off her shoulders.

"Okay," she muttered, and caught the edges of his shirtfront and yanked. All but one snap popped.

Clint laughed. "Okay, so we're taking off the gloves."

"And everything else." She slid her palms up his strong chest. God, he felt so good. She touched the tip of her tongue to his flat dark nipple.

He jerked, grunted.

"Wow, sensitive tonight."

Before she could get to the second one, he started unbuttoning her blouse. Slowly, with the utmost care. Probably worried his callused fingers would snag the delicate fabric.

After he'd set the sweater and blouse aside, he picked her up and laid her on the bed. Getting settled, she accidentally kicked out a foot, making Clint jump back.

"Oops. Sorry," she said. "Good thing you're fast."

"Now that might've ruined the party."

She unfastened her skirt. "Can't have that."

He just stood there looking at her with an odd smile on his face.

"May I help you?" she asked, narrowing her eyes.

"The whole time we were eating supper I wondered which bra you were wearing."

She glanced down at the cream satin demi-cups. "And do you approve?"

He flicked the front clasp and bared her breasts. "I do now," he said, and bent to take a nipple into his mouth. He sucked hard and did something amazing with his tongue.

Warmth spread from her chest to her belly to the dampness between her thighs. She lifted her shoulders off the mattress, enough to reach his ear. She bit his lobe and felt him smile against her breast.

Then he took a slight nip.

"Ouch!"

"That didn't hurt," he murmured, taking a long slow swipe with his tongue.

"It surprised me." She arched her back. "Do it again."

He straightened and removed his shirt. "And have you think I'm a one-trick pony?"

"That particular trick stays in your repertoire. Got it?"

As he unfastened his jeans, he raked a gaze across her breasts.

"You've seen them before," she said, a giggle bubbling at the back of her throat when his mouth quirked up only on one side. That meant she was in for something naughty. Something she was going to like a whole lot.

After unzipping his fly, he sat on the edge of the bed. Keeping an eye on her, he removed the first boot.

She didn't like that he hadn't said anything. She got up on her knees, let the bra slide off, and pressed her breasts against his back and nibbled his neck.

His body jerked, and he laughed.

"Ah…you're ticklish?" She started in the middle of his shoulder so she could get some build-up going. Her lips barely grazed his skin.

"Lila?"

"Clint."

"Listen to me."

"Uh-huh." She bit down.

He had her on her back, pressed into the mattress, restraining her with a palm against her ribs before she could react. With his free hand he tried to peel her skirt over her hips.

"Lift," he ordered.

"Take your jeans off first." The words came out jumbled. She was laughing and hadn't caught her breath from his sly move.

He released her, and feeling triumphant, she got up on her elbows to watch him strip.

His hand shot out. It locked around her ankle, and she gasped. Her left elbow gave out, and she fell back. He grabbed her other ankle and hauled her to the edge of the bed.

She should've known better. So much for enjoying her moment of victory.

Clint didn't tell her to lift her butt again. He managed just fine, stripping off her skirt and her thong. And then stood there like a conquering pirate surveying his spoils while he shoved his own jeans off.

Still wearing his boxers, he spread her legs and stroked the skin of her inner thigh. A slight shiver passed through her. When he dropped to a crouch, she held her breath.

"You're not laughing," he said with a cocky grin, and kissed the sensitive flesh close to her sex.

She'd never felt more vulnerable, more exposed in her life. Swallowing, she lifted her chin. "Never figured you for a sore loser."

"I'm the loser?"

"Who's going down on whom?"

He let out a loud laugh. "Good point," he muttered, still laughing when he pressed his mouth against her core.

Holy crap!

The slight vibration of his lips felt amazing. She squirmed, causing him to look up. "Don't stop."

His mouth was damp, his eyes darker than a moonless night. "I win either way," he said with a sexy smile.

"Me, too. Please, feel free to go to town."

Again he covered her with his mouth and used his tongue to make her squirm. And yowzah, did it feel good.

Lying back, she gasped and writhed. And clutched at his hair at the first signs of a climax. But she didn't want to come yet. She moved back, and managed a quick trick reversal of her own so that she was in a position to take him in her mouth.

He groaned and almost jackknifed when she sucked especially hard.

She glanced up. "Was that a good groan or an ouch groan?"

"It was too good." He pulled her upright and kissed her hard. His tongue chased hers, stroked it, flicked it, then thrust in and out, mimicking everything he'd already done and would do again soon.

Finally they both gasped for air.

"If you're looking for my tonsils, I had them out at seven," she said, barely able to breathe. Laughing didn't help. "Hey." She saw him rolling on a condom. He'd worked fast.

"What?"

"I wasn't finished."

"I'm not either." He picked her up and moved her to center stage. "Two or three pillows?"

"Depends. Where are you putting them?"

Leaning over her, he licked her left breast and tucked a second pillow behind her head. He stacked two under her butt.

Lila grinned. "I'm going to like this, huh?"

Clint's eyes were intense. He was on a mission. He spread her thighs wider and got between them. Before she could take her next breath, he'd found her clit and rubbed it with his thumb.

"Oh," she said with a soft gasp. A jolt of electricity shot up her spine. "You might want to wait on that."

He kissed one breast, then sucked the other.

His thumb increased the pressure.

"Uh, Clint."

"Yes, sweetheart?"

"Clint," she practically yelled and arched off the mattress. "I'm not kidding."

He stroked the hair away from her face and kissed her neck. And then he whispered, "Neither am I."

He entered her, driving in quick and deep, still thumbing her clit. Oh, God, he really had to stop. She drew in the musky male scent of his skin and moaned.

Everything happened at once. The shooting stars behind her eyelids. The fevered rush of pleasure, so familiar, yet new and different. She writhed and begged, and he wouldn't let up.

She started to calm down just as he withdrew. He pulled her legs tightly around his hips and plunged inside her again, then kept moving back and forth, picking up speed, plunging deeper. She liked the angle; he was hitting lots of sensitive places. But he stopped.

Her protest was cut short when he put her legs over his shoulders. He rocked gently against her. "How's this? Okay?"

Panting, she just nodded.

Holding her gaze, Clint leaned down. His eyes were so dark, even this close she couldn't make out the pupils. "I should punish you for wearing that skirt tonight," he said, his voice a hoarse whisper.

"I thought you liked it."

"Your legs are indecently long and very hot." He pushed in farther, and she clutched the sheet.

"So what's the problem?"

"I had to sit through dinner, across the table from my parents, harder than a rock thanks to that damn skirt."

"Well, I'm glad I had nothing to do with it."

A faint smile curved his mouth. He leaned close enough their lips touched, and embedded himself so deep inside her it left her breathless.

She managed a weak whimper. "Please."

Clint pressed his lips against hers. The angle and pressure hit a hot spot that set her insides on fire. He started thrusting and pumping, his face taut, eyes locked with hers. She dug her fingers into his shoulder muscles, clinging to him, as her body roared toward a second release.

They climaxed together, both moaning and murmuring incoherent words. Her hands slid from his sweat-slick skin.

Slowly he moved one leg off his shoulder, kissing the inside of her ankle before lifting her other leg and letting it down.

Clint collapsed beside her, falling hard, as if he had no energy left. Then he pulled her into his arms and cradled her with his body, keeping her close, safe and warm.

17

AFTER WASHING HER brushes and tidying up, Lila stepped out of the trailer and looked up at the overcast sky. Three days ago the news channels had predicted snow for most of the week. So far they'd only had passing flurries, which turned out well for the crew and shooting schedule in general.

For Lila, the shorter days meant she had more time for Clint. They hadn't needed him on the set, so she didn't get to see him until after work. But since dinner with his family, he'd spent every night with her. Lila wasn't sure how she'd feel about running into his mom again. She'd probably blush to high heaven.

She scanned the groups of crew and extras, hoping to spot Erin. They still hadn't talked, though not for lack of Lila trying. Erin had become wily about disappearing the minute they wrapped each day. Lila was beginning to think she should ask Clint for a ride to Shadow Creek so she could corner Erin.

Finally Lila saw Erin conferring with the new camera assistant. They were between scenes, so Lila grabbed a jacket and hurried toward them, hoping to pull Erin aside the second they were finished. The borrowed jacket was big, but Lila wrapped it snugly around her body and pulled up the collar. Just because no snow had fallen didn't mean she wasn't freezing her butt off.

Yeah, so much for her big, fat, glamorous Hollywood life.

Too late she saw Jason approaching Erin from the other side.

He reached her first and barged right into the conversation. "What do you think, Erin? Were you happy with that last take? I'm not sure I was feeling it."

She glanced at him, and without answering, returned her attention to the young assistant. The poor guy shifted nervously. First rule on any set, don't piss off the director.

Lila hung back and imagined the steam coming out of Jason's ears. To say he was pissed would be putting it mildly. He folded his arms across his chest and glared at Erin's back. But he didn't say a word.

It wasn't unusual for him and Erin to get into disagreements. They'd been crossing swords since college. But they rarely argued in public. That was, until a few weeks ago.

Knowing Erin and the terrible mood she'd been in, Lila figured she'd keep talking and make Jason wait. Since Lila wasn't about to get in the middle of their feud and he hadn't noticed her yet, she decided she'd catch Erin later.

She slowly swiveled around and made it a few feet. "Hey, Blondie."

Cringing, she stopped, counted to five and turned to face Jason's silly frat boy grin. "Do you really want to dig out the old nicknames? Let's see, what was yours? I'm sure it'll come to me."

"The grouch must be rubbing off on you," he muttered, glancing at Erin.

"Huh." Lila paused, then moved closer so no one could overhear, even though he didn't deserve the courtesy. "No, it's you. Annoying Erin and me." And most of the crew, but she wouldn't speak for them.

Jason spread his hands. "What did I do to you?"

Interesting. He hadn't included Erin.

"Your lack of communication is unprofessional and rude, for one thing." She waited for the denial, but he just shook his head. "How many people have the final revision?"

He didn't answer, and Lila was fine with stretching out the silence. Hopefully it would make him uncomfortable. Sure, he was under a lot of pressure and worried about the weather. She even sympathized...to some degree.

Erin walked up, looking Jason straight in the eye. "Don't ever interrupt me like that again." Just as she turned to Lila, as though it was an afterthought, Erin added, "The take was fine. Come on, Lila. What is it you need? We'll have to walk and talk. I'm late."

Lila caught a glimpse of anger in Jason's face before she fell into step beside Erin. Her stomach rebelled. She hadn't seen them interact for a while, and the animosity between them was worse than she suspected. Erin didn't hold grudges. She might not agree with something, but she always kept a tight lid on her emotions for the sake of the work.

"What are you late for?"

"Nothing." Erin glanced at her phone. "I just didn't want to talk to him."

"Can you sneak in a break?" Lila asked casually.

"Sure." Erin blinked and slowed down a step. Probably figured out what was coming. "I only have a few minutes, though."

"Baloney. We need to talk, and we're doing it right now."

"Come on, Lila. I'm working. You know this isn't the time or place."

"You've been avoiding me, and you haven't told me anything about what's going on. So no, actually, I have no idea if this is the time or place."

"Look, we'll talk. Later." Erin stopped when Lila did, and they faced each other. "This evening. I promise."

"You'll disappear on me." Lila felt the sting of tears. She blinked them back and held firm. "Now."

Erin's snorted. "Turn off the waterworks. I don't need you playing me, too."

Lila could barely breathe. Shocked and hurt to the bone, she stared at her friend. After several long seconds, afraid she couldn't hold back the tears, Lila turned and walked away.

"Wait. Please, wait." Erin caught up with her. "Dammit. I'm sorry, Lila. I didn't mean it. Jesus. I'm such a shithead."

"Yes, you are," Lila muttered and kept walking, anger overtaking hurt.

"I'm sorry. I really am. You're the last person on earth I'd want to hurt."

Three weeks ago Lila would've believed it. She walked faster, her much longer legs making it hard for Erin to keep up.

"Okay, we'll talk." Erin jogged a few steps ahead and swung around to face her, walking backward. "Right now. Wherever you want. I'll explain everything. God, I'm so sorry," she said, her voice cracking. "Please believe that, if nothing else."

Lila stopped and looked at her friend's stricken expression. Tears glistened in Erin's eyes. She'd cried maybe twice in the twenty years they'd known each other. But it was the crack in her voice that had gotten to Lila.

"I don't have an excuse," Erin said. "I've been horrible, I know, and I—"

"You don't need an excuse. We're friends. You're allowed. I'm sorry, too." Lila swallowed back a lump of tears. "But if you don't follow me to the trailer right this minute and spill everything, I'm going to tell Baxter you have a huge crush on him."

"Huh." Erin sniffed. "I turn my back for a couple weeks and you morph into this evil being."

"Couple weeks, my foot." Lila turned around and resumed her breakneck pace.

Erin sighed and followed.

Ignoring the stares, neither of them spoke until they were inside the hair-and-makeup trailer with the door locked.

Lila sank onto a chair. "Remember, you said everything."

Rubbing her eyes, Erin nodded. She lowered her hands. "Baxter is going to be the first AD for the sequel."

A startled laugh escaped Lila. "Come on...don't waste time joking."

"I wish I were joking. I really do."

"How is that possible? He's an idiot!"

"I'm pretty sure the whole crew and cast agrees with that." Erin exhaled harshly. "His uncle wrote a large check."

"Jason promised you that position and not just because he owes you. You know the job better than anyone, and you've worked harder than anybody else. How many months did you spend scouting locations, living on junk food because there's no per diem money in the budget—"

"It's okay, Lila. Yes, I'm upset, disappointed, all those things. But Jason did what he thought was best for the project. We can't understand what kind of pressure a director is under. In his shoes I might've done the same thing."

"Oh, please. I don't believe that, and neither do you. We've always hated the Hollywood double-talk, the empty promises, using people… You would never have done that to Jason, or any of us."

"You're probably right."

"No probably about it," Lila muttered. "I'm so mad at him."

"See, that's why I didn't want to tell you. Your role is safe. You'll be playing Tara. Don't do anything to mess that up."

"How can you say that? Nothing's sacred. Jason just proved we can't trust him." Lila closed her eyes for a second. "You know, even though he's been short-tempered and annoying, I still believed in him. I wanted him to succeed. He's worked hard since college."

"I *still* believe in him."

"How can you, Erin? Why would you even stick around? Jason needs you. Let him flounder and see just how much."

She turned away.

Lila frowned. "Baxter has no idea what he's doing. The sequel is going to end up a complete mess." She stared at her friend's back. "Erin? What else? You promised."

She cleared her throat and turned around. "Unofficially I'll be the first AD. I'll be paid a salary and everything—"

"And Baxter gets the credit."

Erin nodded.

"You don't care about the money, it was always about the credits for the Director's Guild. What's Baxter going to do with them? Nobody's ever going to hire him to do a film."

"Look on the bright side." Erin smiled. "I'll be making sure our investment pays off. We can get rid of our loans."

Lila stared at her hands. She was almost glad when Erin's phone signaled a text. They probably needed her back on the set, and Lila could use some alone time. How could Erin not be furious and hurt? How could she think Lila wouldn't be, as well? If Jason screwed Erin, then he screwed Lila, too. She didn't even want the role anymore.

"Yep, gotta go," Erin said, looking up from her phone. "Actually I'm glad I finally told you. I've been nasty to Jason, and it's not really fair since I agreed to the deal. We'll all benefit in the end."

Lila forced a smile. It was the best she could do, considering her friend had sold her soul to the devil.

IT HAD BEEN another long frustrating day on the set, and while Lila had avoided most everyone she didn't want to see, she'd had two encounters with Baxter that made her want to FedEx him to Iceland. In his tighty-whities.

At last, though, she was in the right place with the exact right person.

Clint had met her at the motel just after eight, taken one look at her and started running a bath in her heavenly hotel room. He'd gone to pick up food from the diner while she'd soaked and let some of the tension ease from her body.

She'd never been with a man who'd been that considerate without it being about sex. Ever. He'd just been kind, that's all, and here she was, in the throes, as they say, of a very big dilemma.

What she'd like very much to do was lay it all out for him, piece by piece, but since she wasn't sure that any of the pieces made sense, she didn't think it was time. Or maybe it wasn't appropriate. Probably both.

He wouldn't understand, anyway. She'd end up sounding like a Tinseltown flake, which was the last thing she wanted. If she'd really wanted to be fair, she'd tell him they should skip tonight, make plans for tomorrow. But since she'd worked for fifteen hours yesterday, they'd only talked on the phone, and she wasn't willing to do it again.

Not when there were so few nights ahead of them. Maybe if they ate and made love, her mind would just shut off and she wouldn't have to think about how badly she wanted to quit. Walk away. She still hadn't come to terms with Erin's willingness to continue working with Jason.

That backstabbing wiener. How many times had Erin saved his hide on this film? On every project they'd ever worked on, but especially this one. The one that counted. And how did he repay her? By giving her job to a butt-head.

Just thinking about it made her muscles tense—and just when she'd finally loosened up.

Hearing the door to the outer room open, she smiled, ready to get out of the tub and into bed with Clint. She quickly dried off, and just as he knocked, she wrapped the towel around herself. "I'll be right there."

"Take your time. I got the rotisserie chicken you like, and a salad with Italian on the side."

"Sounds great. What did you get?" She wiped off the mirror with her hand, but wished she hadn't when she saw how she looked. Her hair was still in a ponytail, but her eye makeup was smudged, her complexion spotty and she looked about a hundred years old.

But since Clint seemed to like her anyway, she exited the bathroom without giving it another thought.

He'd made the room perfect. The pillows were pushed up against the headboard, the covers turned down, their dinners were laid out on flattened paper bags, complete with a cold beer on each bedside table.

"I got a burger," Clint said, sounding like a manly man. "With cheese and fries."

"Mmm. Sounds yummy. You won't mind if I dine au naturel, will you?" she said, tossing away the bath towel.

He just sputtered in response.

Once she climbed in bed, she pulled the covers up under her arms and watched him strip. Definitely the highlight of her day...so far, anyway.

He uncapped the beers, then joined her. The eating was pretty silent. They both were famished, and as the hunger started to settle, her tangled thoughts took over.

The thing was, quitting was a huge decision. Of course she'd stay until this film wrapped because she'd given her word, but after that? Could she really work with Jason again? And Baxter?

God, the idea was horrible. But bowing out meant leaving Erin on her own, and that would be equally horrible. Plus there was something else to consider. Was she just using what happened to Erin as an excuse for something she hadn't had the guts to do on her own? Spending three months working on location had really opened her eyes. Made her reevaluate what she wanted her life to look like in ten years.

Erin wouldn't understand at first; the role of Tara was too major to give up. She'd advise Lila to suck it up, grab the credit, and after the sequel was finished, Lila wouldn't have to ever work with Jason again.

A very good argument. If Lila still cared about acting.

Honestly? A role like Tara was only going to add to the pressure she already felt. It was such a cutthroat profession, and there was always going to be someone prettier, younger, more connected.

Clint put his beer bottle down loudly on the nightstand. When she looked, she realized she'd eaten half her dinner but hadn't spoken a word to him.

"You okay?"

"Tired," she said. "Sorry. And you were so sweet with the bath and the food. I know I'm terrible company."

"Tired? Is that all? Because you sure seem like something else is on your mind."

"No, there's more. It's about Erin. She's not going to get the job she was promised on the sequel."

"Why not?" He looked stunned. "Everyone says she's the backbone of the film."

Lila grinned. "Listen to you sounding like an insider. But you're right. That's what makes everything so awful. Baxter will be named first AD."

"What the hell? The guy has no idea what he's doing."

"I know. It's all about money. Baxter's uncle's check was big enough to ensure his nephew could have the job. And Erin was the cost."

"Even I know that without Erin, the film's going to fall apart. He's an idiot."

"Which is why Erin's agreed to stay. She says she'll be paid as if she's the first AD, and that will help her get out from behind the loan she'd taken out to invest in the movie. Actually she means for it to help us both pay off the loans. She'll also be calling the shots. Baxter won't override her—he just gets all the credit."

Frowning thoughtfully, Clint finished his beer. "What about you? Is your role affected?"

"Nope. I'll still be in it, but it won't be the same."

"I'm sorry," Clint said, rubbing her arm. "I know how much you wanted this to work out."

"Honestly? I'm not even sure I care. Sometimes I think I'd rather just keep doing hair, which is something I enjoy."

"Do you really mean that?"

She sighed. "This business can be brutal. Erin's going to have to put up with Baxter's incompetence, and knowing every day that Jason sold her out. I don't even know how she's going to do it. She can barely tolerate Baxter or Jason now." Lila began collecting the takeout boxes. "But Erin doesn't give up easily. She can take a lot, always the optimist, waiting for that right door to open."

Clint was finished, too, so she stuffed all the containers back into the empty bags, and set them next to the wastebasket by the dresser.

By the time she was back in bed, she felt as if taking one more step might just kill her. Not that she wanted to disappoint Clint, but she wasn't sure she had it in her to do much more than kiss him good-night.

He smiled at her. "How about we go brush our teeth, then you crawl into my arms and try to get some sleep?"

"You're joking, right?"

"I can see you're beat. If you want to talk, I'll listen until morning, but I'm hoping you'll conk out. You need the rest."

She leaned over and kissed him, and while she meant for it to be a quick peck, she found she wanted it to be more. He tasted like salt and beer, and he smelled wonderful. She wasn't even sure why he was being so nice when she was so preoccupied, but she was grateful.

CLINT WAS TEMPTED to touch her, take the kiss and spin it into what he'd been thinking about for the last thirty-six hours, but she really did sound whipped.

So he pulled back. "Let's go brush our teeth."

She nodded and gave him a soft smile. It seemed like she needed a friendly ear, and that's what she'd get.

Even as he stood next to her in the small bathroom, trying hard not to stare at her breasts in the mirror, it occurred to him that if this thing with Erin blew up and she walked, Lila could leave, too. Go back to California tomorrow. Or the next day.

For a minute he'd gotten excited when she'd claimed she didn't care about the part anymore. But he knew it was just exhaustion and disappointment talking. And even if she'd meant it, that wasn't the same as saying she was done with Hollywood, just this film and Jason.

She would of course go right back home, get her agent or whatever to send her out on auditions. And she'd get roles, too. Plenty of them. Probably do better once she wasn't tied to all the crap going on with Jason and Baxter and everything else. Anyway, like she'd said the other night, she wouldn't disappoint Erin or her parents.

He looked at Lila, met her gaze, but only for a split second, before she made her way back to the bed. She wasn't eager to talk about it, which he understood. She was hurting and probably hadn't meant half of what she'd said. He only hoped she wouldn't be too embarrassed to use him as a sounding board.

Although, what did he know about her situation? He wasn't even in the business. He might be the nice guy who poured her a bath and bought her dinner, but he wasn't her long-haul guy. Never had been, not for Lila. But that was the deal, wasn't it?

He wiped his mouth, then turned off the bathroom light. As for him, it was too late. Foolish, pitiful hick that he was, he'd already fallen for her. Hard.

18

AFTER A SURPRISINGLY good night's sleep, Lila was feeling sort of decent at her 6:00 a.m. call. Her actors hadn't arrived yet, and she regretted not taking time to have coffee with Clint before he'd dropped her off. Annoyed, she refused to drink the craft services coffee when she knew there was really great Colombian in the production trailer. If she interrupted a meeting, so what. Everyone would just get over it.

Walking to the trailer, the only nice one of the bunch, she hurried, more because of the cold than anything, and darted up the three stairs. There was no one inside, but someone had been, and the pot of dark roast was waiting for her as if she'd made an appointment.

She'd just grabbed a mug when the door in the back closed with a bang. Turning her head, she saw it was Jason, and her desire for coffee diminished. Not that she wasn't going to take some; she just couldn't look at him without feeling a little sick.

"Hey, you stealing the coffee again?"

"As if I haven't earned a decent cup," she said. She poured, careful not to let her tremble make her spill the coffee, and by the time she put in a dash of real cream, she couldn't stand it anymore.

She turned to face Jason, who was staring up at the monitor plugged in above the desk.

"Why, Jason?"

He clicked off the dailies with the remote and blinked at her. "Why what?"

"Why was it so easy to sell out Erin? After all she's done for you? After we all swore we'd never become *that*."

"Oh, please. Look, I know you and Erin are besties, and you think I've screwed her, but has she told you that I'm paying her full salary for a first AD? It's not all that terrible."

"Of course it is. Good grief, how you've rationalized everything you used to believe was wrong about the business. Erin is the only thing that truly kept this shoot going. Making Baxter AD is a slap in her face, and you know it."

She could see the red rising up Jason's neck, a sure sign he was ready to blow. Well, she didn't care. Not a whit.

"What, you think it was an easy call for me? Do you have any idea how much money we've got now? Enough to make our budget on the sequel. Without taking out any more loans. Paul Mortimer's check isn't all I've got. He has connections to distributors. My God, after all these years, are you truly this naive?"

"I know who you were. And who you are now. And you used to believe the film would speak for itself. Despite everything, it's a hell of a movie, Jason. You didn't need to sell out. You just got scared and sold your soul for the easier road."

"Christ, what, has Erin been giving you lessons on breaking my balls?"

"I don't need lessons to tell the truth."

"What are you so upset about, anyway? You've still got your part. You're going to get some action on that role, sweetheart. That's what you've always wanted, and I just made sure it would happen. You should be thanking me. I'm giving you a future that's not working in a crappy trailer on some other actress's hair."

For a moment, Lila couldn't catch her breath. Then she got really, really calm. She put her mug down and took a step forward, then another, until she was right up in Jason's face. "You know what? I quit. I'm done. I don't want to work with you ever again. And I sure as heck don't want Baxter telling me what to do for a good eight weeks. I'll finish up on this one, because I've signed a contract, but after that? No more, Jason. Not one extra day."

"You're joking."

"Do I look like I'm joking?"

"This is your shot, Lila. For God's sake, you've got talent. We wrote this character for you. Tara's gonna get as much print as the lead. Don't you understand? This is the part that has all the juice. Don't walk away when it finally matters. You'll be back at square one, can't you see that?"

"I see everything quite clearly, thank you. You're thirty years old and you look like you're forty, you know that? Your affair with Penelope is doing damage to the movie, and your reputation. You sold out your most loyal friend and told her about it after the fact. I'm absolutely certain you knew she'd stick around, because that's who Erin is. Honorable. And you stuck a knife in her back. You—" Her brain and mouth both seemed to quit on her. "You stupid fucker. I'd rather wait tables than work with you again."

Lila's heart was beating so hard she might just have a stroke. She'd never felt better or been surer about anything in her life. And she'd used the F-word. She walked out of the trailer with her head held high.

Until she realized she'd just quit without talking to Erin.

How could she have been so stupid? It wasn't as if she could go back and say, by the way, please don't tell Erin. Pretty, pretty please. For old times' sake. And p.s. you're still a stupid fucker.

Lila sighed.

Crap.

CLINT DIDN'T KNOW what was going on when he saw Lila leave the trailer looking so angry she could spit, but when he saw Jason running after her, Clint jumped out of his truck.

Jason was calling out to her, and she just kept shaking her head, moving fast, without looking back at him. She was at work, Jason was still her boss, and since she didn't appear to be in any danger, Clint had no right to interfere. But that was just too damn bad. She could chew him out later if she wanted.

She was still a good distance away, and he doubted she'd seen him yet. Her head was bowed as she stared at the ground in front of her.

Jason gave up his pursuit, whether it was because he'd seen Clint, he didn't know. Didn't care. As he closed in on Lila, he saw how pale she looked. The violence building inside him wasn't anything he'd ever experienced before, and his fists reflexively clenched.

God help Jason if he was responsible for the stricken expression on her face.

Clint stopped ten feet in front of her.

"Lila?" he said, realizing she hadn't noticed him. "Sweetheart?"

Startled, she glanced up and froze. "Hi. What are you doing here?"

He held up her cell phone. "You forgot this in the truck."

"Oh." She patted her pocket, then held out her hand. "Thanks, I would've been lost without it."

"What's wrong?"

"Nothing." Her shoulders slumped. "Is Jason behind me?"

"He went back to his trailer."

"Good." She drew in a deep breath. "Look, I can't talk. I've got to get to work."

He followed her gaze to the man and woman, actors with small parts, who were here for the week.

Lila touched his arm with an unsteady hand. "Everything's fine," she said. "I promise I'll call you later." She looked as if she was in some kind of daze. "I just quit."

"You what?"

"I quit," she repeated. "You can't say anything."

She smiled at the approaching couple and said, "Go to the trailer, I'll be right there." She looked back at Clint. "Don't tell anyone, okay?"

He was almost too shocked to speak. "I won't."

"It's fine," she said, her face a complete wreck. "I promise."

He might've believed her if her voice hadn't cracked. Twice. Both times when she'd said the word *quit*. Given her loyalty to Erin, he could see her telling Jason to shove it on her friend's behalf. But things sure weren't fine. He recognized regret when he heard it.

Watching her race up the trailer steps, he couldn't make himself move. He had an order to pick up at the hardware store. He'd figured on hanging around and having breakfast at the diner while he waited for Jorgenson to open. But the thought of food didn't agree with him now.

Cast, crew and extras were arriving in herds. He'd left his truck in a lousy spot. He had to move it before he jammed someone up. Part of him wanted to wait around, be available if Lila had a few minutes to talk. But what was the point? Of course he wanted to make sure she was okay, that was a given. It was that tiny niggling of hope that worried him. The hope he still harbored that if she really had quit and it stuck, that could mean something for their future together.

On the other hand, if things went further south with Jason, she could be gone by the end of the day. She wanted to be at home for Christmas. If Jason refused to give her back the role, this was a great opportunity for her to tell him to stick it.

He climbed into his truck and sat there taking one deep breath after another. Just to slow his heart rate. Hell, at least he had the sense to be concerned. Because he knew her quitting didn't change anything. He'd figured that out last night.

Lila had expected to be busy today. But damn, he hoped she took a moment to call him. He sat there for another five minutes, staring at his phone, fighting the impulse to call her. But he was blocking traffic. If he didn't move, someone would be coming to chase him off the lot.

He drove to town, parked in front of the diner and

laid his head back. Lila had slept well, but he hadn't. He needed more coffee, and in a minute he'd rally and go get some.

What he had to remember, Lila may have doubts and regrets over quitting, but he didn't have any doubts about his future. He couldn't afford to, because he belonged at the Whispering Pines, keeping the Landers' name and tradition alive. Clint hoped Lila was right about Seth wanting to come back to the family. But they couldn't count on him.

Anyway, that wasn't the point. Tomorrow made three weeks. That's how long he'd known Lila. And he'd been driving himself insane about *their future*? That pretty much said it all. He was the worst kind of fool.

Clint hadn't realized he'd closed his eyes until someone knocked on the window. He straightened with a start. What the hell?

He let down the window. "Mom? What are you doing here? It's early."

She smiled. "Early? It's eight forty. How about buying your old mom a cup of coffee?"

Clint stared at the dashboard clock. An hour had gone by. How was that possible?

"Looks as though you could use some yourself."

Dazed, he glanced at her. "Sure," he said, and climbed out.

They sat in a small booth at the back of the diner and ordered coffee right away. "I'm so glad I caught you alone," his mom said and reached across the table to pat his hand.

"Is that why you're in town?"

"No," she said, laughing. "I need to pick up a few things at Abe's Variety. Although I wouldn't mind spotting a movie star or two."

Clint smiled. "I don't think any of them are in town today."

"Is Lila working?"

He nodded, hoping the conversation wasn't about to get awkward. "What is it you wanted to talk about?"

"You taking over the ranch."

Clint nodded at the waitress as she set down their coffees, and then he looked at his mom. "Didn't Dad tell you I gave him my answer?"

"He did." She stirred sugar into her cup. "And I'm so proud of him for telling you to wait."

Clint sighed. He knew she meant well, but damn... "It'll be the same answer after Christmas."

"Have you said anything to Lila?"

"She has nothing to do with it, Mom."

"Don't you think she should?"

He turned to stare out the window for a minute. "Look, do I like her? Very much. Can I see the two of us together in a year? No. She's an actress. She plays it down, but in a few months she'll have a part in a movie that will be a major game changer for her—"

"Oh, for goodness' sake, I know all about that," she said, waving a hand. "And about that Caribbean cruise your dad booked, too. So don't let that influence your decision."

"How?"

Laughing, she shook her head. "Your dad, bless his heart, forgets I pay the bills. I saw the charge on last month's statement. In fact, I've got to pick up some Scotch tape to leave around before he drives me crazy looking for it. I'm assuming he wants to wrap the tickets."

"And Lila?"

"We had a few private minutes in the kitchen."

"What did she say?" Clint put down his cup.

"First, the woman clearly has feelings for you, Clint, and don't act like I don't know what I'm talking about. Because you have feelings for her, too—pretty strong feelings that might be making your thinking fuzzy."

"Mom," he said calmly, "what did Lila say?"

"It's more what she didn't say."

His heart sunk. He should've known…

"That girl isn't cut out for show business. You say she plays it down, the big part that's coming up? Lila isn't playing it down, Clinton. She doesn't have the heart for it."

He swallowed. This was torture. He wanted to believe that, even while he told himself his mom was wrong.

"You listen when she talks about being in the movies. It *used* to be her dream. It isn't anymore."

He stared at his cup. Sure, he'd thought the same thing. For a minute. Before he'd realized he was being a fool. "And what if you're wrong?"

"Well, if I am, it doesn't change the fact that Lila isn't Anne."

He met his mom's concerned gaze.

"I know it crossed your mind, and then some," she said. "I'd be worried if it hadn't. Lila is different. She's had a taste of what it's like to be in all the Hollywood hoopla, and it's not for her. She's more of a homebody. Glamour and fame will never take the place of having family around her. And yes, I know you're gonna say I met her for just one night, what do I know, but here's something else to consider. Her looks can be deceiving. Might be hard to imagine her chasing after snotty-nosed kids and muddy dogs."

Clint smiled a little at that. The thing was, he could

see it. Her. Him. The two of them chasing after kids in the damn house he wanted to build. That was the problem. Lila was loyal to Erin, and she didn't want to disappoint her parents. He admired that, but it was another stumbling block. It also lent credence to what his mom said about her losing interest in the dream.

But he'd seen the regret in her face. He'd heard it in her voice. He wouldn't be surprised if she was talking to Jason right now. Apologizing. Trying to get the role back. And if she didn't, she'd always wonder how her life and career could've turned out differently.

That would kill him the most. Watching her spend the rest of her life regretting that she hadn't made it to the finish line. And always wondering what might've happened if she'd just gotten that big break she'd worked so hard to get.

He thought about Nathan and the hell his brother had gone through after Anne died. Not knowing about the yearning his wife had kept secret had almost destroyed him. Clint agreed. Lila wasn't anything like Anne, but to wonder was human nature.

"Clint, do your old mom a favor." She waited until he looked at her. "Before you give up, talk to Lila. Ask her what she wants."

LILA HAD BATTLED against nervous energy all day. That, and guilt. She had to talk to Erin, who was crazy busy. Everyone was, including Jason, so just maybe he hadn't said anything to Erin.

At 5:00 o'clock she texted Erin their SOS signal. It meant drop everything, screw everyone, come now.

As she waited, Lila bit her nails. She'd quit the nasty habit eight years ago. Another reason to hate Jason the

Weasel. "What?" Erin came running up behind her. "Are you okay?"

"Yes. Maybe." Lila swallowed hard. "I love you. You're not like a sister to me, you are my sister. You know that, right?"

"Lila, you're scaring the shit out of me. So just say it."

They were standing between two trailers. People could see them, but not hear the conversation. It was the best location Lila could manage.

"First, promise you won't hate me." Lila wouldn't cry. She'd promised herself.

"You could never do anything to make me hate you," Erin said. "Oh, unless you don't start talking."

Lila gave her a shaky smile. "I quit. This morning."

"You did not."

Lila nodded. "I know I should've talked to you first, but Jason made me so angry I just—"

"Don't worry, kiddo." Erin rubbed Lila's arm. "He hasn't given the role away. I'll talk to him."

"Erin, no. What I'm trying to say is—" She needed to breathe. "I don't want it. I can't do this anymore. I feel terrible. I do. We made promises…we had plans…" Lila sniffed. "Oh, and I called him a stupid fucker."

Erin blinked. "You?"

Lila nodded.

"To his face?"

Lila sighed.

Erin let out a howl and hugged her. "I'm so proud! Pissed that I wasn't there to see it, but really proud."

She freed herself from Erin's strong grasp. "You understand what I'm saying, don't you? It's not just Jason. I don't want this anymore, Erin. I hate being on location. I hate the—"

Erin's and Lila's phones buzzed within seconds of each other. It was the second time for Erin, so she brought out her cell.

Lila read hers. Clint wanted to see her tonight. She felt so giddy with relief, she texted him to come anytime.

"I have five minutes tops," Erin said. "But I have a confession, too."

CLINT'S PALMS WERE SWEATING, so was the back of his neck. He used a towel he had on the backseat, then got out of the truck. Lila's text had said to meet her at the hair-and-makeup trailer. He saw her coming from the back of the lot, but Baxter intercepted her.

For once he didn't want to strangle the guy. Clint slowed his pace and used the extra time to steady his breathing. He was going to do just as his mom suggested. Ask Lila. Straight out. She might give him a pitying look, but she wouldn't laugh at him.

Lila was giving Baxter the strangest look, so Clint sped up.

His back was to Clint. "You know, if you'd just be a little nicer to me, I can make things happen for you," Baxter said, reaching a hand out to Lila, who started laughing.

"You bastard," Clint said, and yanked the guy around to face him. His fist slammed into Baxter's jaw, and the man stumbled back.

"Clint!" Lila grabbed his arm and stopped him from taking another swing. "He's not worth it."

Baxter sputtered, red-faced, trying to breathe. Several bystanders applauded.

"Please," Lila said, trying to drag him away. "I already quit. Who cares what the slimeball says?"

Clint looked at her. Something was different about her voice. She didn't sound upset like she had earlier. She led him to the trailer, but they didn't go inside. "Are you saying you can't get the role back? Is Jason being hard-nosed?"

"Why would I want it back?" She seemed genuinely puzzled.

"You're not having second thoughts? Because you sure looked like it this morning."

"I was upset because I hadn't told Erin first. I haven't felt this good in forever." She laughed, and the happy sound clutched at his heart. "I'm finished. With all of it."

Clint took her hand. "You've worked a long time for this. I hate to see you have any regrets or wonder what could've been…"

"You're right. I've been at this for a very long time. That's how I can be so sure it's not what I want. This didn't happen overnight, Clint. Being on location and away from my family, and seeing the double-dealing up close… I'm not cut out for this."

"What about Erin?"

Tears glistened in Lila's eyes, and Clint felt his little bit of hope disappear. "Erin's quitting, too. She was staying on to make sure Jason let me have the role."

"She's quitting the business?"

"Not completely. She's got a fantastic idea for another documentary. She won an award for her last one."

The new information was making Clint's head spin. He wasn't sure what to say.

"I thought you'd be happy for me," Lila said softly.

He met her steady gaze. "I want you to be sure, sweetheart, that's all."

"Look, you're going to believe what you want, but

I'm telling you, I'm done. And I'm walking away for me." She turned her hand over and entwined their fingers. "Hollywood was a fun dream—the best," she said. "For a kid with stars in her eyes. I'm twenty-eight. I want to get married, have children, and I want to be there for them, always, just like my mom was there for me and my brother and sister. I know it's not chic or popular to admit, but that's what I want."

Clint could barely breathe let alone swallow. Neither of them had looked away once. He thought he could read her. But was he wishing for too much? "What do you plan on doing after you finish here?"

"Well, I miss my family like crazy," she said, and his heart sank. Lila wouldn't leave California. "So I'll go visit them for a couple weeks. When Erin moves ahead with the documentary, I figure I'll help with that."

They had ranches in California, quite a few from what he'd heard. Maybe it was time to have a talk with Seth. "What about after that?"

"I'm not sure." Lila looked nervous. Damn, he'd started sweating five minutes ago. "Have anything in mind?" She put a tentative hand on his chest, her beautiful blue eyes brimming with hope.

Relief and joy flowed through him like a spring river. Clint put his arms around her. "Actually I'm going to talk to a guy about building a house. Wouldn't mind some input if you're willing."

"Yes," she said, smiling through tears and hugging his neck. "Yes."

Clint froze. He did a quick replay in his head. Marriage had been on his mind for a few days. Had he just asked her to— No, he was pretty sure he hadn't done that.

He leaned back and looked at her. "Lila, I love you."

She nodded and whispered, "I love you."

"You know we've only known each other three weeks."

"I keep reminding myself of that," she said. "It seems like so much longer."

"And I think you know I have responsibilities here."

"I do know that," she whispered, snuggling up closer. "But I hope you can take a few days off to come with me and meet my parents."

Clint's chest tightened. He managed to nod. "Lila, will you marry me?"

"Yes," she replied, laughing and kissing him hard.

He held her close, breathing in her familiar scent, long after the applause around them stopped.

* * * * *

HOT HOLIDAY RANCHER

CATHERINE MANN

To my children, the best gift all year round!

One

Esme Perry had basked in the sun on a private beach in the South of France. She'd surfed with the best of them in California, Hawaii and Australia. But not even the threat of heatstroke or sharks had concerned her as much as the rush of water rolling down the country Texas back road toward her low-slung Porsche.

Rain sheeting against her windshield, Esme shifted into Reverse, willing her pulse to slow. *Be calm. Take deep breaths.* A quick three-point turn should have her ready to race out of harm's way. It would be a tight maneuver since the road was narrow, bracketed by a ditch on one side and sycamore trees on the other. It was tough enough to make such a maneuver during the daytime, but after dark? In the middle of a storm?

Not that she had a choice but to move. Flash floods were dangerous, especially in the country.

But her V-8 engine could outrace just about anything. Perhaps the Porsche wasn't the best choice for dirt roads, but she'd been excited about her early Christmas gift to herself.

Two points into Esme's three-point turn, the wave of rainwater slammed into the side of her vehicle. Her stomach clenched. She struggled to control the steering wheel as her car slid along the mud-slicked road. The Porsche's back end fishtailed. Her foot slipped off the clutch, her spiky heel wedging under the brake. The heel snapped. But she didn't have time to mourn the demise of her favorite leopard-print pumps. The Porsche lurched, then spun out, whipping the wheel from her clenched grip.

Her heart rose into her throat with panic as she battled what felt like g-forces slamming her against the door. Worse yet, she couldn't see due to vertigo and the rush of water over her candy apple–red hood. Was she close to the side of the road? How deep was the ditch? Where were the trees?

And, oh God, were those headlights or lampposts?

She braced. Struggled not to close her eyes. And prayed.

The spinning stopped, her car halting with a jolt. But not a crash. She exhaled a shaky breath, her ears ringing so loudly it almost drowned out the rain pounding the roof and a Christmas carol flowing from the speaker.

"Silent Night"?

Hardly.

But she was all right, in one piece, as was her car.

With luck, she could still reach her destination before bedtime. She would have arrived earlier, but an accident on the interstate from Houston to Royal had delayed her arrival. At least she was close enough to her destination to walk. According to her GPS, the front gate to Jesse Stevens's ranch should be less than a mile away.

She pressed the clutch, threw the car into Neutral and pressed the ignition.

The engine turned over. Then spluttered out.

She tried again and…

Nothing. Not even a catch.

She'd bought the stick-shift model, a purist when it came to her sports cars. She liked the control of a manual transmission, a talent she'd learned when teaching herself to drive on one of her father's older trucks on their Houston ranch. She'd been determined to perfect the skill, to win his approval.

Not much had changed on that front, since she was here to please her dad, to bolster his image with the charter branch of the Texas Cattleman's Club here in Royal, in hopes that he could be president of the new Houston branch.

Her PR plan would start with a surprise visit to Royal's own Jesse Stevens, an influential player at the TCC. If she could ever get there.

She bit back a curse, weighing her options. The odds of a tow truck showing up out here in this weather were slim. Should she wait to see if the car started and risk getting hit by another wave? Or start walking? In her broken shoes. In the rain. And mud. Sighing in resignation, she angled to get her umbrella.

Bracing, she opened the door, and rain sheeted inside. She wedged her umbrella through the opening, although it was fast becoming a moot point. Even her Prada trench was losing the fight against the deluge. Frigid water lapped around her ankles, soaking the hem of her slacks as she leaned into the wind, shivering. Still, she was determined to forge ahead, one step at a time.

She couldn't bear the thought of telling her father she needed to postpone the promotion trip. He'd put his trust in her, and even knowing a thirty-four-year-old woman shouldn't care this much what her father thought, she couldn't deny she was still trying to win his approval, to be something other than the often-forgotten middle child.

In college, she'd found her niche with an aptitude for public relations. It was her chance to shine. When her father had taken note of her success after graduation, he'd hired her as PR executive for the family business, Perry Holdings.

And if ever Sterling Perry had needed a promotional face-lift, it was now, when the new Houston Texas Cattleman's Club was cranking up. Fledgling organizations hated nothing more than a scandal.

And her father's good name had taken quite a few blows, first with an arrest on charges of orchestrating a Ponzi scheme that nearly caused a collapse of one of his investment funds.

No sooner had her father gotten out from under the weight of the fraud rumors than he was under suspicion for the murder of a Perry Holdings assistant. And, as if her father wasn't already stressed enough, just last week a Currin Oil executive named Willem Inwood had been arrested under suspicion of being behind the Ponzi scheme. He wasn't talking yet, but already people were coming forward saying he was the one who'd started those nasty rumors.

Now, even though his innocence had been proven on the murder charge and Ponzi issue, he still needed a serious image makeover if he expected to win the club's leadership spot.

And she intended to give him that fresh start, with some help from Jesse Stevens. Wrestling her bedraggled umbrella, she trudged ahead another couple of steps.

Were those lights flickering ahead? Hope and wariness jockeyed inside her. She was so very cold and soggy. But this also wasn't Houston, with her high-rise condo secured by round-the-clock guards.

She pulled one hand from the umbrella and reached inside her coat to her cross-body bag, fumbling for her can of Mace.

The lights drew closer, grew stronger, until the glow focused into two beams. High off the ground. A truck. The driver's-side door swung wide and a large, looming figure jumped out, ducking into the rain while holding his Stetson in place.

She gripped her Mace harder. She'd taken self-defense classes in college, but she was seriously off-balance with one broken heel and the other spiked into the mud.

"Ma'am, what are you doing out here tonight? Are you waiting for a tow truck?"

That voice. It couldn't be… But her ears told her it was. After all, she'd spent countless hours watching videos of Jesse Stevens giving interviews, memorized them, in fact, to decide the best tactic for approaching him. She tilted her head to catch sight of his face below the brim to confirm.

And she gasped.

No picture could do him justice. Even with the Stetson covering his blond hair, he bore the look of a cowboy Viking. An image she found difficult to let go of once it came to life in her mind.

Spluttering on a mouthful of rain, she tucked her Mace can back into her purse, no longer needing protection.

She should have suspected the truck could belong to Jesse Stevens. She was near his ranch, after all. But still, weren't the odds higher it would be one of his employees rather than him at this hour, in the rain?

Yet there was no doubting who this man was, even in the dark with just his headlights slicing through the night. She'd done her research on the man and his spread well before this excursion to meet him, persuade him.

But she wasn't ready to let him know who she was. Not just yet. She swallowed hard. "My car won't start, and the cell reception is garbage out here in the middle of nowhere."

"Speaking as the landlord of the Middle of Nowhere, I've never had any trouble with mine." Rain dripped from the brim of his hat as he towered over her. "You should check with your provider."

Was that irony or irritation coating his words?

Not good if she'd already made him angry. This would be over before it started.

She longed for higher heels to make her taller, closer to his eye level. "I'll be sure to look into my provider as soon as I find dry clothes. If you could just help me call for a tow, I'll get my suitcase so I can change. I'm freezing to death."

It was cold for Texas, even in December.

"Your car's not going anywhere tonight, ma'am. And there's no way either of us should risk walking back over to your vehicle to retrieve your luggage. The ground could give way at any time."

Her foot slipped. She looked quickly at him. "It's just my broken shoe."

Then her other foot shot out from under her. She lurched to the side, her umbrella whipping away in the wind. Her arms pinwheeled as she lost her balance, tumbling toward the rushing swell of water alongside the dirt road.

Strong hands clasped her waist and stopped her fall. Before she could catch her breath, he'd hauled her against his chest. His warm breath fanned her cheek.

"Are you all right?"

Other than goose bumps that had nothing to do with the cold because she was in the arms of a Viking cowboy? "I'm fine." Her words came out husky. "Thank you."

"What are you doing out here this time of night in such crummy weather?" Thunder rolled in the distance.

She braced her palms on his impossibly broad shoulders and looked straight into Jesse Stevens's emerald green eyes. "I'm looking for you."

Jesse Stevens held the drenched woman against him, her willowy body enticing even through her soaked raincoat and his hastily-tossed-on jacket. He'd been making a last check of the horses, concerned about the thunder spooking them, when he'd seen the car lights. He'd been surprised, not expecting anyone until tomorrow. Not that he was complaining.

The matchmaker he'd hired had outdone herself in sending this candidate.

He wondered which of the three contenders this was—the single mom, the veterinarian or the Miss Texas pageant runner-up. This woman certainly could be the latter, and that might explain the high heels and flashy car choice. The height seemed to be right, based on the stats in her profile. Although it was difficult to tell much in the dark. He was definitely curious to learn more about the husky-voiced siren. All the more reason to resist the temptation to hold on for an extra second or two.

Stepping back, he still cupped her elbow. Just to make sure she didn't lose her balance, of course. "Are you okay? You weren't hurt when your car spun out, were you?"

She nodded, pulling one foot, then the other, out of the mud. "I'm fine, thank you. I truly didn't expect the weather to get this bad."

Given her slick trench and Porsche, she had more of a city-girl vibe that he had doubts would hold up out here. But the matchmaker would have told her about him and his rural lifestyle. He'd sure filled out a checklist of his criteria for the kind of woman he was looking for.

"Ma'am, the road is at risk of giving way further. You need to get to safety. My truck can take an alternate path that's not accessible to the public."

"Let's go, then." She started forward, her purse

tucked tight to her side, but her foot sank deeper into the mud, stopping her progress. Sighing, she cursed under her breath. Like a sailor, no less.

An unexpected surprise. She had grit to go along with all of that glam. He could still feel the imprint of her against him.

She glanced up at him, her eyelashes spiky wet, her ponytail slick and sleek down the front of her coat. "The heels aren't holding up well out here."

"Then I'll carry you." He wasn't sure where the invitation came from, but now that he'd said it, the idea had taken root. An appealing option, and with each passing second, an increasingly necessary one.

"Whoa, wait." She held up a manicured hand, with two chipped nails and another broken. "That's a bit extreme."

"Ma'am…" He smiled. "The longer we talk, the worse the roads will be. And I don't know about you, but I'm cold even though I have on boots."

Indecision flickered across her face. But then she shivered and her hand lowered. She nodded quickly, her teeth chattering.

All the invitation he needed.

He scooped her up into his arms, tucking her against him as he made tracks toward his truck. With a squeak of surprise, she looped her arms around his neck, a light scent of something floral and exotic riding the humid air to tempt his nose. Her body fit against him, the curve of her breast pressed to him.

So much for feeling cold. Heat fired through his veins. But he needed to learn more about her. His days of sowing wild oats were in the past. He was ready to settle down, build a family, and he wasn't waiting around for chance to bring him the woman he needed.

He'd contacted a selective, high-priced matchmaker to assist him in the search. His days were packed with running his ranch. His only social life involved the occasional event at the Texas Cattleman's Club and he already knew every one of the members. He wanted a wife, children—heirs. He didn't believe in grand romance or love. But he was a firm advocate of the benefits of a winning partnership.

Yes, he more than wanted a wife. He *needed* a wife and he was prepared to offer that spouse his full partnership in return. A win-win for them both.

Once he found the right candidate.

Stopping by the passenger side of his dual-cab truck, he set the woman on her feet carefully, ensuring the ground beneath her was safe before he let go. The rain was coming down in buckets.

He opened the door for her, offering a hand as she stepped on the running board. Damn, those dainty shoes of hers were mighty mangled. She hadn't been prepared. The clasp of her cold fingers in his hand reminded him of how badly this stormy evening could have turned out for her.

And it still could if he didn't get his butt in gear and drive back to the house. He braced a hand on the hood as he jogged around to the driver's side. Once behind the wheel, he slammed his door closed against the wall of rain being blown inside.

At least the heater was still blasting, since he'd never turned the vehicle off. He swept aside his Stetson, flinging it to the back seat beside a horse blanket and a thermos.

"I'm so glad you came along," she said, her teeth still chattering. She kicked off her broken shoes and wriggled her toes under the blast of warm air circling at the floorboard.

"And I'm glad I saw you out there." He started to ask her name, but the rain picked up pace on the roof. It could wait. "I hate to think what could have happened to you if those waters swept your car away."

As she'd said right away, she knew who he was. So he didn't have to worry about reassuring her she was safe to come with him.

"You were right to question the wisdom of my driving into this storm," she conceded. "I was so eager to get here, I just kept thinking I could outpace the weather."

She shook her head, laughing softly. The husky melody of her chuckle filled the truck cab, stroking his senses. That matchmaker sure had a knack.

He cleared his throat. "And the weather still might win if we don't get moving."

Jesse eased the four-wheel-drive vehicle out of Park and accelerated carefully. The tires spun, then caught, the truck surging forward, toward the dim twinkling of Christmas lights strung along the split-rail fence. The storm smudged the glow until it was just a smear of green, red and white.

"I'm sorry to inconvenience you so late," she said. "I certainly intended to arrive earlier." The truck jostled along a rut in the road and she braced a hand against the door.

"You'd have had better luck with a utility vehicle instead of that sports car of yours."

"It would appear so." She squeezed excess water from her ponytail, her wet hair clearly blond now in the glow of the dash.

But he wasn't any closer to identifying which of the matchmaker's candidates she might be.

"I'm Jesse Stevens, as you already seem to know. And you are?"

"Esme Perry. Nice to meet you, Jesse."

He looked over sharply in surprise at her name. She was not one of the three women the matchmaker had provided. Surely he couldn't have forgotten a recommended candidate. Perhaps he'd missed an email from the matchmaker?

Except… Wait… Alarms sounded in the back of his mind. There were plenty of Perrys in Texas. But one branch in particular was heavy-duty on the radar of the Royal branch of the Texas Cattleman's Club. "Perry, as in…"

"Yes, my father is Sterling Perry. We're very excited about the new branch of the Texas Cattleman's Club opening in Houston. My father sent me here to talk to you. To do a little recon," she said with a sassy smile.

Disappointment churned. She hadn't been sent by the matchmaker. He focused on the path ahead, a back road on higher ground to his home.

"A spy in our midst," he said dryly. Granted, one helluva sexy Mata Hari.

"Not anything so nefarious." She tugged at the belt of her trench coat. "I'm just here to see how you run things at the Royal branch."

"Or to curry favor for your dad."

She straightened in the seat, clearly bristling at the criticism of her father. But it wasn't any secret that Sterling Perry had a sketchy past and a quest for power.

A quest that was currently playing out in a battle with Ryder Currin as they vied for control of the new Houston branch, to be opened in a historic building site, a former luxury boutique hotel. Ryder Currin was a self-made man. Whereas Esme's family was led by the old-money, charming, larger-than-life patriarch Sterling Perry, who continued to grow the Perry fortune in banking, real estate and property development.

Jesse's impression of the man? All show but little substance.

Was this woman like her dad? It seemed so, judging by her car and her clothes and her defense of her father.

He pulled up to his ranch home. More lights glimmered in the trees lining the driveway, and a wreath glowed on the front door of his white two-story house. A sprawling place he'd had built with hopes of one day having a family of his own. His parents were dead. He only had one sister, and while he loved her, she had her own life.

Now he was ready to build a future for himself.

Keeping his eyes off the woman beside him, he steered off the path and onto the driveway, circling around back. More twinkling lights marked the way. He'd arranged for decorations outdoors to make his place more welcoming, but hadn't gotten around to the indoors. His life definitely needed a woman's touch.

He activated the garage door opener, steered into the six-bay garage, and turned off the truck as the automatic door closed behind them. "You can stay at my place until morning…or until the weather blows over."

"I appreciate the offer. Clearly, I'm in no position to turn you down." She gestured to her bare feet and soggy clothes.

"Call it club loyalty. It would be irresponsible of me to send you back out into this weather." He draped a hand over the steering wheel and allowed himself an unrestrained look at the bombshell beside him. "But I don't talk about club business in my off-hours, so I won't be discussing your father or the Houston chapter."

"Fair enough. I just have one question, nothing about the Texas Cattleman's Club." She tipped her head to one side, her raincoat parting to reveal the curve of her breasts in the soaked silk shirt. "Who did you think I was?"

Two

Toying with her seat belt and not in any hurry to leave the truck just yet, Esme waited for Jesse's answer, more curious than she would have liked to admit about what mystery woman he was expecting. Even knowing that cowboys weren't her type, she couldn't deny the appeal of those piercing green eyes.

He cocked an eyebrow as he reached for his Stetson. "I certainly didn't think you were one of the infamous Perry family."

She bristled at the censure in his voice. *"Infamous?"* she repeated, the bubble of romance officially burst. She unbuckled her seat belt and reached for the door handle. "That's rather harsh, don't you think?"

"I didn't mean to offend," he said as his boots hit the pristine cement floor of his six-car garage with a solid thud. "Your father was investigated on fraud charges and the murder of a Perry Holdings assistant not too long ago."

Vincent Hamm had gone missing, the assistant presumed to have quit and moved to the British Virgin Islands to spend his life surfing, based on a text he'd sent his boss. But then his body had been discovered with a bullet wound to the chest, his skull bashed, making identification difficult. But DNA tests had confirmed the man's identity.

Esme slammed the door, the sound reverberating in the dimly lit space. Her damp and muddy feet slipped ever so slightly as she charged forward alongside a speedboat, her toes still so icy cold, her mangled shoes dangling from her hand. An SUV, a motorcycle and a pair of four-wheelers filled the rest of the space. The man sure liked his toys.

Or maybe his family did?

She glanced at his left hand as he tapped the security code at the door leading into the house. No ring. But then, there was still the mystery woman.

Esme pulled her focus back to her reason for being here. To clean up her father's image among the Texas Cattleman's Club members here in Royal.

"My father was cleared of fraud *and* the murder of Vincent Hamm." All hell had broken loose when the body was found at the site of the new Texas Cattleman's Club, where her father's construction company was doing the renovations. The murderer still hadn't been found. "As I recall, you were under suspicion, too, after leaving an angry message on Hamm's voice mail."

"Valid point." He waved her inside with a broad

hand, his square jaw flexing. "Lucky for me, I have an airtight alibi."

While he turned on the lights, she flung her damp hair over her shoulders and unbuttoned her trench coat. "Clearly there's something more you want to say?"

Texas landscapes lined the walls of the corridor, one end leading to a washroom and the other leading into the house. He eyed her for a moment, sizing her up before nodding tightly. "Your father has led a cutthroat life in the business world. Sterling Perry may not be guilty of this, but the man he has been made it easier to believe it could be him."

She couldn't deny the truth in that. But that was still her daddy Jesse was talking about. "You certainly know how to win friends and influence people."

Sighing, he swept off his hat. "Ma'am, you're clearly tired. I'll make you something to drink—decaf coffee? Tea? Hot chocolate?"

She was exhausted. But she had a narrow window of time. If she kept bristling this way, she would lose the chance to plead her father's case to be the president of the Houston branch of the club. It was tough enough already with all the politics back home, given the other contender for the position was his longtime rival, Ryder Currin, who her father felt had unjustly gotten an oil-rich piece of land that should have stayed in the family. It didn't seem to matter to Sterling that he already had more money than royalty and that Ryder had made the bulk of his fortune through savvy investments.

Although they had to get along these days since Ryder was seeing her sister Angela, that didn't change the fact that her dad wanted the position. And Angela would have to live with that, because Esme intended to make this happen for her father.

"Hot chocolate, please, if it's not too much trouble." It sounded like something that would take longer to make. Give her more time to collect herself. Mold herself into the perfect influencer. "And no worries. I'm thick-skinned like my father."

A fib. She actually was the most sensitive of her siblings, but that would smooth things over for now.

As the sensitive sibling, she'd learned early how to play family peacekeeper. To de-escalate tension and defuse situations—even though her heart often thudded loudly in her chest and panic rose in her blood.

With footfalls uncharacteristically silent for such a tall, broad-chested man, he moved into the laundry room. Light flickered on, and Esme peered inside the well-kept pale yellow room with green plant accents. He pulled clothes out of a basket on top of the dryer, then strode with cowboy swagger back to her. He motioned down the hallway. Sconces on the wall provided a warm light as they made their way to the massive kitchen. He placed the neatly folded clothes on the island.

With a surveying glance, she took in the open, sprawling layout. White granite countertops provided a sleek contrast to the dark wood cabinets. Open shelves displayed simple white dishes and mugs. A countertop overlooked a large bay window that, despite the night storm raging outside, offered an enviable view of the large barn and fence. Unlike the interior of the house, the barn and fence sported twinkling Christmas lights.

A thick but unfinished sandwich took up the majority

of a white plate on the countertop. He must have been eating there when he'd spotted her car outside.

Jesse's rough-cut smile lit up his green eyes. "Good, I'm glad to hear you're tough. If we're going to be trapped here together until the road's cleared, it will be easier if we get along."

Trapped? Now, that sounded promising.

"True enough." She slid off her trench coat.

The room went silent as his eyes flickered with awareness, taking in her damp blouse and slacks. Her chilled skin warmed at his gaze.

Then he looked away, clearing his throat as he picked up a remote control off the island and thumbed on the sound system. Holiday tunes played softly, jazz renditions. That surprised her. She would have expected him to pick country music.

Rubbing the back of his neck, he walked over to the double wooden doors of his pantry. Intricately carved, the wood depicted a rearing horse on a landscape. It was a touch of personality in this state-of-the-art kitchen that was otherwise pretty much devoid of personality. He removed a bag of marshmallows and a mason jar filled with hot chocolate mix and set them on the counter. He pulled out milk from the fridge.

"Well, then, Esme, let's agree not to talk about your father." He spun a pan in his hand, setting it down on the front right burner.

Not discussing her dad was rather counterproductive to her reason for braving the storm to see him. But she wasn't going to argue with him. She would work her way back to the subject when the opportunity arose.

"Fair enough." And while she waited, she couldn't resist asking, "Let's start with who you were expecting."

"Actually, three someones." The milk simmered on the gas stove.

He reached up to the open shelves, selecting an oversize mug. His hands were calloused and capable, telling a story. He didn't just own this massive spread. He worked it.

Surprise lit through her. "Three people you didn't know and wouldn't recognize?"

So...mystery *women*. What was this man up to?

Jesse had maneuvered to a well-stocked bar next to the stainless steel fridge. She noticed a sole picture beside it—of a girl in her twenties who shared his intense green eyes. A sibling perhaps? It was the first—and only—sign of personal effects she'd spotted since entering his ranch house/mansion. A private man, then.

He held up a bottle of peppermint schnapps and quirked an inquiring eyebrow. She nodded and he set the bottle on the counter beside the rest of the ingredients.

"In my defense, Esme, it was dark when I found you and you were—*are* drenched. Speaking of which, you should change before you catch a cold. Your hot chocolate will be ready soon." He stood toe to toe, the spicy and damp scent of him teasing her senses. He passed over the stack of clothes—sweats, a tee and socks—his calloused knuckles brushing hers. "I'll tell you all about the three mystery women when you get back."

Her hands still tingling from the light touch, she sure

hoped her father appreciated her efforts here. Because she suspected focus on her task was going to be tough to come by with Jesse Stevens.

She wasn't even one day into this promotional excursion and already she'd made a mess of things. One that not even the longest, steamiest of showers could make right.

Esme was no stranger to luxury, but she still appreciated the plush robe and heated floors in the guest bathroom he led her to.

An all-Texas bathroom for sure, with a touch of modern rustic charm in the form of the polished horns on the wall opposite the luxurious Jacuzzi. But there was also a large tinted window that offered a view of the Christmas lights lining the fence. The only other lights came from a bunkhouse in the distance.

Under this roof, she was alone. With Jesse Stevens.

Exhaling hard, she plucked one of the lotions from the basket on the counter. She opened the top and inhaled the delicious scent of peppermint, which reminded her of that spiked cocoa waiting for her. Along with the man.

Smoothing the lotion onto her legs, she found her thoughts drifting back to Jesse. His broad shoulders. His blond hair spiked and mussed. Her skin tingled from more than the minty cream.

She'd never doubted her professionalism. Her cool head. And while she worked for the family company, she'd allowed this to become too personal. This wasn't even about the business. This was about her father's quest to be the president of a club. Which many would have thought meant she was doing a favor, not a job.

Many would be wrong. This was more than a favor. She was trying to earn her dad's approval. Even knowing that shouldn't matter so much to her, an adult woman, she couldn't dodge the truth.

She risked a glance in the mirror. With her hair wet and snarled, she was a mess. A far cry from how she'd started the morning with a spa day. Even her manicure hadn't survived, one nail broken and two others chipped.

It was almost comical, really, as if all her professional facade had been wiped away. Her slacks were ruined. Her silk blouse very likely unsalvageable, too.

All that was left of the real her were her champagne-colored satin underwear and her diamond stud earrings.

At least she had something to wear other than the robe. She stepped into the baggy sweatpants, then the Texas A&M pullover, the fabric warm and tantalizing against her bare skin. She tugged on the athletic socks, bunching them around her ankles. A far cry from the heels she'd slipped on this morning with such relish. But as least she was warm. And clean.

She left the steam-filled bathroom and returned to her suite. Swiping her phone from the coffee table, she dropped down into the desk chair next to the fireplace. Stones flanked the fireplace, giving the guest suite the feel of a swanky cabin. Her toes sank into the plush rug as she FaceTimed her sister.

Of all of her siblings, Angela Perry worried the most. And judging by the four texts Esme had received while she was showering, her sister was imagining every worst-case scenario.

She propped the phone against a leather-bound book on the desk to free her hands to brush through the rat's nest that had replaced her hair.

Within a few rings, her sister's blond hair and rounded face came into view. Angela sat on the ground in front of the new gas fireplace she'd just had installed, flames flickering. Orchestral carols played softly in the background.

"Well, hello there." Angela stared back at her, her blue eyes flaring in surprise. "You look…not like yourself. No offense meant."

"None taken." Running the brush through a knot in her hair, Esme laughed lightly. Her sister had never been a clotheshorse, preferring an understated style. A love of fashion had been at least one thing Esme could share with Melinda, since Angela and her twin had just about everything else in common.

They even lived in the same condominium building—an upscale thirty-two-floor limestone high-rise with wraparound windows and expansive views. The twins had even chosen the same layout, Angela on the fifteenth floor and Melinda on the twenty-fourth.

"Well, this has been quite a day. Or night, rather." Angela tossed a scrap of Christmas wrapping paper into the fire behind her, then reached for another roll. "Definitely not the image of my glamorous sister."

"Stranger things have happened." But heat still stung her cheeks. One of the ways Esme gained her confidence—and kept her sensitive soul in check—was through a careful curation of makeup, hair and luxurious clothes. The oversize sweats she was wearing rattled her. Threw her off-balance.

Though, if she were being honest, not any more than her sexy host.

Her sister's thin fingers moved deftly over a small stack of jewelry boxes with elegant silver script reading "Diamonds in the Rough." Esme guessed the packages were for her and Melinda, not that she could see inside. Most likely Melinda's contained something to celebrate her baby on the way. The pregnancy had been a surprise to Melinda and her new husband, Slade, but a welcome one. And pregnancy hadn't slowed down her sister's philanthropic works one bit.

To her right, Angela had a bin filled with gold and red foil paper with intricate bows. Designer-level gift-wrapping supplies. A small stack of already-wrapped presents glistened in the fire glow. Esme always told her sister they could afford to pay someone to wrap the gifts for them, but Angela insisted she enjoyed doing it herself, making each one a work of art.

And Christmas was all the more special since Angela had reunited with her former fiancé, Ryder Currin.

Angela ripped clear tape off to secure the golden foil on one of the smaller jewelry boxes. "I'm glad you called. I was starting to get worried. Weather reports are looking terrible in Royal."

Esme thought of the soaked, muddy clothes she had carefully placed in a bag next to the bathtub. She winced a little. "The reports are accurate."

"But you're okay?" her sister asked, genuine worry in her voice.

She nodded, enjoying the soft sounds of violins surging through "Ave Maria."

"I got caught in a flash flood, but lucky for me, I was close to Stevens's ranch. He saw my headlights and came to my rescue."

"Sounds like a close call. I can't imagine your low-slung car held up well in those conditions."

"You can get the judgy tone out of your voice. I know you weren't a fan of my purchase." Esme worked the last of the tangles from her hair, smoothing the brush down the length until she was satisfied that all the knots were out. At least she'd managed to restore some semblance of order in her life.

"It's your money to do with as you please," her sister said as she reached toward a stack of unwrapped presents. Picking up a handsome brass shaving kit, she started sizing up the necessary material to wrap it.

"Well, you can rest easy. My next purchase will come with four-wheel drive." Sporty four-wheel drive.

Angela set down the paper and peered into the screen, her blue eyes fixed but still kind. The look of an older sister. "I just care about you."

"I know." It was tough to discard the defensiveness sometimes, feeling like an outsider with her sisters' twin bond. "And thank you for caring."

Her sister nodded, continuing her methodical wrapping. Without looking up from lining up the edge of the paper with machinelike precision, she said, "So, what's the progress with Jesse Stevens?"

"I've barely had time to shower, much less make progress."

"Shower?" She raised a blond eyebrow. "At Jesse Stevens's house? You're there now?"

"Yes, and no need to sound scandalized. I was drenched. I needed to change." She glanced down at her clothes. When was the last time she'd worn sweats? High school maybe. Or middle school. As rarely as she could manage. "But enough about me. How was your date with Ryder last night?"

Her sister had been engaged to none other than their father's longtime nemesis Ryder Currin, who also happened to be in the running to head the Houston branch of the Texas Cattleman's Club. Angela and Ryder had broken up, but were now back together again with Sterling Perry's blessing. Esme would wager money a re-engagement wasn't too far off.

She just hoped Ryder was really right for her sister. He'd been married twice before—divorced from the first wife and widowed by the second. He had one child from each of those marriages, plus an adopted daughter. All adults. Such a complicated blended family.

Angela deserved to have a man love her unconditionally.

"I never thought he and I would have another chance, but things are good, really good."

Her blue eyes turned wistful and the smile that warmed her face drew a pang of guilt from Esme over her doubts and concerns.

"I wish I could have been there for us to talk all about it in person over lunch."

Angela nodded, her smile still present but soft. "That would have been fun, but I understand."

Her sister leaned back to the pile of gifts—a cashmere scarf, leather-bound books, artisanal reclaimed-wood trays. The silver strands in her chunky gray sweater glimmered.

Christmas was coming at the end of the month and Esme hadn't even begun her shopping. She wished she had her sister's love for organization and gift-giving. Maybe then she would feel more connected to the holiday. "If only I'd waited to leave…"

"Dad appreciates what you're doing for him. This is important."

Was it, though? More important than being with her sister? She'd tried to convince her dad that this could wait a couple of days, but he'd insisted. And she hadn't stood up to him. She'd even had the weather as an excuse and she hadn't taken it.

"Well, I'll be back in Houston before you know it. We can have brunch and chat over mimosas."

"That would great. Just let me know when you're finished there and I'll line it up with Melinda, too. We'll definitely need to make it brunch and not breakfast, since Melinda still gets morning sickness." She chewed her fingernail thoughtfully, then added, "Perhaps we could include Tatiana, as well, if you don't mind."

Esme bit her lip to keep from blurting how she wanted to do things on her own with Angela, without their sister, much less Angela's bestie, Tatiana Havery.

Tatiana, a vice president at Perry Holdings who specialized in real estate, had been going through a tough time ever since it came out that Willem Inwood was her estranged half brother. And now that he'd been arrested last week? It would be petty to exclude her.

"Mimosa brunch with you, Melinda and Tatiana.

Count on it. Maybe we should invite Ryder's two daughters. I could get to know my future nieces better." She chuckled at the irony of that, since Ryder's daughters were both adults. There was an age gap between Ryder and Angela, but since her sister didn't mind, then who was Esme to judge?

"Okay, then. I will." Angela fluffed her golden-blond hair, surveying the mess of ribbon and foil paper strips around her. "All right, sis, I need to clean up this mess. Thank you for checking in. Please stay in touch."

"I will, just as soon as I have something to report." Esme waved before signing off.

Sighing, she swept her hair into a loose topknot. Casual glam, she told herself.

Time to face her sexy host and try not to wonder if a kiss from him would taste of peppermint schnapps.

Jesse stared out the kitchen window at the water pooling outside, covering the driveway. As the storm continued to rage, he was glad he'd reached Esme when he did.

No denying it, the woman who'd crashed into his life this evening had made quite an impression. He thought about the way her wet clothes clung to her, outlined her shapely body.

Not that she was his type. Too city. Too polished for a ranch lifestyle. Not that it mattered. He had three potential matches coming to the ranch.

Still, his thoughts drifted to the way her wet hair fell in waves. No. He couldn't deny being intrigued by the woman who was currently cleaning herself up in his shower as the rain pelted down.

In the oversize mug, he stirred the hot chocolate. The mug in his hand had been a gift from his little sister. She'd made it in a pottery class, rightly guessing that something homemade would mean more to him. He could buy anything he wanted.

His sister had a knack. The pottery was expertly crafted. She'd called it part of her robin's-egg collection.

He wasn't an overly sentimental man, and even though he and his sister weren't close, this mug represented his last link to family. To something grounding.

After giving the hot chocolate a final stir, he popped the top of the peppermint schnapps, deciding Esme should be the judge of her alcohol level. He didn't want to pour too much. Who knew what her alcohol tolerance was? And he wasn't one to take advantage. He prided himself on being a man of honor.

And he needed to stay focused on his search for a bride, someone who wanted to share this lifestyle with him and build a family.

He turned back to the kitchen and poured himself a cup of coffee with a shot of whiskey in it. Then settled onto a barstool at the kitchen island where his half-eaten sandwich still waited. Fried steak between two thick slices of Texas toast. He took another bite and washed it down with his spiked coffee, the taste firing through his veins on this damn long day.

As he continued to eat his sandwich to the rhythm of rain and thunder, he reflected on the events of the last hour. Now he regretted calling Esme's family "infamous." The word had a crueler inflection than he had meant. Especially since Esme's father was no longer a suspect in the murder. He understood too well what it felt like to be wrongly accused.

Tearing into another bite of his sandwich, he went over the events of the murder investigation in his mind.

He'd been shocked when he was questioned by keen Houston detective Zoe Warren. All because of an argument he'd had with Vincent Hamm. Someone he'd thought he could count on. His kid sister just graduated with an MBA from one of the top programs in the country. Not only was she his sister and he had a strong sense of family, but his sister was also brilliant, with a sharp mind for business. Jesse had asked Vincent to help get his sister in at Perry Holdings. But Vincent refused to even set up an interview for Janet.

Jesse took another sip of his coffee, still trying to understand why, despite all the favors Jesse had done for him, Vincent wouldn't lift a finger to help.

Rage had filled him. He'd believed the worst of his friend. That a big-city job with a fancy salary at Perry Holdings had gone to Vincent's head. That he'd forgotten who he was. Jesse had responded with anger.

And then, a few weeks after their strange encounter, Vincent Hamm was dead. And not just dead—murdered.

A brief angry voice mail from Jesse to Vincent had turned up in the authorities' investigation. A handful of words. Crazy. But Jesse, ever a rule follower and ever meticulous, had a solid alibi. He'd been three hours away at a cattle auction. His location south of Houston was certifiable, easily tracked through his purchase records and through his hotel visit. Nearly all his time was accounted for. There was no feasible way he could have been the murderer. As a law-abiding man, he'd voluntarily submitted to a lie detector test, which he'd passed. He wanted Vincent's actual killer to be found. Sooner rather than later.

He thumped the edge of his own mug, heat transferring ever so slightly from the ceramic to his fingertips.

Jesse's attention returned to the present as he heard the creak of the guest suite door and soft footfalls on the hardwood floor. Then there she was. Esme Perry.

He stood slowly. Damn.

The mug was no longer the only thing throwing heat in the kitchen.

Esme walked deeper into the kitchen, looking too damn sexy in his Texas A&M sweats. Even wearing his athletic socks bunched down around her ankles, she somehow made it all work into an elegant ensemble right down to her diamond stud earrings.

"Well, Miss Esme, you are definitely unmistakable now," he said, nudging her mug and the bottle of schnapps toward her.

"It's nice to be dry again." She gestured to her wet hair. "At least somewhat." She poured some of the liquor into the mug, stirred thoughtfully. Almost absently.

She lifted the mug to her lips, and he found himself unable to look away, imagining how soft they would be.

"I'm glad to help." He waited for her to sit before reclaiming his place on the barstool. "Did you reach home to let them know you're okay?"

"I did. Just now. I called my sister Angela. We were talking about plans to meet for brunch." Her delicate nose scrunched with worry. "We haven't had much time to talk lately since she got back together with Ryder."

Everyone in Royal had been blown away at the news when Angela and Ryder had gotten engaged. A Perry and a Currin? Unimaginable. Then they had broken things off, and now were apparently a couple again.

Jesse shook his head. He wanted something more stable in his life. "You and she are close?"

She hesitated for a telling moment. "Angela and Melinda are twins. Then I have a brother, Roarke. We all love one another."

He'd heard the gossip that Roarke was rumored to be Ryder Currin's biological son, rumors so strong they'd taken a DNA test. A test that proved Roarke truly was a Perry. Still, the whole ordeal must have put a strain on their family. "That's not the same as being close."

"The twins are close, and our brother has always gone his own way. He's happy, though, working at Perry Holdings in Houston in a newly formed ethics department. He still does part-time work offering legal, too."

"He sounds like quite the crusading attorney for the underdog. I imagine you're proud of him."

"I am. It wasn't easy for him to find his own path. He and Dad butt heads because our father expected Roarke to go into the family business. But that's enough of our family drama." She shrugged, her hair rippling over her shoulder in a blond waterfall. "So you have siblings?"

Her eyes flickered to the photograph tucked on the marble countertop.

Esme was observant. He'd give her that.

"I have a sister. She's all the family I have left, actually. I thought I was going to lose her not too long ago. Her appendix ruptured and she had to have emergency surgery."

Hospital runs and the smell of antiseptic filled his memory. The bargaining and praying for his sister's life he'd done were still a visceral memory in his stomach.

"I'm so sorry. Is she all right now?"

"She is." He looked at the mug in Esme's hand, thankful for his sister's recovery.

"Thank goodness. Still, that had to have been a scary time for you."

"It was."

Rain continued to fall outside, filling the pause with controlled chaos.

She looked into her mug, swirling the hot chocolate around without meeting his gaze. "Actually, you weren't wrong. My sisters have a special bond. My brother, well, his earlier move to Dallas wasn't all that surprising. Now that he's back, that seems to be changing some. Regardless, I'm still stuck somewhere in the middle. But that's all right. Not everyone has the same relationship."

"You don't sound like it's okay."

She raised an eyebrow in surprise, then took another sip of the hot chocolate as she leaned on the granite countertop. She spread her fingers out wide as if soaking in the cool texture. "About those three someones… I'm dying to know more."

"Dates."

Her eyes went wide, and she inched back. "All three? At the same time?"

"Whoa. It's not what you're thinking." He held up his hands defensively, chuckling. "I signed up for a dating service, a matchmaker. She's lined up a trio of candidates. They were each supposed to come out here individually to meet with me, to see my ranching lifestyle and decide if it's off-putting. It's not for everyone."

Her gaze flickering away at the mention of ranching not being for all, she wriggled her toes in his overlarge socks. "A matchmaker. Seriously?"

"Plenty of people sign up for online services. I opted for the matchmaker because of lack of time." Absolutely the truth. And he found a certain sort of…practicality about having an expert match him with someone with similar interests. It saved time rather than meeting scores of women socially and trusting fate to somehow work out his future.

Her forehead furrowing in confusion, Esme leaned slightly forward. "Why do you want to have a girlfriend if you don't even have time to look for one?"

Well, that was easy enough to answer. "I don't want a girlfriend. I want a wife."

Three

"A wife?" Esme repeated, certain she couldn't have heard him correctly. Hot cocoa cradled in her hand, she studied him through narrowed eyes, but couldn't read if he was serious or not. Which could have something to do with how she kept looking at his impossibly broad shoulders. "You're punking me, aren't you?"

"Not at all." He set his coffee cup aside. "I'm looking for a wife."

A flash of disappointment rippled through her. Silly really, since the last thing she wanted was a rancher. "A wife. Not simply a date. That's just… Well, I'm surprised you're already thinking that far down the road about someone you haven't even met."

He crossed his arms over his chest. "Your shock is a little insulting."

"But you're a man." Her eyes were drawn to his arms

before she could stop herself. His muscular arms. Arms that had carried her so effortlessly.

"And that comment is decidedly sexist." His green eyes flashed with heat.

She grabbed her mug quickly. She should probably hush before she alienated him altogether. "I apologize. I only meant it's a leap from first date to the altar."

"Apology accepted." He reached for the refrigerator door, his flannel shirt pulling taut along his muscular chest. "Whipped cream?"

"What?" she asked, startled, her gaze shooting back up to his face.

"For your hot chocolate." He held out a can, pointing in her direction.

Her mind traveled sexy pathways, imagining things they could do with that sweet treat.

"Uh, sure." She reached for the can, spraying a swirl inside her mug, when she really wanted to fill her mouth with the stuff and quench at least one hunger. "Of course, there's no reason in the world why you shouldn't find love."

"I didn't say anything about love," he said in the most logical of voices. "Just marriage."

Again, he'd surprised her. This man wasn't at all what she'd expected from reading about him online before her trip to Royal. "Marriage but no love?"

The thought of that chilled her with memories of her parents' loveless marriage. Too many nights, her mother had cried herself to sleep over her husband's staying late at the office yet again. Esme wanted more for herself than that and felt sorry for anyone willing to settle for less.

"Why not? I have my life in order—this house, the ranch." He ticked off points one finger at a time. "The timing is right for the next step. A wife. Then kids."

He'd laid out the events as matter-of-factly as he'd laid out the ingredients to make her hot chocolate. He'd described the process of creating a family as if he was listing the week's upcoming groceries.

She raised an eyebrow. "Do these three mystery women know they're expected to pop out children right away?"

Esme imagined what his dream woman was like. What she wanted. What would make her forsake the idea of love.

Not that Esme had had a lot of luck in that department. Still, she wasn't giving up on finding love—when the time was right, with the man who was right.

She gulped down more hot cocoa and struggled not to wince as it burned her tongue.

"We all filled out extensive questionnaires. Our wishes for the future are in line."

Well, now, that wasn't subtle at all. "And I'm in the way."

Esme blinked a sting of jealousy. She'd only just met Jesse. And while he was sure one sexy cowboy with his slightly tousled blond hair, she knew better than to assume they were anything more than two very opposite people stuck together riding out a rainstorm.

With precise, athletic footfalls, he made his way over to the window and looked outside into the tempest.

"In this storm, I seriously doubt any of them will be showing up." He turned to her and his gaze held on her upper lip, and she realized she had a hint of whipped cream clinging there.

Jesse returned to her, offering her a napkin. She took it, dabbing her mouth slowly. His eyes flamed hotter and she wondered what it would have been like to let him kiss her upper lip, to taste him in return.

She swallowed hard to will away the sensation. "How do they feel about being a part of this edition of *Catch a Bachelor: Rancher Style*?"

He shot her an amused glance, easing back a step. "This isn't a reality show."

"Of course not." She rolled her eyes, struggling for levity. "No cameras."

He cocked an eyebrow. "And they're coming at different times so they don't cross paths."

"How very…civil." And cold. "How do your brides-to-be feel about this emotionless transaction?"

"To be fair, they know about the process. No one's being deceived."

He leaned against the island, an arm's length away. Esme's eyes drifted to his shiny engraved belt buckle. Snapping her attention back to their conversation, she considered the less robotic aspects of such an arrangement. All likes and dislikes already sorted. Everyone knowing the rules of the game. Everyone understanding expectations, too. No mystery. Nothing as quirky as fate intervening.

That was something, at least. "Glad to hear it."

A slow, disarming grin spread across his face. "Are you interested in joining the process?"

"Whoa, nuh-uh." She held up her hands in protest.

"I'm in no hurry to fill a nursery, and I've had enough of ranch living."

He tipped his head to the side, studying her, amusement in his eyes replaced by curiosity. "Yet you grew up on a ranch."

Her childhood home on the outskirts of Houston was a sprawling mansion, almost castle-like, surrounded by pastures, elegant barns. The spread was a huge, billion-dollar cattle-and-horse operation started by her maternal grandfather, then passed on to her parents. And even with all of that, Esme had still moved into the city the first chance she had.

"Exactly. No more ranching for me." And that was all the reminder she needed for why she should keep her distance from this man and stay focused on her reason for being here. "Thank you for the hot cocoa and the clothes and the rescue. I should turn in for the night."

She rinsed her mug and made fast tracks for the guest suite before she was tempted to stay in the kitchen. To listen to the warm timbre of his voice.

To imagine the taste of whiskey from his coffee on his tongue if he kissed her.

Sleep had been a difficult commodity for Jesse, with images of his surprise houseguest filling his dreams. Visions of her soaking wet, yet equally enticing in sweats. What would it be like to peel those clothes from her body?

Restless, he'd finally given up sleep just before dawn and gone to the barn to burn off energy.

His cowboy boots reverberated on the cement floor as he approached Juniper's stall. Grabbing the supple brown leather halter and lead, he made his way into the stall of his newest horse.

Juniper, a young dapple gray mare, stretched her neck, giving her tangled mane a shake. She sniffed his hand, her whiskers softly touching his palm. The horse exhaled warm breath against his fingertips, a welcome sensation in the cool, damp morning air. Stepping closer, Jesse slipped the cognac halter on her head and led the mare to the crossties, where his brushes were waiting for him.

He never grew tired of this, the connection with his horses and the land. Ranching was more than a job to him. It was a way of life.

Picking up a currycomb, he moved his hand in circular patterns. Excess hair and dirt gathered in the brush.

Other horses poked their heads from stalls. The barn held two rows of twelve stalls. Buddy, his first gelding, lazily chewed on hay, dropping bits of straw onto the ground. Flash, a muscular chestnut quarter horse, loosed a whinny. Beneath his hands, Juniper sucked in a breath before belting out an answering noise.

Satisfied, Flash moved back into his well-kept stall.

The routine grounded Jesse, reminding him of his reasons for using the matchmaker for a practical choice.

Practical.

That was the mantra he said to himself as he picked up the hard brush. His hand moved in time to the rain pelting the tin roof.

Images of his sexy houseguest kept interrupting his thoughts. *Practical. Practical. Practical.*

How many times would he need to say that until it sank into his brain? He surveyed the barn, wondering if he would need to groom every horse today to refocus himself.

Of course, that was the opposite of practical.

After finishing up with Juniper, he led the mare back to her stall and gave her the carrot he'd shoved in his pocket earlier. The mare crunched her treat, flicking her ears forward in something that seemed like thanks.

Latching her stall, he started to leave the barn. He pushed his Stetson down on his head to keep the cold rain from pelting his ears as he made his way back to the ranch house. The cold nipped at his hands as he moved past the pool, his boots trekking through the muddy earth as he closed the distance to the green door of the back entrance. The matchmaking prospects certainly wouldn't be arriving today, or the next, if the weather didn't ease up soon.

After wicking the rain off his Stetson, he hung his hat on a hook and discarded his leather jacket and mud-drenched boots. The hall led to the kitchen, where he found Esme sitting in front of the fireplace in the lotus position. A plated pastry and coffee mug rested on the mahogany end table to her left.

Damn.

His heart hammered.

Hair drawn up into a sleek ponytail and skin dewy in the firelight, she looked enticing, even in a long slouchy sweater and floral leggings his sister had left behind. Somehow, the pink sweater hinted at her curves, and the floral leggings made her look oddly polished.

His athletic socks still warmed her feet, and he realized he'd have to find her suitable footwear.

Something practical. The word echoed again as he reached for another mug from the open shelf.

"I've had your car towed to my mechanic." He poured himself black coffee, allowing himself to taste the bitter cocoa and fruit undertones. "Carl—who towed your vehicle—said it wouldn't start."

"Oh no, I was afraid of that." She scrunched her nose in dismay. "Because of the flash flood?"

"Most likely." He was drawn to her, this bewitching and beautiful woman. He dropped into the brocade chair on the other side of the fireplace. "If Carl can make it here on his four-wheeler, he'll bring your luggage. Otherwise, you'll have to make do with my sister's clothes for a while longer." He'd offered them to her last night. "I'll see if I can find some rain boots that fit you."

Esme's delicate fingers moved like sultry smoke as she removed her thin phone from where it was tucked under her thigh. "I'll put in a request for a rental car for when the rain lets up. Hopefully they'll have something available."

He stretched his legs out in front of him, powerful legs encased in denim. "You might as well save yourself the time."

"Why?" She hesitated. "Is there a problem?"

"This time of year, with the holidays and all, rentals are all booked for weeks." He flashed her his best bad-boy grin, even though he'd officially hung up his bad-boy ways. "I could lend you a vehicle."

"That would be so helpful." She placed her phone beside her on the armchair. "Thank you."

He watched her through narrowed eyes, unable to

resist. "I have an extra truck. It's twenty-two years old, but runs great. Carl's a super mechanic."

She fidgeted with the end of her blond ponytail, rubbing the strands between her fingers, clearly caught off guard by his offer. "Oh, uh, yes, thank you."

He narrowed his gaze, assessing the impossibly posh woman in front of him. "You've never driven one, have you?"

She arched an eyebrow. "Actually, I learned on an ancient stick-shift truck at Daddy's ranch. A Ford so ancient I figured no one would notice if I added an extra dent or two."

"Touché." He lifted his mug, toasting in her direction.

She eyed him intuitively as the flames licked upward in the fireplace. "You were teasing me."

"Perhaps."

She raised a finger to her lips. "Shhhh. Don't tell your three potential brides that."

A begrudging laugh barked free and before he could second guess himself, he said, "Maybe if the rain lets up this afternoon, we'll get enough of a break to chop down a Christmas tree. That is, if you want to come along?"

"Sure," she said, already launching to her feet. "As long as you don't expect me to load it into the truck."

She flashed him a sassy wink.

"You can just stand there and look pretty." And the thing was, he meant it.

So much for keeping his distance. But something about this woman tempted him more than he wanted to admit.

* * *

Jesse's flirtatious words still echoed in Esme's ears two hours later. Steering the conversation toward her father and the club was tougher than she'd expected.

But she was determined to keep her cool. Slow and steady was her best option. And thanks to their current project sorting Christmas ornaments while waiting for a break in the rain to get a tree, she would have the time she needed.

Despite the rain, light beamed through the floor-to-ceiling windows on two of the four walls of the great room. That, coupled with the cathedral ceilings, made the petal-white room feel impossibly airy.

Which was good considering all the boxes of Christmas ornaments that flanked the white love seat and leather couch. She'd moved the glass-and-wood table in order to create room for the bins Jesse had brought down from the attic, noting as he did so that these were only the tip of the iceberg.

To set the mood and to gain control, Esme queued up her favorite Christmas playlist from her phone, connecting it to the Bluetooth surround-sound system. A hazy, warbly '50s-era carolers version of "Here We Come A-Wassailing" filled the room.

There.

The start of Christmas. And the real start of her mission.

They opened the first box of ornaments. Reaching into the box, she pulled out two silver bells, one with Jesse's name engraved on it, the other with the name Janet etched on it. "Your sister, right?"

"Yes, we split the decorations between us. Somehow

I must have missed giving her that one." His brow furrowed and he tilted his head to the side, inspecting the silver bells. For a moment, she wondered if he'd pull out his phone and snap a picture to send to his sister. But his hands made no move for the phone in his pocket.

"How long until you get to see her over Christmas?" A little prying, but curiosity filled her as she laid the ornaments down with care onto the sofa.

"Like I said, my family wasn't tight-knit," he said, not that it answered her question. "My parents didn't get along. They're gone now." His face hardened, tight lines pulling at the corners of his mouth.

"I'm sorry for your loss. My mother died ten years ago and I still miss her dreadfully." She fidgeted with the thin bracelet her mother had given her so long ago.

Her mom—Tamara—had been a kind and loving mother. Esme knew her parents hadn't married out of romance, and seeing their unhappiness only made her all the more determined not to settle for less than a fully committed heart.

The loss of her mom made Esme cling all the harder to the rest of her family. She couldn't imagine what she would do without them. Her dad and her siblings meant the world to her. Christmases were big, boisterous events for them. Sometimes it had been a challenge to get Roarke to join in, but she and her sisters had worked to wear him down. She had high hopes for him this year, now that he'd found happiness with his new love, Annabel. "That's got to be tough for you and your sister, having lost both parents. I can see how maybe it would have brought you two closer to each other."

She pulled out an ornament tucked in protective

paper. Glitter twinkled as she removed the wrapping to reveal a reindeer towing a sleigh.

"Janet's great, and I do love her, of course. It about killed me to think I might lose her when her appendix burst. But she's well now, thank God." A sigh racked him and he scrubbed a hand over his face.

"That had to be so scary." She stopped unpacking ornaments, searching his face, cradling the sleigh in her hand. "You'll have a lot to celebrate together over Christmas, with her recovery."

He ran his fingers through his blond hair, then rubbed along the back of his neck. "It's unlikely we'll see each other. We don't have much in common. She's a lot younger than I am, and, well, we just have our own lives now."

Jesse looked away and pulled out a snow globe, full of glitter around a tree, a nutcracker and a ballerina. A wistful shadow played across his face.

His thumb stroking the smooth glass, he flipped over the trinket and wound it up. "The Dance of the Sugar Plum Fairy" played as a snowstorm enveloped the little scene.

Biting her lip, she couldn't help but be moved by such a glimpse of nostalgia in this rough-and-tumble man. She stood, reaching a hand to touch his shoulder, then stopping short. "But perhaps the ornaments remind you of happy memories?"

"Yeah, they do." He set the globe on the mantel. "And I look forward to making memories with my own kids one day."

Well, that was sure a splash of cold water, reminding her of his plans. She pulled a smile and tugged at the hem of the pink sweater. "Your sister has nice taste in clothes."

He angled his head. "Are you being sarcastic, Ms. Prada?"

"It's not office wear, but it's fun for ranch work, soft and cheerful."

"That's nice you can appreciate a less flashy style."

"I'm not a snob." She handed him a longhorn ornament.

"Really?" He took the decoration, their fingers brushing.

Her skin tingled even after he'd pulled away. "You don't have to sound so surprised."

The snow globe stopped playing just as the song drifting through the speakers subsided. For a moment, silence filled the great room.

Desire danced in the air, an electricity between them as he moved closer to her. "Would it soften the sting to your ego if I told you how hot you look no matter what you're wearing?"

Music started on her phone again, orchestral carols stroking the air.

She closed her hand into a fist, trying to will away the lingering sensation of that simple touch. "And what about those three bridal prospects of yours, one of whom will give you babies to make Christmas memories with?"

He canted back, nodding tightly. "You're right. It's totally inappropriate of me. I mean it when I say I want to be a family man, and all that entails."

"The epitome of a Texas Cattleman's Club fella."

"Yes, exactly that." His gaze held hers, setting

her skin on fire with just the stroke of his eyes on her face.

Even knowing it was unwise and there were so many reasons they were wrong for each other, she still felt herself sway toward him. His hand lifted slowly, reaching out to tuck her ponytail back over her shoulder. Then his fingers slid to cup the back of her head. Goose bumps of awareness spread over her and she wanted this moment, this connection. Just one kiss.

With luck, it wouldn't even be a very good kiss and she could refocus on her plans to repair her father's reputation. So giving in to temptation was the right thing to do. Or at least that's what she could tell herself as she angled forward the rest of the way for her lips to meet his.

And damn, it was very far from being a bad kiss.

Four

Jesse had expected the kiss to be good. Esme was a sexy woman, after all.

He had not expected that his senses would be set on fire at the first brush of her lips against his. A connection he fully intended to deepen. And explore.

Sliding his arms around her, he drew Esme to his chest, angling his mouth over hers, his tongue tracing the seam of her lips until they parted and…

Thoughts fled until only sensation remained. The soft give of her breasts against his chest. The glide of her hair through his fingers as he cupped the back of her head. He could smell the scent of shampoo and wondered what perfume she chose. What would be in her suitcase once the weather cleared enough to retrieve it. He wanted to feel and learn more about her. More than just the kiss.

Although it was still one helluva kiss.

She tasted of coffee and mint and something innately *her*.

Music hummed softly in the background and rain came down in sheets outside, all almost drowned out by the hammering of his speeding pulse. A breathy sigh whispered from her and he groaned, surrendering to this moment with her.

He swept a hand behind her, brushing away the ornaments and paper, clearing a space to recline her back in the thick woven rug. Her arms twined around his neck and she arched closer, skimming her mouth over his neck up to nip his earlobe.

Irresistible.

Her breasts pressed against his chest in a sweet temptation, her foot stroking the back of his leg as her thighs parted ever so slightly. He'd wanted her since the first time he saw her on the side of the road. The fierce desire for her swept him away as surely as the storm sweeping over the landscape. Until the power of it was ringing in his ears.

Except…

"Your phone," she gasped softly, her breath warm against his skin. "I think that's your phone ringing."

And it was. The text message sound dinged a couple more times. Each successive ring called him back to reality. And each ring raised the level of surprise more and more of what had just occurred. The surprise of the heat that passed between their bodies.

Damn. How could he have lost control so fully? His focus narrowed sharply as he angled off her, swiping his cell off the coffee table. Multiple texts scrolled across the screen and he cursed under his breath.

"Is something wrong?" she asked, elbowing up, her cheeks flushed, her hair tousled from his hands.

She quickly straightened her clothes. The moment had passed. Even if he could stay. Which he couldn't.

He pocketed his phone. "That was my foreman. He and the rest of my crew are cut off from the barn by the rain. I've got to get to the animals." He paused, stroking a finger down her face lightly. "I'm sorry to leave abruptly."

"It's okay. You're needed," she assured him, smiling but inching back. She crossed her arms somewhat protectively around her stomach and chest, as if she were Alice in Wonderland shrinking before his eyes. "And it's not like the kiss was anything more than an impulsive mistake for both of us."

Ouch. That stung more than a little. Because as far as he was concerned, it was a steamy, soul-searing kiss that he wouldn't mind repeating.

But she was right. He'd had no business losing control with her. "If you need anything, call me." He pulled a card from his wallet and passed it over quickly. "All right? Promise?"

"Absolutely." She eased to her feet, backing away. "I should call my sister and check in again anyway." She turned from him, her sun-gold hair glistening.

He reached for her hand, stopping her, not sure what he planned to say until the words fell out of his mouth. "That kiss may have been a mistake, but I don't regret it for a second."

* * *

Hoping her distraction didn't show, Angela Perry half listened to her sister Esme's latest check-in call from Royal while staring out at the Houston skyline from her high-rise condominium. At least they weren't FaceTiming today, so any distraction wouldn't be visible. Esme was going on and on about decorating with Jesse, down to what his decorations looked like.

And yes, Angela was more than ready to embrace the Christmas season, all the way down to the tree behind her with freshly wrapped gifts. She'd had one helluva tough year, caught in the middle of the feud between her father and Ryder Currin. Maybe that was a part of why she was having trouble mustering too much enthusiasm for Esme's call.

Their father's latest ploy to become the president of the Houston branch of the Texas Cattleman's Club was frustrating. Ryder certainly wasn't using a PR expert to sway votes.

Worry gnawed at Angela over what might happen if her father lost. Would he withdraw his recently extended blessing over her dating Ryder again?

A roll of nausea rippled through her. Pain, recent and still tender, colored her memories. Breaking off the engagement had just about broken her heart—and his. Taking a risk on becoming a couple again had been scary.

Though she knew Ryder was her future, emotions still ran high. Angela chewed the inside of her lip, a habit she picked up as a child when nerves got the best of her during school competitions or when she needed an anchor back to the world. Not that this was the best way to cope.

But it was a way.

And she sure as hell needed something right now.

"Angela?" Her sister's voice snapped her out of her reverie. "I'm rambling, aren't I?"

"Not at all," Angela lied, more than aware of how Esme sometimes felt excluded by her sisters. Angela loved both of her sisters, but in her heart of hearts, she knew there was a difference with her twin bond to Melinda. Not that she would ever admit as much to Esme. "I appreciate your checking in and I'll be sure to pass along the update to the rest of the family."

"Thank you. I hope I have something more concrete to share before long."

Hearing Ryder stirring about in the kitchen, Angela figured she'd better cut this conversation short before her sister freaked out that something may have been overheard. "Stay safe and good luck with Jesse Stevens."

She signed off just as Ryder stepped from the kitchen into the living room, carrying a wooden tray of meats, cheeses and olives. He was such a wonderful man. And sexy.

If she didn't already know him, she would have never guessed he had three adult children. Like Brad Pitt, Ryder looked better and better with age.

Even in faded blue jeans and a chambray shirt, Ryder looked like he'd stepped off some movie set. Short, dark blond hair framed his tanned face. Blue eyes as bright as a Texas summer sky met her gaze, just as warm as a summer day, too.

As he yawned, his square, cut jawline moved. Even in these little gestures, he was handsome. He stretched, walking toward her in socks. His well-worn brown boots still took up residence by the fireplace.

Theirs had a been rocky relationship, made more than a little difficult since their families had been bitter rivals for years. Ryder had been a lowly ranch hand on the ranch outside Houston where Sterling Perry—an old-money Houston heir—was briefly the foreman during his engagement to Harrington York's daughter.

As part of a business and social alliance, Harrington had offered his daughter Tamara's hand in marriage to Sterling Perry, as long as Sterling agreed to learn the ranch business from the inside and then live there after he married. When Harrington had died, Sterling had seen Ryder comforting Tamara and assumed they were having an affair, even though Tamara was a decade older.

Discovering that Harrington had willed a key piece of oil-laden land to Ryder had only added fuel to fire, even though Sterling had inherited the bulk of the estate. When over two decades later, Ryder and Angela became an item, Sterling had been enraged. His fury had led to Angela and Ryder breaking up. Finding their way back together had been a long, heartbreaking journey.

But here they were, trying again with the hope of the Christmas season urging them on.

"You're so thoughtful." She extended her legs, wriggling her toes in front of the fire. The rain was making even a Texas winter cold. "I'm starving."

His gaze lingered on her legs for a second beyond casual interest before he set the tray on the end table and sat beside her, his jeans and chambray shirt covering those honed muscles of his. "How's your sister doing?"

Thinking back to the drawn-out conversation with Esme, she tilted her head from side to side. "She's still flooded in at Jesse Stevens's place."

She decided he didn't need to hear all about the decorations.

"Well, I guess that's convenient for your father."

She struggled to hide a wince, concern firing anew. "Please don't say you mean that in a negative way."

He held up his hands, his blue eyes widening. "I get that your dad wants to be the president of the new Texas Cattleman's Club chapter. And we all know that your father can be…determined when he sets his mind to something. Just look at how hard he pushed to break us up."

Angela's mouth tightened at the truth of his words.

However, it hadn't helped that an executive at Ryder's oil corporation had been the one spreading rumors about her father and a Ponzi scheme that had almost destroyed Perry Holdings.

Bringing that up wouldn't be wise at the moment. So she settled on, "But my father relented about us."

"You're right." Shifting his weight, he leaned toward her. "Then he promptly sent your sister to Royal to tip the scales in his favor," he added, his face showing lines of stress and concern.

"It's not like he sent her to seduce Jesse. She's a highly qualified PR executive."

"She's a daddy's girl," he muttered. His jaw became rock solid. Tense.

"And your daughters aren't?" Angela knew otherwise. Both girls loved their dad. And he loved them. He was so proud of Annabel's makeover business, Fairy Godmother. And Maya, his adopted daughter. Things had been in turmoil with them since Maya had demanded more information on her birth parents. But the eighteen-year-old had never doubted her dad's love.

Angela chewed on her lip until she tasted iron. She felt her stomach knotting. "You and my father have hated each other for a long time. I know that's not going to magically go away just because you and I are an item. I only want the two of you to try."

"He and I have come to a truce—"

"It feels more like a temporary cease fire."

A wry grin tucked into his face. "For your sake, we're offering a united, powerful front to get to the bottom of what's going on."

"And after that's been solved?" She didn't want to think about losing Ryder or her father.

"Well, one of us is going to be leading the new chapter. If it's him, I'll be polite. If it's me…?"

She didn't want any part of this conversation anymore. And she had a damn good idea of how to distract them both. She angled toward him, smoothing the collar of his chambray shirt. "Let's stop talking about my father."

"Sure. If you're done with this—" he gestured to the tray of snacks "—then we can head out to finish up the last of your shopping. Although I can't imagine you have more to buy."

"Or we could skip the shopping." She shifted to straddle him, tugging at his shirt.

Grin kicking up the sides of his mouth, he cupped her hips, his eyes smoldering. "Excellent idea."

After her phone call with Angela, Esme had grown restless. It hadn't escaped her notice that her sister sounded breathless and a bit distracted. Ryder Currin's fault, no doubt.

She was happy for her sister, but also concerned for her dad. He was getting older, and this club presidency meant the world to him.

Determined not to waste time, she'd finished getting dressed in clothes left behind by Jesse's sister. She'd even managed to find a pair of rain boots that fit if she put on three pairs of socks. At the thought of seeing her handsome host, her nerves pattered as fast as the rain.

Yesterday she would have sworn she wouldn't be venturing out into the rain again anytime soon. And here she was, pushing out of the door and running through the storm in an oversize slicker that wasn't much more attractive than the sweats she'd worn last night.

Sure, he could most certainly handle things in the barn on his own, but he had saved her. And kissed her.

Who was she trying to kid?

She wanted to spend more time with him. To persuade him for her dad and because he was an interesting, charismatic man. She couldn't remember when she'd been this drawn to anyone this quickly.

She wanted to see if the chemistry of that kiss had been a fluke.

A well-appointed barn stood guardian before a small

patch of trees. As the cold rain continued to pelt down, she widened her stride and dashed for the door.

Once her boots crossed the threshold, she whisked the rain off her body. Drips melted into the floor as her breath slowed. Then she quieted to watch Jesse, unnoticed for the moment.

Hands wringing her damp hair, Esme held her breath as Jesse's muscled form gently stroked a bay horse. Even from a few feet away, she saw the whites of the horse's eyes and the flaring nostrils.

Something had spooked the bay, who kept tossing his head skyward on the crossties, front hooves picking up and down as if he might bolt. Jesse's practiced hand stroked the horse's neck as he spoke impossibly softly in an attempt to soothe the still-frightened animal.

Electricity danced in the air again. Sure, she hadn't anticipated being drawn to him at all. The kiss from earlier drifted back into her mind as this softer-but-still-powerful Jesse filled her vision.

As if sensing her, the bay craned his neck around, nostrils flaring once again, scenting her. Jesse was alerted to her presence and turned around.

"Well, hello, I didn't expect to see you out here. In case you hadn't noticed, there's a crazy-strong storm raging out there."

Grinning, she hung up the slicker on an empty peg along the wall. "I did notice, thank you, and it seemed to me that perhaps you could use some help."

He angled his head to the side, studying her through narrowed eyes. "You realize this isn't glamorous, right?"

"I know what I'm getting in for. I grew up on a ranch, something you seem to keep forgetting. Just because I don't choose to continue that way of life doesn't mean I magically forgot all I learned." Her arms folded across her chest.

"Okay, then," he conceded. "I welcome the extra set of hands. Especially ones so knowledgeable."

She took that as a challenge. A half smile tugging on her lips, she raised a brow. "Point me in the direction of what still needs accomplishing."

After he'd given her a quick rundown of what he'd done thus far—currycombing, hard brush and soft brush on Ace, the bay on the crossties—he launched into how the bay needed to have his hoof wrapped to deal with an abscess.

Reaching back over a decade, Esme remembered when her own buckskin mare had abscessed. If she were being honest, the flow of the care stayed with her but the particulars faded into the background.

Approaching the horse, she offered the palm of her hand to Ace. Sniffing gingerly, the horse's whiskers tickled her palm. But he visibly settled, a great sigh releasing the tightness in his neck. The crossties hung in loose loops for the first time.

"You're a natural." Jesse's eyes showed surprise as she stroked the horse's leg, feeling for the heat of the infection.

Warmth danced on her cheeks, but she willed a casual wink to keep her mind off how close her body was to Jesse's. "Sometimes I get lucky."

Standing up, she looked at the supplies he'd gathered. He bent over, asking the horse to raise the injured foot with a click of his tongue and a tap on the ankle bone. Ace, shifting his weight, complied.

Eyeing the pile, she recognized the Betadine bottle and handed it to him.

"So the city girl does remember her origins after all." He laughed, cradling the hoof as he poured the antiseptic on it.

His muscles rippled with a strength that took her breath away. Which was especially impressive given that she'd spent her life around cowboys, had seen plenty. But he was in a class of his own.

He was more than a figurehead ranch owner.

"Just here for the assist. What is the next step? I'm afraid this is where it gets fuzzy for me."

Looking up from the hoof, he smiled, nodding toward the supply bucket. "I need a pad and tape."

She nodded, handing him the last bit he needed to ensure the horse would heal properly. While he wrapped the horse's hoof, she spoke quietly to Ace, stroking his silky neck until the horse's eyes became heavy.

He finished checking his medical work and then carefully placed the wrapped hoof down. In a fluid movement, he snapped the lead line onto the leather halter and unhooked the crossties. Leading Ace back to his stall, he fished a treat out of his pocket, which the horse happily munched.

After closing the stall door, Jesse led her down the aisle to the wooden door of the barn office. The space was lit by overhead lighting and a blinking Christmas tree in the corner near a sturdy wood desk, scarred from use and full of papers. It had a different vibe than the expertly decorated house and pristine horse stalls. And how ironic that he'd put a Christmas tree in here, but not in his home yet.

She wondered if this might be a peek into his core personality, less constrained, less intent on being analytically perfect in his approach to everything.

He opened a stainless steel refrigerator tucked behind the desk and pulled out two water bottles, one for each of them.

Extending one bottle to her, he leaned on the desk's edge. "Did you reach your sister?"

"I did. You probably think it's strange how often she and I talk—given that you said you're not close to Janet."

"I think if you're both happy with your relationship, then that's awesome." He gestured for her to sit in the leather office chair. "I wish I'd had a houseful of siblings."

"And that's why you've got these three blind dates coming to meet you," she said, trying very hard not to notice how amazing the chair smelled, carrying the hint of him in the leather, like being wrapped in his arms.

"That's the plan." He shook his head wryly. "You were *not* a part of my plan."

"Sorry?"

"I'm not," he said enigmatically, continuing before she had a chance to question him. "You were incredible in there with the horses. Thank you, Esme."

She fidgeted with the bracelet on her wrist. The one from her mom that she couldn't ever remember being without. A small fidget of comfort. "I only did what was needed."

"But you *knew* what was needed, sometimes before I had a chance to ask. That's impressive." He nodded.

"Yes, I know. You grew up on a ranch, but not everyone pays attention. And it's not as if you needed to work."

Helping on the ranch had been yet another way she'd tried to impress her father, only to see he hadn't noticed because, to her surprise, he didn't like the lifestyle. He didn't even like horses, which blew her away because even the city girl in her loved the horses.

All the same, here she was again, still trying to prove she was indispensable. "What's going to happen with the Houston chapter of the Cattleman's Club?" she asked, blurting out what was on her mind.

"I can't predict the election," he said noncommittally.

"Do you think my dad has a chance?" Was she wasting her time here? What if Jesse said no and she would have to leave the second the rain stopped?

"Sure, he has a chance."

"But so does Ryder Currin."

He shrugged.

She sighed, the truth slipping out, frustration and fear of failure weakening her defenses. "I wish someone else was running. If Dad's going to lose, it's going to be so much tougher for him to swallow seeing Ryder at the helm."

"I thought they'd reconciled."

Had she said too much? Would that ongoing battle be a problem for the charter chapter? "They're making an effort for my sister. But they've hated each other for a long time. It's tough to believe they once worked together."

Except her father had known he would marry his boss's daughter. Which was ironic since her father didn't even enjoy ranching, not the way Jesse did. The way Ryder Currin did, too, for that matter.

All a moot point. Her father would make a good president for the new club. Winning would also make it much easier for her dad to accept Ryder with Angela.

And if her dad knew the turn things had taken with Jesse Stevens and that kiss?

Even the word flamed through her, leading her gaze to slide back to Jesse. His eyes met hers quizzically, then knowingly. Heat glinted in his expression.

The air crackled with awareness between them and she couldn't will herself to break away. The tip of her tongue moved over her top lip in an unconscious invitation.

Still seated on the edge of the desk, Jesse angled toward her, his hand sliding to cup the back of her neck. He angled his mouth over hers, and desire radiated through her, driving her to her feet. She looped her arms around his neck and held him close, and somehow, it wasn't nearly close enough. She ached for more of him, all of him. She couldn't stop the sigh of desire from escaping her lips.

A low rumble of pleasure vibrated his chest against hers a second before he swept his arm across his desk. Binders crashed to the floor, papers fluttering before they fell to rest. His arms hooked under her bottom, lifting her and setting her on the sleek mahogany surface.

Surprise flickered through her, excited her, spurred her to demand more, to throw caution to the wind and see how far they could take things. An invitation he seemed to understand, since he lowered her against the desk, then lay over her.

Her world narrowed to the music of the moment.

Her heart hammering in her ears.

Rain drumming on the roof.

A car roaring up the drive...

A car?

She froze, her skin chilling with realization. Jesse angled back, his head turning, his brow furrowed. He started toward the window and she bolted to her feet, making it there only a step behind Jesse.

An SUV was racing up the drive, rainwater sloshing from behind the speeding vehicle all the way to the front porch. She took one look at the sensible four-wheel drive with a cowgirl-hat-wearing woman stepping out from behind the wheel, and Esme knew.

In spite of the weather, the first of those matchmaking candidates had arrived.

Five

In all of his imaginings, this was not how he'd anticipated meeting his potential future bride. With the taste
of another woman still on his lips, the exotic scent of
her clinging to his shirt.

Papers were strewn all over the floor because he'd
been a heartbeat away from taking Esme right here,
right now, on his desk. Practical plans for his future
be damned.

Jesse scrubbed a hand over his face, exhaling hard
over the latest arrival. He should be relieved. The
woman pulling up to the house could be his wife one
day. According to the matchmaker, he had one in three
odds this was it.

Yet Jesse couldn't help but be frustrated over her
timing. He'd been enjoying the afternoon with Esme.
She'd surprised him again today. Not just with showing

up to help, but by being completely unaffected by mud and dung and hard work. He couldn't deny he'd been very impressed. But he also knew he couldn't fall for her. She was all about her job, her glamorous lifestyle, and didn't seem the least bit interested in marriage and children. Or so it appeared from the way she'd reacted to him saying that's what he wanted, his reason for reaching out to the matchmaker.

"Well," Esme said, backing away from the window, rain boots squeaking on the floor with a reminder of all her help, "this is awkward."

Her husky voice turning airy, he could feel the attempt at humor and he appreciated the effort to downplay the situation. But it didn't alleviate it enough.

And it wasn't going to get easier.

He looked out the window at the newcomer again. Given the number of paw print stickers on her back window, he guessed, "That must be Amaryllis Davis. She's a veterinarian, only lives about an hour away."

"Amaryllis? Her name is Amaryllis?" Esme bit her bottom lip for a moment, scrunching her nose before continuing, "Forget I said that. My name's Esme, for goodness' sake. I have no room to tease anyone over what a mama chooses for a name."

He knew he should say something to smooth over this moment, but he didn't have a clue. Never could he have imagined himself in this position. "I'm sorry about the timing."

It was probably the lamest sentence he could offer her. But no other words formed. Comforting her with his touch would cross a line. Again. And he knew he needed to reel back his emotions. Tuck them away. Focus on the future. On finding his perfect mate.

"You were honest from the start about the match-making prospects." Her beautiful face tensed into un-readable lines. She shook her head, honey-blond hair rippling in the office light.

He stared at her for a handful of heartbeats. Not long really, since his pulse was racing from being near Esme. It was so damn wrong that he wanted to steal one last kiss from her. That he was wondering what might have happened if he'd met Esme before contact-ing that matchmaker.

Those thoughts weren't fair to Esme or the woman outside. Or the other two candidates on the way.

Still, he had trouble shutting them down.

With his current luck, they would probably show up early, too.

Esme inched back a step, increasing the distance be-tween them. "You should go meet her without me. I'll just hang here and text my sister." She waved him off like it was no big deal, but her eyes told another story. "I need to firm up plans to meet my sisters for brunch with Angela's friend Tatiana."

"You're sure?" he asked one last time. "We'll talk as soon as… Well, once we see if she's staying or not. You aren't going to leave yet, are you?"

A hopeful question. One he shouldn't ask. One he had to. He straightened the papers on his desk and picked up the binders, looking up at her.

Slender hands twirled her long blond hair. He no-ticed her chipped manicure. She cleared her throat. "I don't have a car and I'm guessing you didn't leave the keys in the old truck."

Her levity during an awkward moment just made her all the more appealing. And he'd only known her for a day. He told himself it was infatuation. Chemistry. Not the stuff practical unions were made of.

Looking down at the scattered ranch documents, he knew the more practical path was the path that continued forward with his plan. Secure a woman who shared his goal to raise a family. Someone who believed in the legacy he wanted to build.

Steeling his resolve, he nodded and turned to leave. To meet the woman the matchmaker had called his 98 percent perfect mate.

Grudges were a bitch. And she knew that better than most. Even if she kept a smile on her face so that no one would guess the person behind all the Perry and Currin grief was actually a woman.

How sexist of them to keep assuming only a man could take them down.

She sat at the conference table in Perry Holdings headquarters in Houston and knew she should be content. Happy even. Her job here at Perry Holdings gave her the money and prestige she'd burned for as a child growing up in poverty.

Listening to all of these entitled blue bloods at work made her blood boil with resentment over all they took for granted. Hearing them bandy about plans to spoil their children at Christmas with extravagant gifts and vacations reopened old wounds and depthless anger. It took all her theater training from college to keep her face neutral. To check the fire that burned in her chest. That resentment had become unbearable when she'd learned how the Perrys and Currins had cheated her out of a chance for a better life.

She eased back in the massive conference chair, the offices radiating the aura of elegance-meets-the-West. Perry Holdings had four floors in a downtown Houston skyscraper. But this could have been her father's business, his success. His *power*.

Or Currin Oil, with its five floors in an elegant brick office building in a more industrial neighborhood on the outskirts of Houston. At least the meeting was finally shifting from discussion of buying diamond earrings for a baby to starting the business meeting.

Such as it was.

Schooling her face to feign interest in the outrageously long discussion about the recent fluctuation in stock prices, she drummed her fingers impatiently along her leg under the table. Bracketed by Ethan Barringer and Roarke Perry, she hoped they wouldn't notice her nerves. She worked to ground herself by fingering the texture of her Chanel linen business suit, the hem just grazing the top of her knees. None other than her boss, Sterling Perry, led the meeting. He was so arrogant, all smiles now that the cloud of suspicion had shifted from him.

But she wasn't surrendering. Not yet. Not ever.

Understanding about the detriment of grudges didn't stop the burning need to take down everyone in the Perry and Currin families. And they had no idea how close danger had been, still was. They were all so damned arrogant that way. They didn't understand what it was like to grow up a joke, her status always one giant step behind that of her so-called friend.

And now, here she sat, right under Sterling Perry's unsuspecting nose.

He was so arrogant, so full of himself in his expensive suits with cowboy shirts and Stetsons when rumor had it he didn't really even enjoy ranching. But he was a formidable businessman, smart and intimidating.

She had barely believed her luck when he'd promoted her to the vice president position. Of course, that arrogance of his made him so confident in his decisions that he'd missed the obvious these past months. Even when it was uncovered that Willem Inwood spread the rumors about Perry that threatened to tank stocks, no one had suspected her of playing a part.

It would almost be amusing how little they suspected her, if only her situation wasn't so dire, her goals finally so close she could almost taste success.

The catalyst for her grudge had come about so unexpectedly, in a quiet moment. She had been nostalgically going through her late dad's things in her attic when she discovered an old letter, from her father to her mother. He'd promised that he would change, that things would get better. She had been stunned to read that her father planned to ask the dying Harrington York for help. The man had promised him a tract of land on the outskirts of Houston that was reputed to be rich in oil.

Harrington York, whose daughter was married to none other than Sterling Perry.

Once a wealthy titan like Harrington and his son-in-law Sterling, her father drank and gambled and got himself into trouble, losing his fortune. But she'd known her dad wanted to reform and that land would have given him a second chance to do just that. But Angela's grandfather Harrington must have changed his mind because when he died that land went to Ryder Currin, who'd developed an oil empire from it. Currin, a nobody ranch hand rumored to be having an affair with Harrington's daughter, Tamara, Sterling's wife. Such pervasive gossip that Sterling's youngest offspring, Roarke, had submitted to a paternity test with Ryder Currin.

Negative.

But still.

Good Lord, these people were like an episode of a reality show. And she had paid the price for their selfishness.

Her mother had never reconciled with her dad, and her life fell apart. She'd lost everything because of Harrington's false promises, and the way the Currins and Perrys had greedily done what was best for them. Her temple throbbed at the thought of how fast her father had been forgotten. How fast her life had taken a downward spiral.

She had even, very reluctantly, given up her baby. She'd had no support system to help her raise her daughter, not like someone at this table would have had. Bitterness soured in her mouth, growing stronger every day.

Within a few years, her father drank himself to death, leaving behind a second wife and a son who she had refused to acknowledge as her brother.

Until this opportunity arose.

She didn't feel guilty about using him in her scheme. Why should she? He had a similar lack of conscience.

Her brother was an easy mark because he'd always wanted the relationship with his sister that she'd denied him since birth. Her half brother had been more than eager to bring down the man "responsible" for destroying their father's future.

Her hands closed into fists under the table. There was still a chance her carefully laid plans could still unravel. Willem was in jail. Staying silent, sure. For now. Eventually the prosecutor would find the sweetspot offer that would make Willem sing.

And then it would all be over. Job lost. Friends gone. Possible jail time for her, too, based on the roll of the dice. No amount of deep breaths could will away panic over the undeniable.

Because once they knew it was she—Tatiana Havery, Willem's half sister, Angela Perry's "best friend"— who'd orchestrated everything? Her time would have run out to make her enemies pay.

Esme was running low on patience. With herself, primarily.

She stood at the kitchen island, chopping a salad and wondering why and how she'd assumed control of entertaining matchmaking contestant number one— Amaryllis, the veterinarian, who was likely perfect for Jesse. Esme diced radishes faster and faster, struggling to appear unaffected by the brunette on the barstool.

Would she be the one Jesse chose for his perfect mate? She seemed right on the surface, given her career. Even Amaryllis's car was a better fit than Esme's destroyed Porsche.

The knife slipped, barely missing her thumb.

Jesse's dating life was not her business. It had no bearing on the situation with her father. She'd just shared a couple of kisses with Jesse Stevens, nothing more. Okay, so it had been, quite possibly, the best kiss of her life. All the more reason she should stay in her suite and work since he had plans to marry and propagate with a stranger.

But curiosity had her out here playing chef on the off chance of finding out why this woman was completely wrong for Jesse.

Radishes reduced to edible rubble, she moved on to cucumbers, still trying to study the woman without being obvious. The last thing she wanted was for Amaryllis to notice. Or worse yet, for Jesse to come back inside and catch her in an unguarded moment. He likely wouldn't be much longer talking to the ranch hands who'd made it back, thanks to their four-wheelers.

When Jesse had asked Amaryllis how she'd managed the drive in spite of the weather, she'd informed him she'd had lots of experience driving in all kinds of storms. After all, her work as a vet extended to farm animals. She'd navigated worse roads to assist in a delivery. Being punctual was important, she'd added, tapping her wristwatch. She had committed to being here at a certain time and she kept her commitments.

No spinning out in a sports car on a washed-out road for her, apparently.

Amaryllis sounded…too perfect.

Even from here, Amaryllis sat too straight. Like a rod shot through her back. Neatly trimmed nails painted a pale pink fiddled with her hair. The first bachelorette glanced down at her watch, then looked impatiently at the kitchen threshold.

Amaryllis broke any stereotypes Esme'd had about vets dressing in baggy scrubs even on their off days. A fitted lavender button-up shirt outlined her curves. Without so much as looking at Esme, the woman scrolled through her phone, pausing to type every so often. She delicately crossed her legs, clad in a pattern of thin black-and-gray pinstripes, as she ignored Esme's presence.

Esme skillfully scraped the chopped vegetables into a large pottery bowl before turning her attention to the grilled chicken breasts waiting to be sliced. "So what made you sign up for a matchmaker? If you don't mind my asking." The words came out of her mouth before her filter could catch them. Slicing the chicken breast into even strips, she waved her free hand. "Wait. Forget I said anything. It's none of my business."

Since walking into this house, she'd lost all damn control of herself. Frustration grew in her chest, and she continued the rhythmic slicing, attempting an air of casual sophistication and disinterest that Esme knew lingered somewhere inside her.

"I'm not ashamed at all. Ask away." Amaryllis pulled out a gold compact from her leather bag. Looking at herself in her reflection, the brunette fluffed her hair and then turned her attention to Esme. Unruffled and precise. "I'm a large-animal veterinarian, which means I spent almost every waking hour of my twenties studying. And now's not much better. I'm a workaholic who loves her job. There's not much chance for me to meet people who aren't affiliated with my practice."

Esme nodded, dumping the chicken into the bowl. Shifting her weight from left to right foot, she shrugged her shoulders, tension growing the longer the woman stayed.

"I would think that would actually give you plenty of opportunities to meet people who share interests with you. You didn't have to drive all the way out here to meet a rancher."

Was she trying to make Amaryllis leave?

Jesse wouldn't appreciate having his plans upset. And it wasn't that she actually had a problem with matchmakers. Plenty of her friends used dating websites, quite successfully. She'd even dipped her toes into those waters a couple of times.

She knew her questions were pushy and not even necessary, but she couldn't make herself stop.

Brows raising, Amaryllis pinned Esme with a matter-of-fact stare that threatened to shut down the conversation. "In my small town, the options are limited. This is the most efficient use of my time."

Amaryllis was too...practical for Jesse. Even though he proclaimed he was going this route for logical reasons, she could tell by his messy desk, it was all an act. He had a freer spirit than he wanted to admit.

"And you don't care that he has two other women coming?" The question sucked the air from the kitchen.

Amaryllis blinked fast, her lips going tight. Apparently, it did matter to her. And Esme felt bad for bringing it up. This really wasn't her business. But something like satisfaction clung to her regret for sharing Jesse's plans.

Which only made her feel worse. Confused her, too.

How did this happen? Esme felt the weight of why she was actually at Jesse Stevens's house crash on her shoulders. Her father's future as the president of the Texas Cattleman's Club. Not to scare away Jesse's suitors.

"I'm sorry," Esme said quickly, shoving aside the bowl and racing to the other side of the island. "That wasn't my place. Talk to Jesse. He'll be back in a moment. I'll just get out of your way."

"I should be leaving." The lady vet moved faster toward the door, tugging her rain jacket on with each step.

Oh, hell. What had she done? She'd ruined everything. This wasn't going to help her father at all. She should have reined in her jealousy, damn it.

"He's a great guy." Esme fast-walked after her, her socked feet slippery against the tiled floor. "I can give you pointers on him, make up for the fact that I shouldn't have said anything."

Amaryllis turned quickly, her eyebrows shooting up in surprise. "So you're going to apologize for meddling by meddling some more?" With a bark of bitter laughter, she shook her head, securing her purse strap over her shoulder. Anger and embarrassment flared in the woman's brown irises. Looking her up and down with an X-ray stare, the woman pressed her lips together. "Wow, you're a piece of work."

Before Esme could think of a suitable response, the door was slamming. Esme tried to formulate a recovery plan. It was her forte, after all. But then she heard the sound of a car engine starting, tires crunching.

Any hope for salvaging the damage she'd caused extinguished as the engine sound faded.

Guilt pinched. Hard. She sagged back against the counter. She'd had no right to be jealous. But the feeling was still there all the same.

Why?

Did she have feelings for Jesse she was unwilling to explore? Yes, she was undeniably attracted to him. And they did have a lot in common, like having been brought up on a ranch. A strong work ethic. Humor.

But she certainly wasn't putting herself on the list of marriage candidates. She wasn't even sure she wanted to have children. Jesse hadn't hidden his plans for the future. In spite of her upbringing, she was a city girl, an executive who loved five-hundred-dollar shoes, in spite of the muck boots she'd worn earlier today.

That seemed like a lifetime ago.

The door opened again and Esme straightened. Had Amaryllis come back? No, the footfalls were too distinctly masculine.

Jesse stepped into the kitchen, sweeping off his Stetson. "Where's Amaryllis?"

Esme cleared her throat, knowing this could hurt her father's bid for a favor from Jesse, but unable to offer anything but the truth and a vow to herself that she would do better with the next two candidates. "I have a confession to make."

Six

A confession? Frowning, Jesse tossed his Stetson onto the kitchen island, keeping his eyes firmly on Esme's face and off the sight of her in jeggings and a long white button-down shirt.

Hey, wait, was that his?

He cleared his throat. "It's okay that you took my shirt."

She blinked uncomprehendingly for a moment. "Your shirt." She looked down and tugged the hem. "It was in the laundry. I hope you don't mind."

"No need to confess about riffling through my clothes. And with luck, your suitcase will be here tonight…or tomorrow." Would she be spending another night?

Not that it should matter. Not with his potential mates coming. Still, he selfishly craved more time.

Esme pursed her lips, her hand moving to the tall glass filled with ice and water. As she swirled the ice against the glass, he watched her grow more tense, her shoulders rising, her jaw clenching.

Her hand shook as she gripped her glass. "That's not my confession. You asked about Amaryllis. She's gone. As in left the property."

Tilting her head, she gestured to the now-empty driveway.

Running a hand through his hair, he tried to make sense of what she was telling him. Had he offended the lady vet somehow? "Where's she going? The Cozy Inn and the Cimarron Rose bed-and-breakfast are probably full with Christmas travelers."

Esme opened her mouth as if to speak, then clamped it shut. He took a step toward her, looking for some clarity.

"She's gone-gone. As in left town, not coming back." Esme crossed her arms over her chest defensively. "She wasn't right for you."

He frowned, surprised and confused. "When I went outside, she seemed quite eager to get to know each other better over dinner. What made her change her mind?" When she didn't answer right away, suspicion nipped at him. "Or should I ask *who* changed her mind? Esme?"

"That's my confession." She inhaled deeply, then blurted, "I let it slip that two other women are coming."

Even from here, he could see the whites of her fingertips as she gripped her water glass.

He rocked back on his boot heels. "That shouldn't have been a surprise to her, though. We both went through a matchmaker. Nothing's exclusive until we decide to date."

She couldn't help but think again how her mother had married her father because it was a practical match that pleased her family. Maybe that had something to do with why she and her siblings had stayed single for so long.

"How very…progressive of you." She nudged the salt grinder closer to the pepper mill.

"I take that to mean you're a romantic, all about the hearts and flowers and being swept off your feet."

"There's no need to make fun of me. I'm very sorry I chased off your new girlfriend. Oops. Not girlfriend. Your potential wife." She winced, resting her hand on his arm. "Wait, scratch that. I'm trying to apologize, not dig myself in deeper."

That small touch sent sensations zinging through him. Her eyes widened with that same awareness he felt, the undeniable attraction.

Then realization dawned. Esme was jealous of the women being sent by the matchmaker, had likely even chased Amaryllis off. That gave him more of a kick than it should, especially when she'd made it clear she wasn't looking for the same things as him in a relationship. Hadn't she?

"So if you don't want me seeing Amaryllis," he mused, heat flaring over his skin at her nearness, "does that mean you want to take that kiss further?"

Her lips worked silently for a moment, color rising in her cheeks. Her chest rose and fell faster, the curves of her breasts enticing. His hands itched to explore.

"You're egotistical." She stepped back. Away from him? Or away from temptation?

He wasn't going to let her off the hook that easily.

"And you like me." The realization was satisfying as hell.

"You're infuriating. And more importantly, you have two more women due here, when?" she asked with a challenge in her voice. She pointed to the window, at the cloudless sky.

"Tomorrow, most likely. The weather app on my phone showed that roads are starting to clear." Esme would be able to leave. "They were supposed to come today, but they texted while I was finishing up in the barn to say they're waiting, just to be safe."

Her jaw dropped. "You scheduled all three women today? At once?"

"I told you Amaryllis already knew about the others. She's a practical, down-to-earth woman."

He needed practical. Stable.

Esme's eyes fluttered closed, then opened again, sparking.

"Knowing about the other women is different than not caring. She had her hopes up, Jesse. You can mock romanticism all you want. It means something to some people, though. It clearly meant something to that woman who ran like hell from the prospect of being a party of some lineup of women for you to pick from."

"What if I were a part of a lineup of men for her?"

"I would find that sad, too," she said without hesitation.

"It doesn't seem like you approve of matchmakers."

She shook her head, her silken hair gliding over her

shoulders. "You misunderstand. I have no problem with a matchmaker. I just think the way you're going about it is…"

"Is what?" he asked, more curious than he should be about how this woman's mind worked. "Spit it out."

"Fine." She braced her shoulders, her chin jutting. "I think it's a recipe for disaster. For heartache. Whatever you want to call it—romantic or practical—it just doesn't seem like something that will work long-term. Not that my opinion matters at all. It's your life."

Her criticism stung. He wanted a family of his own and put a lot of thought into how to approach this. And she just shot it all down in an instant as she stood in judgment of him. "You sure are being confrontational for a person who wants to persuade me your dad should lead that new chapter."

"I'm emotional. I can't make a spreadsheet of my feelings like you do." She grabbed her empty glass and stalked to the sink. "But no worries from here on out. I'll be sure the next two candidates hear only glowing things about you from me."

She stormed across the kitchen and toward the main part of the house without another word, anger crackling off her. His eyes were drawn to the sway of her hips as she walked away. Even after she was gone, her fragrance lingered.

As did his thoughts of what would have happened if Esme had been on that list.

Even two hours later, Esme couldn't believe what she'd said to Jesse. She was normally a calm professional. She was a middle-child peacemaker.

Not today, though.

She'd been hiding out here in her room since their argument, sitting in the middle of the bed and trying to make out a Christmas shopping list. A totally fruitless endeavor since her mind kept wandering back to their fight in the kitchen and how she'd wanted him to...

To what? She hugged the fat pillow, the high-thread-count cotton sensual against her skin.

Sighing, she had to admit the truth. She'd wanted Jesse to agree with her, then sweep her into his arms and kiss her until her knees melted.

The scent of something cooking, something fragrant and full of spices, teased her nose. She glanced at her clock and saw it was approaching suppertime. Would the time apart have hit the reset button for him as it had for her?

There was only one way to find out.

She tossed aside the pillow and slid off the bed, smoothing the shirt, his shirt that she'd pulled from the laundry. Her footfalls soft against the floor, she drew closer until she found Jesse standing at the dark stainless steel stove, stirring a pot of what looked like...

"Is that beef stew?" she asked, gripping and rubbing her wrist, a go-to gesture from when she had heated arguments with her sisters. A self-soothing gesture to calm herself. Not that Jesse knew that. But muscle memory was a powerful thing, and she needed all the smoothing-over vibes she could get.

He glanced back over his shoulder. "It is. Corn bread's in the oven."

"I would have thought you had staff to help you."

After all, he had a bunkhouse for ranch hands, and

he'd mentioned a foreman. But his house was huge and quiet.

He continued stirring, pausing for a moment to smell the deep notes of pepper billowing off the steam. "I do, but they clean and leave. It's just me so they don't need to come often. And I cook for myself."

She stepped closer, dropping her grip on her wrist. "I'm sorry for what I said earlier. It's your life. You know what you want. And that's more than most people in the world."

"Thank you. Apology accepted."

"Does that mean I'm invited to supper?"

"I'm not going to starve you." He tasted the stew and her mouth watered. For him. "My mechanic said he'll get to your car in the morning for a better diagnostic. Unless you have family or friends you want to come get you now. If the rain gets much heavier, the roads could wash out even worse."

Leave? So soon? Apparently, he still was angry, and she couldn't blame him. "Are you asking me to go now? I'm not sure my family could get here safely. But I can still go. There must be lodging somewhere."

"No, that's not what I'm saying. Like I said before, I'm sure everything's booked anyway, given it's the Christmas season." His mouth kicked up into a smile. "And you're chasing women off my property who will need a place to stay since the rain picked up again."

He leaned to pull the corn bread out of the oven, and she couldn't help but check out his butt. No female with a pulse would be able to deny how fine it was, denim cupping the perfect curve in a way that made her long to touch.

She squeezed her hands into fists on the kitchen island.

"Woman," she reminded him. "I've only chased off one woman."

He chuckled softly. "The week is young, Esme."

"It would help if you weren't so funny." Leaning against the cool granite countertop, she shook her head, taking in the subtle pull of his muscles as he stirred the stew.

"And it would help me if you weren't so sexy smart," he retorted.

"What does 'sexy smart' mean?"

He eyed her with a smoky gaze. "You have a brain that rivals your body. Smart women are sexy."

Her skin tingled with awareness. "Thank you for noticing...both. I worry because I work for my father that people may think I don't deserve the job. I try twice as hard to prove myself."

"Word around the club is that you're fierce at what you do. Have you ever thought about looking into switching companies?"

She'd thought of leaving—just once. But duty bound her to protect all that her father had built. Had sacrificed for. She couldn't walk away from the legacy.

"It's the family business. Plenty of relatives work together."

"Okay, fair enough." He leaned back. "So what do you say I dish up dinner and then you can tell me why your father is the best candidate to lead the new chapter of the Texas Cattleman's Club."

Surprise rippled through her. "Really? That simple? You're just asking me?"

"I am. I'll be looking into Ryder Currin. A few other possibilities, too."

"So my dad didn't need to send me here," she said softly.

"It shows how much he wants it. That means something. I get that he's excited about the new chapter. We all are." He passed her a bowl. "Now let's eat."

Companionably, they dished up their dinner, her mind scrolling through what she wanted to say.

Because yes, this club meant a lot to every one of them and she didn't want to say anything to mar the opening.

She could already envision the parties they would have there. The site had been chosen with care, a historic former luxury boutique hotel that fell into disrepair, now almost finished being renovated by Perry Construction. A gorgeous three-story building on a corner downtown. There were suites on the top floor for the president and chairman of the board. The second floor was for board members' and officers' offices and conference rooms. And the first floor contained the ballroom, a bar-style café club for members only, and the main meeting hall.

Stepping into Jesse's dining room, she stopped short at the sight of wineglasses and flickering candles. For a stew dinner?

It was incongruous and charming all at once. A smile lit her from the inside out.

More than just charming, actually. It was dreamy. This man had a romantic side, whether he wanted to admit it or not.

And she needed to remind herself that some other

woman would be the recipient of that long-term. Possibly sooner rather than later, depending on what he thought of those next two candidates.

Resolved, she took her seat at the table to start her pitch on why her father was the person to lead the Houston chapter of the Texas Cattleman's Club.

The very last thing she wanted to be discussing with Jesse Stevens.

The next morning, Esme stared at the two newest matchmaking candidates who'd arrived bright and early, within minutes of each other, and were now getting a tour of the barn. The foreman had just pulled Jesse aside to point out some issue with one of the mares.

Esme was surprised Jesse had left her alone with the two new arrivals after how things went with Amaryllis. He welcomed them and introduced her as a business associate in from Houston before he was called away.

Not that he'd gone far. She felt his gaze on her from across the barn. Warning her?

Biting her lip, she forced her attention back to her side of the stables. This go-round, she wouldn't let so much as a whisper of criticism pass her lips. Far from it, she intended to sing his praises. And to do so, she should learn a little more about them, to get a handle on the best way to help them impress Jesse.

So she flung herself into conversation with the two women in the barn, all the years of training to maneuver through intense situations coming into use now. Not that she could have ever imagined her professional training would prove handy while speaking to matchmaking candidates. But she handled Riley Jean Smith and Michelle Mendoza.

Esme turned her attention back to Riley Jean and remembered the woman mentioning something about having a six-year-old. "Where's your son?"

Riley Jean fluffed her long, wavy jet-black hair. "Staying with my mama. She loves special time with Lonnie Mac."

Esme pulled a smile. "That's what grandmothers are for."

Riley Jean scrunched her pixie-like face, blue eyes grave and serious. "She wants me to have time for myself. And honestly, even though the matchmaking company checks out the prospective dates carefully, I wanted to spend time with him on my own, to form my own opinion."

That made sense. Esme cocked her head to the side, as she petted one of the horses whose head poked out from the stall. The sorrel horse stretched beneath her hands, enjoying the attention.

Shaking her head, Riley Jean held up a hand. "Don't take that the wrong way. It's not like I think he's a serial killer or something. I researched him on the internet. You know, just the basics like his social media pages, his professional profile, college records, friends of his… You're single, too. You understand."

Riley Jean touched a hand to Esme's arm in what seemed like a strange act of camaraderie.

Staying on target was going to be a challenge. More than she had thought. With grit and determination, she willed words to her tongue. "Of course you should meet with him first. Sounds like your mother taught you to be a good mama."

"Thank you. I try."

Actually, the woman sounded a little stalkerish with all that checking up on him. Reasonable safety was one thing. Doing a deep dive into the internet was something else altogether.

Esme shifted her attention to the other woman. "So, tell me more about yourself."

Michelle leaned against the stall door—a vision in heeled boots, jeans and a plaid shirt. Dark waves framed her tan face, making her brown eyes all the more striking. "I'm a former runner-up in the Miss Texas pageant, third runner-up."

"You're lovely. I'm surprised you didn't win."

"Me, too," she said with no indication that she grasped how egotistical that sounded. "I got thrown from a horse the week before the competition, hurt my hip, which made walking in heels a real bitch."

Michelle pushed herself off the stall door, offering her palm to the sorrel horse before petting it. From down the barn, the low timbre of Jesse's voice reverberated, though there was no telling what he was saying.

Esme resisted the urge to shout "fire" and send both women running. But she wasn't going to repeat her mistake by chasing them off. She owed her father—and Jesse—more than that. She needed to be better. She hated being ruled by jealousy whether it was about Jesse, her sisters or her dad.

If this was what Jesse wanted, then she would do her best to help make it happen.

Checking to make sure Jesse was still occupied with

ranch business, Esme leaned closer to Riley Jean and Michelle. "I would like to help you both."

Michelle's microbladed eyebrows rose. "Both of us?"

Esme bit back a sigh. "This isn't *The Bachelor* where you're both trying to outdo the other."

Michelle rocked back and forth in her high-heeled boots with a chuckle. "Speak for yourself."

"Okay, that." Esme tapped Michelle on the arm. "He has a good sense of humor. He'll like that about you."

Michelle shook her hair back over her shoulders with a perfect toss. "I considered doing a stand-up comedy routine as my talent but opted for a patriotic tap dance instead."

"Hmm… I'd say go with your first instinct from now on." Esme bit the inside of her cheek. "Riley Jean? I bet you miss your son."

"I do." She touched a heart locket around her neck. "He's the best thing that ever happened to me, and he's everything to me since my husband died. Do you want to see Lonnie Mac's picture?"

Riley Jean opened the locket to reveal a photo of a gap-toothed boy. A kid who would probably love to have Jesse's attention.

"Cute kid," Esme said, in spite of herself. "Having a family is very important to Jesse. He really wants kids."

A reminder she needed to take to heart.

"Whoa, hold on," Riley Jean protested. "That's getting ahead of things. I only just showed up."

Esme felt the crisis boiling and knew she had to do her best to douse it. "I just meant it's okay to talk about your son. I've seen single-mom friends of mine hold back sharing about their kids for fear it'll chase the guy away. That's not the case here."

Riley Jean smiled impishly. "That's all good to know. Thank you."

Esme fidgeted with the ends of her sleeves, ready for this to be over but knowing there was still a task in front of her. "PR is my chosen profession. It's all about taking the facts and putting the right spin on things."

Michelle looked her up and down. A moment passed before she opened up her bubble gum–pink lips. "I have one last question."

Esme nodded. "Sure. Shoot."

"Why aren't you going after Jesse when you clearly know—and admire—so much about him?"

Surprise slammed into her. A fair question. She looked down the barn to where he worked with a horse. He was so handsome, even covered in dirt, his muscles apparent as he gripped the horse's hoof for more treatment for the abscess.

He was earthy, handsome and, yes, "sexy smart."

As if Jesse sensed her looking at him, he glanced over at her. His green eyes glinted and he smiled. She smiled back. How could she not?

Michelle's sigh and a creak of leather across the room drew Esme's attention back. Riley Jean was gathering her purse and Michelle was tugging on her jacket.

Oh, damn.

Esme straightened quickly and double-timed after them, barely catching them at the barn door. "Where are you going? Did I say something wrong?"

Michelle tucked her head to the side with a half

smile. "Honey, you didn't have to say a word. Your body language said it all. You've got it bad for that man."

Riley Jean nodded. "And by the steamy look he just smoked your way, he has it bad for you, too."

Did he?

She looked over at him quickly, and uh-oh, he was already striding toward her, no doubt because of the rapidly departing women. How had they gotten so far ahead of her already? Panic nipped at her as she called out, "Wait."

But Michelle and Riley Jean were deep in conversation as they moved toward their vehicles, heads tilted together.

"What's going on?" Jesse asked as he closed the distance between them.

Esme met him at the open barn door, chilly air from outside blasting through. "I swear I didn't do a thing to chase them off. In fact, I told them great things about you."

He turned from the door back to her, steam—the sensual kind—smoking from him in palpable waves. "Like what?"

She couldn't believe her ears. She gave him her full attention as the women drove off. Her pulse picked up speed. "You're not angry over them leaving?"

He planted a hand on the doorframe beside her. "Surprisingly, no. Not at all." He stroked back a strand of her hair, drawing two fingers down the lock. "My focus is exactly where it should be."

Butterflies churned in her stomach and she realized, truly realized and acknowledged for the first time, that there was something between them that just couldn't be ignored. Breathless and dry-mouthed, she couldn't deny that she wanted him.

Before she could have second thoughts that could rob her of exploring those feelings, she said, "That's really convenient."

He worked that lock of her hair around his finger, slowly drawing her closer. "How so?"

"Because," she blurted, the words tumbling out of her mouth faster than she intended, "I was thinking perhaps I could try out to be one of your dates."

Seven

Jesse stared at Esme in shock.

Surely he couldn't have heard her correctly. Although the surge of passion shooting through him shouted how much he hoped he had. He wasn't even disappointed to see the three supposedly perfect candidates bail. His thoughts were too wrapped up in Esme.

"Try out?" he asked, pulling the barn door closed, sealing them back inside, a few stray pieces of hay crunching under his boots. "What exactly do you mean by that? Audition to be my wife?"

"That might be a bit of a quick leap down the aisle. But a test run as your girlfriend—your wife, if you will—could give me the chance to see if I really like it." She shifted in her boots. Her blond hair fell over her blouse, hinting at her curves.

"You're certain of what you're suggesting? After everything you said about the matchmaking process?" His brow raised as he leaned against the stall door. Duke poked his head out of the stall, tilting it sideways. The horse chuffed, knocking his muzzle into Jesse.

A wide grin broke across Esme's face, lighting her eyes. She reached up to ruffle Duke's forelock.

"Part of me feels like that's all I want for Christmas," she said earnestly, her blue eyes sparkling. "To be honest, the other part of me isn't sure about anything, particularly life on a ranch and one that's not even near my relatives."

He liked that family was important to her. How ironic that until now he hadn't thought of that being a core part of who she was. So much so that she'd risked her life coming out here in a horrible storm just because her father had asked for her help. He started to churn over the possibility of chucking the matchmaker notion and giving an earnest shot at seeing where the attraction to Esme led.

"And you're okay with this, even though we barely know each other?"

"Seriously? You're asking me that?" She snorted on a laugh. "You were willing to consider marrying someone you'd never even met in person."

"Fair statement." He cupped her shoulders, then slid his hands down her arms, linking fingers.

"Although now that I think about it, your matchmaker had you fill out a profile. So let's do that."

"You want to take a survey now?"

"Not a written one. We can do it verbally." She

leaned closer, the heat of her breath a tempting caress. "Organically."

"Hmm, sounds intriguing. Do you want to go back to the house or to the office?"

She inclined her head, voice husky. "Your office. It's closer."

His heart rate picked up the pace. "After you, ma'am."

He gestured toward his office, following her inside. The Christmas tree lit the room well enough, so he didn't turn on the overhead light.

Esme settled onto the leather sofa, leaving space for him. "I'll start easy. What's your favorite music?"

"Country, acoustic." He sat beside her, stretching his arms along the back of the couch, his fingers brushing against her. "Simple but rich."

"Mmm, sexy answer. I can imagine long, slow kisses with guitar music in the background." Her eyes flamed, lighting an answering fire in him. "I like soft rock, old classics. And there's common ground there to be found in coffeehouse styles of the tunes."

"Favorite author?"

Esme tapped her fingers along a stack of magazines on the table beside the couch. "Jane Austen. Favorite movie?"

"*True Grit*, the original. All Stetsons, all the time." Watching Westerns was a ritual he'd started with his grandfather long ago. Funny how he hadn't thought about that until now.

"What's an absolute no-no in a relationship?"

Her question surprised him, but his answer was easy and earnest. "Lying."

A pained wince twitched at her face. Lines of worry

etched her brow. It made him wonder what had happened in her past to cause them. And made him want to ensure it would never happen again.

She braced her shoulders. "Agreed."

Good. "If you could live anywhere other than Texas, where would it be?"

"There is nowhere other than Texas." Tucking her feet beneath her, she preened like a cat.

He threw back his head and laughed, full-out. He liked the way she could draw that from him. "Ah, perfect answer. Your turn."

Esme pursed her lips. "When was the last time you cried?" Then she shook her head. "Never mind. I don't really expect you to respond to that. Male machismo being what it is."

She might say it didn't matter, but she must have asked for a reason. He'd already gleaned that her father was a controlling type. Certainly, Sterling Perry had a reputation of being all business, all flash. No substance?

Had that question been a Freudian slip? Was Esme looking for more from the people in her life?

Regardless, he had no problem offering her an honest answer. He looked past his desk to a nondescript piece of tack on the wall. "The day my horse Apollo died. I'd had him since I was a kid. I still keep his leather halter hanging there." He pointed to the wall. "I won't be putting it on another horse."

"I'm so sorry for that loss. It sounds like Apollo was an amazing friend to you."

Apollo had gotten him through every tough time in high school. He'd left it all behind when he rode. "I told you my family wasn't close. That led me to spend most of my time in the stables. Everyone there brought me up, taught me a good work ethic, taught me about life."

"You're truly tugging at my heart here."

He traced a finger along her cheekbone, just under her eye. "When was the last time you cried?"

"When my shoe broke in the rain." She angled to nip his finger.

He chuckled, his hand cupping her shoulder and drawing her closer. "Have you considered designer boots? I bet you would rock them."

She flattened her hands on his chest, her palms warm. "Well, thank you for the lovely compliment, cowboy."

"I think we're finding we have more in common here than we expected." Her scent tempted him, enticed him, sending blood surging south.

"And we didn't even need the matchmaker." She stroked sensual circles on his chest that seared through his flannel shirt.

"And you do realize a part of being a wife means being in my bed?"

Her hands slid up his chest to loop around his neck. "That's the part I'm most looking forward to."

Esme didn't consider herself an impulsive person, but she'd never been more certain of anything. She wanted to make love to Jesse Stevens. Here, now, in this office that felt so much more like the essence of him than his perfectly decorated home he'd put together with a laser focus on creating some mythical family.

Reality was better than dreams.

Reality with *this* man.

She met him halfway for the kiss, not that far to move as they were both already angling forward. The hot sweep of his tongue along hers was bold and hungry. His spicy scent filled her every breath. Everything about the moment seared into her senses in a way she knew she would replay in memory again and again.

His fingers speared through her hair, massaging along her scalp as he drew her head closer. She sank deeper into the kiss and delicious sensations licked along her spine. She glided her fingers down his back and tugged the tails of his shirt from the waist of his jeans, tunneling up to stroke the muscled expanse of his back.

A frenzy burned at her even as she ached to savor every touch, taste, caress. Drawing the moment out sharpened the edge of desire, dulled the edge of time until she whispered against his mouth, "I'm ready to show you my sexy brain."

He chuckled, his hands gliding down to clasp her hips. "Oh really?"

"Yes, and more."

He growled softly in appreciation. "I'm looking forward to it."

"You'll reciprocate, of course."

He angled back to meet her gaze. "Am I moving too fast for you?"

She struggled to gather her thoughts and how to express herself when she still had so many questions herself. "To be honest, I've never felt this much for someone so quickly. So yes, my head is spinning more than a little, but I'm sure. Very sure that this is what I want."

"For what it's worth," he said, "even with the whole matchmaker gig, this is moving at lightning speed for me, too."

"But you're sure?" she repeated.

"Absolutely. I want you. Here. Now."

"All I needed to hear."

As soon as she said the words, he slid from the couch to kneel in front of her, the lit tree glimmering behind him.

Between kisses, he eased her sweater over her head, breaking briefly to tug it off and toss it aside. The air was cool against her flesh, then warm as he touched her again, unhooking her bra, freeing her for his touch and gaze. He peeled down her jeggings, his hands warm, launching butterflies in her stomach and goose bumps along her skin.

He reclined her back onto the sofa, his lips grazing her neck, nuzzling aside her sweater to nip along her collarbone. He was definitely overdressed, and she intended to fix that. Immediately. She made quick work of the buttons on his shirt, shoving the flannel off his broad shoulders, flinging it aside. Then... Wow... Just wow... His chest was on display, a feast for her eyes and hands. She arched up for another kiss, desire pulsing through her, demanding more. Of this moment. Of him.

She tucked her hands into his jeans pocket and whispered against his mouth. "Birth control?"

"Yes, I have it."

"So glad." She teased his bottom lip between her teeth.

"Me, too." He rested his forehead against hers for a moment before rolling to his feet.

He fished out his wallet, withdrew a condom and set it on the coffee table on top of a stack of farming magazines.

She swung her legs off the sofa and reached for him, unfastening his jeans. Easing the zipper down. Revealing the steely length of him. She stroked up, then down again. His hands gripped her shoulders, his chest rising and falling faster until he kicked aside his jeans and boxers. He angled back down to join her, stretching out over her in a delicious weight, his bare body meeting hers. She passed him the condom and quickly, he was ready.

And she was more than ready.

His gaze held hers as he slid inside her, filling her in a slow, deliberate stroke. Holding. The sensation of being connected for the first time was so intense, a ripple shimmered through her. Then he moved, and she moved with him, instinct taking over.

His mouth grazed her ear, her neck, before settling, yes, on her breast. Need tightened through her, sending her arching up. Her nails scored down his back lightly, although it was a struggle not to dig her fingers in deeply, anchor them both even more firmly.

She drew her foot up his calf and a husky moan rumbled in his chest. She'd known the attraction between them was strong, but she still hadn't expected the chemistry to be this intense, more than she'd felt with anyone before. Soon, too soon, she felt release building. And as much as she wanted to hold back, to wait, the bliss increased, growing more intense until her head was flung back with the force of her orgasm. Feeling Jesse's hoarse groans of completion heat her skin sent aftershocks along her already-sensitive nerves. Every sense was heightened, honed to right now.

His head was buried in her neck, his breath ragged, until with a hefty exhale, he rolled to his side, taking her with him. He eased a hand away to pull a blanket from the back of the sofa and over them, holding her close, staying silent other than the sound of their hearts galloping in sync.

As she drifted off to sleep, her walls and defenses down, she couldn't escape the niggling voice telling her that this had been a dangerous idea.

And already she wanted him again.

Their interview that afternoon had gone beyond anything he'd imagined. He could certainly check "sexually compatible" off his list. Their lovemaking still lingered in his mind. He already craved her again.

Jesse paced in the sunroom off his bedroom suite, glass walls overlooking his property. In the landscape lights the pool glimmered, spa waters churning. The bunkhouse glowed in the distance. Christmas lights glinted along the split-rail fences, marking the lines of his property out in the distance.

Space, waiting to be filled.

For a moment, he allowed himself to envision what the future might look like. And what it might look like with Esme in it. He dropped into one of the wingbacks, a glass of whiskey in his hand. His memory was full of images of her asleep in his bed, hugging a pillow, her honey-blond hair fanned around her. He wanted to make the most of his time with her, and it would be helpful to know how much time he had before he would have to make some trips up to Houston. It would help to find out about the state of the roads.

Checking the time, he found it just shy of midnight. He didn't want to wake anyone up…but then, his friend was a night owl. He typed out a text to his friend Nathan Battle, the sheriff of Royal.

Are you awake? If not, I'll catch up in the morning.

Seconds after he hit Send, the phone rang, Nathan's number flashing.

Jesse answered. "Thanks for calling. Hope I'm not disturbing you."

"Everyone's asleep or playing video games. What can I do for you?" Nathan was an imposing leader for their police force, with a soft spot for his wife, Amanda, and their children.

Jesse moved out onto the balcony. A few stars peeked out of the nighttime clouds. "How're the roads looking?"

"We have a couple of rural routes that are washed out and a damaged bridge. But we've marked enough detours for people to get around."

"I imagine you've had your hands full."

"Amanda's been on me to take a vacation once this is over." Nathan's wife owned the Royal Diner, an informal eatery where small-town Texas gossip got spread.

"Sounds like you're married to a wise woman." Nathan and Amanda had the kind of rock-solid marriage that was an advertisement for matrimony.

"I'm a lucky bastard," his gravelly voice echoed over the phone line. "But you didn't call me for a weather report. If you wanted to know about the state of the roads you could have phoned anyone in the department."

"What do you think of all the jockeying for power going on over in Houston to decide who's going to head the new club?" Of all his friends, Nathan was like a brother to Jesse. He'd served as sound counsel for years.

"I think we've been lucky to have our group stay local here for a long time. We've got a good town here and the club has made great strides since admitting women. The Texas Cattleman's Club stands for community and family, honor and friendship, a cohesive force to support each other and do good in the community."

Though his friend couldn't see, he still found himself nodding in agreement. For all those reasons he took his role in the Texas Cattleman's Club seriously. "I agree."

"Choosing the person to set the tone in Houston is important. We don't want our brand to be turned into some kind of social club or to lose its values. Houston isn't Royal. It's going to take a strong leader to guide all those larger-than-life personalities."

"Solid insights." His throat tightened. He hesitated.

A yawn echoed from the other end of the phone. "Do you mind if I ask why we're discussing this?"

Shooting a glance at his bed and finding Esme stirring just a bit, he moved farther out onto the balcony and kept his voice low. "I've got an unexpected guest here. Sterling Perry's daughter. She's come to town to lobby for her father."

"What do you think?"

He blinked. How in the hell did he answer that? "What do I think of *her*? Esme's brilliant."

"Uh-huh." Nathan chuckled.

"Uh-huh what?"

Nathan laughed softly again. "My friend, I've been in this job a very long time and that's taught me how to read a person's tone. The sound always tells more than the words. And your tone tells me you are head over ass infatuated with her."

"And if I am? But she's the epitome of Houston glamour." Opposite of everything he thought he wanted during the whole matchmaking process. And yet he couldn't help but feel drawn to her.

"Glamour isn't a bad thing. You've been to enough galas at the club—tuxedos and gowns and jewels. I defy you to find any event more high-end than ours."

"Good point. Esme would enjoy that." He envisioned her in a floor-length ball gown. Dancing. Their bodies in sync as they moved to the music.

"And since you contacted that matchmaker, I assume your interest is still for something lasting. A wife and family?"

"My plans haven't changed."

"Then my advice? Pursue her. Find out if what you're feeling for her is the real thing."

Before Nathan had even finished signing off, Jesse's mind was already churning with ideas and excitement.

Dinner out. Maybe they could even double-date with his neighbor Cord and his girlfriend, Zoe. Cord would be relocating to Houston soon and Jesse was going to miss him. But then, connections in Houston would also give him a reason to see Esme. Houston might have massive department stores, but Royal offered top-notch specialty niche shops, and he wouldn't mind having Esme along as he finished his Christmas shopping. And he still had a tree to chop down for all those decorations and an old-school string of lights like he remembered from childhood.

Full of plans, he pushed to his feet. He intended to show her just how amazing life could be here. That the town of Royal had everything to offer for a full social calendar.

And he very much looked forward to wooing her all the way back to his bed.

Eight

The past two weeks had been a blur of bliss for Esme, a time of discovery, getting to know Jesse, their differences fading in the face of so many shared interests, laughs and kisses. They'd spent nearly every moment together, going on dates, buying last-minute Christmas gifts and adding to the scant wardrobe in her suitcase. Touring his land, decorating his Christmas tree, making love in front of the fire.

He'd learned she had a weakness for flowers and could eat her way to the bottom of a bowl of popcorn. Heavily buttered. She sang Christmas carols with gusto, her pitch questionable, her enthusiasm undeniable.

Her equestrian skills were some of the best he'd ever seen. She was fire in motion on a horse.

Esme was a sensual woman who took pleasure in experiencing life.

Their nights had been spent passionately exploring in a lengthy quest to discover what made the other unravel with desire.

But she knew their time together was drawing to a close. She would have to return to Houston and her job. She'd delayed as long as she could.

Tomorrow, she was due to go back to Houston. Key members of the Royal chapter—including Jesse—would be touring the new club's building renovations. Afterward, there would be a meeting with those Royal players, held at the Houston site.

Cases would be made for who should be the new president. Had she done enough good during her time here? Heaven knew, she'd been focused more on her relationship with Jesse than on her father's bid for power.

She shoved aside the pinch of guilt. There was nothing she could do about that now, and she wouldn't let it steal the joy of this last evening with Jesse.

Tonight, they were enjoying a five-star dinner at the Texas Cattleman's Club—the original branch—in Royal. Music from a string quartet filled the room with classical Christmas melodies.

Looking around, no one would guess the place had suffered a devastating tornado, the fiercest to hit Royal in nearly eighty years. They'd rebuilt, better than ever. Pride surged in her heart at this community, the bonds made in this space. No wonder Jesse felt like these people were family. His comfort here showed in his easy manner, his way of greeting friends who stopped by their table.

The club was housed in a large, rambling single-story building made of dark stone and wood. The interior decor consisted of mostly dark wood floors, leather upholstered furniture and super-high ceilings.

Hunting trophies and historical artifacts adorned the paneled walls. Her favorite was the tooth of an ancient relative of a horse. As a child, she'd been delighted to know herds of horselike creatures roamed the lands she called home. She'd even had her own horse tooth in a small shadow box that always felt strangely comforting to her. That the Royal club boasted a similar horse tooth gave a sense of continuity between the two spaces. A slice of home for her. In addition to the elegant formal dining hall, there were several private meeting rooms and a great room for both public and private Texas Cattleman's Club events.

During her tour of the place prior to being seated for dinner, she'd been most surprised to discover the club had a childcare center for club members and employees, the laughter and squeals broadcasting how much the kids enjoyed the setup.

To see how inclusive the Texas Cattleman's Club had become warmed her even on the somewhat chilly Texas evening.

And of course, that was just the inside. Outdoors there was a stable, a pool, tennis courts and even a playground. Her mind was spinning.

She pulled her attention back to the table, tapered candles flickering in the middle of an arrangement of white poinsettias and holly.

She spooned up the last of her chocolate trifle. "Thank you, Jesse. This is the perfect end to an incredible meal, from the lobster bisque to the filet mignon."

"I'm glad you enjoyed yourself." He stretched a leg out. He'd worn his good boots with the suit.

"This has been an amazing two weeks."

He clasped her hand across the table. "I agree. I don't want things to end just because we're going to Houston."

Her chest grew tight. It was ironic how excitement and anxiety could make such a tangle. "I feel the same." Not wanting to risk wrecking their evening by wading into deep waters too soon, she said, "I'm looking forward to you meeting my family."

"I'm sure they'll be glad to have you back," he said with a pensive look in his green eyes.

She reached for her wine, avoiding his gaze, not ready to have the Houston-versus-Royal discussion yet. She sipped the after-dinner wine, then set the crystal glass on the table again. Her fingers tapped nervously along the gold beading at the glass stem, syncing with the Christmas carol playing softly.

The silence between her and Jesse stretched until she looked up self-consciously, pulling her hand away from the glass and clenching her fingers. She nodded toward the string quartet. "'Silent Night.' It was my mother's favorite carol."

"You must miss her a lot this time of year."

"Very much." She blinked back tears. "We all do. Even my dad, although their marriage wasn't the best. She married him out of duty. He married her for power. It's no surprise things didn't work out well at all."

"Is that why you reacted so strongly to the matchmaker idea?" he asked insightfully.

She could only nod, not trusting her voice.

He clasped her hand again. "Thank you for telling me that."

"Thank you for listening." She swallowed down a lump in her throat, then drew in a shaky breath. "Okay, that's enough serious talk for one night. I just want to enjoy this night of Royal's finest. In fact, I'm thinking we should order more dessert to take home and enjoy later."

"That sounds like an excellent idea. How about you choose for the both of us and surprise me?" Jesse placed his linen napkin by his plate. "And while you're doing that, I need to have a quick word with my friend Cord. I won't be long."

"Take your time." She smiled, soaking up the sight of him in a charcoal-gray suit and festive red tie.

"You really are incredible." Jesse's gaze smoked over her from across the table, lingering on the plunging neckline of the emerald velvet dress she'd chosen in one of the specialty boutiques at the Courtyard Shops. He dropped a kiss on her lips before stepping away.

Her toes curled in her Valentino heels. Tingles spread through her all the way down to her fresh pedicure.

The day had been deliciously pampering from start to finish. While Jesse had had business to attend to at his lawyer's, he'd suggested she spend the day at Royal's Saint Tropez Salon. She hadn't expected such a luxurious, high-end spa in a small town. She'd felt petty for judging so quickly.

Her appointment at the salon had afforded her time for reflection. Something about lavender-scented towels and rubs peeled away stress. And the relative silence had helped. It had forced contemplation. Forced reflection.

Truth be told, these weeks with Jesse had dominated that reflection. How wrong she'd been about him. The silly but serendipitous circumstances of their meeting. How lucky they'd both been to find each other because of the chaos of the storm. Ironic, she'd mused, for a man who craved stability and practicality.

She'd met so many incredible people over the past couple of weeks, some of whom were seated in the dining room tonight. She smiled in response to Megan and Whit Daltry. Megan ran the local animal rescue, Safe Haven. Jesse had brought Esme along when he'd dropped off a donation to help with the rescue's three horses recently taken in. Esme had been amazed at the large operation, one that was apparently growing exponentially under Megan's leadership.

Megan and Whit were dining with Natalie and Max St. Cloud, a fascinating couple. Even though Max was a tech genius billionaire, his wife still owned and operated the Cimarron Rose bed-and-breakfast, with a small bridal dress shop attached. Both couples' children were enjoying a Christmas-themed movie night in the childcare center.

Her heart tugged at the memory of glimpsing those sweet little faces when Jesse had taken a detour there to pass out Christmas candy. They all clearly knew and adored him. And she couldn't deny being enticed by the notion of a baby of her own someday, and celebrating family Christmases.

A cleared throat pulled her attention back. She found Zoe Warren, Cord's girlfriend, standing by the table. The towering brunette looked stunning in a simple gold sheath dress. Esme had enjoyed getting to know her and Cord during a lunch at the Royal Diner.

Zoe smiled genuinely. Drink in hand, she gestured to the table. "I hope I'm not interrupting your dinner."

"Not at all. I'm glad you came over." Esme stood quickly and then greeted her with a welcoming hug. "Have a seat. It looks like our dates are deep in a conversation that isn't close to wrapping up."

"Thank you. I would like that." Zoe settled into a chair beside her. "I enjoyed our lunch the other day."

A phantom gurgle tickled her stomach, even though she was far from hungry. Lunch with Zoe the other day had been at a small, vaguely yellowing local spot. Esme had her doubts as she crossed through the metal door. But after sitting down, her senses had been delighted. She felt as if she'd stumbled upon a contender for one of those reality television shows about stellar restaurants with questionable exteriors.

And the diner's food—she'd ordered the chicken-fried steak and a glass of sweet tea—had been every bit as wonderful as the interior. "The Royal Diner is one of those fun finds off the beaten path of major cities."

Zoe sipped her champagne, bubbles climbing up the crystal flute. "It's incredible how Amanda and Nathan Battle juggle two such busy careers with family life. I've lost count of how many children they have."

Esme toyed with the stem of her wineglass pensively. "It sounds like they have it all."

"That they do." Zoe grinned, motioning to the waiter who was walking by with a tray of champagne. She took another flute before looking back at Esme. "So how are you liking the rest of Royal?"

"Surprisingly very much. It's not Houston, of course," Esme said with a shrug, unworried about judgment since the woman was from Houston, as well, "but I've found there's much more offered here than I expected. It's a unique mix of a small town with some big-city amenities."

"It's quite a haven." Zoe glanced over at her handsome dark-haired boyfriend, concern furrowing her forehead. "I worry he's going to miss Royal and all his friends here. But he insists he's committed to making a move to Houston for me. He's bought the loveliest ranch on the outskirts of town. He's making such a big sacrifice for me. For us."

Zoe was a police detective in Houston. Her investigation into Vincent Hamm's murder had brought her here to Royal. Esme and her family owed Zoe a debt of gratitude, the cop's progress going a long way to help shift the cloud of suspicion off Sterling Perry.

Esme toyed with the placement of her silver dessert spoon. "How incredible that he's willing to move for you."

"We're in love." She looked toward her boyfriend, her face full of emotion. "We found a compromise, because the option of being apart was more than we could bear."

Esme's gaze skated to Jesse deep in conversation with his friend and she wondered…

If Cord was willing to relocate to Houston, might Jesse be willing to make the move, as well? Tomorrow would be pivotal for more than her father.

Her own future with Jesse rode on their trip to Houston.

* * *

Ryder Currin paced through the Houston building of the Texas Cattleman's Club, checking last-minute touches to the structure's renovations before the contingent from Royal arrived tomorrow. Angela walked alongside him, making her own notes in her tablet, the scent of paint heavy in the air. He could hardly believe the plans for starting this Houston branch were coming to fruition. Ryder had been instrumental in bringing the chapter to Houston, and yes, he craved the position as president. He wanted to lead the organization through this transitional time.

But would that ambition threaten his second chance with Angela, given how much her father wanted the same thing?

Telling himself it was pointless to borrow trouble, he pulled his attention back to the building, his boot steps echoing up to the soaring ceiling.

The location and architectural style for the Houston chapter's future home was very different from the Royal club. It had seemed an insurmountable project at first, since the historic former luxury boutique hotel had fallen into disrepair. But all their plans for renovation were coming together, thanks to Perry Construction. The three-story edifice had always been stunning on the outside. Now the inside matched.

The location was practical for so many reasons, including the fact that three doors down was the Houston Galleria Hotel, a medium-sized luxury hotel where members could stay when in town.

Angela's high heels clicked on the floor as she walked ahead of him, caught up in her notes. This club was important to her, too. Ryder understood she was caught in a tough position with both him and her father wanting the lead position here. He didn't want anything to interfere with this second chance they had. He would withdraw if it came to that, but she'd insisted this should play out as the club decided.

He just wanted to make sure there was no negative blowback as they rolled out the official grand opening with a New Year's Eve bash. Press releases for the event had been delayed with Esme Perry out of town for so long.

They'd all been thrown for a loop when Angela's sister had decided to stay in Royal even after the storm passed. And of course, Sterling had been all too willing to accommodate time off work so his daughter could spend more time currying family favor.

Ryder was a man who abided by the rules, so this flagrant lobbying really chapped his hide. It just wasn't fair play.

Angela made everything more complicated. He loved her. Deeply. Truly. In a way that made his soul sing, something he hadn't expected to happen again after his wife Elinah had died. He didn't underestimate how important it was to get this right with Angela. His first marriage had ended in divorce. He couldn't regret the union since his son, Xander, had come from that relationship. But his breakup with Penny was still a failure that marked him.

One he wouldn't allow himself to repeat.

The rumors that he'd had feelings for Angela's mom were true. But he'd never acted on those feelings because of respect for rules and fair play. Honor meant something to him. Besides, his second marriage had shown him what real love was. Elinah. A part of his heart would always belong to her. Their time together had been the best, years that gave him his daughter Annabel and then they'd adopted Maya. Losing Elinah to cancer had almost destroyed him.

He wouldn't go through that heartbreak again. He would do whatever it took to keep he and Angela's love safe. There'd be no repeat of their breakup. Already he could envision her living in his home. His log-style mansion wasn't as fancy as the Perry place. He'd grown up poor and had never been comfortable with ostentation.

Still, the place had been plenty roomy to bring up his children with space to spare. And for more children?

Ryder looked at Angela. He saw the weight that seemed to press down on her, to change her normal happy expression. He hated to see her sad. "I'm sorry your sister missed the brunch she had planned with you, Melinda, Tatiana and my girls."

He was, truly, although secretly he was always antsy when Angela or his daughter Maya spent time with Tatiana. The woman was a shark with the power to upset their lives.

"The brunch will still happen, I'm sure." A brief flash of disappointment flickered in Angela's eyes before she schooled her features. "We haven't set a specific date. Just sometime whenever Esme gets back."

She noticed a paint droplet on a nearby marble plant stand and Ryder watched her as she worked to eradicate it.

"Well, keep me in the loop." A glint caught his eyes.

Stooping down, he picked up a stray nail from beneath a windowsill and pocketed it. Still so much to do.

"About my sister's return?"

Shrugging, he ran a hand through his hair and then stopped at the nape of his neck. "Sure, and the brunch."

Muffled noises grabbed his attention. Shouting and angry voices. He locked eyes with Angela. Her brow furrowed in confusion.

His daughter Maya shouldered past the painters putting last-minute touches on some trim. She raced toward him in a flurry of color with her bold yellow coat and her vibrant red hair. His youngest child had never been one to get lost in the shuffle of day-to-day life.

"Dad, I have to talk to you," she demanded, her raised voice echoing upward as she crashed into the room. Panting and distraught, she wasn't budging.

"Well, hello to you, too, Maya. It's good to see you. Angela and I are almost through here—"

"No, Dad. Not later. Now. There are so many rumors flying around about our family, too many secrets. I can't—I won't—wait any longer. I'm eighteen. It's time we finally had this talk." She stomped her foot in exasperation, but her eyes were filled with tears.

Regret hit him in the chest, that he'd brought his daughter to this level of anxiety.

Angela clasped his arm, a welcome touch when Maya's outburst had him reeling. "I've got plenty to occupy me. Please, take as long as you need."

She gave his arm a final squeeze before walking off toward a pile of plaster dust beneath a gilded mirror, snapping photos with her tablet.

"Thank you," he said, appreciating that she understood and accepted how important his children were to him. He tucked an arm around his daughter's shoulders and guided her to the café area free of painters.

Maya gasped for air beside him, her shoulders shaking in a way that telegraphed how close she was to losing it. He'd put enough bandages over skinned knees and listened to enough of her high school drama to read the signs.

He guided her to a club chair and dropped into another one across from her. "What's going on, Maya? These rumors about the family business have been circulating for a while now. What made today so upsetting?"

Maya closed her eyes tightly. Took a deep breath. Then another.

Ryder could see her mouth moving as she counted to ten before she opened her eyes. His fire-haired child had always struggled to rein in her emotions.

"It's been building up for a long time, and then when the invitations went out for the mother-daughter tea today…" She picked at the wrist of her yellow coat. "I need you to tell me the truth, once and for all."

A sigh all but deflated him. Hearing about the mother-daughter tea sucker punched him, even after all these years since Elinah died. He would always miss her. She'd been a loving wife and mother. He'd tried to make up for what his children had lost…but it was an impossible void to fill.

Then a dark thought hit him. Maya was asking about her biological mother. He'd promised to tell her when she was eighteen and he'd put it off long enough. The pit in his gut grew deeper.

"The truth?" he asked, stalling to give himself time to collect his thoughts for a conversation that would undoubtedly prove difficult. Those secrets had been a heavy weight on the shoulders of a man who prided himself on honesty and honor.

"About my biological parents." Her eyes were clear, her tone steely. "No more delaying. Tell me now, or I'm never going to talk to you again."

There was no missing the vehemence in her voice. Her arms crossed tightly over her chest in a protective hug as she bit down on her lip. Ryder could feel fear and anger radiate from her in waves.

She'd asked in the past, but never pushed. They'd done a kind of dance with the subject, her pressing, then backing away as if she was afraid of the truth.

And there was reason to be wary, the same reason he'd held back telling her until she was old enough to handle the truth. But she was eighteen now, no denying that.

He took her hands in his and thought back to the first time he'd held her and she'd wrapped him around her little finger. He loved all of his children equally, but he'd always felt more protective of his little girl. He wished he could spare her the heartache the truth about her mother might bring.

"Before I start, I want you to know how much I love you."

"I love you, too, Dad." She squeezed his hands. "Now quit stalling." Brows lowering, she fixed him with a stare he recognized. His stare. The one he used to signal he meant business.

"Your biological grandfather was a man named

Sam. Eighteen years ago, he showed up on my doorstep out of the blue one night. Sam's daughter was barely twenty and she'd just given birth to a sickly—" his voice hitched "—but so very beautiful baby girl."

"And my father?"

Here was where things started getting tougher. "He abandoned your mother." He paused for a moment to let that part soak in before continuing. "Your mother was in no position to be a mother. Sam talked her into letting him find a good home for the baby. He said his daughter vowed she loved her baby but knew she couldn't care for a child. He provided documents from both your biological mother and father that signed away their rights to you."

She deflated, tears streaming down her face, her body shaking from the impact of the news. This was a story he wished he never had to burden her with, but he knew she had the right to know. It didn't make the telling any easier, though. He'd give anything to take away the pain snaking its way onto Maya's face. To stop the quiver in her lips.

And his gut knotted since there was still a second shoe to drop once his daughter found out her mother was someone she knew.

"Maya, honey, I'm sorry." He wanted to gather her into a hug and promise everything would be all right, the way he'd done when she was growing up. When she'd trusted him to fight those battles for her. "Sam was drunk three-quarters of the time and had gambled away anything left of the family money."

"But why did he choose you?" The sentence came

out in a rasp. A voice of a much younger Maya cracking through as a sob racked her.

It broke him.

"Harrington York—Sterling Perry's father-in-law—willed me a small parcel of land. Land that Sam swore York had promised to him one day. But the land went to me and that was the start of my oil business."

Ryder hated to paint her biological grandfather in a bad light, but Maya wanted to know the truth and he wouldn't lie to her any longer. "Sam harbored a grudge against the Perrys and me because of that. He told me that I owed him for what happened and this was my chance to repay him by making sure the baby was raised by a wealthy family in a closed private adoption."

As much as Ryder had hated the way the man had gone about things, he couldn't let Havery walk out the door with that infant. The man couldn't be trusted. Ryder hadn't cared about anything else but making sure the baby had a good home.

That she felt loved. Damn it, that still was the only thing that mattered to him in all of this.

He took a deep breath and finished the story. "Sam swore that his daughter—Tatiana Havery—didn't want to know where you went."

"Tatiana Havery?" Maya's face crumpled as the name sank in, as she realized that her birth mother was someone who moved in their world and their lives.

Her shoulders shook harder, sobs racking her. Ryder opened his arms and—thank God—she flew into his hug without hesitation to cry it out. A lump lodged in his throat, too, and neither of them said a word until her tears slowed.

Then she eased back, swiping her wrists under her eyes. "Thank you for telling me, Dad. I'm going to need some time to digest all of this."

Feeling helpless to right this for his child, Ryder watched her rush away, her red hair rippling behind her, hair she'd inherited from her mother. Sighing hard, Ryder sagged back in the chair. He hoped he hadn't lost Maya forever for not telling her the truth sooner.

This whole situation had spun out of control so damn quickly. He rubbed a hand over his suit jacket lapel, still damp from his daughter's tears.

He didn't like or trust Tatiana one bit. But she was also Angela's best friend. And he'd been keeping Maya's parentage a secret from her, too, even when they were engaged, since Tatiana herself was unaware that Maya was hers. If Ryder wanted to have a real chance at a future with Angela, he couldn't hold back about that any longer. He just prayed it wouldn't be the end of them.

Time was definitely running out for him to tell Angela that eighteen years ago he'd adopted Tatiana's child. And he had to pray Angela and his daughter would understand.

Because he loved them both too much to lose either of them.

Nine

Drawing Esme toward his bedroom after their dinner at the club, Jesse didn't want anything to ruin their last night together in Royal. She was excited about returning to Houston, though he wasn't sure he shared that excitement.

Hell, who was he kidding? He wasn't happy about her departure at all, even though he would make the trip with her to review the new clubhouse. Having her here on the ranch had felt too damn right, increasingly so every day they spent together. In spite of what she seemed to think, she fit here. From the way she helped with the ranch to how she blended in with the community, she belonged.

And when she'd looked at the children in the club's childcare center with such tenderness and even a hint of longing, his last reservation had slid away. He wanted her to make that audition for the role of wife to be a permanent one. Which meant he would have to persuade her to come back to Royal. If not permanently, at least for a while.

One step at a time.

Closing the door to his suite behind them, he flipped on the sconces near the headboard, dimming them low as he turned to soak in the sight of Esme shouldering off the sleeve of her green velvet dress. She looked so beautiful tonight and for a moment, he let himself be mesmerized by the sight of her undressing, until she stood barefoot in a black lace bra-and-panties set. It had been all he could do to keep his hands off her during dinner.

With careful precision, she laid the green velvet dress over the back of the chaise longue as he shrugged off his jacket. Before he laid it aside, however, he pulled an envelope from the pocket and stepped closer to her. "I have something for you."

"A gift? Thank you." She looked up in surprise as she took off her chandelier earrings, the jewels throwing multicolored prisms onto her creamy skin. "But it isn't Christmas yet. I don't open my presents until the actual day."

Doing nothing more than standing with her jewelry cupped in her delicate, manicured hands, she made his heart beat faster. A blonde goddess set against the warm brown tones of his bed. Where he longed to be with her.

"It's a 'just because' gift, something you'll need before the twenty-fifth." He pulled out two tickets and fanned them between his fingers.

She set aside her earrings on the mahogany chest of drawers. "Tickets?"

Her voice was neutral. Not a good sign, but he pressed ahead all the same.

"To *A Christmas Carol*. Royal may not be Houston, but we have a good community theater. I thought we could go this weekend after we return from Houston."

And he waited.

"I'm surprised." She smiled, stepping into his arms and wrapping her own around his neck. "This is very thoughtful. Thank you."

She kissed him, long and deep, with a familiarity woven from their past two weeks as lovers. The caress of her fingers along the back of his neck was cool, the press of her breasts a sweet temptation against his chest.

Much longer and he would have her against the wall before he'd locked in her return to Royal.

He angled back, stroking her blond hair over her shoulders with a caress down her spine. "Would you rather do something in Houston? I have no problem going back to the drawing board. We could make the plans together."

"You're asking me to come back here for Christmas?" Blue eyes searched his.

He couldn't quite make out the hesitation or confusion he saw brimming in her face. He prided himself on being an adept observer of body language. Except he couldn't hold on to a thought long enough to press his agenda, not with his mind scrambled by Esme's touch, the press of her breasts against his chest.

"Yes, I'm asking you to come back."

"Let's worry about the future later. You're welcome

to pamper me right now any other ways that come to mind. I'll be much nicer about accepting your present," she said with an unmistakable invitation in her siren's voice as she tugged him toward the bed, walking backward.

And he didn't need any encouragement to follow, his gaze drawn like a magnet to the sway of her hips. The narrow indent of her waist. The long, smooth line of her thighs. By the time he tumbled with her onto the mattress, he couldn't think about anything but pleasuring her. Making her remember how this connection they shared could burn away everything else.

Tunneling his fingers into her hair, he angled her head to kiss her long and slow, deeply and thoroughly. He took his time lowering the strap of her bra, cupping each breast in turn, savoring the shivers that went through her. He liked the feel of her hands on him as she peeled off his shirt, stripped off his belt.

By the time he moved lower to kiss his way down her shoulder, they were both breathing hard, the whisper of exhales mingling with the slide of fabric across the duvet as they swept away the rest of their clothes. Fevered touches gave way to more demanding kisses. His. Hers.

He felt the taut need in her movements as her hips nudged his thighs. Obliging her unspoken demand, he curved a palm over her hip and traced his way to the juncture of her thighs, and he teased her there.

Fingernails bit into his shoulders, a welcome counterpoint to his own need firing through him. He sensed how close she was to finding her release, so he stayed right with her, whispering into her ear how much he wanted her.

When the soft shudders racked her body, the sense of triumph was almost as fierce as his own desire. He didn't let go for long moments, helping her find every last sweet sensation from her orgasm.

As she stilled, he angled back to glimpse her, to memorize this moment. Her flushed cheeks. Her lips swollen from his kisses. A protective surge fired through him.

He never tired of seeing her in his bed.

Her bed, too, now.

For how long?

He brushed aside the thought that threatened to steal this perfect moment from them both. He refused to accept it could be the last time he had her in his home. Having her stay in Houston was unacceptable.

All the same, there was a frenzy between them tonight. She reached into the bedside table and passed him a condom, urging him to hurry, her voice breathless and encouraging as she sheathed him. Her touch was slow and deliberate. Knowing and tempting.

"Jesse…"

She didn't need to ask him twice.

He rolled her under him in a smooth sweep, sliding inside with a sense of home. Her legs glided up and around his hips, holding him, syncing them both into a perfect rhythm. Flesh against flesh. Heartbeats racing against each other.

They'd made love in every room of his house in every position and still each time with her was as exciting as the first. And while he wasn't a romantic, there was something special between them. Something unique. He would be a fool to let it go. To let her go.

Purring her pleasure, she urged him to his back and straddled him. She rode him, fanning the blaze inside him that begged for release.

His hands dug into her hips, guiding her faster as he thrust upward. Even as his eyes grew heavy with the need to seal in this moment, he couldn't tear his gaze away from the sight of her over him. Her blond hair over her shoulders and along her breasts. Her chest rising and falling faster. Her pale flesh flushing. Her release was close. He knew her body that well now. And seeing her orgasm was the sexiest thing he'd ever experienced.

So much so, it sent him crashing into his own climax, sensation surging through him as he plunged into her. It was more than sex. It was— He stopped the thought short, too dazed to let his mind travel that path. She'd already rocked his world beyond measure in a few short weeks.

His life had been forever changed by the rainstorm that had landed her on his doorstep. And now everything was riding on their trip to Houston and being able to persuade her to leave it all behind.

Because he couldn't imagine his life without her.

Tatiana was seething over the board meeting about to take place, bigwigs from Royal in Houston to represent the charter chapter of the Texas Cattleman's Club.

And she wasn't welcome.

She tried her damnedest to scrub out any trace of the woman she was before she rose to power in Perry Holdings. She'd shed family mementos. Opted for all new things. Posh designer fixtures. Symbolic, partly, of creating the life she wanted. It still counted for nothing. Got her nowhere. As if not being born into the world of the Perrys meant she could never fully enter the rarefied realm of Houston's wealthiest society.

Angela called herself a friend, but hadn't gotten Tatiana a ticket to the inner circle. No matter how much money she made, how high she rose in the Perry firm, she was still an outsider. She'd never felt that more than today. Her fist clenched around a crystal paperweight. Waterford. For once, though, her designer-decorated town house brought her no comfort. She struggled against the urge to hurl the paperweight through the window.

Instead, she strode over to her white Christmas tree decorated with monochrome lights, with silver tinsel and pale blue ornaments. Normally, the twinkling delighted her. An anchor in an ocean of chaos. Today, even as she straightened the ornaments, Christmas magic held nothing for her.

Her doorbell rang, the high-pitched bell chimes cutting her thoughts short and launching a wave of panic through her. Could it be the police? She had spent the past nine months looking over her shoulder. She wasn't sure how much more of this she could take.

With a deep breath, she steadied her nerves and scraped her red hair back into a sleek ponytail. Not a strand of hair out of place.

She looked through the peephole.

It wasn't the police. Far from it. A stranger, a teenager, stood in the corridor. Her long red hair and mustard-yellow coat were definitely not cop material, even if she'd been older.

Curious, Tatiana opened the door. "Yes, what can I do for you…"

She let her question drift off, a hint for the teen to introduce herself.

"Maya," she said, jamming her fists into her yellow coat. "My name is Maya Currin."

Currin? Maya Currin, as in Ryder's daughter? Tatiana had heard Angela talk about her future stepdaughter. But other than that, Tatiana had had no contact with the Currin family all these years.

But something brought the girl here today and Maya could use a distraction. "Come in, dear. What can I do for you?"

Maya stepped over the threshold warily, her hyperfocus on Tatiana unnerving. Just as she considered asking the girl to leave, Maya turned her attention to the condo, walking to the massive wall of glass, flattening her palm against it.

"I'm Ryder Currin's youngest. I've been away at college for my freshman year, but I'm home for Christmas."

The girl looked around the apartment, staring unabashedly, her gaze lingering on the white plush sofa.

What the hell was going on? Was the girl unhinged? "Are you looking for someone?"

A shaky sigh rocked through her before she continued. "I've always known I was adopted. My father always swore he would tell me about my biological family once I turned eighteen, but he's been putting it off. Until yesterday, when I insisted." She turned back to

Tatiana. "I stayed awake all night working up the nerve to confront you."

Tatiana's scalp tingled with premonition. This conversation couldn't be headed where she thought... Still, she started shaking, staring at this beautiful girl with red hair and brown eyes.

Practically a mini version of her.

Tears misted her eyes as the undeniable truth hit home. "Are you my daughter?"

She didn't even need Maya to respond. She knew. Could sense it between them. Her heart fractured all over again at the time they'd spent apart. And how close her child had been all this time.

Kept from her by Ryder Currin.

Maya nodded slowly. "Yes. My father can confirm it."

Fat tears rolled down Maya's face and she flew into Tatiana's arms with zero hesitation. The one thing that was hers, that no one could take from her. Tatiana held her tight with a possessive urgency. Her child. Grown, safe and beautiful. She'd led the pampered childhood Tatiana hadn't had. If only Maya's childhood hadn't been with that horrid Ryder Currin.

Regret threatened to level her. The choices she'd made had been impossible. Unfair. The reality of how much she'd lost stood in front of her now, a haunting reminder of how truly she'd been robbed.

"I wanted to keep you. I loved you so much." Tatiana held her hands tightly, hardly able to believe she was truly touching her baby girl. "But I had no money. I was alone. My father was on his last legs healthwise." A nice way to gloss over her father's alcoholism. "I begged him to let me give you to a good family to raise."

And her father had promised her he would. Then he'd turned around and given her baby to Ryder Currin. The betrayal cut deeper than any other.

Fury rose in her, only tempered by the joy of meeting Maya.

"Thank you for letting me in and telling me," Maya said. "There are so many questions I want to ask, but I have to get back to my dad. I—I—" The teen stuttered with nerves. "I hope we can get to know each other."

Tatiana's broken heart warmed, and she was filled with pride over this beautiful child she had created. "I would love that."

She hugged her daughter again, transported back to the day she'd held the infant bundle in her arms, her heart broken, her life wrecked. The memories lingered long after she'd escorted Maya to the door, leaning against the frame to watch her child walk to the elevator, step inside and disappear from view.

Overwhelmed by emotion, Tatiana backed into her condo and leaned against the closed door, unable to think straight. The man she despised was raising the daughter she'd always loved. It wasn't fair. Her whole damn life wasn't fair right now.

For the first time since she'd decorated her apartment, she felt weighed down in this space, in spite of the pristine white decor she'd chosen for a sense of freedom, of a fresh start unsullied by the past. Normally, it soothed her, giving her a sense of control.

Instead, right now the piercing all-white motif made her feel as though she'd been trapped in a hospital, about to undergo surgery. Except the surgery was a painful montage of every moment in her life that went so damn wrong.

She couldn't escape the cornered feeling that her brother might give her up to avoid jail time. The more she thought about it, the more freaked out she became until she surrendered to the fear. Racing around the condo, she threw a haphazard collection into her suitcase, then frantically searched for her passport. She had to leave the country. Now.

But…

How could she? Her daughter, her baby girl, was here in Houston. And after all this time, she had the chance to get to know her. Her mind whirled all over the place with questions. Had Angela known about this? All this time? That her boyfriend had been raising Tatiana's daughter?

The fury raged. Angela had to have known. The bitch.

Someone had to pay for all Tatiana had been through. Angela had a golden life, full of advantages from being Sterling Perry's child, and now from being with Ryder Currin. Both men disgusted Tatiana. They'd stolen that parcel of land from her father. If he hadn't been cheated, then her family wouldn't have fallen apart. She wanted Sterling and Ryder to hurt as much as she did right now, as much as she'd always hurt when she'd thought of her daughter.

Her fury focused on the perfect way to make both men suffer. By taking from them someone precious. Angela. If Angela were to die…

Tatiana's hand tightened around the paperweight

again, the crystal cool in her grip, like a rock in her hand with enough heft to bash in a head. She forced her hold to relax. Whatever happened next was totally in her control.

She'd killed once. She could do so again.

Esme could hardly believe she was back in Houston. Home. And that Jesse was with her.

It seemed like a lifetime ago that she'd left for Royal. So much had changed since then, hell-bent on making a difference for her dad. She still wanted that for him. In fact, she looked forward to seeing the two most special men in her life—Jesse and her dad—making a difference in the club.

Her family, Jesse, even her brother and sisters.

The gathering would be like a family reunion.

Her suede pumps click-clacked musically against the tile floor in the Houston club building. A tour of the facility had gone well, and now they were meeting in a conference room. Every reverberation made her feel more at home, more comfortable with her newfound happiness. As she turned the corner, she saw a familiar silhouette.

Angela dressed with her pitch-perfect fashion sense in a black-and-white A-line dress with a small clutch. Her sister noticed her nearly at the same moment. A wide grin pulled the corners of her mouth skyward.

With determined steps, Esme closed the distance between her and Angela, wrapping her older sister in a tight hug. She'd missed her and wanted to share the latest news about the burgeoning relationship with Jesse. She just knew Jesse and Ryder would enjoy each other's company, too, both such down-to-earth men with a love of the land. So much joy and hope for the future coursed through her heart. But as she eased back and looked more fully at her sister, she could sense something was off with Angela.

"What's going on?" Esme prodded gently. Possibilities cartwheeled through her mind.

At the simple question, Angela's face paled. Deeper concern rose in Esme's chest, and she maneuvered them to one of the decorative palms out of earshot of the people milling in the halls as guests from Royal began arriving at the Houston chapter clubhouse for the tour of the new facility.

A somewhat nervous laugh trembled from Angela's lips. That's when Esme knew something serious had happened. Top of the list of her guesses? "Are you and Ryder okay?"

If that man had hurt her sister again, Esme would never forgive him.

"Well…that's a million-dollar question. I'm still reeling. Prepare yourself. Turns out Maya, Ryder's adopted daughter, is actually Tatiana's daughter. Tatiana. My best friend. And Tatiana never told me." Angela's voice shook. "She never even hinted she gave up a baby. And Ryder… I just… I just can't believe he didn't tell me before now. I'm trying not to feel betrayed. But it's just… a lot of information to digest."

Esme blinked. Then she immediately scanned the room for Ryder Currin, who was deep in conversation with a group of people down the hall. That bastard had actually once been engaged to Angela and hadn't opened up about his life—about something that would have a deep impact on his fiancée. Sure, his children were all adults now, but they would have been Angela's stepchildren, an important connection. He'd expected Angela to give her all to a relationship, yet he'd held back about this tie to her best friend.

And where did that leave them now?

Her sister's breakup with Ryder had been rough. That was no secret. They'd fought for their relationship, though, made it back to a promising forever. But she imagined information like this didn't do a lot in the way of bolstering trust in a relationship that still needed healing.

Esme schooled her features into PR neutrality. The last thing Angela needed was Esme's anger piled on top of all the turmoil she must be feeling. Esme just wanted to be here for her sister. "Are you having second thoughts about being with Ryder?"

Angela wrung her hands until her knuckles turned pale, nerves clearly rising hard and fast. "I know that I love him."

Esme pulled her gaze from her distraught sister to Ryder Currin again. Did the man love Angela as much? Was he the man Angela deserved? He inclined his head to the rancher he chatted with, his black Stetson obscuring his face.

Esme wished she had the answers and assurance. Love was a risky prospect. Even thinking about a future with Jesse was scary—and exciting. There was so much potential for heartbreak and failure. And opportunity for happiness.

She turned back to her sister. "What can I do for you?"

Her sister let out a breath. "Just be here for me. Be

my sister." She pressed a trembling hand to her chest, the absence of her engagement ring so very sad. The tan line even remained. Faint, but there, if one looked close enough. "I can't say this hasn't thrown me. I feel like I barely know him."

Throat bobbing, Angela's voice trailed off.

Esme struggled for the right words. Just being there somehow didn't seem like enough. "I realize this is un- believably hard. I'm here whenever you need to talk."

Never had she been more grateful for her siblings to support one another, to continue the family bond. They needed one another.

Jesse was right that family was everything. And if he moved here, he could share in all of hers.

Esme squeezed Angela's hand in more unspoken support.

"I'll be okay. I'm glad you're home." Angela squeezed back in understanding, the sibling connec- tion never more tangible. Esme felt like finally she and her sister had related without any barrier, no more being an outsider to Angela and Melinda's twin bond.

She wasn't going to let that go and hoped the same progress could be made with Melinda.

Esme made a mental note to talk to her sister more about this later, and they made their way into the confer- ence room. Esme was drawn into a conversation about the press releases she needed to send out while some- one tapped Angela with a question about the order of events. Giving her sister one last glance before they parted ways, Esme had to admire Angela's strength through so much adversity.

Then, turning her attention from the influx of people

on-site for the meeting, Esme took a moment to admire the renovations. There was still some work to complete before the holiday party a couple of days before Christmas, much less in time for the official opening at the huge New Year's Eve blowout gala.

But it was still already an impressive conference room, from the lengthy wooden table to the massive chairs all around. Crystal pitchers of water were placed strategically, but she was too nervous.

She was actually listening to her first Texas Cattleman's Club business meeting, with all the influential players on hand, including the current Royal chapter president and board members. Familiar faces, new friends even, after her time at Jesse's. Cord and Sheriff Battle sat on either side of her father. Ryder Currin scowled from the other side of the table where he sat with Angela. It saddened Esme that her sister seemed a gulf away, but they would mend that with time. Angela had to understand Esme's reasons for rooting for their father.

Then the gavel sounded, startling Esme and pulling her upright just as the meeting was called to order.

Ten

Echoes of Houston traffic pierced the walls of the historic site of the new Texas Cattleman's Club. One of the many reasons Jesse avoided Houston. Too much traffic. Too many people. Too many buildings.

Not enough sounds of crickets and birdsong. Not enough roaming horses and cattle. Not enough intentional living. He wouldn't even know it was Christmastime here, the only nod to the season the massive tree in the lobby.

He couldn't wait to get Esme back to Royal where they could celebrate the holiday together, under the spruce he'd cut down himself. The one they'd decorated together in front of the fireplace, sharing memories from their childhoods as they did so.

The sooner he finished this meeting, the sooner he could hit the road with her. Jesse hung back in the meeting room, the rest of the board from the Royal chapter seated around the conference table listening to pitches for leadership positions. Leaning against the wall, he studied the players. There were more contenders than just Sterling Perry and Ryder Currin to consider for the role. Venture capitalist Camden McNeal. Or Lucas Ford, an investigator and security mogul. Plus there was a wild card in the mix with Cord Galicia moving from Royal to Houston. He could well be a strong candidate to see the club through the start-up, since he had firsthand experience with the inner workings of the Royal chapter.

Jesse couldn't quite comprehend how his neighbor was going to make big-city life work. Even living on the outskirts of Houston. The hum, bustle and lights of the urban area radiated outward in palpable bands.

Jesse was already feeling claustrophobic, ready to get back home. To take Esme to that Christmas play and continue his campaign to persuade her to move.

Settling his weight onto the heels of his best pair of boots—a thoughtful gift from his sister three Christmases ago—Jesse scanned the crowd. He attempted to read the reactions of his fellow members. It seemed he was not the only one keeping a tight rein on his emotions during the candidates' speeches. Members listened attentively, doing their part to hear the unique plans each potential president would do his best to execute.

As Ryder Currin finished his pitch to run the new club and returned to his seat beside Angela, Esme took the floor. Apparently, Sterling intended to let his daughter put her PR skills to work and do the talking for him.

Jesse worked to keep his face neutral, which was tough to do with Esme using all of her job savvy to lobby for her father. She was poised. Articulate. Convincing.

Damn. This woman enchanted him. Seeing her here today was more proof of her sexy-smart charm. He couldn't even detect a trace of nerves as she adjusted the microphone at the lectern to make herself better heard. Of all the places he'd seen her, she looked like she was born to be in the spotlight.

Crossing his arms over his chest as he leaned against the back wall, he focused on Esme in action. She looked stunning in her sleek black power suit. Her sky-high heels reminded him of meeting her for the first time, her broken shoes sinking into the mud, her beautiful blond hair soaked. She'd been a drowned rat, but somehow managed to keep her composure.

That charisma was in full wattage today, and not just her poise, but her keen mind. Her father watched her with unmistakable pride. Jesse took the measure of the man from a different perspective now, as Esme's dad, rather than just an infamous figure in the news.

Sterling had aged well, his brown hair graying at the temples. His blue eyes were the same shade as Esme's, and he also seemed to share her appreciation of style. His suit had a custom cut, his cowboy boots expensive without even a scuff. He may have worked as foreman of the ranch to prove himself to his father-in-law decades ago, but Jesse doubted Sterling was much of a hands-on ranch owner these days.

He looked 100 percent a powerhouse Texas businessman. And that's how Esme was pitching her dad to the Royal chapter board. As a successful, ambitious entrepreneur who'd expanded beyond just the ranch. Always striving for perfection, her father didn't know the meaning of the word "enough." Perry Holdings included real estate as well as banking, property management and construction.

In fact, Perry Holdings was responsible for the stunning renovations of this very building, with the help of Ethan Barringer, CEO of Perry Construction. Originally from Royal, Ethan made for a nice connection between the two worlds in tackling this project.

Esme painted her father as a visionary who knew how to put together a winning team, this historic building a symbol of his plan to grow the Houston branch of the Texas Cattleman's Club into the future.

In total Perry Holdings PR mode, Esme had them eating out of the palm of her hand.

Jesse realized *this* was the essence of who Esme really was. A city woman. A businesswoman. And no matter how sweet it had been to have her in his bed, in his house—in his life—he couldn't escape the deep-seated sense that eventually she would be miserable out on his ranch, far from the work she obviously did so well.

She completed her presentation and returned to sit beside her father. His smile of appreciation and pride brought a light to Esme's eyes. Even her sister nodded approval during the applause from across the room.

Esme blinked fast, a sheen of tears in her eyes. She was clearly choked up. Emotional.

She'd warned him about that, about her romantic side. She had a heart that was easily touched, and he'd grown to appreciate that about her. But how could he justify taking Esme from these people she loved? He recognized how selfish it would be. From a job she was born to perform. His freshly formed dreams of building a life with her at his side faded. He cared for her too much. His heart ached already at the thought of saying goodbye. But he wanted her to have the life that would make her happy.

Unable to take another moment of this meeting, Jesse ducked out into the hall, his focus homed in on the exit, on getting away from there as quickly as possible. Just as he reached the door, he heard the sound of fast-clicking high heels on the floor, growing closer.

"Jesse," Esme called. "Jesse, where are you going?"

He turned in the lobby—empty save for a towering Christmas tree—and the sight of her glowing smile poleaxed him. He swallowed down a lump in his throat, unable to push past the emotion.

She reached him and rested her palm on his chest. "What did you think of my presentation? I really think it went well, but I don't want to be overly optimistic. Still, I think a celebration is in order. Dinner out at my favorite Houston hot spot. My treat."

She looked so happy. So hopeful. The knowledge ate away at him.

"Esme." He clasped her hand and removed it from his chest. "I have something to tell you."

Her smile faded as she glanced down at the way their hands were suspended in air. "You look serious. Is something wrong?"

Everything. He'd made a huge mistake thinking he could change her, that he could transplant her to his world and mold her into the kind of woman he'd always imagined at his side. To do that would be a disservice to the bright, beautiful, smart woman she was.

So even though it hurt like hell, he forced himself to say the words that would send her out of his life for good. The quicker the better. Rip that bandage right off. He did his best to take a page out of her book. Keep his tone neutral. Final. Definitive. Sure. "I've made my decision about a wife candidate. And I'm sorry, but it's not you."

Her gasp of surprise cut through the silence between them. Shock froze her features, followed by a wash of pain in her eyes at his rejection of all they'd shared over the past couple of weeks. That glimpse into her heart damn near broke his, but he told himself she would be happier this way.

Living her own dreams instead of his.

Then her shoulders went back, her chin tipped with pride. A feral smile brushed over her lips though pain shone in her pretty blue eyes. "Congratulations," she said bitterly. "I'm glad you got exactly what you wanted."

She adjusted her jacket, sweeping her blond locks over her shoulders. Without another word, she brushed past him, striding past the towering Christmas tree and out the door.

And out of his life.

Weary, physically and emotionally, Angela punched in the code to her condominium. Latches releasing, she pushed inside, ready to put the events of the last twenty-four hours behind her. Far, far behind her. She needed space and a moment to breathe and process. Once inside, she dropped her purse on the floor and reached to turn on the lights.

She startled in surprise, the shock followed by a twinge of fear. Someone was huddled on her sofa. Fear slammed into her chest and constricted her breathing. She'd seen enough crime shows to know victims usually had a small, narrow window of escape. She reached for the doorknob behind her, quietly...

Then recognized the female curled up on her couch among the holiday throw pillows and sighed in relief. Her jagged heartbeat returning to normal, she laid a hand on her chest, her linen dress rough against her fingertips. "Esme, you scared me for a moment."

Her youngest sister looked up, her eyes red from crying as she hugged a red velvet throw pillow with a silver embroidered reindeer. "I hope you don't mind that I used your spare key. I couldn't bear to be alone."

Fresh sobs rolled out of Esme. Her normally perfect makeup was smeared across her face. She looked so different from the woman who had just delivered a fiery and impassioned speech on behalf of her father. Something was seriously wrong for Esme to display such unfettered emotion.

Worry filling her, Angela crossed into the living room and nudged aside the ceramic snowman to reach the box of tissues on the coffee table. "What's wrong?"

Esme drew in a ragged breath, gripping the velvet pillow tassels. "It's over between Jesse and me."

Angela's eyebrows raised in surprise. But then she pushed aside her thousand questions to be there for her sister. Reaching a protective arm around her sister, she gripped Esme in a side hug. "Oh, sis, I'm so sorry."

"We haven't even known each other long." Her face was lined with pain. "It shouldn't hurt this much."

"Our hearts aren't tied to time." She understood too well about love and heartbreak because of her rocky relationship with Ryder. Angela stroked her sister's shoulder, attempting to soothe her as much as she could.

Wishing she could take her pain away.

Losing their mother early on had forced them to be close. And Angela was grateful for that closeness. But at times like this, her heart ached for their mother. What would Tamara have said to soothe Esme? To soothe Angela, even? She tipped her head closer to Esme's, doing her best to comfort.

Clutching a tissue, Esme blew her nose. Tears still leaked down her face. In a cracked tone, she continued.

"Thank you for understanding, for not writing me off as histrionic."

"Of course not. I'm glad you reached out to me. You shouldn't be alone." She plucked another tissue from the box and passed it over.

Her cell phone rang from her purse back at the door. She glanced at it, but looked away fast, not wanting her sister to feel like she had anything other than Angela's full attention. It was rare that Esme showed vulnerability to her. She had always seemed a bit jealous of Angela and Melinda's bond.

Esme dabbed at her eyes. "Please take the call. It'll give me a chance to pull myself together."

"If you're sure…" Angela hesitated.

"Absolutely." She nodded, standing and grabbing her purse.

"Okay, then, but I'll make it quick. Don't go anywhere." She retrieved her own purse and fished out her phone. Her eyes scanned the screen. Tatiana? Angela still hadn't quite wrapped her brain around the fact that her friend had given up a baby for adoption and never told her about it. She would have wanted to help, even if just to listen. Maybe that's what this call was about.

She answered. "Hello, Tatiana, what can I do for you?"

"Angela, I need you." Tatiana sobbed hard on the other end of the phone.

She bit the bullet and plunged right in, her gut telling her the timing of Tatiana being this upset couldn't be a coincidence after Ryder's conversation with his youngest child. "Is this about Maya Currin…about your daughter?"

"Yes," Tatiana whispered. "That's exactly what this is about. And I really need to talk to you. Everything is so out of control. My half brother's in prison and he's clearly mentally unstable. He's been threatening to say all sorts of awful things about me."

"I'm so sorry you're going through that. Let's meet for breakfast in the morning."

Tatiana hiccuped on another sob. "I need to talk to you now. In person."

Angela glanced to her still-hurting sister standing at the kitchen counter wiping her tears around her eyeliner. Shaking her head, she answered her friend. "I'm afraid I—"

Esme turned, her brave face on. "It's okay. Go. I know she's your friend and it's okay."

"But you're my sister." She wanted to be with Esme.

To find out why things had ended so quickly between her and a man she'd been so excited about.

"Thank you," Esme said with a watery smile. "How about we go over together?"

Angela nodded, relieved not to be torn between her sister and her friend. Of course she would choose Esme, but with Willem in jail, Tatiana didn't have any family left.

Other than Maya.

Her heart pinched at the thought. "Tatiana, Esme and I can come over right now. Just let us know where you are."

Angela reached for a notepad and jotted down the location and time. The new club. In a half hour. So simple, she wondered why she'd bothered to write it. She was such a jumble of emotions today.

But it helped take her mind off her own relationship to be there for others.

Angela ended the call and turned to her sister. "We can talk in my car on the way over." Then she grabbed her purse and went to the door.

Esme followed close on her heels. "Getting to be with you helps. Even if we don't talk. I just don't want to be alone right now."

Taking Esme at her word, when Angela got to her car, she turned on soft Christmas carols. Esme sat silently beside her, her head resting against the window, her sniffles further and further apart.

Angela's cell phone rang a couple of times with calls from Ryder, but she wasn't ready to talk to him, not yet. The third time he called, she sent him straight to voice mail and turned off her cell. She couldn't handle another emotional conversation sidetracking her tonight. It felt like the whole world was falling apart.

A half hour later, Angela pulled up outside the back entrance of the club, the historic building rather foreboding at night. While Christmas lights lined the street and lit up the other buildings, the club was pitch-black inside, the only illumination a Christmas tree in the lobby. She was glad she'd brought someone along with her. Tatiana's car was parked in back, too, so she had to be inside the building already. Why would she be sitting in the dark?

Arriving at the back door, Angela tapped in the security code, something Tatiana would know, too, since she was with Perry Holdings.

"Tatiana," Angela called as she walked inside, her sister following a step behind.

A faint light shone from the back parlor, the dim glow giving the place a creepy vibe that reminded her that the body of the murdered Perry Holdings assistant had been found in this building. Of course she had to think of that now, when she was already uneasy.

"Tatiana?" she called again, reaching for a switch to flip on the lights.

Tatiana stepped into view, her red hair in wild disarray. A step closer and she was bathed in light.

And her arms were extended, a gun held with steady hands.

Esme gasped behind her. Shocked and confused, Angela couldn't figure out what her friend was doing.

Tatiana waved the gun, gesturing toward the parlor. "Both of you. In there."

What the hell was going on? Was Tatiana unhinged?

Angela cast a quick glance at her stunned sister. She wasn't sure how they were going to get out of this, but she had to believe they would figure something out.

Angela kept her voice low even though her heart pounded so very hard with fear. She needed to stay calm. Stay in control of her emotions and de-escalate the situation. Giving herself completely over to fear would only immobilize her. Which might interfere with any way to keep her and Esme safe.

Her hands clenching so hard her nails cut into her palms, Angela struggled for the right words for a situation she never could have imagined happening. "Tatiana, my friend, whatever you're feeling, I understand—"

"Shut up," Tatiana shouted.

Angela snapped her jaw shut. She tried to get a read on the events quickly spiraling out of control. The woman who stood before them might as well have been a stranger. Her expression, her tone, her actions… Angela didn't recognize any of them.

"You're not my friend, Angela, and you can't have any clue what I'm feeling, or what I've been through. Showing up here with your sister when I said I needed you? You've just proven what I already knew. Perrys always look out for Perrys and to hell with the rest of us."

Fear for her sister constricted her throat.

If only she hadn't brought Esme along, she wouldn't be in danger. "Esme has nothing to do with whatever grudge you have against me. It's not fair to keep her—"

Tatiana closed herself inside the empty parlor with them, the gleam in her eyes vicious. "Nothing in my life has been fair. My father lost everything because the land he was promised by your grandfather went to that idiot Ryder Currin instead. And your sister Melinda gets to have a baby when I had to give up mine."

Tatiana Havery was a madwoman, and Angela had never seen it. Never known. She felt stupid and foolish, all the more so because she couldn't focus on getting out of this situation. Panic clogged her airways, making it hard to breathe.

Esme took a step forward with the signature calm that stood her in good stead at work. "What can we do to make this right for you now?"

She was buying them time. Angela looked around the room, taking in the high windows and lack of furnishings. Tried to formulate a plan that didn't end in death and gunshots. And so far, she came up empty.

She wanted Ryder. Why hadn't she taken his call in the car? If something happened to her and she never got to speak to him again… The hurt of that made her legs wobble beneath her.

Tatiana's gaze swung wildly to her. "It's too late. I thought I was going to get my revenge by bringing down the Perrys and Currins for taking what was rightfully my father's. Yes, I was responsible for spreading all those rumors with the help of my brother. And it was working, too." She pointed the gun back and forth between them. "But then that stupid Vincent Hamm overheard one of our conversations. So I had to kill him."

Angela swallowed down a knot of horror as she looked around and realized that Tatiana had brought them to this building, where Hamm's body had been dumped, with a grisly purpose. And there was nothing in this empty room to defend herself with. She gripped her purse harder, trying to remember what was inside, what might be used as a weapon, all the while trying to keep track of what Tatiana was saying.

"I tried to pin the murder on your father but of course Mr. 'Teflon' Perry got away with it. The Perrys and Currins get everything and my family got nothing. That land would have given my dad a fresh start."

But Tatiana's father had lost everything because of his addiction. He'd gone broke just as Tatiana finished boarding school. She must have had her baby not too long after that.

"Tatiana," Esme said softly, "I remember your dad. We were all so sad when he died in that accident. It had to have been hard for you."

"Accident?" Tatiana shrieked. "It wasn't an accident. He killed himself. Because of your family…and that vile Ryder Currin, who got the land my father should have had. And now Ryder has my daughter, too?"

Esme backed up a step, no longer the conciliatory, smooth businesswoman.

Angela agreed. Talking wasn't going to work. Tatiana was crazed, her speech dripping with bitterness and hatred. She had already made up her mind to murder them.

Angela's purse slid from her shoulder, hitting the floor with a thud. Her cell phone skittered out, a reminder of all those missed calls from Ryder. She would give anything to hear his voice one more time. But she was never going to see Ryder again, never have the chance to hold him, tell him how much she loved him.

She reached for Esme's hand, needing to feel her

sister's presence. Wanting to offer whatever love and comfort she could.

Tatiana's face spread in an evil smile. "It's time Sterling Perry and Ryder Currin learn what it feels like to have their hearts torn out by losing what's dearest to them."

Eleven

Ryder tossed his uneaten supper in the sink.

The dish clanked, the sound jarring in his too-still, too-quiet home on Currin Ranch.

Damn it, he was tired of being ignored. He'd phoned Angela repeatedly since the meeting ended and she wasn't answering. She hadn't called back, much less sent a text in response to his voice mails.

Angela was going to have to talk to him eventually, so it might as well be now. The longer silence stretched between them, the tougher it would be to bridge that gap.

Sure, she'd sat at his side during the meeting, but other than that, she hadn't spoken to him since he'd told her about Tatiana being Maya's biological mother. Angela hadn't even allowed him to apologize for keeping the secret from her. She'd just walked away, refusing to talk to him.

He could see how it would seem that he didn't trust her not to tell Tatiana—her best friend—where her baby had gone. He couldn't help but wonder if he'd kept the information from her because on some level, he had still been holding back from committing.

Whatever the reason, he owed her an apology. They had been engaged. He should have honored that commitment he'd made to Angela. It hadn't been fair to expect her to build a relationship with Maya without all the facts.

He stalked to the foyer to snag his jacket and pluck his keys out of the carved wood bowl in the entryway. He pulled open the door and stopped short. Maya stood on the other side, her keys in hand.

Given how upset she'd been, he hadn't expected to see her so soon. Except she didn't look at all distressed. In fact, she had a hopeful gleam in her tired eyes. All that emotion in a short time must have been draining.

She pushed past him into the house, turning back to him, tentative but with a growing excitement building. "Guess what?"

Shrugging, he tried to imagine. A boy, maybe? Final grades were posted and she made the president's list? Anything was possible. "I haven't a clue."

"I went to see my birth mother," she blurted. "I told her I'm her daughter."

He went cold inside. He'd figured she would want to meet Tatiana, but he hadn't thought it would happen this soon, before she really had the chance to think through all the implications of the meeting. To prepare herself for her birth mother's potential reactions. He wanted Maya to be happy, but he also wanted to protect her from hurt. What if Tatiana didn't want Maya in her life?

Although based on the happiness on his daughter's face, it seemed the meeting had gone well. "What did Tatiana say?"

"She was so shocked." Maya's hands moved a million miles a minute as she spoke. "She definitely had no idea that you were raising her biological daughter."

It had been her own family's stipulation. Ryder had kept it a secret for good reason.

"And?" Questions piled up inside him, blanketed with a deep sense of foreboding. He could never place his concern, but something about Tatiana had always sent his senses skidding.

"She was glad to meet me. She said she'd never stopped loving me. She cried." Maya swiped away a fresh stream of tears rolling down her cheeks. "She seemed happy, but something in her face made me really believe she regretted the decision, too, you know? Like maybe she'd begged her dad not to send me away? She seemed so overwhelmed, I decided to give her some space to digest."

Thinking of Tatiana's pain sent his thoughts spiraling. His daughter continued to share information about the meeting, but Ryder lost track of her words as bits and pieces of what had happened over the past several months swirled through his head. Vincent Hamm's death. His employee Willem Inwood going to prison for his role in a Ponzi scheme, a scheme he'd attempted to blame on Sterling Perry.

Decades of controversy over that one damn piece

of land Harrington York had willed to Ryder, but both Sterling Perry and Sam Havery thought was rightfully theirs. The land had proved to be rich in oil, stoking the bitterness Perry and Havery harbored.

And the oddest piece in this whole puzzle. Inwood was Tatiana's half brother. Ryder had thought it strange Inwood would do something that could jeopardize Tatiana's position at Perry Holdings. But what if they had been colluding to get back at both Ryder and Sterling because of that land?

He could feel the blood drain from his face as he wrapped his brain around the possibility—probability—that Tatiana could have orchestrated those rumors to avenge what happened to her father. For having to give up her baby since she couldn't offer her a future.

An even more horrifying prospect occurred to him. Could she have even killed Vincent?

No. That was a stretch. This was Angela's best friend he was talking about...

Oh God. Angela.

He focused on his daughter again. "Maya, kiddo, I am so glad you're happy." He didn't even want to think of what it would do to his daughter if it turned out her newly found biological mother was a criminal. "I want to hear all about it. But I need to take care of some quick business. Will you wait for me here?"

"Sure, Dad." She backed away, smiling. "It's okay, really. I have tons of things I want to write in my diary so I don't forget anything about this day."

She faded from sight in a flurry of teenage energy and red hair. A surge of protectiveness shot through him. For her. For Angela.

Heaven help anyone who tried to harm his family.

Gathering his keys and wallet, he tried to call Angela again. It went straight to voice mail. He tried Melinda's number, willing her to pick up.

"Hello?" she said, her voice so like Angela's, a shared twin timbre. "What's going on, Ryder?"

His boots ate up the space to the garage. "Is Angela with you? She's not answering her cell and I need to talk to her."

"No, she's not, but I'm at my condo with Slade packing up a few last things before I sell the place." Melinda's condo was in the same building as Angela's. "Do you want me to go check on her?"

"Yes, please."

"I'll call you back from her place if she's not there."

"Thank you." He didn't want to worry Melinda, given her pregnancy, but he also didn't want to waste a minute more.

Waiting for her to phone back felt like an eternity. He threw open the door of his truck and settled behind the wheel, ready to tear out of there if he needed to start a search.

His cell rang from where he'd placed it on the dash. Melinda. He jabbed the screen before the second tone could chime.

"Did you find her?" he asked without preamble.

"She's not here, Ryder." Melinda's answer ramped up his concern. "But I found a note she left behind about some kind of meeting? It says, 'T at the TCC building at 8 p.m.' Does that make any sense to you?"

His grip tightened on the steering wheel. He didn't want to believe the worst. But he knew in his gut, Angela was in grave danger. "Thank you, Melinda. You've been a big help."

Without a second to waste, he peeled out of the garage. Plowing down the drive, he called for backup to meet him at the club.

Houston police detective Zoe Warren.

Royal sheriff Nathan Battle, who, thank God, was still in town.

Ryder knew they wouldn't question him or write off his suspicions the way someone on the other end of a 911 call might. And sure enough, they agreed without hesitation. Zoe had been with Cord and Jesse, who were coming, as well.

The drive felt like an eternity even though he knew he'd made it in half the usual time. Pulling up behind the TCC building, Ryder didn't know whether to be relieved or horrified to find Angela's car parked beside another vehicle. Tatiana Havery's?

Two more cars swept in, doors opening, as his backup arrived. Sheriff Battle raised a finger to his mouth for silence, then motioned for them to follow him.

Ryder's heart raced as they entered the building, fast and silent, everything inside him telling him he needed to get to Angela. Now.

Muffled voices echoed down the corridor, female voices. Coming from the parlor.

Ryder bit back bile while the group crept closer. He kept his footfalls quiet as he picked his way forward, praying there wouldn't be a squeaky floorboard. The voices grew louder, more distinctive.

Tatiana.

Angela.

And Esme?

Nothing about this scene made sense to him. How had it gotten to this point? How had Angela found herself in the crosshairs?

Another rolling wave of protective urges washed over his body. He needed to make sure Angela—and Esme—made it out alive. And in one piece.

Ryder shot a quick look at Jesse Stevens, the Royal rancher who was Cord's close friend. His face was pale, his jaw flexing.

But he looked every bit as hell-bent on getting to the women as Ryder.

The door had a vintage stained glass inset. Shadows moved on the other side, muffled sounds seeping through…

"The Perrys and Currins have to pay for what they did to my father. To me. To my child."

Tatiana.

Every muscle in Ryder tensed for action. He burned to push through that door now and to hell with caution.

Zoe paused, holding up a hand for them to wait. Nathan Battle nodded. This was Zoe's jurisdiction. Her case. Her bust. But Ryder intended to be right on her heels.

Nathan's lips thinned as he checked his weapon. Tension was so thick that it was tangible in the air.

Withdrawing her weapon, Zoe mouthed silently, "One, two…three."

They moved as one, bursting into the room. Ryder's hungry gaze devoured the sight of Angela. Alive.

And held at gunpoint.

"Tatiana," Ryder called, distracting her for a split second, willing to risk taking a shot without hesitation. Angela's life was at stake.

That second's distraction was all it took for Zoe and Nathan to tackle Tatiana while Jesse pushed the two sisters out of the way of any potential gunfire. A single shot went wild and shattered the stained glass.

Then silence.

Sulfur from the gunfire tinged the air.

Adrenaline burned through Ryder as he braced a hand against the wall to keep from sinking to his knees in relief. Angela was safe. Thank God, she was safe. Only a couple of strides away.

"My daughter," Tatiana whimpered as Zoe handcuffed her, reading Tatiana her rights. Glass crunched under their feet on the way out, Tatiana's sobs growing fainter.

But Ryder didn't have the least bit of sympathy for her and didn't intend to waste so much as a single thought for her. His focus was on Angela, barely registering Nathan and Jesse helping Esme to her feet.

Ryder reached for Angela, hauling her close, his heart slamming against his rib cage. "Thank God you're all right. I was so damn scared when I couldn't reach you."

The memory of that interminable drive to the club sucker punched him all over again. He knew with certainty he loved this woman deeply.

"How did you know where to find me? Find us?" Angela looked over at Esme deep in conversation with Nathan Battle. Her sister's arms moved in sweeping gestures, no doubt recounting the story of how they'd wound up at gunpoint. A story he, too, wanted to hear.

An unexpected distance gaped between Esme and Jesse. Maybe they hadn't been as close as everyone thought and it had only been a fling.

Ryder buried his face against the top of Angela's head and breathed in the scent of her shampoo, like an exotic flower. "You left your note with the address and time at your place."

"I'm so glad you made it in time," she whispered, trembling in his arms. "I really believe she would have killed my sister and me."

And if Melinda hadn't discovered that little scrap of paper, he could have lost Angela forever, a blow his heart couldn't have withstood. How could he have let her get away before? Their broken engagement was the biggest mistake of his life.

One he didn't intend to repeat. He would do whatever it took to win her back. To build a life with her. A strong partner, his lover, his love.

With Angela's help, he would need to tread gently with Maya about her birth mother and what had happened over the past months, culminating in the most horrifying night of his life.

Unwinding the events of the last few hours would take patience and finesse. Traits he deeply admired in the woman he loved. The one who made his life so much better.

His eyes held hers. Throat bobbing, he strung together words. Knowing it would never be enough to explain how he felt about her.

"Angela, you have to know I love you. I've known

love before and this is the real thing. Something worth cherishing. And I'll be damned if I'll throw that away again. We're the forever deal. And whatever I need to do to convince you to marry me—"

She pressed her fingers to his mouth, her eyes on him. "Ryder, stop." She eased her hand away. "You don't have to convince me. I love you, too. I want nothing more than to be your wife."

A swell of relief filled him. Along with gratitude for this second chance with Angela.

He pulled out the engagement ring he'd given Angela, a ring he'd kept with him since the day she'd taken it off. "I've kept this with me even though I was the one who called off our engagement. I couldn't seem to let it go, to let *you* go."

"And now you never have to." She smiled up at him, her hand outstretched for him to slide the ring back in place.

Where it would stay for a lifetime.

A week later, Esme stood in the middle of what she'd once thought would be her dream come true—a holiday party held at the beautifully renovated building for the Houston branch of the Texas Cattleman's Club. Tomorrow was Christmas Eve. At the very least, she should be celebrating having survived Tatiana's attack.

She truly was grateful for her family's safety, her father's cleared name. Still, the revelry echoed hollowly around her without Jesse by her side. But she hadn't heard even a word from him since Tatiana held her and Angela hostage.

A harp played Christmas songs as Texas Cattleman's

Club guests from both Houston and Royal filled the room to celebrate the completed renovations. The formal grand opening was scheduled to ring in the New Year, the entire memberships of both chapters invited. Would Jesse attend? Would she have to see him with whatever "perfect" woman he'd chosen? The thought sent her stomach plummeting. Thankfully, so far, he was a no-show tonight.

The attack had drawn Ryder and Angela closer, though. Angela had gone through so much heartache over the last year that this warmed Esme's soul for her. They were so rock solid these days. Things had been difficult for Maya, but Ryder's older two children had been a wall of support, perhaps having gained strength from their own happiness. His son, Xander, who'd mourned the loss of a fiancée two years ago, had even found love again with cowgirl tomboy Frankie Walsh.

She stepped aside for waitstaff walking by with a silver tray of bacon-wrapped prawns, another carrying flutes. Even the champagne didn't tempt her. While she was happy for her sister, watching the in-love couple reminded her of a very real absence in her own life. The pain was made more palpable when Cord and Zoe romantically sipped from each other's champagne flutes.

The jabs to her heart just kept coming.

Cupping her crystal glass of sparkling water, she tucked herself farther away from the partiers. She needed to put in an appearance for her family's sake, but she wanted to remain as inconspicuous as possible. She'd even chosen her clothes with just that in mind, settling on a basic black cocktail dress. Her only nod to the party and the season was her red Gucci heels.

She was still raw inside from Jesse's rejection, heart-broken in a way that grew more painful every day. She felt adrift. After the vibrant days on Jesse's ranch, she found city life noisy and crowded. Even her job felt soulless now that she'd moved beyond seeking her daddy's approval.

Maybe she should buy a ranch of her own, work in philanthropy like her sister Melinda. Her sister might even welcome her help as Melinda's pregnancy progressed. She could spend more time with her husband, Slade.

Esme pressed her palm to her forehead, her thoughts all over the place. She had no idea what to do with her future, couldn't even think straight. She'd been so hopeful she and Jesse could build a life together. Seeing him walk away after the police hauled off Tatiana had been the worst pain she'd ever endured. He'd meant what he'd said about not wanting her.

How could things be so awful and perfect at the same time? Her father and Ryder were continuing to strengthen their reconciliation, much to Angela's joy. Their dad had even managed to repay the investors who'd panicked and lost so much money, an empathetic move that had people wondering if Sterling had become more than an empty suit after all.

After all the bad blood between the two families, it still felt surreal to Esme that her brother, Roarke, was engaged to Ryder's older daughter, Annabel.

Perry Construction CEO Ethan Barringer and his fiancée, Aria, were deep in conversation with Liam Morrow and socialite Chloe Hemsworth, both engaged couples radiating such happiness it made Esme ache all over again. An animated Paisley Ford held court with both of them, no doubt sharing news of the latest wedding fashion from her boutique. Her husband, Lucas, smiled proudly, as supportive of his wife as she was of him.

It seemed the whole room was full of couples, making her recent breakup all the more difficult to bear.

Venture capitalist Camden McNeal, his new bride, Vivianne, at his side, had his phone out showing everyone who would look the family photos of the two of them with their toddler daughter. Esme thought of the childcare center in the Royal TCC building, a benefit the Houston chapter didn't offer. She would have never thought to miss it before knowing Jesse and hearing his plans and yearning for a family.

"Can I get you a refill?"

Her father's voice startled her from her pity party. She hated feeling so morose but couldn't seem to shake herself out of it. "Thanks, Dad. I'm good."

He adjusted his tie, ever the clotheshorse. "You really did a top-notch job over in Royal on behalf of our chapter."

"But I didn't do anything that secures the presidency for you. It's still up in the air who'll lead this chapter."

"I can't deny that I would like the position, but I'm okay with however things shake out." He reached for his whiskey glass and finished off the last swallow without even a wince. "You made all of us look good in Royal and laid the groundwork for a great relationship between us."

The two clubs had worked together to draw up nomination papers for board positions and officers, creating the new club's rules and regulations.

His praise meant a lot to her. "Thanks, Dad. I'm glad you're pleased. But I'm not sure what I did."

"Houston and Royal are two very different towns. Forging a strong tie could have been rocky. But you've helped all of us—in both cities—form new business connections and new friendships."

Uncomfortable with praise she wasn't sure she'd earned, she shook her head emphatically. Pieces of her upswept hair loosened, tumbling in front of her eyes. Coming undone, for a change, gave her strange comfort. "It wasn't as difficult as you make it sound. We aren't really that different, Dad."

"If you believe that, then what's kept you from going back to Royal and that man you're obviously so taken with?"

She stared at him incredulously, surprised he'd noticed. She found herself aching to confide in her father, even knowing he couldn't fix this for her. "Dad, he doesn't want me."

"Huh, could have fooled me. Whenever he looked your way, he seemed besotted." He placed his hands on her shoulders. "And even if he's on the fence about committing, when did a child of mine ever back down without a fight?"

She stared back into her father's eyes, the same color as hers, and let his words sink in, really sink in. About Royal and Houston being similar. About fighting for what she wanted.

He continued, "I made the mistake of paying more

attention to business than to my marriage and I paid the price for that. So have you kids. Learn from my mistakes."

The rare glimpse of vulnerability in her father touched her heart and pushed aside barriers of her own making. She'd enjoyed her time at Jesse's ranch, working alongside him, riding to check the cattle, watching sunsets together on his porch.

Dreams spun into possibility. Esme Perry—a wife, a mother, an entrepreneur. Maybe she could have the best of both worlds by working remotely. Why had she gotten it into her head that she had to wait to establish her career before even considering motherhood? They could also share in the Texas Cattleman's Club world and she would still be connected to her family.

She arched up on her toes to kiss her dad on the cheek, a plan to woo Jesse already forming in her mind. "Thanks, Dad. Do you mind if I borrow that old truck of yours I used to learn to drive? I think my Christmas plans just changed."

"Sure," he answered without hesitation. "Just remember, even restored, that sucker's got a tricky clutch."

With a final look at the room full of her family and friends, at the stunning renovations now complete and the club ready to launch, Esme felt her world settle into place. She would always enjoy Houston, but her heart was in Royal now.

She had fallen head over heels in love with Jesse Stevens. And damn straight, Perrys fought for what they wanted.

The night was still young. If she made good time, she could be in Royal to celebrate Christmas Eve with Jesse.

* * *

Jesse was decidedly lacking in the holiday spirit, in spite of his decked-out house. The decorations only served as a reminder of all he'd left behind in Houston and how he would be spending Christmas Eve alone. He'd called his sister, exchanged holiday greetings, but then she was off to enjoy her vacation.

Why in the hell he'd thought coming to the stables would be better was beyond him. Esme had permeated every part of his world until there was nowhere to step without thinking of her, wanting her. Ghosts of their time together whispered from every corner of his ranch. And he had no idea how to find peace with her absence.

The familiar scents and sounds of his stable at night did little to soothe his restless spirit. He just kept thinking of how he would want to share the moment with Esme.

He stroked Duke's nose, wishing those wise brown eyes could offer him some wisdom. "Well, boy, I've made a mess of things, haven't I?"

The horse whinnied in response, shaking his mane. When he was a kid, he used to do this with Apollo. Tell his horse his secrets, dreams, regrets. The act steadied him. At least, a bit.

"I'm already regretting my decision to let her go." He couldn't sleep. He couldn't eat. His life was empty without her. "This ranch means nothing to me without her."

Never had he imagined a moment where the ranch felt like it wasn't enough for him. Sure, he appreciated his horses, his house, the rolling grounds. But he couldn't help but notice its expanse. How big it was. How empty it was.

Pawing the ground, Duke swung his head toward a mare in the next stall. The Appaloosa mare nickered softly.

Everyone was partnering up. Horses included, it seemed. "I want what my married friends at the Texas Cattleman's Club have. A sense of belonging to a family."

That hadn't changed. He just wanted it all with Esme.

Duke nuzzled Jesse on the shoulder. Those brown eyes stared back at him, catching him up short.

He knew the horse couldn't answer. Not really. Still, the flick of Duke's ear let him know he was listening. Stroking the horse's neck, he kept replaying the memory in his mind of meeting Esme. Of all that life with her seemed to promise. Of all that he'd thrown away.

Jesse's mind circled back around to how this ranch meant nothing without her. How he'd wanted that family with Esme. And everything clicked into place with startling clarity.

For some lame-ass reason, he'd thought that he could only have his dream family here in Royal.

As he rocked back on his boot heels, taking in his stable, thinking about his ranch, he also thought about the club here and the branch starting in Houston. And he realized the heart of that organization beat in either location.

Friends. Family. Community. Home wasn't about a building, or even a plot of land. It was about loving people and having them return that love.

It was still a few minutes shy of Christmas Eve, but there was nothing to say he couldn't make his holiday miracle happen now.

After shooting off a text with instructions for his foreman, Jesse made fast tracks outside, toward the house. He could be packed and on the road in less than ten minutes, but even that felt like an eternity.

Ten minutes later, he settled behind the wheel, a thermos of coffee beside him for the nighttime trip to Houston. Only a few hours separated him and Esme.

Mind made up, he turned the ignition key. He was ready for the journey. He needed to see her. To fight for her. The woman who made every room and space light up with energy and love. He'd been a fool to cast that aside, but he wouldn't let that get in the way of winning her back and healing her heart.

Just as he hit the gas, headlights shone in the distance, barreling down the long drive toward him. He scratched his head, frustrated at what might be a delay. He wasn't expecting anyone.

The vehicle stopped in front of him, his eyes taking a moment to adjust to the bright lights from what appeared to be a restored classic truck with a big red bow on the grille. He held up a hand, blotting out the glare as the door was flung open and a pair of shapely long legs stepped out.

A woman wearing sky-high red leather heels.

Jesse put his truck in Park, a smile building inside and spreading to his face. His heart slugged in his ears, each beat an echo of her name.

Esme.

He didn't know what she was doing in a vintage truck, a magnificent ride that at another time he would have been jonesing to drive. It was on the complete opposite end of the spectrum from her Porsche.

But then, everything about this woman was unpredictable. Perfectly so. He wouldn't have her any other way.

He hit the ground running, his strides eating up the space between them as she ran into his arms, leaping into his embrace. He spun her around, his face buried in her hair, the scent and feel of her filling his senses just as she filled his life.

Easing her to the ground, he sealed his mouth to hers and she met his kiss fully, her hands on either side of his face. No hesitation. He didn't know why she'd forgiven him. He was just glad to his soul that she had.

Jesse skimmed a final kiss over her lips before angling back, enjoying the way the stars were reflected in her eyes. "Nice ride."

"Turns out I'm a fan of trucks and a certain cowboy." She tapped his Stetson.

"And I'm a fan of you." He ran his hand down her sleek blond hair, burying his fingers in the silken strands. "I was just coming to you, but I'm glad we don't have to wait any longer. Every day without you has been miserable. I've been a brooding mess since you left."

"Oh, Jesse," she sighed, looping her arms around his neck. "I've—"

"Shhh." He kissed her quiet. "I need to speak first, especially after you took such a leap to drive all the way here. I didn't mean what I said about wanting someone else to be my wife. I was just afraid I couldn't make you happy here in Royal. So I want you to know I'm willing to move, like Cord is doing."

Eyes dancing, she drew teasing circles along his

back. "Thank you for that beautiful offer, and a couple of weeks ago, I might have been wrongheaded enough to have accepted. But now I know my heart and my future are here in Royal."

He couldn't believe his ears or his luck. More than luck, this was a Christmas miracle beyond any he could have imagined. And right on schedule as the night slid into Christmas Eve.

Jesse looked into the eyes of the woman he knew he would love for the rest of his life. "Merry Christmas, Esme. You're the best gift I could have ever received."

"And Merry Christmas to you, cowboy." She pulled his Stetson off and dropped it on her head. "I can promise you, the celebrating has only just begun."

Epilogue

Esme clutched Jesse's hand, eager to hear the announcement of the Houston chapter's president, the news to be revealed just before the stroke of midnight at the New Year's Eve soiree. She was doing her best to seem even-keeled and not at all on edge.

The ballroom was packed with members from both clubs, wall-to-wall Texas powerhouses mingling under crystal chandeliers. The men were decked out in tuxedos and their best Stetsons. Designer gowns and jewels to rival royalty draped the women.

But no one outshone the man at her side. She stole a look up at Jesse, her heart in her throat. They'd had a blissful Christmas week together before driving to Houston yesterday for this evening's New Year's Eve gala.

Esme had gotten dressed twice tonight. The first

time, Jesse had peeled off her gown and messed her updo. But she didn't mind. Not one bit. She and Jesse had thrown their clothes on quickly, barely making it to the gala on time. Trying to restore order to her hair in the car ride over, she'd given up and brushed it into a sleek, straight fall down her back. She'd smoothed the wrinkles out of her maroon gown with her hands, the silver embellishments glistening in the dash lights.

No one seemed to notice her hastily-put-together look. She slid a smoky-eyed glance up at Jesse. His knowing smile promised a repeat of earlier. An answering heat rose in her.

Her father and Ryder both appeared to be a bundle of nerves, even though they were making nice with each other, Angela smiling between them.

Her sister seemed happy. Genuinely happy. A sight that had been missing for what felt like ages.

And Jesse stepped right up like he'd known them forever. She appreciated how supportive he was of her family as a whole, and hoped to help him grow closer to his sister, Janet.

The music shifted from a fast dance number to a softer tune as the chairwoman for the nomination committee walked around the champagne fountain. Abigail Langley Price, a stunning redhead in a bold sequined gown, had been instrumental in allowing women to join the Texas Cattleman's Club.

Abigail climbed the steps to take the microphone. "Well, I imagine everyone is eager to hear the election results." She paused playfully before continuing, "And I won't keep you in suspense a second longer. I'll start with the board members."

She pulled out a card and slid on cat's-eye reading glasses. She read name after name off the list with a flourish, waiting for the applause to wane after each announcement. And every time neither Ryder nor her father was called, nerves ratcheted higher in Esme's stomach with the growing possibility the president would be one of them.

The woman smiled out at the audience. "There are only two more board positions to fill before I announce the first president of the Texas Cattleman's Club, Houston branch. Are you ready?"

The crowd roared in response. Esme's gaze skittered over to her father. She mouthed "good luck" from across the room. Sterling winked at her, inclining his head before turning his attention back to the stage.

Jesse squeezed her hand, a gesture of warmth and support that flooded her. Made her feel invincible. Like anything and everything was possible.

"There's a bit of a twist. We have a tie for the last two board positions, both having gained equal support. Our last two positions will be filled by… Sterling Perry and Ryder Currin."

Neither man had won the bid for president?

Shock tingled through Esme, a sentiment she suspected she wasn't alone in feeling. Whispers zipped from person to person. If not Sterling or Ryder, then who?

The woman tapped the microphone to regain control of the room. "It is now my honor, as one of the first women to be admitted to the Royal chapter of the Texas Cattleman's Club, to announce your president…" A drumroll rippled from the band, then stopped. "Elected with an overwhelming amount of write-in votes… Angela Perry."

Angela?

Without a second's hesitation, the crowd erupted into deafening applause and shouts of approval. And as Esme thought about it, she couldn't imagine anyone better for the job than her sister. She hoped her father and Ryder would be supportive, as well. Angling to look, she found both men holding their hands high in applause as Angela made her way to the stage.

Her sister was a vision in an off-the-shoulder gown of gold tulle with the tiniest shimmer. "Thank you, everyone, for the vote of confidence." Angela pressed a hand to her chest, breathless with surprise. "I'm stunned, to say the least. But honored and excited to lead the Houston chapter as we launch."

She waited for the applause to die down. "I'm especially pleased to serve with my father and my fiancé on the board."

More applause and cheers rippled through the partiers. Jesse let out a whoop. Esme's heart nearly burst as her smile grew even wider.

"I hope you'll indulge me a moment longer as my fiancé and I share some news of our own." Angela held out a hand to Ryder, her engagement ring glinting. She waved for him to join her on stage. He climbed the steps, his face beaming with pride.

Angela looked up at him, their love for each other clear for all to see. "We were given the best Christmas present of all. We're expecting our first child together."

The cheers and applause doubled in a rousing endorsement followed by glasses lifted in toast. Partiers converged around the couple and Esme knew she didn't stand a chance of getting to her sister anytime soon. But that was okay. They had months to celebrate.

Plans were already flowering in her mind for a joint baby shower for both of her sisters. Twins celebrating the births of their first children. Esme was truly happy for them.

Just as she knew they would be happy for her when her day came.

She looked up at Jesse, wondering aloud, "Are you feeling the baby urge? I know you want children. And so do I."

Jesse kissed the inside of her wrist before drawing her hand to rest against his heart. Stars and promises glimmered in those green eyes.

"Someday. But first, I want us to have time together, to get to know each other, to build a foundation for our future." He kissed the tip of her nose. "But at the risk of sounding too practical, I want us to have time to savor falling more and more in love with each other."

"That's beautiful. Underneath all that rancher practicality, you really do have a sentimental heart, full of emotions as messy as your desk."

"My desk?" He cocked his head to the side, a laugh spluttering out.

"No need to look offended. I think all that clutter is endearing." She remembered the time they'd gotten hot and heavy there, a place that had helped her see who Jesse Stevens really was inside.

"Well, then, I'm more than happy to have a messy office."

The countdown to midnight started, the partiers

chiming in until the forty-five-second mark was a thunderous echo of numbers. He pulled her close, swaying with her to the music, then spinning her out onto the balcony.

"How smart of you to have come out here ahead of the crowd to see the fireworks."

"Actually, I brought you out here to tell you how much I love you."

She smiled, her heart full of happiness like a champagne glass full of bubbles. "You've already told me."

"It's something I look forward to telling you every day." He held her tighter. Closer. Their bodies melting into one. Into a promise of forever.

"Now, isn't that convenient? Because I love you, too, and I enjoy telling you again and again." She teased her fingers along the hair at the base of his neck. "I can't believe how lucky we are."

"What a way to ring in the new year."

"And how wonderfully perfect we'll get to share the midnight kiss."

His low growl of approval rumbled between them as he angled down to take her up on that kiss.

A kiss that set her senses on fire. Their love made everything all the more special.

And as she arched up on her toes to press herself even closer, she could have sworn the fireworks had already started.

* * * * *

COMING SOON!

We really hope you enjoyed reading this book.
If you're looking for more romance
be sure to head to the shops when
new books are available on

Thursday 20th November

To see which titles are coming soon, please visit

millsandboon.co.uk/nextmonth

MILLS & BOON

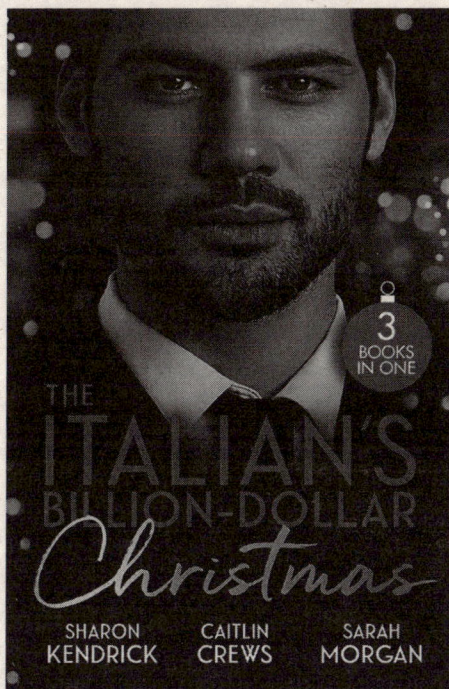

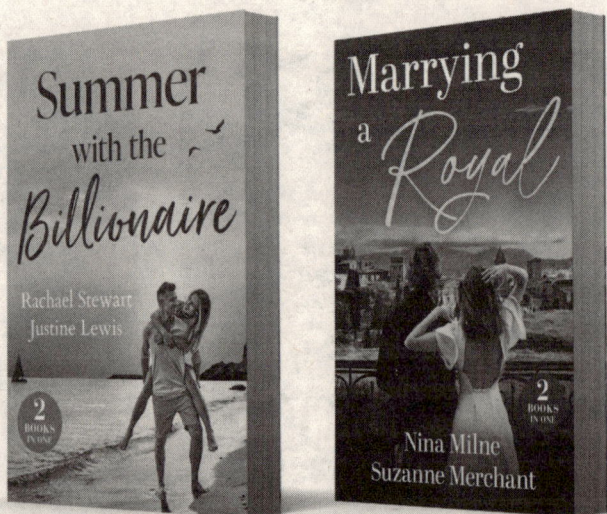